TW...
W...
...

BADMAN'S HOLIDAY

"Get set. There'll be only one shot fired," Fineen whispered, picking up the huge gun. He inserted the homemade cartridge.

"Be careful," someone said.

"I'm always careful," Fineen replied. He led the way through the mud. "Be sure and let him get almost past," he said. "He won't be going fast."

The rider was close now, almost obscured by the rain. He was moving slowly, almost leisurely.

And Fineen was waiting for him, the long muzzle of the terrible gun braced on a log, his finger carefully closing on the trigger.

THE WIND RIVER KID

"You after somebody, Marshal?" Bess Jamison called with a cold, calculating look that hit the Kid's stomach like a fist.

Marshal Boomhauer chewed at his cigar for a moment. "We have reason to believe the Wind River Kid is in the vicinity."

"Reason?" Bess threw her head back and gave a short bitter laugh. The Kid held himself rigid. This was it. And he couldn't blame Bess. Few people could resist such a temptation.

Bess didn't. She pointed to the Kid. "There's your Wind River Kid, Mr. Marshal." She threw the Kid a look of icy triumph. "Let's see you get out of this one!"

BADMAN'S HOLIDAY/
THE WIND RIVER KID

WILL COOK

LEISURE BOOKS ▮ NEW YORK CITY

A LEISURE BOOK®

May 1994

Published by special arrangement with Golden West
Literary Agency.

Dorchester Publishing Co., Inc.
276 Fifth Avenue
New York, NY 10001

BADMAN'S HOLIDAY

1.

AFTER eleven years' residence in Two Pines, Lincoln McKeever had grown accustomed to a life of quiet boredom, and during his three and a half years as sheriff, McKeever had now and then been irritated by the deadly monotony, for all infractions of the law were petty, and the West's wildness seemed to circumvent Two Pines. McKeever suspected that this was because Two Pines lacked allure, the easy-money kind that drew the toughs and the gunmen and the card sharks. Or perhaps the people of Two Pines had something to do with this serenity; they were so settled in dull routine that life had anesthetized itself, and moved only in the rut of habit.

The trouble with Two Pines, McKeever decided, was that there was too much of a good thing there. No one really had to hustle for anything; the challenge was gone. Why, there hadn't been a new business established in seven years. People went on working, making about the same wages, spending about the same, saying what they had always said, thinking what they had always thought. And I'm as bad as the next guy, McKeever thought.

Unlike most towns, Two Pines did not depend on any one thing for its revenue. To the south was the cattle country, good graze, plenty of water, and the men who worked the land were "stayers," even the working hands. McKeever had roamed enough to know men who followed cattle. Loose-footed usually, always quitting, moving, hiring on someplace else—but not around Two Pines. They just seemed to fit in, coming to town every Saturday night, having their drink, playing a few hands of cards, making no fuss. McKeever always watched them, for they'd stand around on the street corners, talking about the weather or cattle, the things they already knew about, week after week; and McKeever wondered when they'd break, do something different, maybe something illegal, just to be doing it.

5

But this never happened.

To the north was the timber. McKeever had originally come to Two Pines to work in the woods, but he'd stayed on as sheriff even when his good sense told him to go someplace else. Logging was good. Not spectacular, but there were a hundred years of it if a man held himself back and didn't get greedy and cut it all down in the first ten years. And they held back, taking it out slow and enticing the weekly-pay, bread-and-butter-on-the-table kind of logger to stay on.

These men were another concern for Lincoln Mc-Keever, for he knew the breed—tough, and mean sometimes, a pot of trouble just waiting for an excuse to boil over. Only it never did. Saturday nights they'd come into town, walk up and down the streets, talk, loaf, buy in the stores, then go home. Now and then there would be a fist fight, but it never went any farther. At one time, a few of the sporting bloods rode over to Woodland, a neighboring town, to let off a little of the hell that is in all men, but McKeever noticed that they soon stopped this. The ride was long and it was a lot of trouble for nothing, so they stayed in Two Pines, leaning against the same lampposts week after week, talking to the same men about the same things, and doing the same work day after day.

Logging and cattle—two fine, stable industries that had never mixed, but in Two Pines they did, as though it were too much trouble to fight. Still there was more, to the west—the galena mines. Through Two Pines came the long ore wagons hauling the stuff to the smelters to be fired down into lead pigs; there they were shipped eighty miles overland to the railroad. McKeever had been in boom camps; he knew miners and teamsters and during his first year in office he had kept an eye constantly on them, especially on Saturday nights, but he was wasting his time.

The miners had their saloon, the cattlemen had theirs, and the loggers liked a place on the edge of town. Even McKeever's routine was well established. He sat on the hotel porch each Saturday evening until seven, then he made his rounds. His first stop was The Palace, the cattleman's place. The four "big" men had their poker game going; same table, and about the same level of win or lose. Now and then fresh blood would be invited to enter, but not often; people in Two Pines wiggled and worked until things were just right, then worked harder to keep them that way. At the cattleman's place, the drinking men would be drinking, the talking men talking, and the listeners listening; this never varied, and Joel Lovering, who ran The Palace, knew what his Saturday night take would be even before the first of the hands drifted into the place. Now and then the sameness of it all would get someone down and he would look for something to change, something small, like the color of a man's eye.

These minor fights were no problem to McKeever, who broke them up and let it go at that.

At the miners' place, a man ran into a little of the old country, Welsh songs, rough Irish jokes, and men who liked to bear-wrestle; the events started at seven-thirty and McKeever watched them in case someone lost his temper.

For a man just turning thirty, Lincoln McKeever figured that he had most of his troubles behind him, and it was a satisfying thought. McKeever was long and lanky, with a shock of unruly hair that hung in a lock beneath the sweatband of his hat. He moved slowly, talked slowly, and some people had once made the mistake of thinking that his mind worked at that pace. But those men were now in jail, with eleven more years to go before their sentence was up.

Twice, after he had been elected sheriff, two strangers passing through had made the fatal mistake of believing that because McKeever carried his pistol in his coat pocket he would be clumsy at it. They were buried, at township expense and only Mrs. Moody, who thought about those things, placed flowers on their graves each Easter.

THE sun finally slid behind the hills and this announced McKeever's supper hour; he walked a block west to the Hanover House and took his usual table next to the door. He did not order, for years of eating here had established his likes and dislikes as firmly as anyone else in Two Pines. McKeever could look out the window and see the main street, or a good part of it. Everyone was in his place, like actors waiting for the first curtain to go up. One of these days, he thought, someone is going to forget what he always says or does, and then there'll be hell to pay.

Between his apple pie and his coffee there was a lull of several minutes during which Lincoln McKeever kept looking toward the door, and when a heavy, bluff-faced man came in, McKeever smiled and toed a chair away from the table.

"Don't you ever eat anything but apple pie?" the man said, sitting down. He put his hat on a vacant chair, then signaled the waiter to bring his cup of coffee.

"I could set my watch by the time you come through that door," McKeever said softly. "You want to do me a favor, Finley?"

"What kind?"

McKeever smiled. "The next time you buy a new coat, make it something else besides brown corduroy."

"I like brown corduroy," Finley Fineen said. Then he laughed. "Lincoln, suppose I bought blue serge. Do you know what would happen? No one in town would know me. Man, you don't think that they look at your face any more, do you? You see a straw hat walk past, that's Huddlemyer, the butcher. He's worn straw hats since anyone can remember. You see a parasol and it's Richardson at the bank; he carries the damn thing during August dog days, when it hasn't rained in thirty-one years in August." Fineen shook his head, a bit sadly. "We've got to stay the same, Lincoln. Lord, if anyone changed it would upset the whole damned township." Then he shrugged. "I'm too lazy to scratch anyway. The lead mine ordered four new wagons this afternoon. A nice profit there." His coffee came and he softened its heat with water. "Poker game tonight, Lincoln?"

"You ask that every Saturday," McKeever said. "Finley, don't we always play poker?"

Fineen laughed. "Yeah. But I guess I keep hoping you'll shock me and say to hell with it, just to be different."

"If it bores you, then cut it out."

"Bores me? My God, this whole damned town bores me." He drank some of his coffee. "Ah, what difference does it make? If we weren't playing poker, it would be something else. Don't you get tired of one day following another, with tomorrow so damned predictable?"

"No," McKeever said. "I like·Two Pines, Finley. I

kicked around for a long time; my father was a restless man. It's good to find a rut that fits." A rumble rattled dishes in the kitchen and McKeever raised his head. "That thunder?"

"Yeah, it was clouding up," Fineen said. "Damn, I hope it doesn't start to rain. I've got some oak outside that I want kept dry."

"It sometimes rains on Saturday nights," McKeever said.

The hotel clerk came into the dining room, had a quick look, then went out to stand on the porch, peering up at the dark sky. Fineen studied the man briefly. "You know what he'll say when I leave?"

McKeever nodded. "Looks like we're going to have some rain after all."

"That's it exactly," Fineen said. "You know something, if he says that to me I think I'll hit him."

"Better not," McKeever said gently, but the warning was there. "Finley, a man's what he wants to be. If you want them to talk about something different, go out in the middle of the street and take your pants off."

"To hell with you," Fineen said, smiling. "Around nine?"

"With the usual boring punctuality," McKeever said.

Fineen went out, pausing in the doorway to look back; McKeever was having his coffee. The clerk, still on the porch, turned and said, "Looks like we're going to have some rain after all, Mr. Fineen."

"Samson, you're an alert bastard," Fineen said then walked on down the street. He was a tall man, over two hundred pounds, and muscled by twenty years of blacksmithing and carriage-making. There were some people in Two Pines who thought a man with Fineen's money ought to quit manual labor and spend his time behind a cloud of expensive cigar smoke, with his feet elevated to a desk, but Fineen's habits were too well set to be broken.

HE STOPPED at the drugstore, then stood on the porch as the first spatter of rain dimpled the street's dust. Then he went inside and into the back room where Bill Daley sniffed with his eternal head cold. He packaged medicines that cured others, but not himself.

Daley was thin, almost sickly in both physique and

complexion. He had thin red hair and a nose reddened by constant blowing. He looked around when Fineen stopped in the doorway.

"It's beginning to rain," Fineen said.

Daley looked at him for a moment, then said, "You know, if you hadn't come along, Finley, I'd never have been able to have figured that out for myself."

"All right, all right," Fineen said. "I'm going over to the office. You be over in half an hour?"

"I always am," Daley said. "My wife's over to Bertha Mailer's gossiping as usual, and my help is dipping their fingers into the till, as usual. As usual, I'll be there in a half hour. Wade Stanton too?"

"Of course," Fineen said. "Bring the stuff."

"What? Tonight?" Daley spoke sharply, with a touch of apprehension.

"It's raining, isn't it?"

Fineen walked out and down the street, not stopping until he came to his office. His mill and carriage yard was behind the main building; he unlocked the door and went into the back room, there turning up the lamp he had left faintly burning.

The rain was coming down steadily now, drumming on the roof, turning his yard into one big mud puddle. He listened to the rain, then smiled and went across the compound to his small machine shop where he made carriage parts. A huge screw press sat in one corner, and in the darkness he disassembled the handle, a six-foot length of steel pipe. Taking this into the office, he locked the back door and the front door, and then went to his desk. From the bottom drawer he took a walnut stock and fitted the pipe to it, but before he fastened it securely he took out a steel gunlock and screwed it onto the pipe. With this seated into the stock, he locked the two small wing clamps and set the thing in the corner.

Someone knocked on the front door and Fineen opened it. Wade Stanton stepped inside and flogged water from his wide-brimmed hat. He was cattle, from boots to hat, thirty-some and wealthy enough to have considerable say in Two Pines. "Have you seen Daley?" Stanton asked.

"He'll be here," Fineen said. "Come on in the back."

Stanton followed him and Fineen closed the separating

door. Stanton's eyes went to the gun in the corner. "That's an ugly thing," he said.

"It'll do the job," Fineen said casually.

Stanton turned and looked at him. "This doesn't bother you at all, does it, Finley?"

"No. Does it you?"

Stanton shook his head. "No, we've gone over it so many times that I wake up at night believing it's already been done." He put his hands in his pockets. "Where's Lincoln McKeever?"

"Now, you know where he is," Fineen said. "He's over to the teamsters' saloon watching them knock bottles off the bar with a bull whip. You ought to get around this town, Wade. See what's going on."

"I know what's going on," Stanton said sourly. "Nothing's going on around this damned town. I get sick of doing nothing. I've thought about staying home one of these Saturday nights just to listen to the speculation on why I didn't come to town."

"Habit can be a blessing," Fineen said. He cocked his head to one side. "That'll be Bill Daley." He went to the front again and came back with the druggist. Daley and Stanton looked at each other, then Fineen motioned for them to sit down.

"We've got an hour," he said. "Relax." His glance touched Daley. "Let me have it."

DALEY took a package from under his coat and laid it on Fineen's desk. After unwrapping it, Fineen said, "You sure this will go off?" He turned the small brass projectile over, examining it carefully.

"Damned sure," Daley said. "Finley, it'll kill the horse. Blow him to hell and gone."

"But will it make smoke?"

Daley nodded. "Like a choked-off brush fire."

"That's good," Fineen said. "Everything going on as usual out there?" He nodded toward the street.

"The rain doesn't change much," Daley said.

"All right," Fineen said. "Now let's go over the whole thing again, from top to bottom."

"Hell, we've been over it a hundred times," Stanton said.

"We'll go over it once more," Fineen said, not arguing.

"Dalridge will leave town at eight-thirty, as usual."

"We hope," Daley said.

Fineen's expression mirrored his impatience. "He has for the past year and a half, and that's good enough for me. Look, he can't help but do what he always does. He'll take the south road." Fineen laughed. "Last time he took the lane out by Miles' place. This time it's the south road. A while ago I was talking to Lincoln McKeever about us—you know, being creatures of habit. This whole thing is based on habit. The habits of all of us. Now you take Dalridge, he's been taking the mine's money to the railhead for nearly four years, and I'll bet he'd swear that he's never established a pattern. Yet he has, for in spite of his taking different roads, he's developed a sequence. I believe we can predict where he'll be tonight at twenty minutes to nine."

"We've waited long enough for rain," Stanton said. "Especially rain on an alternate Saturday night."

"Well, we've got rain tonight," Fineen said. "There's no better cover than a rainy night. We all agreed to that."

"What about McKeever?" Daley asked. "What if he comes early?"

"Has he ever come before nine in the last four years?"

"No," Daley said, "but he could—"

Fineen shook his head. "Gentlemen, we've agreed to use logic, haven't we? All right, then, let's stick to the plan. McKeever knows that our poker game starts at eight and he always comes in at nine, with Doc Harris. We'll take twenty-eight minutes to do the job and get back here. All right?"

"I'm sold," Stanton said. "I see no flaw in it, Finley."

"There isn't any flaw," Fineen said. "We'll take Dalridge on the south road because it's close to town. We'll bring the money back here, split it as we planned, then sit on it for five years. After that, we can mix it in with our spending and no one will ever know the difference." Fineen leaned back in his chair. "I think we all agree that criminals are caught trying to flee the scene of their crime. We won't flee at all." He spread his hands. "A man steals because he wants money. None of us needs money, we have plenty already. I'll bet McKeever drives himself ragged looking for the robbers, and all the time we'll be laughing at him."

"Not out loud," Stanton said. He got up and walked around the office. "You know, I get so goddamn bored, the same thing all the time, the same talk." He laughed. "I wonder if you know how much I've been looking forward to this just because it'll be different." He made a sweeping motion with his hand. "I've thought a lot about robbery since we first talked about this. This is different than just deciding to stick up the stage or something. Kind of a work of art, like a painting, or a poem."

"I like the idea of the money," Bill Daley said, sniffing. "This'll be the first dollar I've had in fifteen years that my wife won't get her hands on first. I'd like to go to St. Louis and—"

"None of that!" Fineen said sharply. "Damn it, this will work only if we stay here and keep our cover. Understand that, Daley?"

"Yeah, yeah, I understand it. I was only wishing, that's all."

"This is one time when you're not permitted to wish," Fineen said. "Bill, this will work if we stick to our cover. But the minute one of us breaks away from our usual routine, we'll draw suspicion like—"

"We know that," Stanton said irritably. "Finley, how much do you suppose Dalridge will be carrying this time?"

"Close to sixty thousand," Fineen said. "It'll take that much to cover their subcontracts, teamsters, supplies, and all. I make it that they'll take nearly sixty thousand out of that vault." He laughed. "This way is better than going out to the mine and blowing it open, isn't it?"

"I never liked hard work anyway," Stanton said.

Finley Fineen consulted his watch. "Two minutes. Dalridge is halfway to town by now." He picked up his hat, then took three slickers from a closet; they slipped into them. From his desk he took out three revolvers and made sure they were unloaded.

"Don't you trust us, Finley?" This was Stanton's question.

"There'll only be one shot fired," Fineen said, picking up the huge gun leaning in the corner. He inserted the cartridge Bill Daley had made, and the druggist grew nervous.

"Be careful of that, Finley."

"I'm always careful," Fineen said, and led the way into the muddy yard. He hitched a team to a light, covered buggy. Stanton drove while Fineen lay flat in back, a tarpaulin over him.

Stanton knew where he was going and took all the back roads to get there. He left town and drove for nearly a mile, then parked at the junction, where a back road ran into the main road to the railhead.

From under the tarp, Fineen said, "Be sure and let him pass, Wade. He won't be going fast."

"I know how to do it," Stanton said with annoyance in his voice.

Bill Daley began to cough and Fineen said, "For Christ's sake, cut that out. That's a dead giveaway."

Daley choked his coughing, then Wade Stanton spoke, excitement in his voice. "God, here he comes!"

"Get set!" Fineen said, and by feel he checked the mechanism of the homemade gun to see that it was set to fire.

A buggy and driver passed, nearly obscured by the rain; then Wade Stanton lashed the team into motion. He drove like a wild man, skidding back and forth across the road, then controlled them enough to pass Dalridge. Fineen was waiting, the long muzzle lifted over the rim of the rear wheel, and when Stanton pulled slightly past Dalridge's rig, Fineen fired.

2.

FINLEY FINEEN had been right; the one shot killed the horse, upset the buggy and broke both of Dalridge's legs when it toppled over on him. Stanton sawed the rig to a halt, made a wild U turn and drove back; Fineen was out of the back before the rig stopped.

They put on bandannas quickly and ran to the overturned buggy. Stanton searched for the money sacks, and found them. Bill Daley heard Dalridge groaning and bent over him, a mistake if he ever made one, for Dalridge snatched the bandanna away, recognizing Daley.

Stanton had the money. Fineen looked at Dalridge for a moment, then said, "Nothing to do now but kill him."

The thought frightened Bill Daley. "Finley, that wasn't in the plan!"

"You damned fool, the plan's changed! You going to do it or am I?"

"I—I couldn't do it," Daley said.

"What're you going to kill him with?" Stanton asked. "You unloaded the guns."

Finley Fineen hesitated an instant, then clubbed Dalridge across the head with the barrel of his gun. Daley watched, his expression frozen as Fineen's gun rose and fell; he sounded as if he were smashing honeydew melons on a brick walk. Then Daley turned away and threw up and Fineen put his gun away.

"Let's go," Fineen said. "We're a minute off schedule now." He looked at Daley, then slapped him hard. "Snap out of it!" He shoved the man into the buggy, then crawled back under the tarp as Stanton drove back toward town, again taking the side roads.

He used the back door to Fineen's carriage yard and parked the rig. Daley stood coughing and sniffing while Fineen unhitched the team and put them in the barn. Stanton was standing by the back door when Fineen motioned him inside.

They put their slickers away and Fineen said, "There's a mop in back, Bill. Clean up that water on the floor."

While Daley worked the swab over the floor, Fineen took the home made gun apart and put the steel pipe back into the press. He disassembled the firing mechanism and put that away, then he took the three sacks of money from Stanton and dropped them into the bottom desk drawer.

Daley was through mopping and at Fineen's nod, he took his place at the table. Stanton was shuffling cards and dealing the first hand. "Here," Fineen said, handing each of them a cigar.

"I don't smoke," Daley said. "Bad for my health." He took a bottle of pills from his coat pocket and popped one into his mouth.

"Smoke that cigar," Fineen said. "When McKeever gets here, I want this room full of smoke."

"He's right," Stanton said. "It's always foggy in here when McKeever arrives."

Fineen took a sack of cigar butts from his desk and filled the two metal ashtrays. Then he threw the sack away. "Let's get some money on the table." He looked at his watch while they laid out coins and bills. "Don't divide it evenly," he snapped. "We've been playing poker for an hour, and who heard of three even winners." He gave most of the money to Daley and then picked up his cards.

"I'll never get that sound out of my mind," Bill Daley said softly. "His head just busted wide—"

"Shut your mouth!" Stanton snapped. "Finley did what he had to do."

"I know, but we didn't figure on murder."

Fineen looked up and his eyes were gray glass. "God damn you, Bill, don't crack on me. McKeever will be here in two minutes. You act the same as always."

"All right," Daley said. "But I'll have to work at it."

"Then work at it." Fineen said flatly. You expect to get that money for nothing?" He made a fan of his cards and Stanton opened.

T HE room was full of smoke when McKeever arrived. He shook his head and squinted at them, then pulled his chair aside and sat down. "Doc Harris will be along in a minute," he said. He looked at Daley's pile. "Are you winning?"

"It looks that way," Daley said, pausing to cough.

Fineen looked at McKeever. "Bill's luck has changed, Lincoln."

"I guess it has," McKeever said, smiling. "I was counting on taking twenty or so off him tonight."

"Still raining?" Stanton asked.

"Just listen to it," McKeever said. "The creek'll be up when you go home, Wade."

Stanton shrugged. "My horse has long legs."

Everyone looked up when Doctor Harris came in, pipe going, water shedding off his coat. He put his hat and black bag aside, then draped his coat over the back of a chair before taking his place at the table. He was a dry-skinned little man who always squinted when he talked. Noticing Bill Daley's pile, Harris said, "You been eating meat, Bill?"

"Huh?"

"You're winning," Harris said. "That will spoil a beautiful friendship quicker than anything, Bill. What makes you such a delightful poker partner is that you consistently lose." He slapped the table. "Let's deal, huh?"

McKeever took his cards, made a modest bet after Harris opened, then said, "Good thing you don't have any house calls tonight, Doc."

"The hell I don't. Mrs. Ludlow's going to have another any time now. I left word that I was here." He nodded toward his bag. "Got my tools and eveything."

"How's your wife?" McKeever asked.

Stanton looked up. "You talking to me?"

McKeever winked at Harris. "Now who else here has a wife young enought for me to be interested in?"

"If you want her," Stanton said flatly, "you can have her."

"Hey," Fineen said. "This started out to be a joke." His eyes warned Stanton. "What's got into you, anyway?"

"Nothing," Stanton said. "Betty gets on my nerves once in a while. We had a fight before I left for town tonight."

Harris squinted. "Wade, all husbands and wives fight. Didn't anyone ever tell you that?" He checked his hand. "How long have you been married now? A year?"

"Closer to two," Stanton said. "Hell, do we have to talk about it?"

"It was your topic," McKeever said. "Let me have three cards, Bill."

"What do you tell your wife when you lose at poker, Bill?" This was Harris' question, an irritating one, because they all knew that Daley never spoke to his wife unless she invited him to speak.

"Want to know something?" Daley asked. "One of these days she's going to say something to me and I'll beat her damned brains out!" He closed his mouth suddenly and looked stricken, his complexion chalky.

"What's the matter with you?" Harris asked, his professional interest aroused. "Taking too many of those damned patent pills? Or maybe you ought to take one now."

"I don't feel good," Bill Daley said lamely.

Finley Fineen said, "Hell, you're always sick or complaining. You're all right, Bill. You just keep telling yourself that."

"Sure," Daley said. "Sure, Finley."

McKeever played for an hour, a dull game with dull

people, made so by constant association, by wearing out all avenues of conversation. He listened to the rain on the roof, and to their talk, and managed to stay out of it whenever he could.

SOMEONE came to the front door and pounded on it. Finley Fineen, turned his hand face down and went out to see who it was. He came back with a worried-looking man in a rain-soaked coat.

"Been some trouble," Fineen said and sat down at the table.

McKeever looked at the man. "What's wrong, Ben?"

"An accident, Sheriff." He looked at the others, as though wondering whether he should talk or not.

"It's all right," McKeever said. "Better tell me about it."

"My wife and I were driving into town," the man said. "Got a late start because one of my cows was about to drop and I had trouble—"

"Spare us the details of this bovine delivery," Harris said dryly. "Get on with it, Ben."

"Well, it's Dalridge, Sheriff. He's dead. We found his rig overturned on the road south. I didn't look at him too good, but he sure was dead."

McKeever sighed and got up, putting on his slicker. "I'd better get out there. This is the second Saturday in the month and Dalridge would be carrying a lot of money."

"You think someone around here has light fingers?" Stanton asked.

"No." McKeever said, grinning, "but the mine owners will feel better if it's locked up in my office." He touched Ben on the arm. "Thanks for stopping, Ben."

"It was the least I could do," the man said and went out.

"This makes four-handed poker," Harris said. "Damned dull."

"I'm for closing it up," Daley said suddenly, and then looked as though he wished he'd kept quiet.

Harris was putting on his coat and hat. Fineen made an appeal. "Hell, you stay, Doc."

"No," Harris said. "Better get out to Ludlow's place. Shouldn't keep a woman waiting, or so they say." He glanced at Stanton. "Wade, what's your wife going to say if you come home early tonight?"

"We're not speaking," Stanton said flatly. "The first peace I've had for two weeks, believe me."

"I believe you," Harris said and went out with Mc-Keever.

Fineen waited until he heard the front door close, then put the cards away. The shine of sweat appeared on his face and Wade Stanton laughed. "Nerves, Finley?"

"It was tighter than I thought it was going to be," Fineen said. "A lot tighter."

"Let's look at the money," Daley said. "I want to go home."

"In a minute," Fineen said. "We want to make sure we got everything straight. All right?"

"Sure," Stanton said. "There's nothing like a straight story."

"The rain will wash out the tracks," Fineen said. "And that's important. Now there's no use fooling ourselves; we counted on McKeever finding out that Dalridge was robbed. Had everything gone as we'd originally planned, it would have turned out no different than now."

"Only Dalridge is dead," Daley said.

"So he's dead," Stanton said. "Hell, a man of sixty is about through anyway, ain't he?"

"That doesn't matter," Fineen said flatly. "McKeever will know it wasn't an accident when he finds the dead horse. But we're in the clear. Just keep remembering that."

"I'll remember it," Stanton said. "Now let's split the money."

"All right," Fineen said and went to the desk to get it. He took it from the sacks and stacked it neatly, then began to count. Stanton and Daley watched, nervously, until it was placed into three equal piles.

"Nearly eighteen thousand apiece," Fineen said. "That's profit."

"I thought it was going to be twenty," Daley said. Stanton looked at him sharply. "What's the hell's the matter with you, Bill? You getting greedy all of a sudden?"

"Oh, shut up, both of you," Fineen said. "Now I'll leave it up to each of you to hide this right. If it's found by anybody, we're all in it together." He leaned forward. "Now listen to this. We trust each other; there's no other way. As long as we go on trusting each other, we'll come out fine. But I know McKeever, and if anything ever leads him to any of us, he'll start hammering away. We've got to make damn sure that nothing leads him here, understand?"

"Yeah, we understand," Stanton said.

Fineen looked sharply at him. "Wade, don't take this lightly."

"Who the hell's taking it lightly?"

"You are," Fineen said.

"Dalridge is dead," Daley said.

Stanton looked at him. "S'matter, you afraid to use the word murder?"

Daley looked as if he was about to strangle. Fineen's scowl was like a rain cloud forming. "You got a blunt mouth, Wade."

"Yes, I have." Then he smiled. "It doesn't take much to get us arguing, does it?"

"You trying to prove something?" Fineen asked.

"No," Stanton said, "but I'd like to point out a few facts, Finley. Granted that you figured a lot of things right, like the habits Dalridge got into without knowing it, and making the gun out of that hunk of pipe, so it could be put back afterward and no one would ever know what it was used for. And the way we hit Dalridge—all very neat, with the rain to cover us, and our own habits to back 'em up. Hell, I'll bet McKeever would swear on a stack of Bibles that we never left this office, because we've met here every Saturday for years." He shook his head. "That was real good planning, Finley. But you made a couple of mistakes."

"Like what?"

"Like misfiguring the money. You're right so much of the time that I thought you'd be right there too."

"You complaining because you're short a few thousand?"

"No, just pointing out that you could make a mistake. You made another when you killed Dalridge." He held up his hands when Fineen started to speak. "All right, you had to do it; I won't argue that, but it was a mistake."

He got up and began to put on his hat and coat.

Fineen watched him carefully. "Don't blow this, Wade. I mean it. Watch that wife of yours."

"Hell, she'd be the last one I'd ever tell."

After he left, Bill Daley slipped into his coat. Fineen said, "Don't let this work on your mind now."

"How can I help it?" Daley asked. He looked along at Fineen. "Finley, what in God's name ever led us to this moment?"

"Does it matter? We're here." He made a motion with his hand. "Go on, get a good night's sleep. I've got some cleaning up to do."

He went out in back after Daley went home, and took a shotgun bore brush to the pipe, scouring it so that all trace of powder was gone. Then he went back into his office and took out the three guns they had used. He recognized the one he had carried; the barrel was matted with blood and hair, and a few other things he didn't want to look at.

A strong drink of whisky helped; then he sat down to clean the .45. By the time he was ready to reassemble it, he found himself thick-fingered, for he had drunk nearly half the bottle.

"Get ahold of yourself," he said softly. "I mean it, Fineen."

3.

A DOZEN men joined Lincoln McKeever around the upset buggy. and a ring of lantern light illuminated the scene. McKeever motioned for Jim Singleton, a young man who ran the hotel and doubled as deputy sheriff. McKeever was examining the horse, and Singleton cast the glow of his lantern over the animal.

"Someone must have used a stick of dynamite," McKeever said softly. He raised his head and looked at those crowded around the buggy. "Keep away from there! Too many tracks already!"

He listened to their muttered resentment and understood the reason for it. Even Jim Singleton said. "Lincoln, to hell with the horse. Hadn't you ought to get Dalridge out of the mud?"

"In a minute," McKeever said. "Jim, see if you can't send that crowd home."

He stood in the rain while Singleton argued in his mild voice. Finally a few men returned to their buggies; others followed once the movement commenced. When Singleton came back, he was alone.

"This damn rain has washed all tracks away," McKeever said. "Even the ones Dalridge made when he went off the road." He took the lantern from Singleton's hand and walked over to the dead man, examining him carefully. Jim Singleton looked over McKeever's shoulder, trying hard not to lose his supper.

"Ain't his legs busted, Lincoln?"

"Yes. I guess the wheel caught him when the buggy went over." He held the light closer to Dalridge's head. "He didn't crack his skull in the fall though." McKeever pointed. "There's nothing but mud in that ditch, Jim."

"Yeah." The young man swallowed hard. "This ain't no accident, is it, Mr. McKeever?"

"No, it's murder. And robbery, unless we find that money." He turned to his horse. "I'm going to leave you here until I can send Doc out with the ambulance."

"Gosh," Singleton said, "I ain't even carryin' a gun."

"You won't need a gun," McKeever said, and then turned back. "Here." He took a break-open .32 Smith and Wesson from his inner coat pocket and handed it to Singleton. "This ought to make you feel better. It is damn dark out here, and the rain makes a man jumpy. And I can think of better company than a dead man."

McKeever mounted and paused to look back. Singleton was standing by the edge of the road, lantern in one hand, pistol in the other. McKeever kicked the horse into motion and rode back to Two Pines.

He could tell by the milling, muttering crowd that the word had gone around, and as he rode down the street, men followed him, pushing questions at him, questions he did not bother to answer. . . .

There was a telegraph in Two Pines, owned jointly by the Idaho Lumber Company and the Galena Mining Company; McKeever dismounted in front of the building and turned in the doorway, facing the men crowding up. "There's nothing you can do," McKeever said. "Why don't you go about your business? Everything's being taken care of."

"You goin' to leave Dalridge out there in the rain?" one man asked.

"Doc Harris knows about it." McKeever said. "He'll go out there with his ambulance as soon as he's able to." McKeever went inside the telegrapher's shack. To the telegrapher, he said, "Did you notify Burgess at the mine, or Kelly at the mill?"

"No, sir," the telegrapher said. "This office only transmits messages; we don't originate 'em, Sheriff."

"You're a good man, Larry. All right, let me have a blank." McKeever wrote for several minutes, then gave the messages to Larry, who tapped them out to a mute length of wire. Immediately he was answered; the camps were only a few miles away, and they kept an operator on duty all the time.

McKeever waited for the answers, read them, then dropped the paper into his pocket. When McKeever turned to the door, the telegrapher said, "Mr. McKeever, someone killed Dalridge for the money, huh?"

"Yes. There's no use in trying to keep it a secret. I'll be at the Hanover House if anyone wants me."

He stepped out into the downpour, but kept under the overhangs as he walked toward the hotel. There was a mild-mannered crowd on the porch, full of unspoken questions, but McKeever passed into the lobby and hung up his dripping coat. The dining room was dark, closed for the night, but McKeever knew there was coffee in the kitchen; he went there, turned up the lamp, and took a cup from the cupboard.

WHILE he drank, light steps drew nearer, and Nan Singleton paused in the doorway. She was tall, like her brother, and fair-haired. Her eyes were large and her lips full. "Where's Jim? Out there all alone?"

"He'll be all right," McKeever said.

"Because you say so?"

"There's nothing out there to harm him. Nan, he's twenty. Let him be a man."

"I suppose there was nothing out there to harm Dalridge either?"

He shrugged. "I won't argue with you."

"Some of the men think it wasn't an accident."

"It wasn't," McKeever said. "The old man was killed for the money he carried."

Nan Singleton seemed horrified. "Lincoln, the murderer might still be out there someplace."

"I doubt it. Likely he's on a fast horse and riding as far as he can go."

"Then why aren't you chasing him?"

McKeever smiled. "After I talk with Burgess and Kelly, I'll telegraph to all the towns within a hundred miles and tell them to look for strangers who have a lot of money to spend, or are in a hurry. The fastest horse alive can't outrun the telegraph."

"That's a lazy man's way of doing a job," Nan said, and went back to the lobby.

McKeever took his time with his coffee and when he was through, he washed the cup and laid it on the drainboard of the sink to dry. The lobby was crowded; every chair was taken, and men stood in small groups talking earnestly. When Lincoln McKeever stepped into the room, they stopped talking and looked at him, their expressions curious, and annoyed, and angry.

Sam Richardson, who ran the bank of Two Pines, as mayor spoke for all of them. "What are you going to do about this, McKeever?"

"Catch the man," McKeever said. He peeled the wrapper from a cigar and put a match to it.

"Then why ain't you out looking?" one man asked.

McKeever raised his eyes and looked at the man. Nan Singleton stood behind the mahogany counter, waiting. "Which direction did he take?" McKeever asked.

Richardson snorted. "How in the hell would Pete know? McKeever, you move too slow to suit me. You always have."

"What do you want me to do?" McKeever asked. "Richardson, when a man asks for a loan you just give it to him, or ask a few questions first?"

"This isn't the same thing," Richardson said. He shook his finger at McKeever. "Dalridge had a lot of friends around Two Pines, friends who'll want to see someone hang for this. He carried a lot of money in his day, and not one penny stuck to his fingers."

The lobby drained by common consent; they all followed Richardson outside. When the door closed, Nan Singleton said, "You're not the most popular man in town right now, Lincoln. I feel a little sorry for you."

"Do you?"

"Yes, you have a large responsibility."

Lincoln McKeever smiled faintly. "That's a refreshing change, Nan. You usually believe that I have too little responsibility." He put on his hat and coat and went outside, discovering that the rain had stopped. Eaves still shed water, and it drained away in the gutters, but the clouds had broken, allowing a moon to shine through.

He walked two blocks over to his office and let himself in. The room contained a damp chill and after lighting the lamp, he built a small fire in the pot-bellied stove. Settled in his chair, with his cigar, Lincoln McKeever wondered where a man started to unravel a murder.

Of course the money was motive enough. McKeever wasn't certain of the exact amount, but it was always enough to make carrying it risky. Still, old man Dalridge had been carrying money for years, and never lost any of it. There was that time when a lone man tried to hold him up and got both barrels of buckshot in his chest for his trouble. After the county buried the man, no one else ever bothered Dalridge.

And Two Pines wasn't the kind of town where violence spawned. It was dull, but so were a lot of towns back east that had long ago settled into their comfortable rut. McKeever's home town had been like that, so dull that his father couldn't stand it any longer and had pulled out. Things like murder and robbery happened in Tombstone and Dodge City and El Paso, but not in Two Pines.

McKeever's cigar turned into a sour stub and he went to the door to toss it into the street. While he stood there, Doctor Harris drove by with his ambulance. Across the way, Wade Stanton observed this passage from his saddle. Stanton saw McKeever and came over and dismounted. As he stepped inside, Jim Singleton came down the walk, his long step quick and determined.

Singleton closed the door, then laid McKeever's pistol on the desk. "Jim," McKeever said, "when Doc finishes, I want a report."

"What for?" Jim Singleton said. "Hell, you can tell that the knock on the head killed him."

"Tell Doc I want it in writing," McKeever said. "You'd better go on over to the hotel, Jim. Your sister's worried about you."

"Let her worry," Singleton said and slammed the door as he left.

"There's a damned fresh kid," Wade Stanton said. "He's shot his mouth off to me a couple of times. One of these days I'm going to set him down, hard."

"Jim's just crowding his growth," McKeever said. He picked up his gun and broke it open, spilling the cartridges onto the desk top. He got out cloth and oil and dried it thoroughly.

"Why don't you carry a man-sized gun?" Stanton asked.

"What's wrong with this?"

"A thirty-two? Hell, when you go up against a man, you need a bigger gun, that's all." He shook his head. "Dalridge's killing's sure got this town jumpy, you know it?"

"I didn't think they'd take it calmly," McKeever said. He reloaded the Smith & Wesson and slipped it into his pocket. "They'll cool down in a day or two, after they get a chance to think about it."

"Who could have done a thing like that?" Stanton asked.

"Someone who wanted money," McKeever said.

"Maybe some down-and-outer passing through," Stanton said. "That could be worth thinking about, Lincoln."

"Oh, I'm thinking about it," McKeever admitted. "But that poses a lot of unanswered questions. How did he know Dalridge was carrying money?"

Stanton shrugged, then said, "Could be he was hoping to get a few dollars and hit a bonanza."

"Mmmmm," McKeever said. "A possibility there. Then, I have to ask myself who would be carrying a stick of dynamite around just in case he wanted to hold up someone."

Wade Stanton laughed. "I'm going home. Everytime I suggest something, you blow it apart for me." He got up and turned to the door. "Betty's been asking why you never come out any more."

"Wade, don't you know?"

Stanton shrugged. "Hell, Lincoln, there was never any jealousy on my part. I thought that was over with you. Over a long time ago."

"Sure, it's over," McKeever said. "She made her choice and I let it go at that. But it might start talk."

"To hell with the talk," Stanton said. "I enjoy your company, Lincoln. So does Betty. How about tomorrow; it's Sunday. Right after church, huh?"

"All right," McKeever said and watched Stanton leave.

He looked at his watch, and wondered whether or not he should wait for Olin Kelly and George Burgess. Then he decided that they'd be here when he got back, so he slipped into his coat, got a lantern out of the back room, and went to the stable for his horse.

McKEEVER left town, taking the south road, and when he got to the wrecked buggy, he dismounted, tied his horse and put a match to the lantern. His curiosity was jabbing him sharply, and he didn't like it, especially his curiosity about the dead horse.

The dead animal had attracted his attention from the beginning, so much so that he had glossed over his examination of Dalridge. And even now, he could not clear his thinking of the dead animal. Every time he tried to think of a possibility, the horse kept cropping up, as though begging him to come back for a closer look.

Damned funny, McKeever thought, that a holdup man would choose this way to stop a horse and buggy. Shoot the horse, perhaps, or the driver, but to blow up the horse—only a warped mind would think of that.

McKeever spent twenty minutes examining the animal, especially what appeared to be an entrance wound just behind the left shoulder. A very big hole, too big for a rifle. He measured it with his fingers and found it to be nearly an inch and a half in diameter.

He disliked this work, the blood and the torn flesh, yet it was necessary; his curiosity was stronger than his distaste. Quite obviously this was not the work of dynamite; some kind of a projectile was used, and McKeever could not find an exit hole.

The horse's back had been broken from inside, which suggested an explosion to McKeever. This had led his original thinking to dynamite. The intestines were ruptured, and much flesh had been torn away. He did not doubt it now; the animal had been killed by a fired shell.

McKeever stood by the road, thinking about this. A damned big gun was needed to shoot a shell that large. Too big for a man to handle easily, or get rid of in a hurry.

He blew out the lantern and rode back to his office.

Doctor Harris was there, his foul pipe filling the room with shag tobacco. His report was on McKeever's desk. As McKeever hung up his hat and coat, Harris said, "The head injury killed him. I'd say he was struck repeatedly by a gun barrel, or an iron rod."

"How big a gun?"

Harris shrugged. "A handgun. Of course, it could have been an iron rod."

"All right; that's something anyway." McKeever bent over the lamp to get a light for his cigar. "Doc, go get Jim Singleton and a couple more men from the stable. They'll loan you a block and tackle and rope. Get that horse on a wagon and cut him open. Bring me anything you find."

"What? Lincoln, I'm a doctor, not a vet!"

"Will you do this? For me?"

"All right," Doctor Harris said, edging toward the door. "Have you lost your mind? God, the people here'll howl their heads off when they find out you're investigating the death of a horse."

"Let 'em howl," McKeever said. "Did Kelly or Burgess get into town yet?"

"They're at the hotel," Harris said, and stepped out. He paused to look back. "Do you know what you're doing, Lincoln?"

"No," McKeever said. "But don't worry about it."

4.

WADE STANTON's ranch lay in the fork of two valleys, less than an hour's ride from Two Pines; yet he loitered, not wanting to arrive home too early. Betty would want to know why, and Wade Stanton wasn't too sure he could carry off an excuse.

Then there was the money; he'd have to hide that before he went into the house. He wasn't worried about the four paid hands; they had been in Kincaid's saloon and had a four-hour thirst to quench.

The mud made his approach silent and he dismounted by the barn, turning the horse into the stall before unsaddling. With the saddlebag over his arm, Stanton walked around the barn to the corral. With a shovel he dug a hole at the base of the manure pile, then went back to the barn for half a dozen burlap sacks. He wrapped the saddlebag carefully and then covered it, smoothing manure over the spot.

After he put the shovel away, he walked to the house, noticing that the parlor lamp was still lighted. He scraped the mud off his boots, then paused just inside the door to take them off. No need to get Betty started by tracking in mud.

He went into the parlor, and a moment later her bedroom door opened and closed. She came in, eyes pinched to shut out some of the light. "You're early. Lose all your money playing poker?"

"The game broke up," he said. "There was some trouble."

He looked at her briefly. She was small and shapely, dark-haired and quite tan. She was young, in her early twenties, which was an immature age as far as Wade Stanton was concerned. "Why don't you go back to bed?" he asked.

"I'm awake now," she said and sat down. She let the robe fall away from her legs, long enough for him to have his look, then she pulled the folds tightly around her.

Stanton said, "You do that on purpose, don't you?"

"Do what?" She looked at him innocently.

"Never mind," he said. "You'd say I was making it up."

"Well, you make up so many things," Betty Stanton said. . . . "What kind of trouble?"

"What? Oh, Dalridge was killed." He forced his voice to be casual.

"That's terrible! Does Lincoln know who did it?"

Stanton shook his head. "I invited him for dinner tomorrow."

"Why did you do that?"

He shrugged. "I thought you'd like it, that's all."

"You're lying to me, Wade. It's over between Lincoln and me, and you know it. It was over when we got married."

"I suppose," he said. "But it seems a shame. You'd have made a fine pair."

"That was meant to be unkind," Betty said. "But if I had it to do over again, you know which way it would go, don't you?"

"Yes, you've told me often enough," Stanton said. He turned to the sideboard and a glass of whisky. "One thing that's never occurred to you, Betty, is that I'm as sick of you as you are of me."

"Can you really be, Wade? I don't think it's possible."

He sat down across from her, his expression serious. "Betty, where did we go wrong?"

"I really don't know, Wade. You haven't changed a bit, so I guess it must be me. Yes, I think that's it. I wouldn't marry Lincoln because of his job; I thought it was insecure."

"Why don't you be honest and say he didn't make enough money?"

She stared at him for a moment, and then said, "All right, so he didn't make enough. You did. You rode a fine horse and sat a silver-mounted saddle, and I wanted the things your money could buy. But I never got them, Wade. I never got to touch a damned dollar, did I?"

"Betty, you have credit in all the stores. Anything you want to buy is there waiting for you. Hell, I've never denied you anything."

"You've denied me money," she said flatly. "I just want to hold it in my hands, to feel it, to know it's mine. Wade, do you know what I'd do if I could get my hands on some cash?"

"No, what would you do?"

"I'd leave you." His startled expression pleased her. "I'd leave you to your damned Saturday night poker buddies, and your man talk, and your damned man town." She got up then. "Good night, Wade. And don't bother to pound on my door."

When her bedroom door closed and the lock snapped, Wade Stanton poured himself another drink and sat with it in his hands, wondering how a man ever got into such a mess. Take that little tramp he'd known a few years back over in Woodland; she could cook the finest meals a man ever ate, sew on a button in nothing flat, make a man laugh when he felt like slugging the world, and give him one hell of a time in bed. But she was just a nester's daughter, who could hardly write her name, and who'd never dressed decent in her life.

No, Stanton decided, a man had to have better, especially when he had a big place and a bank account, and a responsibility toward the community. So a man chose someone else, Betty Richardson, who some day would inherit a bank. But the old man would sure have to die first because he was too tight-fisted to give away a nickle, even to his own daughter. Maybe that was just as well, Stanton figured. If Richardson ever gave Betty twenty dollars in cash, she'd light out and leave him standing there while everyone laughed.

Wade Stanton was a man who never let a thing bother him until he was ready to let it, and in the silent house, with the lulling effect of the whisky, he thought about Dalridge and the furious, well-planned twenty-one minutes out of his life. Twenty-one minutes that he could never recall or change or wipe out or even forget, for in those minutes a man had died while three other men had taken a step that was final and absolute.

With numbing clarity, Wade Stanton realized that he had known his last restful night on this earth; from that moment on he would have to be on guard for that small mistake every man might sooner or later make.

"Only my mistake will hang me," Stanton said softly, and then went at the rest of the bottle in earnest.

DAL LEGGITT reminded Lincoln McKeever of an undertaker, not a newspaperman, for Leggitt was very tall and always wore somber clothes. McKeever opened the hotel room door and found Leggitt there, ink stains on his shirt sleeves, paper and pencil in hand.

"I understand that Mr. Burgess and Mr. Kelly are here, Sheriff. I thought maybe I could get a statement."

"Let him come in," Burgess said. "That all right with you, Kelly?"

"Who can hide this?" Kelly said, and McKeever closed the door.

Kelly and Burgess were both big men, money big, physically big. Forty years of hard work and hard living and a hard heart had elevated them to a position of importance in Two Pines, and wherever lead or timber was sold.

"Have a chair, Mr. Leggitt," McKeever said, and sat down on the edge of the bed. "You were saying, Kelly?"

"I was saying that we ought to post a reward," Kelly snapped. "Dalridge worked for both of us; we split his salary right down the middle. And he was carrying money from both our companies."

"How much money?" Leggitt asked.

Kelly pursed his lips. "I'd say nearly forty-five thousand from me. How about you, George?"

"About that," Burgess said. He made a fuss with his cigar before he put a match to it. "Ninety thousand is a fortune, gentlemen. I hardly need say that I'm more interested in catching Dalridge's killer than I am in recovering the money. A firm in San Francisco has insured all my finances while in transit. I'll file a claim tonight with them."

"Then they'll send an investigator?" Leggitt asked.

"I suppose so," Kelly said. "I'm insured by the same firm." His glance touched McKeever. "I wouldn't let any grass grow under my feet if I were you, Lincoln. Hate to think of an outsider poking his nose into our business. I'd like to see this cleared up locally."

"So would I," McKeever said. "And believe me, gentlemen, I'll do my best."

"Just get the killer," George Burgess said. "That'll satisfy everyone."

"Sheriff," Leggitt said, "I'd like a statement from you. Any leads?"

"Nothing definite," McKeever said smoothly. "However, I've sent telegrams to all the law enforcement agencies within a hundred miles in every direction, warning them to be on the lookout for anyone who spends money freely, or acts suspicious. I'll question them as they're picked up."

"Seems to be a long way around the track," Kelly said, then popped the lid on his watch. "I want to get off a telegram tonight. San Francisco won't do a damned thing until Monday morning. Probably won't send a man until Tuesday, or even Wednesday." He pursed his lips. "If he takes the train to Woodland, it'll be Friday before he gets here. That gives you a little less than a week, McKeever. Better get on your horse."

"Yes, it isn't much time." When Burgess and Kelly got up to leave, McKeever said, "Ah, about the burial, gentlemen. Do you want the county to take care of that?"

"County be damned," Kelly snapped. "Dalridge was our employee, and we'll see that he gets the best planting possible. I want this town closed up tighter'n a drum tomorrow. Set the funeral for eleven o'clock and pass the word around that I want everyone to be there."

"Why bury him so soon?" Leggitt wanted to know.

Kelly stared at him. "Why not? He's dead, ain't he? And you give the funeral a nice coverage in the paper, understand. And don't put it on the back page, either."

They went out and after the door closed, Lincoln McKeever said, "Don't take Olin Kelly too literally, Dal."

"Oh? Why don't you let me be the judge?"

"All right," McKeever said. "You do as you please. You will anyway."

Dal Leggitt smiled. "McKeever, we never liked each other, but I'm not going to use this killing as a club."

"Well, thanks."

"You just do your job and I won't complain."

Lincoln McKeever smiled. "Did you ever hear the one about not being able to please all the people all of the time?"

"I know that one," Leggitt said. "But I've never jumped on a man's back without a good reason." He stood up then and put away his writing material. "I'll stay out of your way, Lincoln. I imagine you have things to do."

"I have, for a fact," McKeever said and went down to the lobby with Dal Leggitt.

Nan Singleton stopped McKeever before he could make the sidewalk. "Lincoln, it's after eleven. Where's my brother?"

"With Doc Harris."

"Send him home."

"If Doc's through," McKeever said.

Temper bloomed in Nan Singleton's eyes. "I said send him home." She whirled and went into the back room, slamming the door behind her.

The clerk, who had observed this with a smile, said, "What makes you two fight?"

"Ask her."

"Wouldn't do any good," the clerk said. "You know, I think you're both afraid you'll stop fighting."

McKeever frowned. "What the hell's that supposed to mean?"

"You figure it out," the clerk said, and then laughed.

Doc HARRIS was operating in the stable, with Jim Singleton handing him instruments and seeing that the lanterns were shining properly. Harris looked up briefly when McKeever came in. A cloth had been spread on a cobbler's bench, and bloody pieces of metal were piled there.

"How's it going?" McKeever asked.

"You want to know something?" Harris asked. "You've got me curious now. This horse is peppered with hunks of metal." He dug for another piece. "I'll be at this all night, the rate I'm going."

"It'll help if you get all the pieces you can," McKeever said.

Doc Harris squinted. "What you going to do, Lincoln? Make a puzzle out of this?"

"It's been floating around in my mind," McKeever admitted. He glanced at Jim Singleton. "Your sister wants you home."

"I'm helping Doc," Jim said. He was a round-faced young man, in spite of his height. "Do I have to go?"

"Not unless you want to," McKeever said.

He watched Harris work, then he heard the town clock strike midnight. A step in the stable archway made him turn, and Nan Singleton stopped there.

"I thought I said that I wanted Jim home."

McKeever walked over to her. "He's busy. We're all busy, so you go on and mind your own business, Nan."

She sucked in her breath and glared at him. "I'm not going to argue with you, Lincoln."

"That's a change," McKeever said. He took her arm and turned her away, but she tried to twist out of his grip. He held her, until she tried to kick him, then he unexpectedly pulled her against him and kissed her. For a second she was passive in his arms; then she writhed away, pawing the back of her hand across her mouth.

"Don't you ever do that to me again!"

"Afraid you'll get to liking it?"

"Lincoln, I hate you!"

"What for? Not because I kissed you. Or is it because I didn't kiss you soon enough?"

"I'm not Betty Stanton," she snapped. Then she looked at her brother. "Jim, you come home, you hear?" When the boy didn't answer, or turn his head, she stamped her foot. "Then stay, damn it! See if I care."

"Nan—" McKeever began.

"Shut up! Just leave me alone." She turned and ran down the street, her skirts lifted above the mud.

Doc Harris turned his head and smiled. "She likes you, Lincoln."

"Oh, to hell with you," McKeever said.

"Don't be stupid as well as blind," Harris said. "She likes you too much, and you hurt her at one time or another." Then he turned back to his job of probing the horse's carcass for bits of metal.

5.

LINCOLN MCKEEVER had his horse saddled before dawn, and when a wan, cloud-filtered sun rose, he was again examining the overturned buggy in which Dalridge had died. The rain had washed out all the tracks, leaving the road a smear of undefinable gouges, and McKeever did not favor them with even a moment's attention. He looked along the road in both directions, looking for a hiding place, a haven for ambush; he was sure that Dalridge had been taken by complete surprise, for no other way would have succeeded.

McKeever thought about this. How did you take an old Indian fighter by surprise? No place for a man to hide, unless he crouched in the ditch, and McKeever scratched that out for two reasons: a man on foot is in a poor position to escape, and then there was the gun— how big he wasn't sure, but certainly bigger than a heavy rifle. With that ruled out, McKeever thought of a horseman and immediately discounted it because of the gun.

Another buggy? That was worth considering; he mounted and rode back a piece until he came to the lane leading to the main road. Stopping there, he could see the wrecked buggy, and the elements began to fall into place, at least enough so that every idea he got wasn't automatically shot full of holes by conflicting evidence. In the first place, Dalridge wouldn't be alarmed by a buggy coming up behind him. McKeever stopped. A buggy would be just right to carry an infernal gun the size necessary to shoot an exploding shell.

Then he took out a cigar and began to gnaw on it. Why an exploding shell? Why not just shoot Dalridge? Hell, he was clubbed to death anyway. McKeever's brows wrinkled as he thought about this. Then an answer came to him. Confusion was what the robbers were after, something to confuse the hell out of anyone trying to make head or tail of this. Killing the horse to stop a man was something new and confusing in highway robbery, McKeever had to admit.

McKeever puffed on his cigar and considered himself to be a robber, bent on robbing but not on killing, and then in the end forced to kill. What would make a man kill? Recognition? McKeever slowly took the cigar from his mouth. By God, how simple could he get? Of course that was it! Dalridge recognized one of the men and was killed because of that.

The facts then piled up in McKeever's mind too fast to sort.

This was no outside robbery; the men who robbed Dalridge lived in Two Pines. Men? The fact that he had thought of them in the plural surprised him, and he groped for the reason his thinking had automatically taken that turn. In a moment he had it—the gun. Too big for one man to handle and drive at the same time. Two men anyway, he decided; one to drive and one to kill the horse.

Mounting his horse, Lincoln McKeever rode slowly

back to town, kicking possibilities around in his mind. The more he thought about it, the clearer it became. Almost everyone in town knew that Dalridge carried money from the mine and the logging camp, and the robbers would have to know that in order to set their trap. Know the back roads too, in order to get in and out of town without being seen.

McKeever almost wished that some stranger had killed Dalridge; finding him would be easier than ferreting out someone in Two Pines. He knew everyone, yet he knew none who seemed capable of this robbery and deliberate murder.

"But it's my job to find out," McKeever said softly, and then rode on to his office.

He shaved and changed into his best suit, and when he was wiping the mud off his boots, Doctor Harris came in, bleary-eyed and in a foul humor.

"I said it would take all night." He set the metal fragments on McKeever's desk. "You have a good sleep?"

"I didn't bother to lay down," McKeever said.

Harris packed his pipe and lit it. "What you going to do with all that scrap junk, Lincoln?"

"Try and put it together," McKeever said.

Doctor Harris shook his head. "Lincoln, you'd better not spend your time fooling around with that thing. Folks would like it a lot better if you started hunting around for Dalridge's killer."

"I intend to get to that too," McKeever said.

"Well," Harris said, "I never knew a man who could tell you what to do. Me, I'm going to shave and get ready for the funeral. When Kelly and Burgess say for a man to be someplace, it pays him to listen."

McKeever grinned. "They don't scare you, Doc. Who're you fooling, anyway?"

"Kelly and Burgess," Harris said and went out.

McKeever unwrapped the cloth and spread it out on his desk, sorting the pieces carefully. Harris had washed them in alcohol to clean them, and McKeever chose the largest fragment as the starter. He sorted and fitted until he found another fragment that seemed to fit properly, then he stopped, wondering how he was going to glue this together.

Finally he got the idea of using putty; he got a half-used can from the storeroom. He scraped the dried stuff off the surface and then molded a piece into a ball, pressing the metal fragments into it. They clung to the putty, and he began to put his puzzle together.

McKeever had fit four pieces together when Dal Leggitt came in. He sat down and said, "McKeever, I want to put the paper to bed this afternoon and I wondered if there was anything you wanted to add to it?"

"Nope," McKeever said. "You may say that this office has no leads. I'm completely in the dark."

Leggitt's brows furrowed. "You want to admit that?"

"Why not?" McKeever asked. "Don't you want to print the truth?"

"With election only six months away, I thought you'd have something better than that." He looked at the scattered fragments of metal. "What the hell are you doing?"

"Trying to find out what killed Dalridge's horse."

"Good God, who cares about the horse?"

McKeever looked at him. "I do, Dal. Don't you?"

"To hell with the horse! What do you think the readers are going to do when they hear you're investigating the death of a horse?"

"Mob me?" McKeever shook his head. "Why don't you go print your paper, Dal? I'd hate to think that the women in this town would be without it to wrap their garbage in."

Color ran into Leggitt's face, and he stood up quickly. "All right, McKeever. I'll give you war, if that's what you want."

"You just do that," McKeever said. "You intended to anyway, in spite of the speech you made for Kelly's benefit." McKeever bored the man with his eyes. "You know something, Dal? If Nan would marry you, you'd get off my back, wouldn't you?"

Leggitt stood there and for a time McKeever thought he wasn't going to answer. Then Leggitt said, "I don't like you, McKeever. I don't like any man who takes what I want."

"I have no claim on Nan Singletón, and you know it."

"You've got the kind of a claim I can't break," Leggitt said. "But I'll break it, Lincoln. I'll break it and you at the same time." He rubbed his thin, ink-stained hands across the front of his coat. "You hurt her, McKeever, and you're going to pay for it."

"Get out of here," McKeever said. "Go on, beat it."

"All right, but remember what I said." He backed to the door, then eased out, as though he were afraid to turn his back on McKeever.

FINLEY FINEEN's head felt like a number-two washtub when he awoke, and his mouth seemed stuffed with cotton. He got up, stood for a moment in his underwear, then staggered to the wash basin and soaked his head in the cold water.

Then he realized that he hadn't even gone home; he didn't want to think of what his wife would say. Dressing, he threw away the empty whisky bottle, then went out through the yard in back, took a side street to his house on Locust Street, and tried to ease in the side door without making any noise.

His wife was in the kitchen; she came to the hallway, flour-covered hands on her hips, and the very devil in her eye. "Finley Fineen, where have you been?" Without waiting for an answer she approached him, sniffing suspiciously. "You smell like a mince pie!"

She was a small woman in her middle thirties, and still pretty in a sun-bleached way. Fineen looked downcast. "I got drunk, Madge."

"Finley, you didn't?" She seemed horror-stricken.

He nodded. "I did, Madge."

"You gave me your pledge the day we were married, Finley."

"Aye, and for eleven years I've kept it." He raised his head. "By God, Madge, a man's got a right to go on a toot once in a while!"

"I'll have no drunks in my house," Madge Fineen said. "You know I feel strongly about liquor, Finley." She compressed her lips in that firm way she had. "Now you march right upstairs and take a bath and change your clothes. They're burying that poor Mr. Dalridge this morning and the whole town will be there."

"This morning?" Fineen straightened. "I didn't know."

"Of course you didn't know. How could you, being drunk?"

"Ah, Madge, are you going to harp about that for the next twenty years now? If it isn't one thing, it's another."

"Now, Finley, you're a respectable man, and you've got to set a good example." She made shooing motions. "Go on now. We haven't much time."

He sniffed. "Is that pie I smell?"

Her smile started slowly; she could never long contain anger. "I thought you'd like it, Finley."

He came to her then and put his huge hands on her shoulders. "Madge, you're a woman in a million, do you know that?"

"I don't think I ought to let you touch me," she said, then came against him, her arms around him tightly. "You worried me so, Finley."

"Now, now," he said, kissing her briefly. "You're not really mad at me, are you?"

"Well, since this is the first time in eleven years—"

He laughed then and went on up the stairs, whistling.

Fineen brought his clothes down to the small room off the kitchen, and there filled the wooden tub with water. He sang in an off-key baritone while he scrubbed, then dried himself and slipped into clean underwear. While he was buttoning up, he suddenly stopped singing and jerked open the door leading into the kitchen.

Madge Fineen had her back to him and she was pummeling a piece of bread dough on the table. Finley Fineen locked his hands against the door frame and closed his eyes as her fist beat the dough with a dull sloughing impact. The sound beat against his ears and brought sweat to his forehead and upper lip.

Finally he could stand it no longer. Roughly he shoved her aside, unmindful of her surprised cry. Then he picked up the bread dough and threw it out into the back yard.

"Finley, have you lost your mind!" She tried to take his arm, to pull him around to face her, but he jerked away.

"Don't ever make that stuff when I'm home, you understand?" He shouted.

"Finley, you lower your voice! You want the neighbors to hear?"

He looked at her, his expression set. "I don't give a damn about the neighbors! Now you mind what I say!"

"What in the world's gotten into you, Finley?" She

shook her head and tried to laugh. "I've made bread every Sunday morning for twenty years. My mother made it on Sunday morning, and her mother before that."

"I don't give a hoot what they did," he said. "I'm telling you, Madge, don't ever make that stuff again while I'm in the house."

"Finley, I don't understand you at all," Madge Fineen said. "I just don't understand you at all. I can't see what making bread has to do with you getting so upset."

"Just never mind," Fineen said, calmer now. "Madge, I've never been a demanding man, and you seem happy with me."

"Oh, I am, Finley. You've been all a woman could ask in a man."

"Then just mind me this time, huh? Is it so much to ask?"

"No, but I don't like to break my habits, Finley. No more than you do." Her brow wrinkled slightly. "What would you say if I just asked you to give up something, without telling you why?"

"Madge, you can buy your bread from Hanson's Bakery!"

"I prefer to make my own," she said, then smiled. "Go get your clothes on, Finley. A man looks so funny in his underwear." Then she looked out the door at the bread in the yard. "My, and it would have made such pretty loaves too."

Fineen went into the side room again, closed the door, and, leaned against it a moment. When he felt that his control was restored, he slipped into his suit, then went out so that Madge could knot his tie.

She was in the yard gathering the pad of dough, her expression sad, as though he had destroyed something fine. When she came in, she dumped it into the garbage pail and put the lid on.

Fineen said, "Madge, honey, don't be angry with me, please."

"If drink does this to you, Finley—"

"Yeah, I guess that's it." He licked his lips. "I told Bill Daley I'd drop over this morning. I'd better do that, I guess."

"Land's sake, don't you see enough of him on Saturday night? All right, you'd better go; you'd just faunch around here if you didn't. But you come back here in time to take me to the church."

"Sure," he said, and turned to the door.

"Finley Fineen! You come here and let me fix that tie."

6.

McKEEVER was standing on the porch of the Hanover House when Finley Fineen turned the far corner. Wade Stanton was coming down the street in his buggy and when he saw McKeever, he pulled over to the hitch-rack and stopped. Betty sat beside him, a wide hat shielding her face. She smiled at McKeever and said, "I got up early this morning and baked an apple pie for you. I expect you to appreciate it."

"I'll show that appreciation by eating two pieces," McKeever said. "Going to the funeral?"

"Of course," Stanton said quickly. "I liked Dalridge too, you know."

Fineen crossed the street, nodded to McKeever, then said, "Don't you think that striped shirt is a little gay for a funeral, Wade?"

"That's what I told him," Betty said, "but he never listens to me."

"Funerals are too sad anyway," Stanton said. "They can stand a little cheering." He glanced at Betty. "And don't start crying; you didn't know Dalridge that well."

"One is expected to cry a little," Betty said.

"A barbaric custom," Stanton said. "I'll bet half the women have onions in their handkerchiefs."

McKeever seemed offended. "You have a practical mind, Wade. Too damned practical."

"Well," Fineen said, "I'll see you at the funeral, huh, Wade?"

"Why, sure."

Fineen nodded to Betty and walked on.

Bill Daley lived over the drugstore, and Fineen went up the outside stairs. Daley's wife answered the door, a pleasant-faced woman with the sharpest tongue in town, a startling contrast to her gentle appearance.

"Oh, it's you," she said. "Come on in."

"Is Bill up?"

"Yes, but he hadn't ought to be," she said. "I told him to stay home last night, but he had to play poker. This wet weather raises hob with his health, but poker's more important." She snorted. "Seems to me he's trying to make a widow of me before my time. Deliberate, if you ask me."

"I'd never make the mistake of asking," Fineen said.

She glared at him, hard eyes in a sweet face. "He's in the parlor. Go in if you want to."

Bill Daley heard them talking and came to the hallway. He had a towel around his throat and a thermometer in his mouth. He spoke around this. "I'm not long for this world, Finley. Didn't sleep a wink last night."

"You coming to the funeral?"

"I'd better not," Daley said. "This cold's worse. Real bad."

"You'd better come," Fineen said. He glanced into the kitchen to see if Daley's wife listened. "You want this to look good, don't you?"

"Hell, it'll look all right if I'm not there," Daley said softly. "Everyone knows how sickly I am."

Fineen tapped him on the chest with his finger. "Bill, you show up at the church and at the cemetery, you understand?"

"Oh, all right." He had a fit of coughing. "I ought to go to a dry climate, Finley. Arizona or someplace where the air's good."

"To hell with that," Finley Fineen said. "Once you got clear of Two Pines you'd start spending that money."

"I wouldn't," Daley said. "Honest, I wouldn't, Finley."

"Where would you get the money to live on then? You think your wife would give it to you?" Fineen laughed softly. "She's got you buffaloed, Bill. I'll bet she prays you'll come down with something and die, leaving it all to her."

"Ah, you got no right to talk like that," Daley said. He shook his head. "Must have got wet last night. I've got no resistance for these things. Doc Harris said so." He took Fineen by the sleeve. "Look, if Doc advised me to go to another climate, who'd suspect, huh?"

"We'll talk about it later," Fineen said. "Now get dressed for the funeral."

He went to the door and and let himself out. Daley's wife waited until Fineen's step faded, then came into the parlor. "I don't think much of your friends."

Daley looked at her. "That's not surprising, Ethel." He went into the bedroom and laid out his dark suit.

"You're going to the funeral after all?"

"Yes," he said.

"Fineen talk you into it?"

He turned to her, exasperated. "No, Fineen didn't talk me into it. I feel better, that's all."

"My, what a miraculous change. A few minutes ago you felt too bad to answer the door. Made me come all the way in from the kitchen to open it."

"Ethel, don't make it sound like a twenty-mile hike."

"You're sharp to criticize, aren't you?"

He bit his tongue and slipped into his pants and shirt. "I wouldn't criticize you, Ethel. Some people are just born perfect, and you're fortunate that you're one of those rare jewels."

"That's right, throw it up to me. Always throwing it up to me. What do you have to go to the funeral for? What was Dalridge to you?"

Daley hesitated, then said, "I don't want to go, Ethel; I wish I didn't have to go. But I'm a business man and it would look bad if I didn't." Then he shrugged. "Besides, birth and death are events that happen only once to a man. What's in between doesn't matter very much."

He knotted his tie, picked up his hat and coat and went to the door, his wife trailing him.

"I suppose you'll stop off for an afternoon with your crowd. I won't see you until suppertime."

He paused in the doorway. "Will that break your heart, Ethel?"

She looked at him a moment, then her lower lip began to quiver and tears dammed up against her lower lids. "It just breaks my heart to see us this way, Bill. I don't mean to be talking all the time, picking at you, but I just can't help myself. Sometimes I think you'd be happier if I was dead."

This talk alarmed him, although he had heard it before and recognized it for an attention-getting device. He put his arm around her and patted her on the shoulder.

"Don't think about things like that, Ethel. We get on as good as most."

He left her at the top of the landing and went on down to the street, coughing into his handkerchief.

THE minister preached a fine sermon, a little on the solemn side, but fine, the kind every man wanted spoken over him, glossing over his bad points and stretching his good ones as far as credulity would allow. McKeever sat through it, his attention wandering, and after the church emptied, the minister came up to him, speaking in that soft, confidential voice he had so patiently cultivated. "Sheriff, I haven't had time to select the pallbearers. Kelly volunteered, and Burgess, but I wondered if I could count on you?"

"Certainly," McKeever said. He looked around and saw Finley Fineen talking to Wade Stanton and Bill Daley. "I'll get the other three for you." He walked over and they broke off their talk. "Goodnight wants some pallbearers. I've elected you three."

"Hell," Stanton said quickly, "I don't want to carry a casket."

Fineen fixed him with a sharp eye. "What kind of talk is that, Wade? Sure, Lincoln, we'll serve. Be proud to."

"I don't think I ought to lift anything," Daley said. "Feeling the way I do."

"A sixth of two hundred and fifty pounds isn't much," Fineen said. "You can count us in, Lincoln."

"Thanks," McKeever said and walked away.

Wade Stanton glanced around him to make sure no one was near enough to overhear. "My God, Finley, where's your feelings?"

"Hidden," Fineen said. "And that's where yours ought to be." He looked at Daley. Wipe that sick look off your face, you hear?"

"Finley, I—I don't want to carry him."

"By God you're going to carry him," Fineen said softly. "This isn't what I want, but if it has to be, then we'll do it." He discovered sweat on his face and wiped it away. "I got drunk last night." He was instantly sorry that he made the admission, for both Daley and Stanton looked sharply at him.

"I didn't sleep a wink," Daley admitted. He glanced at Stanton. "How about you?"

"I never thought about it," he said quickly. Then he chuckled. "I think both of you have paper guts."

Fineen tapped him on the arm as Lincoln McKeever came over. "Goodnight's ready. Wade, you want to pick me up at the office after the funeral?"

"Sure," Stanton said. He took Bill Daley by the arm. "Come on, let's get Dalridge in the ground respectful-like."

McKeever was not fond of funerals, and the crying, but he endured it, and as soon as possible he walked back to his office. He barely had time to light a cigar when Olin Kelly and George Burgess walked in and sat down.

They looked sad-eyed and silent, as though their dearest friend had just passed away, and this annoyed McKeever and goaded him into speaking. "You can quit acting now."

Both men looked at him, offended. Kelly said, "What a hell of a thing to say. Dalridge was our employee."

"He was a man who worked for you and now you'll hire another one." McKeever leaned on his desk. "Have you notified the insurance company?"

"Yes," Burgess said. "I expect a telegram tomorrow. I'll let you know if they're sending a man or not."

"It won't make much difference if they do or don't. I think our man is still in town." He put it out for its shock value, and found that it had plenty.

Both men tried to talk at once, but McKeever quieted them and told them why he thought the killer was still in Two Pines.

"By God, McKeever," Kelly said, "this is horrible. I thought we had honest folks around here?" He turned his head toward the door as Stanton drove up in his buggy. Kelly and Burgess put on their hats. "We'll see you later, Sheriff," Kelly said. "Come on, George. I want to think about this for a while."

"Make sure you don't talk," McKeever said. "And I mean to anyone."

"Don't worry about that," Burgess said, and they went out, meeting Wade Stanton as he came in the door. McKeever put on his hat while Stanton took a look at the clay and metal fragments on McKeever's desk.

"What you making, mud pies?"

"Just something to pass the time," McKeever said.

When Stanton went to pick up the clay, McKeever said, "Don't do that, Wade. I don't want it disturbed."

"Hell, I was only looking," Stanton said, frowning.

He walked to the door with McKeever, then stood there while McKeever locked up. Betty was waiting in the buggy, her hat in her lap.

"I'll get my horse," McKeever said.

"Ah, Lincoln, I want to stay in town for a while. Why don't you drive Betty home and I'll ride your horse out when I come?"

McKeever frowned. "Wade, I can wait if you won't be long."

"I don't know how long I will be," Stanton said. "Hell, I trust you, Lincoln."

Color came into McKeever's cheeks and he glanced at Betty Stanton, but she was studying her fingernails. Without looking up, she said, "Am I going to have to waste the pie?"

"All right," McKeever said and climbed into the rig. He lifted the reins and drove out of town.

FINALLY Betty Stanton said, "Don't look so glum, Lincoln. There are men who would like to be alone with me."

"Men you were once engaged to?"

"That was two years ago," she said. "I thought it was all over."

"It is, but people still like to talk."

She laughed. "Lincoln, a little talk would liven up this dead town."

"It's lively enough to suit me," he said.

She made a half pout with her lips. "Now you're talking like Wade. All he wants to do is eat, sleep, and raise hell with the boys."

"You're complaining?"

"I get lonesome," she said. "Don't you?" She took his arm and tugged. "Stop this damn thing for a minute."

He hauled on the reins and then she turned in the seat and put her arms around him. Her lips came against his, warm and working, speaking to him without words. Then she drew away, laughing, her hands smoothing her hair. "You know, I needed that, Lincoln."

"Now you've made me sorry I came with you," McKeever said.

"Why? Are you afraid Nan Singleton will find out?"

"What do you have against Nan? You've been digging at her for two years."

Betty Stanton shrugged. "Lincoln, I made a mistake, marrying Wade."

"So?"

"So I'd like to straighten that out."

"What's that got to do with Nan?"

"Well, she's in love with you, Lincoln, and I don't want her to be." She touched his cheek gently, then kissed him again, lightly. "I want to get away from Wade. And when I do, I'm going to make right the mistake I made two years ago. I want you, Lincoln. And I want you unattached. To get you that way I have to say just the right things to Nan Singleton. Not lies, really, but I want her to think the worst. And Lincoln, I don't think you really mind. Do you?"

He blew out a long breath and sat with the reins lax in his hands. "Betty, I wish I could get over you."

"You never will," she said. "Now come on, let's go home. Wade may stay in town for hours yet."

7.

WADE STANTON walked to Finley Fineen's office, hoping to find him there, but Fineen was home, with his wife. Stanton stood by the door for several minutes, trying to decide whether to go to Fineen's house or send for him. He decided that sending for him was safer, so he collared a boy and gave him two twenty-five-cent pieces, one for fetching Fineen and the other for fetching Bill Daley.

For ten minutes Stanton waited, and he forced himself to appear unconcerned. It wouldn't do to seem nervous; someone might see him and remember it; for the town was full of people who liked to look in on everyone else's business.

Bill Daley arrived first, a trace of annoyance in his expression.

"What the hell is this?" Daley asked. "I had a devil of a time explaining to my wife. You know I'm not good at thinking up excuses."

"Do you have to tell your wife everything?" Stanton asked. Then he saw Fineen coming down the street.

Fineen frowned and said. "There's no reason for this, Wade. What excuse are you going to offer for this?"

"I'll tell you inside," Stanton said.

"Not to me, you fool," Fineen said. "What are you going to say when someone starts prying into your reason for coming here today?"

"Nobody will," Stanton said.

"The hell they won't. Before the day's out you're going to be asked. How about it? What's the excuse?"

"Oh, tell 'em that Bill ordered a new buggy for his wife."

Daley looked surprised. "Buggy? I haven't given Ethel a gift for ten-twelve years."

"Then it's time you did," Fineen said and unlocked the door. He said no more until they were in his back office, with the door closed. "All right, Wade, what's up?"

"I just came from McKeever's office. You know what he's doing? He's putting together the pieces of that shell."

"So?" Fineen said.

"So he'll find out about it!" Stanton snapped.

"By God, I made that shell," Daley said, alarmed. "Finley, what are we going to do?"

"We're going to do nothing," Fineen said. He looked at each of them. "What the devil do you expect me to do? Steal it from him?"

"Why not?" Stanton asked. "Finley, McKeever's at my place, with Betty. He'll stay there until I get home, so we've got the time."

Finley Fineen frowned. "What's this? About McKeever being with your wife, I mean?"

Wade Stanton waved his hands. "It don't have anything to do with us, Finley. But we can take advantage of it."

"Everything the three of us do and say has to do with all of us, and don't you ever forget it, Wade." Fineen's frown was intense. "What are you cooking up for McKeever's benefit anyway?"

Wade Stanton hesitated, then said, "Well, Betty and

I don't get along; I'd be better off without her. But she's expensive, Finley. I'd have to kick her out without a cent, but I need a reason to do that."

Fineen blew out his breath. "So you want to involve her with Lincoln McKeever, is that it?"

Shrugging, Stanton said, "Well, hell, they were pretty sweet on each other once, so I thought—"

"You're bragging!" Fineen snapped. "No one ever accused you of thinking, Wade. Now you listen to me, both of you. Don't cook up any schemes of your own, understand? We made a plan and we're going to stick to it. So McKeever's putting together the pieces. All right, what does he have when he gets through?"

"Something I made," Daley said. "And I don't want it traced to me."

"He can't trace it to you," Fineen said quickly. "You made that shell in my shop, in the hours when you were supposed to be playing poker, in the hour before McKeever came here each Saturday night. Now, I mean it, we don't get panic-stricken over this."

"I still think stealing it—"

Fineen cut Stanton off. "That would be the worst thing we could do, Wade. Then and there McKeever would know that the men he wanted were right here in Two Pines." He shook his head. "We leave him alone, you understand. I'll go see Dal Leggitt at the paper; he's always had it in for McKeever. If I drop the hint that McKeever's wasting his time putting pieces of metal together, Leggitt will blast him with his paper."

"But if he can rebuild the shell," Daley said, "he might find the gun."

"What gun? There isn't any gun," Fineen said. "That was part of the idea, using parts of this and that to fire the shell. A gun is something that has to be gotten rid of, but not our gun. There's nothing for him to find. Hell, he could use my press for the rest of his life and never suspect that he was handling the gun barrel." He took each of them by the arm, steering them toward the door. "I tell you not to worry about this. I'll see Leggitt and get him stirred up, and you two just stand back and watch the fireworks; we'll keep McKeever on the fire until he's tired of jumping around."

"All right," Daley said, "but I still think—"

"What can we do?" Fineen asked. "What can we possibly do that won't throw suspicion our way? We must make sure that McKeever never knows for sure that the men he wants are still in Two Pines." He patted their shoulders. "Now get out of here, and Bill, tell your wife in a roundabout way about the new buggy."

"Lord, that's expensive."

"You can afford it," Fineen said. "In fact, you can't afford not to buy it." His glance touched Stanton. "And you came here to see it. After all, everyone knows we're close friends." Fineen smiled. "Relax, Bill. When that mouthy woman of yours gets through telling it all over town, no one would ever think of questioning us about this meeting."

"You're too damned careful," Wade Stanton said.

"Careful?" Fineen shook his head. "I know how people like to talk, that's all. Now go on, get out of here."

AFTER they left, Fineen sat down at his desk and tried to straighten the facts out in his mind. Somehow he could no longer say which was important, to lead McKeever astray, or to sit back and rest in the knowledge that McKeever could never trace the killing to his door.

He was disturbed, now that McKeever was piecing together the shell; Fineen hadn't figured on his doing that at all. To his way of thinking, McKeever was just a man coasting along in a soft job, not particularly smart, and certainly without any experience when it came to catching criminals. The way Fineen had it figured, McKeever would tear up the countryside looking for Dalridge's killer, but he had fooled everyone by staying around town and apparently doing nothing.

Only McKeever wasn't idle; Fineen knew that now. Neither idle nor stupid, and the fact that he lacked experience didn't seem to slow him much.

He believed he knew a way to throw Lincoln McKeever off the track, although it violated his original plan. But after thinking about it, he decided it would be foolproof, and he didn't have to tell Wade Stanton or Bill Daley; what they didn't know wouldn't hurt them.

Removing the money in broad daylight, even with all the doors locked, wasn't the smartest thing Finley Fineen ever did, but he figured that it was necessary. He took

eight thousand dollars and set it aside, then put the
rest of the money back in its hiding place. Carefully he
stripped the band from one package, but made certain
that a portion of it, with the mine's name, was placed
between the layers of bills as though it had accidentally
been caught there and overlooked.

With brown butcher paper he wrapped the money
securely, then penciled a note:

> Mr. Lon Beasley
> Attorney at Law
> Woodland, Wyoming
>
> Dear Mr. Beasley:
> Here you'll find eight thousand dollars to buy me
> a ranch with. I hear you buy property and sell it
> and I've been looking for a place, now that I have
> the money. You just hang onto it for me and I'll
> be in a week come Saturday to get the deed. I'll
> identify myself to you.
>
> > Yours,
> > Peter Hotchkiss

Fineen read it over a few times and seemed satisfied,
both with the wording and his disguised handwriting.
He tied the bundle and tucked it into his coat pocket,
feeling, as he let himself out, that this would draw Lincoln McKeever away from Two Pines like a good dog
on coon scent. Fineen was sure that most of the news-
papers would carry a story of the robbery, so every
sheriff would be aware of what that binding ribbon
meant, as would Lon Beasley.

Getting the package mailed presented a problem to
Finley Fineen, but he solved it by cutting through the
Wells Fargo stage yard on his way home. This was not
an uncommon route for him and he would arouse no suspicion, particularly when he stopped and looked at the
coaches.

The mail was carried in the well beneath the driver's
feet, and Fineen knew that the rocking now and then
broke open the bags, at least often enough so that the
drivers always looked for scattered pieces. Sidling
around the coach, Fineen saw that no one was watching
through their front windows. He quickly tossed the

package into the footwell, knowing that when it was found in Woodland, the driver would assume that it had been spilled out of the sack.

No one would be able to trace the package to Finley Fineen.

WALKING the rest of the way home, Fineen was troubled, for McKeever had driven him to doing something he swore he would never do: depart from the original plan. From the beginning he had figured that most men got caught because they panicked, and sooner or later, broke cover to run. This was one mistake he was not going to make, and yet he had already made it by allowing McKeever to jar him.

As he approached the house he remembered that he had to see Dal Leggitt, and turned about, walking back up town. Fineen knew better than to go to the newspaper office; this was Sunday and Leggitt would be trying to make time with Nan Singleton.

Leggitt was on the porch of the Hanover House, Nan beside him in one of the wicker chairs. Fineen made his approach casual, and his halt one of those spur-of-the-moment things. Taking off his hat, Fineen inspected the band for sweat stains. Then he said, "Pretty good funeral, huh, Dal?"

"As good as you'll ever see in Two Pines," Leggitt admitted. "The best thing that can happen to a man around here is to die with Olin Kelly's and George Burgess' blessing. Everyone attends then."

Fineen laughed because he was supposed to, then looked at Nan Singleton. "You're a mighty pretty thing today, Nan."

"Thank you, Finley. It's nice of you to say it."

"How many times has Dal proposed this month?" Fineen asked.

"Now cut that," Leggitt said, somewhat quickly. "Damn it, doesn't a man have any business of his own around this town? Seems to me that there ought to be something else to talk about besides each other." He shook his head as though this were a sad state of affairs. "By golly, I can walk into Huddlemyer's place to buy me a new derby, and the whole town knows about it before I can put it on."

"Yeah," Fineen said, "it's a fact all right. But we're all

guilty, Dal. We all talk too much." He squinted a look up and down the street. "I guess you heard about Mc-Keever's new project."

"What project?" Leggitt asked.

"You mean you haven't heard?"

"Get to the point, Finley!"

Fineen grinned. "I couldn't believe it when Wade told me. Betty invited Lincoln out for dinner, but Wade stayed in town." He paused, leaning forward to lower his voice. "I guess it's sort of a secret, but Bill Daley's getting a new buggy for his wife. A surprise. I—ah, had a picture of it in a catalog and Wade wanted to see it."

"Will you quit beating around the bush?" Leggitt demanded.

Finley Fineen acted like a man whose best story is being ruined by impatience. "I'm getting there. Let me tell it my way. Well, when Wade went over to Mc-Keever's office to tell him to go ahead with Betty, he saw this thing McKeever was working on. A hunk of clay with little pieces of metal sticking to it. Now ain't that a funny think for a man to amuse himself with when a murder's been done?"

"By golly, it sure is," Leggitt snapped. "I'm going to talk to McKeever about this and he'd better have a good explanation ready."

"Well, you'd better let someone else find out for you," Finley Fineen said. "McKeever and you are sort of out of sorts."

"He'll be more than just out of sorts when he reads the paper," Dal Leggitt said. He glanced at Nan Singleton. "I told you he wouldn't stay away from her."

"Please, Dal." She spoke softly, and did not look at him.

"Did I say something wrong?" Fineen asked, the soul of innocence.

"No, I'm glad you said it," Leggitt said. "Nan, listen to me. I never wanted to hurt you, and I still don't, but you've got to realize that McKeever's not an honorable man. What man would see another man's wife when the husband is away?"

"That's pretty strong," Fineen said. "I'm a friend of both McKeever and Wade Stanton, and talk like that will start trouble." He scratched his head. "It's no secret that McKeever threw Nan here over for Betty, then got pushed out by Wade, but there's been no trouble over it. And I wouldn't want to see none start now."

"There is a thing called honor and decency," Leggitt said. "Would you excuse us, Finley? I want to talk to Nan alone."

"All right," Fineen said. "I'll see you around, Dal."

He turned and walked back to his home, and after he passed out of earshot, Dal Leggitt took Nan Singleton's hand. "Isn't this enough to convince you, Nan? I mean, all she has to do is to whistle and he runs."

"Yes," she said. "I'm sorry I've been so foolish, Dal. Very sorry."

"Nan, Nan, I've waited a long time to hear you say that. Perhaps now you'll think more—kindly of me."

"Kindly?" She smiled and squeezed his hand. "You're good and gentle. I'll marry you, Dal. Whenever you say."

He came closer to shouting then than he ever had in his life, but he was a man nearly incapable of expressing his emotion, never elation such as he knew then. He merely smiled with his eyes and his lips, and said, "This is May. We'll have a June wedding. Tradition, you know."

"Yes," she said softly. "We wouldn't want to start off by defying tradition, would we?"

8.

As soon as Wade Stanton got Lincoln McKeever's horse from the stable and rode out of town, Bill Daley let his worry come out in the open, for this was what he did best—worry. If it wasn't about his health, it was about his wife, but now he had something else to grow concerned about, the scattered bits of the projectile that McKeever was patiently reassembling.

Making the explosive hadn't been at all difficult, since he had training in chemistry; the projectile itself was an eight-gauge brass shotgun shell with a metal detonator. Still, Bill Daley had fashioned it with his own

hands, and because of this, he felt that it could lead the
law directly to his door. He wanted to believe Fineen,
but he still knew he would sleep better if he had those
metal particles in his own possession to destroy.

Getting into the sheriff's office on a Sunday afternoon
presented more of a problem than he had first imagined;
too many people sat on their porches and saw everything that went on within blocks of the place. Still, fear
of one thing can drive a man past another fear, and Bill
Daley walked slowly, boldly, down the street, tipping
his hat now and then, speaking occassionally to those
who spoke to him.

McKeever's door was unlocked and Daley went in, his
eyes going immediately to the desk where the scattered
pieces lay. The thought that he should just jam the
whole thing into his pocket and run was uppermost in
his mind, but caution took hold of him, and held him
from that bit of foolishness. Too many people had seen
him come in; he now wished that he'd gone home instead. If he took it, McKeever would have no trouble at
all finding out who the thief was, and Daley didn't want
that finger pointed at him.

Instead he took only a handful of the pieces, enough
of them so that McKeever would never be able to as-
semble the thing to the point where he could positively
say how it was made, and what it was made of. Daley
turned to the door, ready and eager to leave, but stopped
when he heard steps coming toward him. Quickly he
began to whistle in a sub-tonal key and examine the
reward dodgers on the wall.

When the door opened, he turned his head, feigning
pleasant surprise. "Hello, Doc. McKeever's out."

"I can see that," Harris said dryly. He squinted at
Daley. "What did you do, break the law?"

"Why, no. What made you think that?"

"Just a joke," Harris said and crammed tobacco into
his pipe. He sidled over to McKeever's desk and looked
at the clay and metal. "Wish to hell he'd hurry up and
get that thing finished. I'd like to see what I worked
all night to get."

"What's that?" Daley said, turning.

"This—thing," Harris said. "It killed Dalridge's horse."

"No fooling? But who the hell cares about the horse?
What's McKeever doing about Daldridge?"

"You'd have to ask him," Harris said. He disturbed the pieces with his finger. "Funny, but I thought I dug out more chunks than that. Anyway it seemed like I did."

"What did you do? Count 'em?"

"I didn't get finished until daybreak," Harris said, stepping to the door. "When McKeever comes in, tell him I want to see him."

"Might as well leave myself," Daley said. "I'll walk with you, Doc."

"All right," Harris said, "but I'm too tired to be much company."

When they approached the hotel, Harris stopped to talk to Nan Singleton and her brother. Bill Daley smiled and went on toward his place. Harris looked at Jim and said, "You get out of the doghouse yet?" He winked. "If it gets too tough, come over and bunk with me."

"You're a bad influence," Nan said. "Between you and Lincoln McKeever—"

"—we'll make a man out of him," Harris finished for her. "It isn't Jim you're worried about, it's McKeever."

"Doctor, you ought to mind your own business."

Harris laughed. "Why? No one else does in Two Pines. By the way, where is McKeever? Haven't seen him since the funeral."

"He's out to Stanton's place."

"Stanton's?" Harris frowned. "Hell, I saw Wade less than fifteen minutes ago—" He stopped talking and pursed his lips. "Oh, I see what's eating you."

"You don't see anything," Nan snapped. "It's all over between Lincoln and me. I'm going to marry Dal Leggitt in June."

Harris' expression did not change; he sucked on his dry pipe and then put it into his pocket. "Good luck then. You'll need it."

When he walked on down the street, Jim Singleton said, "You sure judge Lincoln fast, Nan."

"Do I? I don't think so. I've had two years, Jim. And two years is a very long time." She got up and started to go inside. "Now don't go running off; there's work for you to do."

DOC HARRIS was surprised to find Bill Daley waiting for him. Harris hung up his hat and tossed his bag onto a low table. Daley said, "I guess you think it's funny, me coming here like this, but I haven't been feeling too well, Doc." He sniffed to prove it.

"You've got a store full of pills," Harris said, "and you've tried them all. What do you expect me to do, Bill?"

"I don't know," Daley said. "Maybe I ought to go to Arizona for the dry air."

"Then go."

"Well, I wanted a doctor's advice first."

"I just gave it to you," Harris said. "Pack up and go."

Bill Daley moved his hands briefly. "I don't know what Ethel will say."

Harris blew out a long breath. "Bill, that's your problem. Why bother me with it? I'm dog-tired." He shed his coat and then rolled his sleeves to wash his hands and face.

"I sure wish you'd examine me," Daley said. "A man likes to know what ails him."

Harris raised his head and looked at him, water dripping from his face. "You want to know?"

"Sure."

"You want it straight? All right. The only thing that's bothering you is yourself. Get out of this damned dead town and go somewhere. Get yourself a woman, one of those wide-hipped wild ones who'll take your money then run off with another man. And when that happens, get drunk and stay that way until you land in jail. When you sober up enough to know who you are, you'll be a well man."

"What would I tell Ethel?"

"Tell her? Hell, hit her on the head with something—" Then he shook his head. "No, don't do that. Don't do anything. Just go on listening to her yapping at you all the time and go on selling pills and licorice sticks and coughing when there's nothing to cough." He yanked a towel off the wall rack and dried his face. "This is a tough world, Bill, but be glad you're alive to enjoy it. A man dies too damned quick as it is. I was thinking of Dalridge, working steady, saving his money—and what did it get him but a smashed head."

"That sure isn't pleasant to think about," Bill Daley said.

"No, it's not," Harris said. "Now I'm a tough man when it comes to seeing people die, but I'll tell you, Daldridge's killing got me here." He thumped himself on the heart. "It's one thing to crack a man over the head when you're mad at him, but it's another to keep clubbing to make sure he's dead."

Daley looked at Harris with a set expression. "Is that the way it happened?"

"Yes, it is," Harris said. "You know, a doctor can tell a lot from a wound. I've just figured it all out, what was used, and what kind of a man did it."

"Is that a fact?"

"Yep. He used the barrel of a forty-five and he was a big man, six foot and at least a hundred and eighty-five pounds. I could tell by the damage; a man would have to be that powerful to crack a man's head that bad. Literally pulped the bone."

"I—wish you wouldn't talk about it," Daley said.

"Huh? Oh, sure." Harris chuckled. "I get a little clinical at times." He reached for his coat. "But I guess McKeever will be glad to hear it though."

"Yes," Daley said. "I guess he will." He got up and as he did, he brushed his coat against the back of the chair; the metal in his pocket grated with the musical sound that brass always possesses.

Harris frowned. "You got a pocket full of nails, Bill?"

"Just some junk," Daley said. "Well, I'll see you later, Doc."

Harris opened his door leading onto the outer office. "You ought to take my advice."

"I might," Daley said and offered to shake hands.

The offer was unusual and Harris hesitated, then gripped Daley's hand, glancing at it at the same time. Daley struck him then, the blow catching Harris alongside the jaw. He reeled back, stunned, coming against a glass-faced cabinet full of instruments. The cabinet went over with a crash and Daley drove into him, hitting him again. When Harris fell to the floor, Daley bent and picked up a scalpel, slashing with it before Harris could duck.

He opened Harris' face to the bone, then struck him in the throat, trying to reach the jugular vein. Daley wanted to make this quick, but that wasn't the way it was to be; Harris fought like a wild man and Daley plunged the knife again and again until Harris lay still.

Slowly Daley got to his feet and threw the scalpel

away from him. His sleeves were soaked with blood and he quickly shed his coat and shirt. Going to Harris' closet, he put on a clean shirt, then one of Harris' coats, a brown one like the one Daley discarded.

He wrapped his own clothes in a newspaper, then let himself out through the back door where the alley was protected by a long, high wooden fence. At the end of the alley he had a quick look in both directions, then stepped boldly to the walk. At the next block he crossed over and entered the alley behind his own place, and let himself into the back of the store. He could hear his wife walking around upstairs, and quickly rolled up a newspaper to start a fire in the furnace.

The coat and shirt were burning well before he realized that the metal pieces were still in the pocket. Then he decided that it didn't really matter; they would be melted in the fire, destroyed beyond hope of recovery.

Ethel Daley came to the top of the landing and yelled down at him. "Bill, is that you?"

"Who did you think it was?" He wished she'd fall over the railing and break her neck.

"What in the world are you doing?"

"Building a fire," he said. "What does it sound like?"

"In May? Daley, I've got the windows open."

"Well, I'm chilly," he said. "Go in and quit hollering."

"Don't give me any of your sass!" she snapped and slammed the door.

When coat and shirt were completely burned, Daley went to the wash stand and carefully scrubbed his hands. Reaction was beginning to maul him now and the enormity of his act came home to him.

I made a mistake; this was his thought, and he felt a need to talk to Fineen, only he dared not. Fineen had told him to leave this alone, and he had meant to, only Fineen would never believe that. He hadn't meant to kill Harris. Or maybe he had at that, especially after Harris caught him in McKeever's office.

Bill Daley knew Harris; the man never let go of an idea once his mind locked on it, and Harris would think some more about those pieces of metal, the ones that were missing. And Harris would add them to Bill Daley, more especially after they jangled in Daley's pocket. I had to kill him; Daley rationalized to himself. But it was bad, very bad. Worse than Fineen breaking Daldridge's skull with that .45 barrel. Then Daley remembered Harris' talk. No need to worry about that now; no need to tell Finley Fineen a thing.

But Fineen would know. As soon as someone discovered Doc Harris' body, Fineen would add two and two and come up with the right answer. Bill Daley didn't like to consider Fineen's anger when he did.

He went upstairs then, but left Harris' coat behind. I'll have to get rid of that, he thought; Ethel will know it isn't mine.

She was in the kitchen and glared at him as he stepped into the hall. "I swear, Bill Daley, sometimes I believe you've lost your mind."

"Don't start nagging, Ethel. I don't feel well."

"Have you ever felt well? I ask you, have you ever felt well? Since the day we've been married it's been complaints day in, day out."

"I think I'll go to Arizona," Daley said. "I was talking to Doc Harris and he said I could clear up this cough in the dry air."

"Go. See if I care."

"But I need money, Ethel. Maybe a thousand dollars. You've got that much saved."

"I'm saving that money," she snapped.

He looked at her for a moment, then a hardness came into his voice. "By God, Ethel, don't fool around with me! Don't drive me now! Just don't!"

She put down her spoon and came up to him, her expression puzzled. "Bill, what's come over you? Your expression, your voice—why you sounded ready to kill me."

"Don't tempt me, Ethel." He whirled away from her, afraid again that he had gone too far, revealed too much.

9.

L INCOLN McKEEVER did not like walking, and the two-mile hike back to Two Pines was no exception. The walk was of his own choosing but the distance was an accident, brought about by his stopping the buggy, handing the reins to Betty Stanton, then dismounting and saying a brief good-by.

She was an angry woman, and he was a fool, he told himself as he walked back to town. Hell, even a dog will catch a bone if it's thrown at him. But I'm not a dog, McKeever decided.

The walk left him sweating and muddy so he went directly to the Hanover House for a bath and a change of clothes. When he came down the stairs, he found Nan Singleton behind the counter, trying to make the books balance.

"Lincoln, is seven times nine fifty-six or sixty-three?"

"Sixty-three," he said. He looked out through the front window. "The town's like a tomb."

"This is Sunday," Nan said. Then she looked at him quickly, a hardness in her eyes. "You didn't stay long."

"I never got there," he said.

For a moment she just stared, then said, "What?"

"I said I never got there." He smiled. "And I walked back." She closed the ledger with a snap and started to turn away, but McKeever took her arm, holding her. "Betty's a liar."

"About what?"

"About the things she likes to brag about."

Color came into Nan's cheeks. "Lincoln, there must be some truth there."

"No truth," he said flatly. "But you believe what you want to."

"Lincoln, I want to believe—" Then she shook her head. "But it's hard sometimes." She bit her lip briefly, then added, "I told Dal Leggitt I'd marry him, Lincoln."

For a moment he thought he had heard incorrectly; this stunned him more than he believed it would. "I—wish you the best, Nan."

"Do you? Lincoln, let's be honest this one time."

"All right," he said. "I hope Leggitt drops dead before the sun sets."

Then he wheeled out of the lobby and went out to the porch where a cooling breeze fanned him. Jim Singleton had his feet cocked to the railing; he shot a glance at McKeever, then toed the chair around.

"You going to bite somebody, Lincoln?"

McKeever laughed; he felt he had to, or explode.

"Not today," he said and stripped the wrapper from a cigar. "How'd you like to be a paid deputy, Jim?"

"You mean it?"

"Yes," McKeever said. "I can use you, Jim, and you might as well get paid for it."

"Wow! Can I carry a gun?"

"I expect you ought to," McKeever said softly. He looked across the street as Dal Leggitt came from his small newspaper office; he had a paper under his arm and headed directly toward McKeever.

"Nan tell you about her and Dal?" Jim said.

"Yes," McKeever said.

Leggitt came up with his prancing step and plopped the newspaper in Lincoln McKeever's lap. "Read that and laugh, if you can," Leggitt said.

McKeever calmly unfolded the paper and read the headlines.

"Sheriff incompetent, eh?" He rolled the cigar from one corner of his mouth to the other. "Violation of public trust? Your punctuation is excellent, Dal, and I believe your spelling is picking up."

Jim Singleton sniggered, then choked it off.

"Irresponsible and lax in his duties—" McKeever looked up. "Dal, don't you think lazy would have been a better word? Right here—" He turned and pointed to the printing. "You've got to choose your adjectives more carefully. Now shiftless is a good word if you want your writing to have impact." He folded the paper carefully, then quickly reached up and slapped Dal Leggitt across the face with it before throwing it into the gutter.

LEGGITT raised his hand to his stung cheek, then said, "McKeever, you shoudn't have done that." He shed his coat, popped his cuff links and then carefully rolled his sleeves.

Jim Singleton, with all the foolishness of youth, raced off the porch and down the street, yelling, "Lincoln McKeever's going to whip the hell out of Dal Leggitt!"

Had he sounded the fire bell he wouldn't have attracted more attention. Leggitt stepped forward and cocked his fists. "I'm ready whenever you are, Lincoln."

"You've been ready a long time," McKeever said, and hit him.

Leggitt went into the porch rail, and over it, arms

flailing for balance, legs dancing. Nan Singleton came out in time to see this brief flight to the boardwalk.

"Lincoln, how could you hit a man unaware?"

Without glancing at her, he said, "When a man takes off his coat and rolls up his sleeves, he's hardly unaware."

Leggitt was getting up, coming up the steps, and a crowd was gathering. McKeever's sweeping arm pushed Nan back out of the way, and left himself open to Dal Leggitt's charge. McKeever was carried against the wall, lip bleeding from Leggitt's blow; his head buzzing, he managed to wiggle free and block Leggitt's jabbing fists.

Somewhere along the line, Dal Leggitt had taken more than a few boxing lessons from a man who just wasn't shooting his mouth off when he claimed to be a fighter. Leggitt had the footwork and the strength to sting McKeever, keep him back where the kicking jabs were most effective.

McKeever's mouth and nose were bleeding and he hadn't got in any more than that first lick. A new caution took hold of him and he realized that he could easily lose this fight if he didn't watch himself more carefully. Leggitt wasn't the kind of a fighter you could walk into, place your toe against his, and swing until the weakest man fell. Leggitt's skill and ability more than made up for his weaknesses, and McKeever started backing up, making Leggitt come to him, making Leggitt carry the fight.

The crowd was thick and interested and shouted a continual encouragement with a divided sentiment. Jim had his sister backed into the doorway where she would be out of the way, leaving the porch to the two fighters.

McKeever had a cut over his left eye, and a nose that felt like a wet sponge. Try as he would, he could not seem to mark Leggitt at all; every time he swung, the man wasn't there.

And every time Leggitt ducked, he found an opening and laced McKeever again, usually drawing blood. Jim Singleton, whose loyalty was with McKeever, had a hard time saving his face, for there was not a man there who doubted now how this was going to turn out.

McKeever was winded and Leggitt seemed quite fresh. He shifted about in that crazy dance of his, feet whispering lightly on the flooring, fists reaching out and connecting with a sound like a slap.

Unable to take much more of this, McKeever stepped in; he had to finish it now or never. He caught another one on the mouth and shook it off, but he couldn't shake off the one under the heart. A clamp came down on his lungs and his mouth flopped open for an instant and he stood there, looking at Dal Leggitt with completely blank eyes before he began to fall.

Someone generously threw a bucket of rain water in his face and McKeever found that he could breathe again, although painfully. He looked around for Leggitt and failed to find him. Then he heard Nan's voice in some faraway place, pleading with Leggitt. An upstairs window banged open and someone in the crowd yelled as clothes began to rain down, and boots, an old rifle, satchels, a small trunk; everything Lincoln McKeever owned cascaded into the street.

Then Dal Leggitt came down, calmly refastened his pearl cuff links, put on his coat and snapped the lapels flat, and spoke to McKeever in a calm, flat voice. "I've just thrown you out of this establishment, McKeever. Find a place to live somewhere else. If I see you here again I'll take a buggy whip to you."

He brusquely pushed his way through the crowd and stalked back to his newspaper office.

THE crowd began to thin rapidly; every fight had to be talked over afterward and none of them wanted to do it in front of the loser. Jim Singleton helped McKeever to his feet, and there was a sharp disappointment in the young man's expression.

McKeever said, "One thing you learn, Jim, is that you can't win them all."

"I thought you was better than him," Jim said hotly.

"Is that the measure of a man, his ability to fight?"

"Jim," Nan said, "go on inside. Go on, now. I'll take care of this." She waited until young Singleton went on in, then she said, "I didn't want this to happen, Lincoln, but now that it has, I have no regrets."

"I didn't expect you would have," McKeever said. He stanched the flow of blood from his nose, then said, "Do you suppose I could wash up?"

"Of course. Do you want Jim to pick up your things?"

"Yes," McKeever said. "Tell him to take them over to the jail. I'll stay there."

Nan was turning to the door; she stopped and turned back. "Are you afraid of Dal?"

"No," McKeever said.

"You don't have to move out of here," she said. "Dal Leggitt isn't running this hotel."

"Yes, he is," McKeever said. "I just never realized it."

He went into the kitchen, took off his coat and shirt, then washed carefully. His face was badly bruised and his nose was as spongy as an old potato, much too tender to fool with other than a gentle washing.

Nan Singleton stood by the sink, her arms crossed, watching him closely. "What was the fight about, Lincoln?"

"I like to think that my half of it was inspired by Dal Leggitt's newspaper article."

"I didn't ask you what you'd like to think," she said. "Lincoln, somewhere along the line we've lost the knack of talking to each other."

"Maybe we've said all the things there are to be said. Or perhaps we've said too many of the wrong things. Things we can't forget."

"You're right. I wanted Dal to hurt you, Lincoln. Do you understand that? I wanted him to pay you back for the times I stayed awake with the hurt you gave me."

"And it was all pretty needless," he said, dressing again. "The way it turned out, I mean." Then he shrugged. "But we never know how a thing is going to turn out, do we?"

"No. I suppose that's what makes life so interesting."

"Or so full of pain."

He went out then and found Jim carting his belongings to the jail in a wheelbarrow. McKeever looked up and down the street once, then followed the young man, picking up a shirt, one slipper, and a small box that had dribbled off the load.

The storeroom was suitable for quarters and McKeever spent the rest of the afternoon moving in a cot and making the place livable. Jim Singleton didn't stay, and he failed to mention the swearing-in as a deputy. McKeever supposed now that the young man had lost interest; young men considered a job in the light of reflected glory first and remuneration second, and McKeever had recently lost his lustre in Jim Singleton's eyes.

WHEN darkness came, McKeever lighted the lamps in the outer office and began to work on his puzzle. He fitted pieces for several hours before he became aware that many were missing. He could not be sure of this, but he seemed to find the pile thinner, the puzzle twice as difficult.

His head ached and his stomach was still upset; he discounted the bruises on his face, and the stiffness. At eight, Olin Kelly and George Burgess came in, their expressions serious; they took chairs and came right to the point.

Kelly did the talking. "McKeever, we heard about the fight you had with Leggitt, and we know the reason behind it."

"Oh?"

"You're taking this calmly enough," Burgess said. "Olin and I read Leggitt's account of your activities; perhaps you could explain them to us. We want to be fair about this."

"What is there to explain?" McKeever asked. "I believe it's important to piece together these pieces and Leggitt believes it's more important to chase all over the country after men who do not exist there. What can be more simple?"

"You're twisting this, McKeever," Kelly said. "George and I have talked this over with several responsible people, and we feel that your affair with Leggitt was more personal than a matter of law-enforcement policy."

"I can't help what you think," McKeever said.

"Let me tell it," Burgess said. "You're getting nowhere, Olin. McKeever, since this crime occurred, you've sent a few telegrams to outlying peace officers, then set on your butt as though you were investigating a hog theft. Now we told you once before that we wanted action. We meant it. And if you can't give it to us, then we'll put someone in office who will."

"I see," McKeever said. "Maybe you gentlemen would like to run this yourselves?"

"Now don't get huffy," Kelly said. "We didn't say that at all. McKeever, did you go out to Stanton's place this afternoon?"

"It's none of your business if I did," McKeever said.

Kelly and Burgess looked at each other. "I thought you'd take that attitude," Burgess said. "McKeever, in view of the fact that you're doing next to nothing about Daldridge's killing, we think it would be best for all concerned if you stepped down."

"Resign? What if I say no?"

"Then we'll put you out of office," Kelly said. "McKeever, there are enough moral people in Two Pines to back us, but we'd rather not drag up anything that would be embarrassing, you understand. Betty Stanton is Sam Richardson's daughter, and we don't want to embarrass innocent people." He paused a moment. "Make up your mind, McKeever. Do you go out the nice, easy way, or the hard way?"

"Will you answer one question?"

"If we can," Kelly said.

"Who suggested this?"

The two men looked at each other. "Dal Leggitt. Who did you think?"

McKeever nodded, then said, "All right, you'll have my resignation in the morning."

10.

BETWEEN the hours of nine and eleven Monday morning, Dal Leggitt's paper appeared on the street and was promptly read by every serious-minded citizen in Two Pines. Not that there was ever anything in the paper that the citizens didn't know about, or hadn't talked over already, but it was nice to see it in print. Made it permanent, sort of.

Leggitt was a little put out because he didn't have time to set up a piece on the front page about Lincoln McKeever being asked to resign, but he talked it up, making certain that everyone in town knew about it. At his own expense, Leggitt telegraphed San Francisco and learned the name of the investigator they were going to send; he had a word profile of the man, Charles Boomhauer, on the front page. Leggitt enjoyed giving a story the personal slant; his paper was a small-minded, opinionated rag but the people of Two Pines excused this, feeling that it was better to have a biased paper than none at all. According to Leggitt, the investigator was a whiz who always got his man, and the town of Two Pines would soon see a lawman of genuine caliber in action; this dig at Lincoln McKeever did not pass unnoticed.

Bill Daley caused a mild stir in town by taking delivery of a new buggy, the first new rig he had ever bought, as far as anyone could remember. He parked it in front of his drugstore so that everyone could admire the brass fittings, the red wheels and the shiny black body. Daley stood proudly by while the crowd gathered and he was disturbed to find that the buggy was not the drawing card; people were curious as to why he had abandoned his tight spending habits, and Daley found this hard to explain. He thought he would just say that he bought it for his wife, but everyone knew that they fought, that she wore the pants and that Daley wouldn't give her the time of day. The purchase of the buggy became as big a mystery in Two Pines as the robbery-murder of Daldridge.

Just before noon, one of the men at the mine dropped a setting maul while shoring staging and put a slight dent in Swan Jaccobbson's head, and it was only when they sent a man to fetch Doctor Harris that anyone discovered he had been killed.

Lincoln McKeever was having a mid-mornng breakfast at a small restaurant on Ash Street—he'd felt too creaky to get up earlier—and his attention was pulled to the commotion on the street. But he did not leave his table to see what was going on, for Jim Singleton came charging through the door, more than eager to relate the news.

"Somethin' terrible's happened," Jim said.

"What? Leggitt's newspaper office burn down?"

"I'm not joking. Doc Harris is dead."

Lincoln McKeever put his fork down. He saw that Jim Singleton was serious and reached for his hat. They went out together and Jim told him how Harris was discovered as they hurried to Harris' office.

A jam-packed crowd fronted the place and McKeever rammed a way through for both of them. Dal Leggitt was inside, snooping around, and he frowned when McKeever stepped into the room.

"What are you doing here? This isn't your business any longer."

McKeever did not bother to answer him. He pushed him aside and looked at Harris, who was stiff and blood-caked. It didn't take much of a brain to figure out how Harris had died, but when and by whose hand was some problem.

Jim Singleton looked pale, but more controlled than when he had looked at Daldridge. "Let's go," McKeever said.

As they stepped to the door, Olin Kelly and George Burgess came in. "A terrible thing," Burgess was saying. "Who'd want to kill Doc Harris, the best friend this town ever had." He glanced at McKeever. "You see him? What do you make of it?"

"I could give you only an unofficial opinion," Mc-Keever said and tried to press through.

Kelly stopped him half angrily. "Man, this is no time to get proud."

"Ask the new sheriff," McKeever said.

Burgess frowned. "You know we haven't appointed a man yet. Hell, there's no need to be sore about this, Lincoln."

"Who's sore? Coming Jim?"

They skirted the crowd and stopped on the main stem. Jim Singleton said, "Lincoln, you suppose Doc found out something? About Daldridge, I mean?"

"He wasn't killed for fun," McKeever said. "Well, there's nothing to be done while that crowd's littering up the place. I'll go back later when they quiet down."

Jim Singleton shifted his feet. "Lincoln, you've re-signed. You're not forgetting that, are you?"

"No, but I knew Harris pretty well. He liked to write things down. Some men are like that, Jim; they'd rather write a report than tell something." McKeever looked down the street and saw Finley Fineen come out of his office and stand on the walk's edge. The street was de-serted except for these three men, and as McKeever turned to walk toward Fineen, he noticed a fourth, Bill Daley.

HE STOPPED by Daley, merely because he was nearer than Fineen. Daley said, "Your face looks like hell, Lin-coln. Better let me give you something for it."

"Maybe later. You been over to Doc's house?"

Bill Daley shook his head. "I don't have the stomach for it. Besides, a dozen people will insist on telling me about it."

"In this town you'd better make that two dozen," McKeever said and walked on. Jim Singleton decided to go back to the hotel; McKeever sided Fineen and prepared a cigar for a match. "Messy business, huh, Finley?"

"Yeah." Fineen looked at Bill Daley for a long moment, not dropping his glance until Daley went back into his store. "Who could have done a thing like that, do you suppose?"

"A badly frightened man," McKeever said softly. "You know anyone who's frightened, Finley?"

"Not that scared," Fineen said. "Hey, you suppose Doc's death had anything to do with Daldridge's being killed?"

"I'd say so," McKeever agreed. "But the question is, what was the link? What tied the two together and made killing Doc necessary?"

"Gives a man the creeps, don't it? I mean, a man could wake up dead damned easy."

"Only if he knew too much about the wrong things," McKeever said.

"I guess that's right. If it gets any tougher around here I think I'll move south to Tombstone and do something safe, like drawing on Wyatt Earp." He laughed at his own joke, then choked it off since McKeever didn't think it was funny. "You see Daley's new buggy?"

"I never paid any attention to it," McKeever said. He shifted away from the wall, ready to leave.

"Where you staying now?" Finley Fineen asked.

"A rooming house on Pine. Poker this coming Saturday night? I can come an hour earlier now."

"I don't know," Fineen said. "We'll see, Lincoln."

"What do you mean, we'll see? We've been playing Saturday night poker for years."

"Well, I guess we'll have a game," Fineen said and watched Lincoln McKeever walk away.

As soon as McKeever passed on down the street, Bill Daley returned to his doorway. Fineen cupped his hands around his mouth and called over to him. "A quilted lap robe and a buggy whip goes with that rig, Bill. Come over and get 'em."

Daley hesitated, then said, "There's no one to mind the store."

"Hell, everyone's over to Doc's house." He waited, and finally Daley crossed the street, his expression filled with apprehension and alarm. "Come on inside," Fineen said and closed the door. He speared Daley with his eyes and spoke softly. "I don't have to look far to find the man who killed Harris, do I?"

"I—I didn't mean to kill him," Daley said quickly, softly. "Finley, you've got to believe me."

"Well, I guess no one saw you coming or going," Fineen said with surprising mildness. He smiled and clapped Daley on the shoulder. "You let something stampede you; don't do it again. McKeever's out and there's nothing to worry about. Did you cover your tracks? I mean, you didn't leave anything behind, did you?"

"No," Daley said. "Finley, I'm glad you're not sore. I thought you would be."

"It's all right, I tell you. Look, Bill, we'll just keep this to ourselves. What Wade Stanton doesn't know won't hurt him, huh?"

"Yeah," Daley said, vastly relieved. "It wasn't easy, Finley. God, it sure wasn't easy."

"You'd best forget about it," Fineen said. "Wade will surely suspect that you did it, but that'll be as far as it goes." He smiled briefly. "We're in the clear now. Nothing to worry about. If Doc knew anything, he sure as hell will never tell it. And McKeever's still in the dark. Sure, he might have been getting a lead, but that was all. Now you go on back to the store and keep everything normal, you understand?"

"Sure," Daley said. "How about the robe?"

"That was just something to get you over here in case someone overheard.

"Then let me carry a robe back in case someone looks," Daley said.

Finley Fineen lost his humor. "You tight bastard, you'd milk your mother." He went into the back and brought out a robe, throwing it on the counter. "Take it and get out."

Daley smiled and walked out. Fineen went to the

door to stand and when Olin Kelley and George Burgess came toward him, he stepped aside so they could enter.

"Don't tell me I can sell you·some more wagons?" Fineen asked.

"No, we're going to try to sell you on something," Kelly said. "All right to sit down?"

"Sure," Fineen said, pushing out chairs. "What's on your mind?"

"I'll come right to the point," Kelly said. "This town needs a law officer. We'd like to have you fill McKeever's shoes."

Finley Fineen had an excellent poker face, and he was smart enough to say just the right things, and exhibit an embarrassed reluctance. "Gentlemen, if it came to hitting a man on the jaw and dragging him off to the lock-up, I guess I could do it, but to investigate—"

"We've thought that all out," Burgess said. "Finley, there's a crack investigator coming here from San Francisco, and he'll take over the case completely. But we want a good local man on the job, one that we can trust. Now Olin and I have known you for years. A family man, churchgoer and a responsible business man who's pretty well fixed for money. How about it, Finley?"

He shook his head and frowned; his stalling was misinterpreted for modesty. But beneath it all Fineen was more pleased than he had ever been; they were making everything so simple for him. "Can I think about it?" he asked.

"We'd like an answer now," Kelly said. "Hate like hell to push you this way, Finley, but we talked it over with Leggitt and Richardson and they're for it a hundred per cent."

"Well," Fineen said, smiling, "I can't buck the local dignitaries can I?"

"Wonderful," Burgess said and offered his hand. "It won't take long to swear you in, Finley." He stuck his thumbs into the armholes of his vest. "The star will look good on you. Takes a big man to represent the law. I guess that's McKeever's main trouble; he just never did look like a sheriff ought to."

"I wonder what my wife'll say?" Fineen said.

"She'll be pleased," Kelly said. "Come on, Finley. We'll get the formalities over with."

Sam Richardson, as mayor of Two Pines, officiated, and afterward he pinned McKeever's star onto Finley Fineen's coat front. There was handshaking all around, and a sample of Richardson's bourbon, which he reserved for state occasions, weddings and funerals. As soon as was possible, Finley Fineen left Richardson's bank, walked a half a block to the hardware store, and there bought a cartridge belt and holster, and a pearl-handled .45 to fit it. With this buckled on the outside of his coat, he stepped to the sidewalk and the admiring citizens.

To HIS surprise, small boys followed him, for a lawman is youth's highest throne of worship. At the doorway of Daley's drugstore, Fineen shooed them on their way, then went inside. The place was empty of customers and Daley was behind the counter, filling bottles.

He spoke with only half a glance. "Something I can do—" Then he stopped, his eyes fastened on that star. "This a joke, Finley?"

"No," Fineen said. "I was appointed not five minutes ago to take McKeever's place."

"But—but why you?"

"Why not me?" Fineen asked. "I'm a respectable citizen."

Daley looked around, even cocked his head toward the ceiling to determine where his wife was by her footsteps. When he spoke, it was little more than a whisper. "But, Finley, it don't seem right after—"

"It couldn't be more right," Fineen said flatly. "This is a windfall I hadn't counted on, not in a million years. Bill, no one ever suspects a respectable man; I told you and Wade that from the first. Now that I'm sheriff, even temporarily, I'll investigate Harris' killing my own way."

"Finley, I thought you said we'd forget it!"

"Forget it? How can I forget it now? I've got a responsibility to the citizens, haven't I?" He leaned forward. "But don't you worry about it, Bill. I'll confiscate all of Doc's papers and go through them, just in case there's anything there. You know how Doc was, always writing everything down."

"Sure," Daley said, moving his hands nervously. A coughing spell seized him and he fought it under control. "Only this kind of puts us on opposite sides."

"That's all in your head," Fineen said. "You know nothing's changed."

"Hell, everything's changed," Daley said. "God, I only went into this thing because I wanted to see if I could do something by myself. You don't know what it's like to be a little man, Finley. Your wife yaps at you all the time, and kids talk smart to you. Hell, I've never even been in a fight in my whole life."

"Look, don't get stewed up. You know it wrecks your health." He patted Daley on the arm. "You just think about how this is going to be now, Bill. You just think about it and see if it's not better."

Bill Daley shook his head. "I don't know, Finley. I wish to God we'd never started this thing. I don't want the damned money. I don't want any of it, but now I've got it all."

Finley Fineen studied Daley carefully, then said, "There's no out, Bill. If you ever thought there was, you were fooling yourself."

"I know it, and that's what I was doing. Three days ago you and Wade were the best friends I ever had. I mean that, Finley. As long as we just talked about it, it wasn't so bad. But now I don't want to talk to you, Finley, or to Wade. I don't want to even see you any more. You figure that out?"

"Yes," Fineen said softly. "But it's all right, Bill. I'm your friend, you just remember that. One of these days it won't matter."

"What do you mean?" Daley asked.

Finley Fineen shook his head. "It'll work out all right. You'll see that I'm right."

Then he turned and walked out.

11.

WADE STANTON picketed his horse within visual distance of his ranch, then hunkered down to wait until nightfall. He could see the buggy parked by the porch and this was enough to satisfy him that Lincoln

McKeever was still there. Stanton didn't like to wait, but if the prize was big enough, he could do it. He watched the lights go on in the bunkhouse and when he judged that the hands were bedded down for the night, he stepped into the saddle and rode on home.

Easing into the barn, he put up the horse without disturbing anyone, then walked to the house with an eager step. There was a light burning brightly in the parlor, but he expected that. Going around to the back door, he eased it open and catfooted his way down the hall to Betty's room. For a time he stood with his ear to the panel; then he tried the knob, feeling it give in his hand.

With a rush he flung the door open, letting the hall light rush into the room with him. Betty sat up in bed and then laughed.

"What did you expect to find, Wade?" She swung her legs to the floor and turned up the lamp on the night stand. Slipping into her robe, she pushed past him, going into the kitchen.

He followed her, his expression bewildered. "Where's Lincoln McKeever?"

"I wouldn't know," Betty said.

"What do you mean? He came home with you, didn't he?"

"No," she said and stirred the fire. After she placed the coffee pot on the stove, she turned to him. "I've had a bad afternoon, Wade. Very bad. But I've figured it all out now and it's funny. Real funny."

"I don't think it's so damned funny."

"Don't you?" She laughed without humor. "Wade, I wanted to make love to Lincoln, but he got out of the buggy and chose to walk back to town. Can you imagine that, a man walking home? I thought women were supposed to do that. You and I have both been fools, Wade. I want to get rid of you and you want to get rid of me. I wanted Lincoln to take me away and you wanted me to run away with Lincoln."

"Well, as long as it's out in the open, why don't you go?"

"Because he won't have me." She made a wry face. "Honorable men! You can have 'em." The coffee began to boil and she pulled it to one side of the stove. "You looked funny, Wade, sneaking in like a thief, expecting to catch a sinning wife red-handed."

"That's all right," Stanton said. "I can afford to make a fool of myself. You can't."

"I suppose," Betty said. "But I can afford to wait, Wade. Can you?"

"Sure. I'll tell you one thing, though, Betty; you'll never get a nickle of my money."

She smiled and poured herself a cup of coffee. "Want to bet?" She sat down at the table and looked up at him. "This is the kind of a game we're playing between ourselves, Wade, and it'll be interesting to see who wins. You want to make everything my fault, to be the injured party. That way you can slam the door in my face and leave me with nothing. And I want it the other way around. I want to sit in this parlor and own it all, only I don't want you around. Fair enough?"

"That day'll never come," Wade Stanton said flatly.

"Oh, I think it will, if we both work at it," Betty said, then smiled with her eyes as she lifted the coffee cup.

To most people's way of thinking, Finley Fineen was the kind of law officer Two Pines had always wanted, a man on the go all the time. He turned his business over to his foreman, and began a fevered investigation. He went to Judge Harper and got an order to confiscate all of Doctor Harris' papers and belongings, then spent the next two days asking endless questions, especially of the people who lived near Harris. Did they see anything? Hear anything?

Dal Leggitt followed Fineen like a well-trained dog, taking it all down for his paper.

Lincoln McKeever spent his daylight hours in the saloon, playing endless games of solitaire and drinking beer, and to many people in Two Pines this substantiated their earlier belief that McKeever was at heart a lazy loafer.

Now and then Jim Singleton came in with a word about this or that. He disliked the idea of McKeever sitting around doing nothing, and he resented Finley Fineen. This amused McKeever, and he asked, "Fineen turn you down, Jim?"

"Huh? Turn me down for what?"

"You asked him for a job as deputy, didn't you?"

"How did you know that?"

McKeever shrugged. "It just figured. What did Fineen say?"

Jim Singleton frowned, then said, "He told me to get the hell out before he kicked me out. Lincoln, he had no call to talk like that."

"No? You'd better just stay away from him, Jim."

"I will," Jim Singleton said. "Hey, he was asking me what happened to that thing you was working on. You know, that piece of putty and the metal parts."

"It's safe," McKeever said.

"You'd better hand it over before he asks for it."

"If he wants it bad enough," McKeever said, "I'll let him ask." He leaned forward and spoke more softly. "Jim, one reason I've always liked you is that you can keep your mouth shut."

"Yes, sir. I don't say anything I'm not supposed to."

"I know that," McKeever said. "And that's why I'll tell you this. Let's try to put this thing together using the pieces of knowledge we have. We'll have to assume a lot, but that's all right as long as there's no contradictory evidence. You go along with that?"

"Sure."

"In the first place, we'll assume that the robbers and Daldridge's killers are someone from Two Pines. All right? Second, the only thing we have to work on is the pieces of metal which made up the shell that killed the horse. Now get this clear, Jim: we have no other suspicion; none at all."

"You can say that again. They sure didn't leave anything behind."

"That's fine, but people leave behind more than they figure. A man can leave nothing physical behind, yet leave himself open to suspicion. Those pieces of metal were the one actual link we had with the killer. But what was there about them to make a man afraid? Some of them are missing, Jim. I'd say about half, because I haven't counted the ones that are left."

"Then how can you know that half are gone?"

McKeever smiled. "Doc Harris' report. 'Removed from carcass of dead horse, forty-one assorted pieces of un-identified brass.' That's how I know that half are gone. Look, Jim, you're fresh on this. Let's see what you can make out of this. Harris' killing, I mean. Give me a reason for anyone to kill him."

"Gosh, I don't know, Lincoln. I really don't. Unless Harris knew something that was damaging to someone in town."

"But what could he know?" McKeever asked. "Come on, Jim, think! I want to see if you reach the same conclusion I've already reached. Remember the bits of brass now. Try and take it from there."

"Well, we're supposing that your having them made someone nervous, huh? All right, then is it so farfetched to suppose someone would try and steal them?" He snapped his fingers. "Sure, someone did steal 'em!" Then his elation faded. "Well, they only stole half of 'em."

McKeever was smiling. "All right, why, Jim? Why just steal half?"

"Hell, I don't know, Lincoln."

"Jim, suppose a man was fixing his watch and he had the parts scattered all over the table and you wanted to play a joke on him, mix him up. What would you do?"

Jim Singleton sniggered. "I'd put in an extra screw." He laughed, conjuring up a mental picture of a man holding a completed, operating watch in his hand and wondering where that extra screw went.

"Suppose you didn't have a screw?"

"I guess I'd swipe some of the parts so he couldn't put it tog—" Then he slapped his forehead. "Sure! Why swipe 'em all when just a few would do the trick?"

"Now you're thinking," McKeever said. "All right, supposition one is that our man swiped some of the pieces, but where does Doc Harris come in? What have the pieces to do with his killing, anyway?"

"Well," Jim said, "Doc could have come into your office while the man was there."

"No reason to kill for that," McKeever said. "No, Jim, I don't think that's enough. Our man killed out of desperation, out of panic."

"How in the hell can you figure that, Lincoln?"

"Because the job was messy. Jim, if you had a real hate for a man, how would you get rid of him? A man you were really scared of?"

"I'd probably shoot him."

"Well, yes, but you'd do a more deliberate job of it than someone did on Doc Harris. Harris' killer was panic-stricken. He made a horrible mess of Doc's killing. One of those messes a man makes when he's scared to death. You saw the stab wounds, how scattered they were, and you saw Dalridge, and how one spot had been beaten to mush."

Jim Singleton swallowed hard. "I sure don't like to think about it, Lincoln. My stomach ain't none too good around things like that." He shook his head slowly, coming back to the main issue. "Maybe Doc noticed some of the pieces missing? Of course he'd have to say something or the killer wouldn't get jumpy."

McKEEVER reached for his beer glass and leaned back in his chair, a smile widening his lips. 'Jim, you've got a head on you. I reached that very same conclusion; no other seems to fit. Of course we're guessing all the way."

"A guess won't hold up in court," Jim Singleton said.

"Sure, but let's see if we can't crowd our man a little. He was scared once. Let's see if we can't scare him again."

"Yeah, but who do you scare?"

"I don't know," McKeever said. "But I'll work on it."

"Maybe Finley Fineen's working on it too."

"Maybe," McKeever said. Then his glance went past Jim Singleton's shoulder to the door. "Here comes Fineen. We can ask him."

Fineen came over to McKeever's table and sat down. He shifted his pearl-handled gun around to the front of his thigh and then leaned his elbows on the table. "Ain't it about time you got a job, Lincoln?"

"I thought I'd live off the fat of the land a little," McKeever said. "You don't object to that, do you, Finley?"

"I got where I am by hard work," Fineen said. "As your friend, Lincoln, I can only say that if you'd applied that rule to yourself you'd still be wearing this badge."

"True," McKeever said. "I'm a product of a mispent youth, Finley." His glance touched Jim Singleton. "Let this be an example to you, son. Work hard, save your money, and stay away from strong drink, fast women, and cards."

"Oh, cut it out," Fineen said. "McKeever, don't you ever take anything seriously?"

"Sure. I take you seriously, Finley."

Fineen frowned. "What the hell's that supposed to mean?"

"Finley Fineen, the intrepid lawman," McKeever said. "I always thought of you as a good carriage maker and nothing else. You look different carrying a gun, Finley. You pretty fair on the draw?"

"Don't play games with me, Lincoln. You'll stretch a long-standing friendship out of shape." He looked then at Jim Singleton. "Why don't you go take your big ears for a walk?"

"Huh?" Jim said, startled.

"Lay off the boy, Finley. He's not bothering you."

Fineen's glance returned to McKeever. "I was talking to him, not you. Besides, I've seen you roust plenty of fellows around."

"No one that didn't have it coming," McKeever said flatly. "What do you want, Finley? My beer's getting stale."

"All right," Fineen said. "Be a sorehead because I got your job."

"Sorehead?" Jim piped in. "Hell, he ain't—" Then he caught McKeever's look and closed his mouth.

Fineen said, "Lincoln, I want those metal pieces Leggitt says you're fooling with."

"Don't have 'em."

"What do you mean, you don't have 'em?"

"That's what I said. Someone stole 'em a couple of days ago."

This made Finley Fineen angry and he didn't try to hide it. "By God, you could have said something to me about it!"

"Well," McKeever said, "you never asked me and I never thought to mention it. Anyway, they got me in trouble with Leggitt and his damned paper. I didn't care either way, if you know what I mean."

"Those pieces were evidence," Fineen said. "Good God, Lincoln, no wonder Leggitt wanted you kicked out, as sloppy as you are." He pushed himself erect. "I don't suppose you have any idea who took 'em?"

"None whatsoever," McKeever said gently. "You think they were important, Finley?" Then he shrugged. "I guess not. But it was fun trying to put 'em together. You know how I like puzzles." Then he switched the subject quickly. "How you coming along with Doc's killing."

"Nowhere," Fineen admitted. "And you're no help to me." He turned and stalked out, banging the doors as he made his exit.

Jim Singleton lowered his voice and said, "How come you lied to him, Lincoln? I never knew you to tell anyone a lie before."

For a moment McKeever sat in silence, his eyes thoughtful. "I don't know, Jim. Ever play hunches? You know, it's funny to me that Finley would take those pieces of brass so seriously. What I mean is, even Doc Harris treated it like a joke; he never could get serious about it or believe they'd lead to anything. Leggitt didn't, and neither did anyone else."

"I did," Jim said.

"Did you really?" McKeever shook his head. "If I hadn't insisted on you helping Doc you'd have gone home to bed. Isn't that right?"

"Yeah," Jim said. "It's right."

"But Finley's real interested. Makes me wonder why." McKeever stood up, leaving his beer and unfinished game. "Be real interesting to find out, huh, Jim?"

12.

THURSDAY morning the telegrapher copied a message received from the marshal at Woodland concerning the eight thousand dollars turned over to him by the local attorney. The telegrapher took the message to Finley Fineen, and then spread the news all over town.

Lincoln McKeever was at the cemetery, sitting on a small headstone near Doc Harris' grave when Jim Singleton came up, out of breath and full of talk. McKeever listened with quiet attention, and when Jim Singleton finished, McKeever just sighed and stood up.

"For Pete's sake, doesn't this mean anything to you?" Jim demanded. "Some of the money's turned up. This kind of throws your theory into a cocked hat, doesn't it?"

"No," McKeever said softly. "Not yet, Jim."

"What do you mean, not yet?"

"It all depends on what Finley Fineen does," McKeever said. "Go keep an eye on Finley for me, Jim."

"Hell, what am I looking for?"

"See if Finley Fineen leaves town," McKeever said. "If he does—" McKeever shrugged.

"And if not?"

"Then I can assume that Finley has reached the same conclusion I have concerning the whereabouts of the killer, or he knows that the money that turned up in Woodland was sent there as a dodge."

"Gosh," Jim Singleton said. "How could he know a thing like that if he wasn't—"

McKeever's glance cut him off. "Don't say it, Jim. It might slip out when you didn't want it to." He gave the young man a push. "Go on now and keep an eye on Finley Fineen. I'll take it from there."

"All right," Jim said and walked on down the street. . . .

Dal Leggitt was on the porch of the Hanover House with Nan Singleton, and on impulse McKeever went over there. Dal Leggitt stopped talking when McKeever hailed in earshot, then gave him a blunt stare.

"You're not wanted around here, McKeever."

"Oh?" McKeever was the model of mildness. His quick glance went to Nan. "Dal the boss yet?"

"No," Nan said. "I was going to bring out some tea and cake. Care for some, Lincoln?"

"Why, I sure would." He stepped up on the porch and brushed Leggitt's arm aside to pass. "You don't mind, do you, Dal?"

"I do mind. McKeever, I whipped you once. I can put some more marks on your face if that's what you want."

McKeever regarded him solemnly. "What are you going to do after you marry her, Dal? Keep her locked in the closet for fear some man will look sideways at her?" He sat down then and cocked his feet to the railing. "Ahhhh, there's nothing like a good chair." He motioned to a vacant one. "Why don't you sit down, Dal? You look like a dog guarding his dish."

Leggitt hesitated briefly, then sat down. "You know, you don't seem so big without the badge, Lincoln."

"That so?" He glanced at Nan Singleton. "Didn't you say something about tea and cake?"

"Yes, but I was just waiting to see if you two were going to fight again."

"I'm a peaceful man," McKeever said.

"He doesn't like a licking," Leggitt offered. "Isn't that right, Lincoln?"

"If you say so, Dal."

Leggitt stared at McKeever. "You're too damned agreeable."

"Oh? And I guess you're never satisfied. A minute ago you wanted to know if I wanted to fight and now you want to know why I won't."

"I'll get a tray," Nan said and went on inside.

"Happy with your new sheriff?" McKeever asked.

"Anything's an improvement over you," Leggitt said.

"Now you don't mean that, Dal. If I hadn't been engaged to Nan once, you'd think I was a nice guy." He stripped the wrapper from a cigar, then offered one to Dal Leggitt. For a moment it seemed that Leggitt would refuse, then he took it without thanks. "Pretty exciting news, that money turning up in Woodland, huh?"

"Yes," Leggitt said. "I wish I could find Fineen and talk to him about it."

McKeever's interest sharpened. "Where is Fineen?"

"Out to Wade Stanton's place," Leggitt said. "Here's the tea and cake." He got up and made a fuss by taking the tray from Nan Singleton.

"Well, I don't see any blood," Nan said.

"There'll be no trouble," McKeever said. "Now that we all understand which burr's under Dal's blanket." He leaned against the porch railing. "What's Fineen doing out at Wade's place?"

"I don't know," Leggitt said. He glanced at his watch and then slipped it back into his pocket. "Wish he'd get back. I'd like to get some material for next week's paper." His glance touched McKeever. "When are you going to get a job?"

"You're the second man asked me that," McKeever said. "Does my loafing bother you, Dal?"

"It's none of my business what you do," Leggitt said flatly.

"Then why ask?"

Leggitt had an answer, but withheld it, for Finley Fineen drove onto the main street in his buggy. "I'll see you later, Nan," Dal Leggitt said and put his cake dish aside. He dashed off the porch, following Fineen's rig down the street.

"There goes a very busy man," McKeever said. He looked at Nan Singleton. "Aren't you going to argue with me?"

"No," she said softly. "Does it give you pleasure to run him down, Lincoln?"

"Maybe I'm as small as Dal," McKeever said. "Might as well be honest, huh? You want to know something? I'm jealous of him."

"You have no right to be," Nan said. "And you made the choice."

"True," McKeever said, rising, setting his cup and plate aside. "I was a fool, Nan. Can you believe it?"

"That you were a fool? Yes, you were. But you don't get a second chance with me, Lincoln. Be sure you understand that."

"Oh, I understand that all right," McKeever said.

He stepped off the porch and walked down the street.

McKeever wondered if he wasn't playing a fool's game, just standing around and waiting for something to happen; but then he considered all available facts and decided he had no other choice. There wasn't a man in town he didn't know well, yet at least two of them had banded together to rob and to kill. Two men carried this on their minds day and night. Two men watched themselves to make sure they let nothing slip, made no mistake that would trip them up. To McKeever's way of thinking, this was hardly different from a good stiff game of poker, where a man had to do plenty of close guessing if he expected to end the evening with two dollars in his pocket.

One thing for sure about Dalridge's death, it hadn't been decided and executed on the spur of the moment. A lot of thinking and a lot of talk had gone into it, not to mention considerable work with the outsized gun and the shell. Time was a factor; a man could spend it, waste it, hoard it, but he couldn't squeeze it or stretch it. Neither could he destroy it. The more McKeever thought of this, the more he became convinced that he was looking for men who had time and a place in common where they could spend time without anyone's ever guessing how it was spent.

McKeever covered his thinking and his searching by hanging around the saloon with a beer glass at his elbow and a deck of cards in front of him. He thought about all these people that he knew so well, especially the ones who always spent a lot of time together. There were those checker games that were played over the feed store Monday and Wednesday nights, but they went right on, same time, same place, same four people. McKeever felt he could rule them out.

During the two days Lincoln McKeever held the town under the magnifying scrutiny of his thoughts, he found that everyone seemed to be going on just as they always did. Kelly and Burgess moved about, making big talk. Sam Richardson made a speech on the saloon porch; he usually made one a week, just to keep himself in the voters' eyes. McKeever began to run out of ideas, and people who shared time together. . . .

The investigator from San Francisco was expected to arrive on Saturday. Everyone was at the stage depot, but he came in on horseback, unnoticed, for he was a thin, stringbean of a man in his late twenties, looking more like a whisky drummer than an insurance detective. He wore a flat-brimmed hat and a serious manner. He put up at the hotel, and had a bath, shave and a haircut in the barbershop before someone happened to look at the hotel register and then realized he had arrived. Then no one remembered what he looked like, except Lincoln McKeever, who had seen him ride in and spotted him right away.

McKeever stayed near the saloon until evening mealtime, then ate in the small restaurant down the street. Around eight he drifted toward Bill Daley's drugstore, bought a few cigars, then paused to pass the time of day with Daley.

"You see the insurance detective yet?"

"Yep," Daley said. "He came in here and bought a package of cough drops, and I didn't even guess who he was."

"Did he ask any questions?"

"Not a damn one, except where was a good place to eat. I told him the Chinese joint on Ash Street."

McKeever was lighting his cigar. "He disappointed some folks, who expected a real two-gun man."

"You want to know something?" Daley said. "People

are easily disappointed." He sighed and shook his head.

"I'll walk over to Finley's with you," McKeever said.

Daley looked at him blankly for a moment, then said, "I—I'm not going to play tonight, Lincoln."

"What? Hell, Bill, we've played poker every Saturday night for years."

"Count me out tonight," Daley said. "I told Ethel I'd drive her over to her sister's place in Woodland. Figured to stay the weekend."

McKeever went out, scratching his head. Finally he cut across the street to Finley Fineen's office and found the place dark. He banged on the door for a while, then walked back toward the Hanover House, puzzled by the sudden shifting of a familiar routine.

INSIDE the Hanover House, in the dining room, McKeever found Wade and Betty Stanton having dinner. Wade looked around, then said, "You want to sit down, Lincoln?"

"Ah, no," McKeever said. "You going over to Fineen's tonight?"

"We're not playing," Stanton said. "Didn't Finley tell you?"

"No, I guess he forgot about it," McKeever said. "How come, Wade? Someone get sore about something?"

"I don't think so," Stanton said. "Maybe it was Bill's idea. Why don't you ask him?"

"I might," McKeever said.

"Anyhow, it wouldn't be the same without Doc Harris," Stanton said. "I guess it had to break up sooner or later."

"Yeah," McKeever said and walked out.

At his table in the saloon, he laid out his spread of cards and lifted a fresh beer. He kept kicking Stanton's reason around in his mind, trying to get it to settle down, but it seemed as if Harris was reaching out of the grave to upset it every time it started to jell. The more McKeever thought about it, the more troubled he became, until he was forced to start at the beginning again and admit a few things to himself. First, in looking over the town, the quiet gatherings, he had missed one, or had deliberately dismissed it; he wasn't sure which. But the fact remained that he had disregarded the Saturday poker games in Fineen's place.

The thought seemed ridiculous, yet he could not seem to put it aside. Habit was a funny thing, the way it took hold of a man, made him dress a certain way, talk with a certain quaintness, and even think along clearly outlined patterns. Then all of a sudden something changed, without a reason. McKeever could remember plenty of times when a good reason came along to miss a poker session, yet no one had. Then all of a sudden Daley wanted to drive his nagging wife over to her sister's place. And Fineen wouldn't miss his poker; it was the only place in town where he could nip at the bottle without his wife's finding out he'd skipped the pledge. McKeever didn't even know Stanton's excuse, if the man had one; only the fact remained that three men suddenly got tired of playing poker, and all at the same time. If one man had dropped out, McKeever supposed he'd consider that natural, but the excuse of Doc's not being there didn't fit because Doc didn't always show up.

McKeever didn't like to think about time just then, because it made him consider three men who had been his long-time friends in an unholy light. Yet he did think of them, and of the time they spent together when he wasn't around, and all the talk that must have gone on between them. After he had circulated the thought a moment, the rest wasn't so difficult to consider. Instead of two, there was three: Daley, Stanton and Fineen.

The reason for it all was the stickler, and he could think of none. They all had enough money to make most men happy. They had wives and respectability and certainly no criminal pasts, which made all this speculation a little hard to believe. Maybe that's why they did it, it was so completely out of character for them; or better still, all part of a character that had remained hidden.

McKeever disliked the neatness, the ease with which all the pieces went together without one shred of proof, or anything beside his basic suspicion. Fineen could have supplied the buggy, maybe even the gun; Stanton probably drove, and Daley went along because they had to do something with him.

He felt almost a sense of betrayal for thinking these things, yet the feeling was too strong to put down. McKeever didn't know exactly how to go about finding out the truth, but he knew that one of them, if his thinking was right, had gotten scared enough to kill. Maybe he could scare them again.

His hand of solitaire didn't come out, but then he didn't mind since everything else seemed to be falling apart at the seams. He redealt, then looked up in time to see the San Francisco investigator come through the door and head for his table.

An outthrust hand came first, then a brief shake. "I'm Charlie Boomhauer, from San Francisco."

"And you know who I am, or you wouldn't be here," McKeever said. "Quite an entrance you made. The town was disappointed; they expected something more exciting."

"We're both too old to believe in fairy tales," Boomhauer said. "Mr. McKeever, I'll be brief. Just a few questions, if you don't mind. I think it's a relatively simple case and should be cleared up shortly. The crime started in this town, and it'll end here. I cannot see any outside forces at work."

McKeever laid a black queen on a red king. Without taking his attention from the game, he said, "My sentiments exactly, Mr. Boomhauer. What do you want to know?"

13.

THE appointment as sheriff gave Finley Fineen the license he needed to move around without question, and when he saw Wade Stanton talking to Bill Daley in front of the drugstore, Fineen crossed over. Daley was standing by his new buggy, waiting for a fussing wife; both men turned as Fineen came up in a foul frame of mind.

"The damned gall of Kelly and Burgess. You hear about it?"

"Hear about what?" Stanton asked.

"They turned in a claim to the insurance company of over forty thousand apiece," Fineen said. "Boy, if that ain't crust, I never seen it." He slapped his hands together. "You know, there's a lot of profit in being robbed, when you get it back with interest like that."

Wade Stanton smiled. "Well, Finley, why don't you go tell the insurance investigator. Boomhauer, was that his name?"

"Very funny," Fineen said, scowling. "But it sure gets me, that's all."

"It ought to make you feel good," Bill Daley said. "I mean, now you know that you're not the only crook around Two Pines."

"You could write Boomhauer an anonymous letter and tell him about it," Stanton suggested.

"That would be real smart," Fineen said flatly. "Real smart."

Stanton shrugged. "About as smart as mailing some money to Woodland to make everyone think someone there tried to spend some of it."

"You seem damned sure of that accusation," Fineen snapped back.

"I'm pretty sure," Stanton said. "I know I didn't send it, and Bill's too tight to spend a dollar, so it must have been you. Finley, you'll have to go over to Woodland and fuss around to make this look good."

"Yeah, I'm riding over Monday with Boomhauer." He raised a hand and mopped his face. "McKeever made me jumpier than I thought, but it's all right now."

Daley tipped back his head and looked at the upstairs windows. "Wonder what's keeping Ethel?"

"You in a hurry to get out of town?" Fineen asked. "I'd hate to think you were going somewhere else to live, Bill."

"You think I'd take her along if I was?" He nodded toward Fineen's shoulder. "Here comes Lincoln McKeever. I can do without him right now."

McKeever had a cigar locked between his teeth, and a smile for them. "Together again," he said smoothly. "What are you doing, Finley? Talking about how to get rid of the money?"

Bill Daley took a deep breath and held it. Stanton's expression froze, but Finley Fineen's remained unchanged. "What the hell you talking about?"

"The money Dalridge was carrying." He pursed his lips briefly "Come on, Finley, it wasn't so hard to figure out."

"That's a damned serious accusation to make against a man without proof," Stanton said.

McKeever glanced at him, smiling. "Now, you know me, Wade. Do I ever bluff without the cards to back me up? How about it, Finley, you going to cut me in, or do I talk?"

"You're beating the wrong bush this time," Fineen said flatly. "Lincoln, I'm willing to forget you ever said this, but I'll tell you now that if you spread talk about us, I'll kill you."

"You may think that's cheaper than making another split," McKeever said. "I'll give you an hour or two to kick it around."

"I don't need an hour," Fineen snapped.

Lincoln McKeever looked at Stanton and Daley. "You two don't have much to say—especially you, Bill. I always thought you were real touchy, but now you don't seem to care." He rotated the cigar between his lips. "Let's see now, what would you do with the money? You don't trust your wife and you wouldn't take it to a bank. I'll bet you got it stuck away in a jar someplace where you can take it out now and then and count it." He studied Daley's expression while he spoke, then still smiling, he turned to Wade Stanton. "I think you'd bury yours, Wade, because you're a miserly bastard who likes to have things just to be having them, even when they don't do you a damned bit of good. Money or a wife, it wouldn't make much difference."

"You've said too much," Fineen said. "Get away from us, Lincoln."

"In a minute, in a minute," McKeever said. He took out his watch and looked at it. "I'll give you an hour, gentlemen. You name the place. I'll be at Hanover House. Send a boy when you make up your minds."

McKeever turned and walked away, leaving silence behind him.

WADE STANTON spoke first. "I told you that you made too many mistakes, Finley."

"Shut up!"

"How did he know?" Daley asked. "How could he know?"

"He's guessing," Fineen said quickly, "nothing more."

"You guess that close, you've got a hit," Stanton said

softly. "You played poker with him, Daley. Can't you figure it out?"

"What are we going to do?" This was Daley's one concern.

"We're going to do nothing," Fineen said. "Damn it, how many times do I have to tell you that as long as we don't break and run for it we're safe? All right, so McKeever was smarter than I gave him credit for, and so he guessed the truth, but he won't say anything. That was a bluff to make us break."

"He sounded serious to me," Daley said uneasily.

"It was a bluff, I tell you," Fineen insisted. "He don't have one damned thing to go on. Not one damned thing. And he won't talk because he hasn't anything to talk about." He took Daley by the arm and shook him slightly. "You go get your woman and drive her to Woodland, just as if nothing happened. By the time you get back, this whole thing will be done with, finished."

"What you going to do, Finley?" This was Daley's question.

"I'm going to meet him in one hour, as he asks. Then I'm going to run a bluff of my own."

"I don't think you can get away with it," Stanton said.

"No? Who asked you, anyway?"

"Maybe if you'd have shut your mouth once in a while instead of doing all the talking we wouldn't be in this spot now," Stanton said. "You've got to run everything, Finley, and always your way."

"Is that the way you feel about it? Then take your share and shift for yourself. And don't come to me when McKeever starts stepping on your toes."

"I'm not scared of McKeever," Stanton said.

Bill Daley interrupted. "Wade, Finley, don't talk like that. We've got to stick together."

"The hell we do," Fineen said. "If Stanton wants out, then he's free to go. I don't want a man around me who doesn't trust me."

"You said yourself that the worst thing that could happen was for us to fight among ourselves," Daley said. "Finley, Wade didn't mean anything by what he sa—"

"Look, Bill, I'll decide what I meant and didn't mean." He looked at Fineen. "The trouble with you, Finley, is that you figure everybody needs you. Well, I don't. I can handle McKeever by myself, and I won't have to ask you for advice either."

"That suits me," Fineen said. "By golly, I've been a man of honor all my life, and I won't let a crook like you call me a fool." He waved his hand. "Go on, Wade. But walk away now, and it's for good."

"Oh, you're getting me all choked up," Stanton said and stalked down the street.

"I can patch this up," Daley said quickly. "Finley, let me go to him and I'll get it all straightened out."

"No," Fineen said, his eyes following Stanton. "I didn't know it until this minute, but I never liked him. Not one damned bit I never."

LINCOLN MCKEEVER waited on the porch of the Hanover House as he had promised, only he did not wait alone, for Betty Stanton sat close beside him. They talked in low tones and she laughed repeatedly and Nan Singleton, when she brought out the tray of coffee McKeever ordered, set it down a little harder than was necessary.

To anyone passing along the walk, and there were many who noticed, Lincoln McKeever was carrying on an obvious flirtation with Wade Stanton's wife, and she was enjoying every minute of it. McKeever kept a well disguised attention on the street, and saw Wade Stanton approaching on the opposite boardwalk. He stopped at the base of the steps, one hand on the porch rail.

"You two amusing each other?" Stanton asked. Nan Singleton came to the door and Stanton glanced at her, then back to McKeever.

"Your wife is charming company," McKeever said, "but I don't think we'd ever quarrel over that point, would we, Wade?" He eased out of his chair then and stood near Stanton. "Did Fineen send you?"

Wade said, "This is between the two of us."

"What is?"

Wade Stanton glared for a moment, then said, "McKeever, I'm tired of having you fool around my wife."

This was the kind of talk to make people interested, and Wade said it in a voice that would carry. Several men stopped, looked at each other, then decided to remain to see what came next.

"Take this someplace else," Nan Singleton said. "I run a decent place here."

A few more men attached themselves to the lingering group on the walk, and a crowd attracts a crowd. Within half a minute, twenty-five men stood there, smoking, looking, waiting.

"Wade, you're making a fool of yourself," Betty Stanton said. "And you're embarrassing me."

"Too bad about you," Wade said. "How about it, Lincoln? We going to settle this man to man?"

"If you think there's anything to settle," McKeever said. He smiled thinly. "What are you going to do, Wade? Whip me with a gun barrel?"

"I don't do things that way," Stanton said flatly.

"Well, I didn't think you did," McKeever said softly. "But if it's a fight you want, I'll accommodate you."

"I'm not carrying a gun," Stanton said, "but I'll sure get one."

"Gun? Fineen wants this done permanently, huh?"

"Fineen doesn't give me orders," Stanton said. "This is purely my pleasure." He spun around and went across the street to his buggy. From under the seat he took a cartridge belt and buckled it on. Nan Singleton came out and took McKeever's arm. "You fool, would you fight over her? Kill for her?"

He wanted to tell her the truth, but he could not, and he knew that if he didn't tell her in this moment, she would never believe it later. "Get back," he said softly. "Take Betty inside."

"No," Nan said. "She wants to see it. She's waited long enough to see it."

A lane opened up for Wade Stanton; he stopped at the walk's edge.

McKeever stood with his hands in his coat pockets. "Wade, you're a damned fool. You haven't got a chance and you know it."

"What kind of a chance will I have if I don't go through with this?"

"All right, you figure it that way if you want," McKeever said. "But there's only one way for you to find out, Wade, and this time it could be with your life, not just a few dollars."

There was a hushed period when both men waited; then Wade Stanton reached for his gun. He wasn't fast, but he was good, and as the barrel came level, his thumb eared back the hammer while Lincoln McKeever remained rooted, his hands in his coat pockets. An instant before Stanton fired, McKeever shot, right through the pocket, leaving a burning eye of cloth. Stanton staggered back and sent his shot into the porch planks. He quickly clasped his left hand over his breast and stared at Lincoln McKeever.

"Damned . . . pea-shooter anyway," he said, and then fell.

The crowd broke, and Lincoln McKeever flogged the pocket of his coat, beating out the smoldering ring. He broke open the .32 and replaced the spent cartridge from the few spares he carried in a pocket. Betty Stanton stood by the rail, staring at her dead husband.

"Now you've got it all." McKeever said softly. "All of that money." He started to turn, then stopped to add, "Get a shovel and start digging. You might be surprised at how much more you'll find."

Her expression was blank, mirroring her lack of understanding. Then he stepped inside the hotel and looked toward the desk where Nan Singleton stood.

"Well," Nan said, her voice softly bitter, "she finally got you to kill for her, didn't she, Lincoln?"

14.

FINLEY FINEEN heard about the shooting within minutes, and the news was like a blow to the face; the fact that Wade Stanton was so quickly dead was almost beyond belief. Evidently Bill Daley thought so too, for he defied his wife by cancelling the ride to Woodland.

As Fineen stepped out of his office, he met Daley coming across the street.

"What are you going to do about this?" Daley wanted to know.

"Arrest McKeever," Finley Fineen said. "What the hell can I do?"

"Did you ever think that maybe he wanted to be arrested?"

"Yes, I thought of that. It's a chance I have to take," Fineen said. "God, you're not going to get as nervous like Wade was, are you?"

"No," Daley said. He put his hand to his face. "Finley, I've got to get out of here. Go to Arizona. Ethel can have the place. I'll take my share and—"

"You spend one cent of that money and I'll kill you," Fineen said.

Daley backed up a step. "Now hold on there. You sent that lawyer in Woodland eight thousand dollars. That wasn't in the damn plan."

"Neither was killing Doc Harris!" Fineen calmed himself. "Let's not start pulling apart, Bill. Wade did, and got himself killed for it."

"McKeever's got to be shut up some way," Daley said. "I mean it, Finley. He's dangerous."

"You don't have to tell me about McKeever." Fineen wiped a hand across his mouth. "I'd better get over to the hotel before someone sends for me. I want to talk to McKeever alone."

"Don't let him get your goat," Daley warned. "That's his game, getting us to do something foolish, and Wade fell for it."

"Don't keep telling me stuff I already know!"

He wheeled away, toward the hotel. Several men were carrying Wade Stanton away when he arrived. Charlie Boomhauer was there, his face more grave than usual.

"Where's McKeever?" Fineen asked, speaking to anyone who would answer him.

One man nodded toward the inside. "In there."

Fineen went in and found McKeever in the lobby, alone. As Fineen came up, McKeever took his watch from his pocket and consulted it. "I thought you'd get here sooner than this," he said.

"I want to talk to you, alone," Fineen said.

"We're alone here," McKeever said.

"Let's take one of the empty rooms," Fineen said. "And keep your damned hands out of your coat pockets."

"You arresting me?"

"We'll talk first," Fineen said. "Come on."

FINEEN went behind the counter, snagged a key off the hook and led the way down the hall. He unlocked the door and went on in to light the lamp. Then he closed the door and locked it before speaking. "Wade was a fool. I told him I'd handle it."

"Yeah, he was a fool. So you handle it."

Fineen said, "What am I going to do with you, Lincoln?"

"I was waiting for you to figure it out," McKeever said. "I don't think the judge will hold me. Too many witnesses to the shooting. You see, I had the drop on Wade and told him so, but he drew anyway. I had to shoot in self-defense."

"You're damned smart," Finley Fineen said. "I wish to God you were stupid." He sat down then and studied his huge hands.

"How did it ever get started, Finley? You know, talking about it?"

He looked up quickly, then laughed. "Why shouldn't I tell you? If you repeated it I'd call you a liar."

"Did you think of it first?"

"No," Fineen said softly. "I think Bill Daley did. You know how he is, sometimes. Full of big talk." Fineen shook his head. "I've thought about it a lot, Lincoln, how it worked up from just talk to—"

"—to murder?"

"It didn't start out that way," Fineen said quickly. "We kept kicking the idea around just to have something different to talk about, I guess. Lincoln, didn't you ever get tired of this damned town, and the same people and the same conversations all the time?"

"Yes, but never that tired."

"Then we're not alike," Fineen said. "Hell, I go home at night and Madge says, 'How did it go today?' Every night for eleven years it's the same damned question."

"And the same answer, Finley?"

"Huh?"

"What do you say in answer?"

He thought a moment. "I say, 'Fine. Just fine.'"

"Maybe you ought to have brought your wife in on this too, Finley. She'd have the same reason as you."

Fineen looked at McKeever. "You want me to confess? Say I'm sorry?"

"No, you're not sorry, Finley. You're not sorry because underneath all that good will and fine citizenship you're nothing but a thief and a killer, I think you enjoyed beating Dalridge's brains out with a gun barrel. I think you've always wanted to beat someone's brains out." Fineen started to get up, but McKeever's voice drove him back. "Sit down! I'll tell you when you can get up. Finley, you know and I know all about this. And you know I can't even open my mouth about it because everyone would laugh at me; I couldn't prove a thing. But I want to tell you something. You and I are going to play a little game. Bill Daley's in it too, because I think he killed Doc Harris; you wouldn't have done such a messy job of it. This little game is for keeps, Finley, like the one I played with Wade Stanton. I'm going to hound you until I make you break and run. And when you do, it'll be out in the open and then every peace officer west of the Mississippi will join in with me. It's going to be a grand hunt, Finley. You, me, and Bill Daley. I'll never let up on you, so watch yourself." Then he went to the door and flung it open. "Get out of here. And don't make any mistakes, Finley."

Finley Fineen sat in the chair, sweat bold on his forehead. He said, "Suppose I drew on you now, Lincoln?"

"Too late," McKeever said, turning so that Fineen could see the pocket that had a moment ago been hidden from sight; McKeever's hand was in it, and Fineen understood what that meant. "A thirty-two is small, but it does the job." He nodded again toward the open door. "All right, now get going."

Fineen got up and stepped to the hall. "Lincoln, you chose the odds, two against one."

"You're scared, Finley. How do you sleep at night? Do you ever worry about talking in your sleep?" His smile was mocking.

Spinning on his heel, Finley Fineen walked rapidly down the hall, then took the stairs two at a time. McKeever blew out the lamp and locked the door before returning to the lobby. He rehung the key, then on impulse he turned toward the kitchen.

HE SAW Dal Leggitt first, seated at the table, then when McKeever stepped deeper into the room he saw Nan Singleton, her back toward him. When she turned around to see who it was he noticed that her eyes and nose were red from crying.

"Get out of here," Leggitt said bitterly. "McKeever, you spoil everything you touch."

"Why don't you just shut your mouth for a while," McKeever said.

Nan took a final sniff, a final dab with the handkerchief and said, "Betty's at her father's house. Why don't you go there, Lincoln? Don't stand on formality now."

"Nan," McKeever said, "I wish you'd listen to me."

"She doesn't have to listen to you," Leggitt said. "I told her time and time again how this would end; maybe now she'll believe me." He got up and put his arm around her, but she shrugged off his embrace.

"Just leave me alone, Dal."

"With him?"

This made her angry. "Oh, don't be stupid!"

He was easily offended. Taking up his hat, he stepped to the door. "Very well, Nan. When you come to your senses, call me."

When Leggitt's footfalls faded, McKeever said, "Nan, will you listen to me?"

"No," she said. "I meant you too when I said I wanted to be left alone." She faced him quickly. "Oh, Lincoln, I wish I hated you."

He had no words for her, no ready explanation; he went out and paused on the boardwalk. From the shadows of the porch, Charlie Boomhauer spoke.

"Got a minute, McKeever?"

"Sure. Here?"

"No," Boomhauer said. "Let's walk."

He fell in beside McKeever and they started down the street, Boomhauer remaining silent until they came to the residential district.

"How much money do you think the robbers got?" Boomhauer asked.

"Don't you know?"

"I know what Mr. Kelly and Mr. Burgess claim was stolen," he said, "but I haven't had a chance to check it. Those things take time, you know. I'll have to audit all the accounts listed in their books, then check the balance owed against their claim."

"Why ask me?"

"Because you know this town. And because you were the sheriff when this happened." Boomhauer paused to light a cigar, and then he walked on, his step slow and even. "That quarrel you had with Wade Stanton—was that as personal as it looked?"

"No," McKeever said. "But I couldn't prove anything."

"That's often the case," Boomhauer admitted. "I'm interested in finding the money and absolving my company of a large claim payment. Catching killers I leave to marshals and sheriffs. You follow me?"

"Maybe I do," McKeever said. "You want me to go ahead with what I'm doing, and you'll follow along to pick up the pieces. Is that it?"

Boomhauer chuckled. "That's the general idea, as long as the pieces are money." He paused to draw on his smoke. "This Stanton, was he in on the robbery?"

"Yes, he and two others."

"Suppose you name them to me."

"I'll name Stanton. The other two I'll deal with my own way. As you said, Boomhauer, there's murder connected with this. And that's my department."

"It's the law's department. And you're not the law."

"There are times," McKeever said, "when the individual must be the law."

For a time Boomhauer said nothing, then he posed a question. "Are you going to make me hunt the money that was Stanton's share? Or are you going to tell me where it is?"

"I don't know where it is," McKeever said.

Charlie Boomhauer chuckled. "McKeever, you were smart enough to put this together so far. I assume you're smart enough to take it the rest of the way. Where do you think the money is hidden?"

"Go buy a shovel," McKeever said.

Boomhauer threw his cigar into the street. "I believe I will. And it's been pleasant talking to you."

When he turned to leave, McKeever took his arm. "There might be others digging."

"I'll enjoy the company," Boomhauer said.

Lincoln McKeever laughed. "Nothing much bothers you, does it?"

"No," Boomhauer said. "I think that's a trait we share in common. And incidentally, if you settle with the other two as finally as with Stanton, will you please bear in mind my interest in the money?"

"Yes," McKeever said. "That won't be difficult."

Boomhauer headed back toward the central part of town, and Lincoln McKeever remained under the trees.

The shot came as a complete surprise, a carnation of flame and an echo that slapped among the quiet houses. McKeever assumed that the bullet was meant for him and pulled his pistol from his pocket, but before he could even aim it in the general direction of the assailant, Boomhauer had his .44 free of the shoulder holster and was rolling a cylinder full of lead at the trees twenty yards beyond.

This sudden volley was enough to make the trees untenable, and a man quickly dashed down the street, his steps spanking the boardwalk. McKeever started to race after him, but Boomhauer called him back.

"No use, McKeever. The night's dark and there're too many alleys down there to duck into. Hell, he could hide behind someone's rosebush and you'd walk right by him while he aimed at your back."

Booomhauer was punching the empties from his gun and after he reloaded it, he replaced it in the holster.

"I didn't know you were carrying that," McKeever said.

Boomhauer smiled. "I just look innocent."

Lights popped on and a few people stuck their heads out of upstairs windows, but after a moment they ducked back inside, convinced it was all over.

"Whoever it was, his aim was sure lousy," McKeever said.

"Really?" Boomhauer lifted the tail of his coat and poked a finger through the hole. "It seems, McKeever, that we have more than one thing in common. We are alike in appearance just enough so that in poor light, I could be mistaken for you, and you for me."

"Come on," McKeever said. "I owe you a drink."

"And a needle and thread," Boomhauer said.

15.

AT NINE o'clock the next morning, the judge held an inquest and heard witnesses testify that Lincoln McKeever was justified in shooting Wade Stanton, since

Stanton had picked the quarrel and then tried to draw against the drop. The verdict was not difficult to reach and McKeever walked out twenty minutes later, Charlie Boomhauer at his elbow. They walked down the street to the saloon, ordered two glasses of beer, then went to McKeever's favorite table.

Boomhauer said, "This newspaperman, Leggitt, he's going to stir up all the feeling against you he can."

"I expect that."

"You changed your mind yet and decided to work along with me?"

"I'd like to work with you," McKeever said, "but you'll have to do your job your way and let me do mine my way."

"That sounds reasonable," Boomhauer said mildly. "I don't think we'll get in each other's way."

"I think Bill Daley and Finley Fineen are the other two we want."

Boomhauer's eyes widened. "Fineen? Why, he's the sheriff!"

"He wasn't sheriff then," McKeever said. "Look, Charlie, you've got to go along with me, all the way. Either I have that or you can figure it out for yourself."

"Just give me something to go on," Boomhauer said. "I'm a reasonable man."

Lincoln McKeever did. He outlined his way of thinking, and one by one, pointed out the conclusions he had reached. Boomhauer was quick-witted and ready to find fault, but there was none. Because he knew these men, and this town, he had arrived at some startling answers.

"All right," Boomhauer said, when McKeever finished. "I'll buy it, McKeever. But where do we go from here?"

"I think you'd better get a restraining order from the court to keep Betty Stanton's hands off Wade's property. At least until you have time to look for the money."

"That won't be difficult. And you?"

"Well, Bill Daley is the weak link, so I'm going to start to lean on him and see if I can break him off at the ankles."

Charlie Boomhauer raised his coat and indicated the bullet hole. "Don't forget this, McKeever. Either of them will kill you if they get the chance." He hunched forward. "If you were killed, I couldn't do a thing about it. There's no evidence against them now, and if Fineen is running this, as you say, he's smart enough to make sure no one drops anything." He shook his head. "Your way's pretty risky, McKeever. I'd advise against it."

"I didn't ask for that. You said you'd go along."

"And I won't go back on it," Boomhauer said. "Do you have a plan?"

McKeever admitted, "The way I figure it, if Fineen and Daley sit tight, we'll never get anything on them, and my accusation won't mean a thing if I can't prove it." He rubbed a hand across his face. "My only chance is to make one of them break, and that would be Daley. I think he got scared enough once to kill Doc Harris, and I'm going to scare him again."

"He knows you're on to him," Boomhauer pointed out. "And he'll know what you're trying to do. McKeever, I don't think it's going to work."

"Yes it is," McKeever said, then leaned forward to tell why in little more than a whisper. Boomhauer listened with a quickened interest, then he slapped the table and laughed. "Well?" McKeever asked. "How about it?"

"I think so," Boomhauer said. He scraped his chair back. "I'd better get that restraining order. Good luck, McKeever."

AFTER he left, McKeever had a refill on his beer, then played solitaire until noon. One of the town barflies mooched two drinks off McKeever, then he sent the man on an errand.

Ten minutes later Jim Singleton came in and sat down. "You wanted to see me?"

"Like to do a job tonight? It might be risky."

Jim Singleton didn't hesitate. "Sure. You name it."

McKeever did. "Spend the night in my room. Keep the lamp going until around midnight, then lock the door and go to bed."

"That's risky?"

"Someone took a shot at me tonight," McKeever said. "They may try it again."

Jim Singleton swallowed hard. "Can I have a gun to shoot back?"

"There's a rifle and a box of shells in my room," McKeever said. "Jim, I want you to stay in that room until I tell you to come out."

"Yes, sir."

"All right," McKeever said. "Sneak in right after dark, and make sure the lamp is on."

Jim Singleton nodded. "Can I tell Nan?"

"God, no! Look, keep this to yourself."

"What you up to, Lincoln?"

"I wouldn't say," McKeever told him. "Go on now."

He killed the afternoon by loafing in the saloon. That evening, when he went to the restaurant he met Dal Leggitt having an early supper. In passing Leggitt's table, McKeever said, "How come you're not over to Nan's place sponging a free meal?"

This drew a frown across Leggitt's forehead. "Sit down, McKeever. I want to talk to you."

After a moment's hesitation, McKeever took the chair across from him. He gave his order to the waiter; then McKeever said, "What's on your mind, Dal?"

"What to do about you," Leggitt said.

"I didn't know you could do anything about me," McKeever said.

Leggitt speared a piece of steak with his fork and chewed violently. "McKeever, you're the worst thing that ever happened to this town. If I ever needed proof, I had it when you shot Wade Stanton down in cold blood."

"You're doing a lot of guessing there," McKeever said. "Dal, you don't even know what's going on around here. All you ever think about is yourself. That lousy little paper of yours is just a showcase for your own small-minded opinions."

Leggitt was quietly angry; his eyes took on a brilliant sheen. "Lincoln, that lousy little paper, as you call it, is just big enough to run you out of town. That's my ambition now."

"Well, it's growing, anyway," McKeever said. His supper arrived and he began to eat. "At first you were just interested in bucking me when I ran for sheriff. Then you decided you'd grown enough to throw me out of office by getting Kelly and Burgess stirred up."

"And now I'm big enough to push you all the way out of town," Dal Leggitt said. "Why don't you go out to Stanton's place and live with Betty? I wouldn't want to think you killed Wade for nothing."

McKeever's first impulse was to hit him, but he had

too much to lose by embroiling himself with Dal Leggitt.

And Leggitt was the kind who would mistake judgment for cowardice. He placed his hands on the table and said, "You're yellow, McKeever."

Now that the first shock of anger passed, McKeever was almost amused by Leggitt. The man was like a small boy approaching a strange dog, timidly at first, then with increasing boldness. McKeever believed that a sudden move on his part would make Leggitt jump.

But McKeever did none of these things. He merely shrugged and went on eating, unmindful of the other diners who were listening to every word said.

Dal Leggitt found something more interesting than food, a person he could torment and get away with it. "Your presence here offends me," he said. "Get up and get out of this restaurant while I'm eating my supper."

Even the dishwasher stopped and came to the kitchen door to see this. Lincoln McKeever wiped his lips with his napkin and slowly stood up. Someone gasped and someone else groaned while Dal Leggitt smiled.

McKeever took Leggitt's plate from the table and set it on the floor. Then he looked at Leggitt and said, "That's where the dogs eat. Get down there."

For an instant Leggitt just stared and wondered how this could have happened, and what he was going to do about it. He found out when McKeever hit him, driving him out of his chair. Before Leggitt could clear the buzzing from his head, McKeever grabbed him by the hair and pushed his face down to the plate.

Leggitt clawed and tried to fight back, but McKeever's anger was too strong, his strength too determined now. Hauling Leggitt erect, McKeever shoved him toward the front door while potatoes and peas and gravy dribbled off Leggitt's face. Not bothering to open the door, McKeever merely drove Leggitt against it with enough force to carry away the hasp; then they were crossing the walk and Leggitt was propelled by McKeever's foot into the street. He struck and rolled and then sat up, stunned, shamed, afraid to get up.

"You want me to wait?" McKeever said. "Come on, Dal, you wanted trouble. Here's a big bundle of it." He stepped toward Leggitt. "Show me how a dog walks,

Dal. Go on, show me!" He gave Leggitt a kick to get him started.

On hands and knees, Leggitt started to move away, but McKeever stepped up and grabbed him by the collar, hauling him back. Leggitt struck at McKeever's legs and earned a clout on the ear for his trouble. The crowd had come outside the restaurant to see this and all the business houses along the street hurriedly emptied.

"See that hitching post over there? Go over and show everyone how a dog takes a leak," McKeever said. "Damn you, Dal, you'd better do it!"

"Ain't he had enough?" one man asked.

McKeever's glance whipped around and singled this man out. "*I've* had enough. You want to join him?"

"I was just sayin'," the man murmured and fell silent.

Leggit was still on his hands and knees, head raised, watching McKeever. Let me up and I'll fight you," Leggitt said.

"You like to fight with your mouth," McKeever said. "Get over to that post."

"I won't do it," Leggitt said dully. "You do what you want, but I won't do it." He raised a hand to mingle dust with the food still stuck to his face. "Let me have a gun, somebody. For God's sake, let me have a gun!"

McKeever waited, then a man spoke up. "How about it, McKeever? You want me to give him mine?"

"Do as you damned please," McKeever said.

The man hesitated, then took a long-barreled .45 from his waistband. "A man ought to have the right to settle a thing anyway he wants." He tossed the gun into the dust by Leggitt's knee.

"Well?" McKeever said and stood there.

Leggitt looked at the gun for a long moment, then raised his eyes to Lincoln McKeever. "You want to chalk up another killing, don't you?"

"No," McKeever said. "But I'll let you start anything you think you can finish."

Leggitt's hand came out briefly and almost touched the gun, but then he started to shake. Suddenly he clasped both hands over his face and rocked forward on his elbows and knees. The man who had tossed the gun stepped forward and picked it up.

The crowd seemed to melt then and McKeever turned

back inside the restaurant to finish his meal. One man stopped by his table and said, "You'd have been a lot kinder if you'd just shot him, Lincoln. Dal's through in Two Pines. Won't be anyone who'll listen to anything he has to say from now on."

"Yes," McKeever said, somewhat sadly. "Remember that when you feel like talking too much."

His meal ended, McKeever paid the counter man and went out. At the stable he rented a horse and a saddle, then went to his room and changed clothes. He slipped into a pair of levis and a tan canvas brush jacket. From the bureau drawer he took a worn .38-40 with belt and holster and buckled this around his waist.

When the door opened he turned quickly, then relaxed when Jim Singleton stepped into the room. The young man's face was serious. "Heard what happened to Dal. I wouldn't go near Nan for a while if I was you."

"I don't intend to," McKeever said. "That's the part I don't like, what she's thinking."

"You done that awful hard," Jim said. "Nan says too hard. Dal didn't have it coming."

"I thought he did," McKeever said.

"Sure, I understand all right." He nodded toward McKeever's worn clothes. "Never seen you in anything but a suit before, Lincoln."

"I wore these clothes when I came to Two Pines."

"You leavin'?" Jim asked.

"For a while," McKeever said. "I'll go out the back window. You sure no one saw you come in?"

"No, I sneaked in. Where you going?"

McKeever shook his head. "I'll be back. Remember what I said about the lamp, and stay here until I tell you to leave." Then he opened the window and left.

16.

Lincoln McKeever didn't often get to Woodland, at least not more than two or three times a year. The town was built on the flats, which extended on for nearly eight miles before they were broken up by low rolling hills. This was cattle country, rough country, with a man's nearest neighbor ten or twelve miles away. The men here were loners, and they liked it that way.

Riding down the main street, McKeever stopped at the saloon, for at a quarter to three in the morning, only the saloon stayed open. He tied his horse and went inside. A sleepy bartender racked glasses while a long-winded poker game went on in one corner.

"Whisky," McKeever said, and then with his drink paid for, he felt free to venture the next question. "Marshal Green around?"

"Went to bed two hours ago," the bartender said.

"He still sleeping in the office?"

"Yeah," the bartender said. "Say, ain't you the sheriff from Two Pines? Didn't recognize you without your suit on."

McKeever lingered a moment longer, then went out and down the dark street. The marshal's office and two-by-four jail sat near an alley and McKeever pounded on the oak door until he heard Green's outraged voice: "All right, all right, I'm coming!"

A lamp was lighted, then Green flung the door open and thrust his belligerent face and a pistol at McKeever. "What the blue blazes you want? That you, McKeever? Come on in." He put the pistol down and hitched up his suspenders. "Couldn't it wait until morning?"

"You sleep until noon anyway," McKeever said. "I came after that money, Ben."

"The eight thousand? It's in Lon Beasley's safe."

"I'd like to get it tonight," McKeever said.

"Well, Lon ain't going to like being got out of bed," Ben Green said. "You can't wait, huh?"

"I'm going back as soon as I can get a fresh horse."

"All right," Green said and put on his shirt and hat. He sat down on the edge of his cot to wrestle on his boots, then blew out the lamp and walked three blocks south with Lincoln McKeever.

Lon Beasley took his time about answering the door, but his annoyance vanished when he saw who it was. He shook hands with McKeever and said, "I expected you before this, Sheriff."

"Been pretty busy," McKeever admitted. "If I can

sign for the money, I'll be on my way so you can get
back to bed."

"Hell, the damage has been done," Beasley said. "I'm
awake now. Care for a drink?"

"Had one at the saloon," McKeever said.

Beasley shrugged. "Have a chair. I'll go get the money."

After he left the room, Green said, "Been thinking
about that money, Lincoln. Seems damned funny a
man would send an amount like that through the mails.
Especially when he was so careless as to leave a strip
of the binder that made identification easy."

"He wanted you to identify it," McKeever said. "I'm
getting pretty close to my man, Ben. But I need this
money because there's an insurance investigator from San
Francisco snooping around and he's getting real nervous because it isn't where he can put his hands on it."

"Don't blame him," Green said. "A man could take
eight thousand and live out his life in Mexico. Live
damned good too."

Lon Beasley came back with the money. "You want
to count it, Lincoln?"

"No, just wrap it in some paper and put a string
around it."

"Trusting soul," Beasley said and bound the bills
tightly.

"Can I rent a fast horse here?" McKeever asked of
Green.

"I've got a bay you can have, but she's a little spooky
yet."

"Can she travel? I want to get back to Two Pines by
noon."

Beasley looked up. "Trying to set a record?"

"Trying to get back before I'm missed," McKeever
said.

The good-byes were brief, and McKeever went to
the stable with the marshal, the package under his
arm. Saddled, he stepped aboard and swung out of town,
letting the bay work off her ginger.

BEN GREEN hadn't been stretching the truth any; the
bay had heart and all the staying power a man could
ask for. He stopped now and then, to rest himself more
than the horse, and for over a mile he walked in an at-

tempt to restore some of the feeling into his legs.

Dawn pushed over the rim of the land and he figured up the miles traveled, subtracting them from the total, and found himself nearly an hour ahead of what he had figured.

At ten-thirty he sighted Two Pines, and ten minutes later he was easing through all the back streets to his own room, taking the back window for an entrance.

Jim Singleton was asleep on the bed; he jerked awake, rifle flourished when McKeever's boot rapped the dresser. "Hold it," McKeever said, and saw Jim's face go slack with relief.

There was broken glass on the floor; this crunched beneath McKeever's boots. A bullet pucker dimpled the opposite wall. "You had company, I see."

"Twice," Jim Singleton said. "Man, was I scared!"

"Did you shoot back?"

"Yeah, but I didn't hit anything."

"It's just as well," McKeever said. He took off his hat and jumper.

"Where the devil you been?" Jim Singleton asked. "Kelly and Burgess were here looking for you."

This filled McKeever with alarm. "You didn't let 'em in, did you?"

"Hell no," Jim said. "I figured you wanted to hide, so I just gave 'em a growl and told 'em if they didn't get the hell away I'd shoot through the door."

Lincoln McKeever smiled. "Good boy, Jim. Were they sore?"

"I'll say. Kelly was cussin' you a blue streak."

"He'll get over it," McKeever said. "Jim, I want you to leave now. Walk up and down the main street twice."

"Huh?"

"Now you just do as I tell you. Stop on the corners and loaf a few minutes, and when you're through, go on home."

"Nan'll be scalding mad. What'll I tell her?"

"Tell her you stayed with me last night."

"She won't like that."

McKeever smiled and pushed him toward the door. "She'll get over it, the same as Kelly and Burgess." He took and set the rifle in the corner, and after Jim left, he swept up the broken glass. He waited then, but not long, no more than a half hour. A knock gently rattled his door and McKeever drew his gun. "Who is it?"

"Charlie Boomhauer."

McKeever opened the door and Boomhauer stepped quickly inside. He smiled. "As soon as I saw Jim, I knew you were back. Did you get the money?"

"Yes. Did you get a restraining order?"

Boomhauer nodded. "Mrs. Stanton is fit to be tied. She wants to see you right away."

"She'll have to wait. Did you bring paper, pen and some ink?"

"Got it right here," Boomhauer said, taking the items from his pocket. He saw the package. "That the money? Boy, if the home office ever finds out I'm going along with you on this, I'll be looking for another job—after I get out of jail." He shook his head. "I've been asking myself why I let you talk me into this. You know I'm supposed to impound all money that was stolen until the case is closed."

"You impound that, and you'll never close the case."

Boomhauer held up both hands. "I'm sold, I'm sold."

"You'd better write the notes," McKeever said. "My hand's pretty well known around town."

"Who'll I start out with?" Boomhauer said, uncorking the ink bottle.

McKeever thought a moment, then said, "Make one out to Cris Meyer, the stableman."

"How much and for what?"

"A new harness, say. Make it expensive, at least two hundred dollars, and specify a lot of silver work." He frowned. "Maybe he'd better have another horse too, a blooded animal. Add another five hundred to that and have Meyer send to Kentucky for a real fine animal."

"You sure can spend someone else's money," Charlie Boomhauer said. He wrote the note, then opened the package of stolen money and put in the right amount before sealing it.

There were other notes to write, to the tailor for clothes, nearly four hundred dollars' worth. The watchmaker was given two hundred for the finest watch and gold fob. And Huddleton, who sold some jewelry, was paid five hundred dollars for a diamond ring to be ordered from Kansas City.

T HE LIST was long, for McKeever had an active imagination, and, as Boomhauer said, he was spending someone else's money, a delightful position for any man to be in.

Finally Boomhauer called a halt to it. "You've spent nearly three thousand, Lincoln; let's call it quits. What's this luggage for?"

"In case our friend wants to take a trip," McKeever said and picked up his hat. "You see that those are quietly delivered. I'm going out to Betty Stanton's place."

"All right," Boomhauer said. "Where will you be when the fireworks start?"

"In the saloon where I can keep an eye on things."

"I'll see you there then," Boomhauer said and tucked the letters into his pocket. He smiled and picked up the rest of the money. "You don't mind if I keep this, do you?"

"Not at all. I never use the stuff."

Boomhauer grinned and let himself out. Lincoln McKeever waited for a few minutes, then used the window again. Mounted on the bay, he cut along the back streets to the road out to Wade Stanton's place.

His good sense told him not to go, but then he knew Betty and didn't want her to kick up a needless fuss before Boomhauer and a crew could search for Wade's share of the money. . . .

The four paid hands were lounging near the bunkhouse door when McKeever rode into the yard. One of them, the foreman, came over as he was tying up his horse.

"Wade was a good man. You didn't have to kill him."

McKeever looked at him steadily. "What should I have done?"

The front door opened and Betty came out. "Eddie, go mind your own damned business! Come in, Lincoln. It's been hell, alone like this."

"I thought you liked it alone," McKeever said, entering the house.

She poured a drink for him, and one for herself. "I wanted you to shoot him, Lincoln. And I'm glad you did."

"You've got a surprise coming," McKeever said. "I didn't shoot him because of you, Betty."

She regarded him, surprised. "Well, I guess it isn't too important, is it? Do you know what that Boomhauer did to me? He had a restraining order slapped on the place. I can't even draw a damned dime of Wade's money out of the bank."

"Why don't you hire a lawyer?"

"With what? If I didn't have credit at the stores, I couldn't eat. Lincoln, you don't know how tight-fisted Wade was with a dollar."

"Oh, I know." He downed his drink and put the glass aside. "Why don't you get out for a while, Betty? Oh, yeah, no money. Well, would you take a loan from me?"

From her smile, her relief, he knew that this was what she wanted to see him about, to put the bite on him, and every instinct told him to tell her to go to the devil.

"Lincoln, would you?" She came to him and touched his arms, then pressed against him. "Darling, I knew I could count on you."

He eased away from her, gently. "How much?"

"Four hundred?" Her voice was timid. "I know it's a lot, but after this is cleared up, you'll get it back, and more."

"That'll be something to look forward to," he said. "All right, Betty. You come into town tonight and I'll have it for you."

"I'll pack," she said. "I think I'll go to Cheyenne. Would you come to me in a week or so?"

"Why not?" He smiled. "We can figure something out from there, huh?"

"It won't be difficult, Lincoln. I know it won't."

She walked with him to the door. He stopped and said, "I wouldn't worry about the restraining order if I were you. Once Boomhauer leaves Two Pines, the judge will lift it for you."

"I think I'll sell the place. How much will it bring?"

He made a hasty guess. "Eighteen thousand, I suppose, for a quick sale. Wade must have more than a little put away besides."

She laughed then, for the thought of so much money pleased her. "We can live pretty high on that, Lincoln."

"High enough anyway," he said and stepped off the porch to his horse. "If you want to pay the men off, I'll tell your father at the bank to take it out of my account. We can add that to the four hundred."

She touched his cheek with her hand. "Dear Lincoln. I owe you so much. And I always pay. You know that, Lincoln, don't you?"

17.

THE last person Lincoln McKeever wanted to see was Nan Singleton, yet from the way she waited on the Hanover House porch, McKeever knew that she was waiting for him. He dismounted and tied his horse. Nan said, "Come in, Lincoln. I want to talk to you."

He followed her inside and into her room off the lobby. She closed the door then moved around, her manner restless. "I had a lot of things to say, Lincoln, but now I don't know where to start."

"Start anywhere," he invited. "Maybe we can rearrange the pieces afterward."

"All right, suppose we do it that way then. I thought there was kindness in you, Lincoln. And understanding."

"I take it we're going to talk about Dal Leggitt?"

"That's right. Dal Leggitt."

"Then what's there to talk about? If you love the man, then hate me for making him small and let it go at that."

She looked steadily at him, no longer angry. "Lincoln, I don't love him and you know it. If I had loved him, I don't think you would have treated him like that."

"He got what he asked for," McKeever said. "If you want me to say I'm sorry, you're wasting your time, Nan."

"I don't expect you to be sorry," she said. "Lincoln, if everyone got what they had coming, we'd all be so bruised and battered we couldn't walk." She made a brief fan of her hands. "Maybe we'd better forget it, after all. What will it settle?"

"A long-standing quarrel between us," he said. "Nan, you said that if everyone got their lumps we'd all be pretty bruised and battered. All right, I agree, but at the same time, if everyone tried to even up all the hurt they'd known, they'd be hitting everyone. Once I threw you over for another woman, but if you remember I came here and told you to your face, not meaning to hurt you at all. And since then you've been getting back at me, one way or another. Leggitt wasn't much of a man, just a poodle dog for you. Did you enjoy seeing him fight over you, Nan?"

"You have no right to say that to me!"

"And what right do you think you have, waiting on the porch like some irate wife? Damn it, Nan, people would think we'd been married ten years the way you take me to task all the time."

Color came to her cheeks and she looked away from him. "Does—does it really look like that, Lincoln?"

"You know it does, and you like it." He put his hat aside and stepped up to her. "Now I'll tell you one thing, Nan, it's going to stop. If you want to fight with me, then marry me."

"You don't love me," she said.

"No? Nan, how can you be so sure of everything? When I shot Wade you were so sure it was over Betty. You still think so, don't you?"

"I don't know," she admitted. "I really don't, Lincoln. But I wish I could hate you. It'd make life a lot easier."

"Nan, I'm going to give you some time. Not much, but a little anyway. Then I'm going to ask you once more. If you marry me, I'll stay. If not, I'll move on and get out of your life." He picked up his hat and put it on. "There are a lot of things in this world that'll dazzle a man and Betty was one of them. I'm the kind of a guy who won't guarantee a thing, Nan. If you marry me, I won't promise not to look at another woman or to give up beer and cards. Don't marry me to make me over; I wouldn't do that to you."

He went out then and paused on the porch. Boomhauer exited from the saloon and teetered on the walk's edge, a cigar fragrantly ignited. McKeever crossed over. "Anything stirring?"

"Give it time," Boomhauer said softly. "You see Stanton's wife?"

"Yes," McKeever said and told him what had happened.

"You'd better make the arrangements at the bank, then."

"All right."

Sam Richardson was a little on the unfriendly side, since Lincoln McKeever had made a widow out of his daughter, and his frown was thunderous when McKeever told him why he wanted to draw out the money. Richardson completed the transaction and McKeever returned to the saloon to wait. Charlie Boomhauer was already there and he shuffled the deck of cards for the first of endless games of double solitaire.

ETHEL DALEY began her shopping at eleven, leaving her order with the grocer, who would send the delivery boy around with it later in the day. She had money and everyone knew it, but she never spent much of it, keeping the merchants' favor only by the veiled promise that someday she might spend some of it.

Finley Fineen watched her move along the street; his doorway was a vantage point from which he could observe the town. He saw nothing to arouse his interest until Ethel Daley hurried back toward the drugstore, her step firm and rapid, an unusual pace for a woman who liked to live life leisurely. Fineen watched her ascend the stairs, and a moment later the argument started, loud enough and violent enough to raise heads along the street.

Expecting this to be one of those quick-tempered storms, Fineen waited a few minutes for the quiet he knew would come, but there was none. Ethel Daley was wound up and now Fineen detected the crashing of dishes, the ring of a hurled pot. Amid this sound came Daley's pained yelp, proof of his wife's accuracy.

Leaving his doorway, Fineen moved on down the street, idly curious as to what had set this off. He stopped when the saddlemaker came out of his shop, plainly eager for talk. The saddlemaker nodded toward the drugstore and said, "Funny, you'd think Daley was smarter than that."

"What are you talking about?" Fineen asked.

"Swiping his old lady's money."

"Where'd you hear that?"

"Hear it? Hell, I didn't hear it, Fineen. I added two and two and got four." He turned inside the shop. "Come here. Want to show you something." He walked over to his bench and slapped a fine saddle tree. "I'm making this up for Bill Daley. Won't be anything like it in the county. Silver mountings and all." He winked. "Making him a harness too. Nigh onto six hundred dollars' worth of stuff." He poked Fineen in the chest. "After all these years, Bill found where she's hid the money. That's what she's mad about. I told Ab Larkin in the store, and he must have said something to Daley's wife."

A DULL alarm tolled in the back of Finley Fineen's mind, yet he moved forward with great caution. "Collins, you've been taken in. Daley won't ever pay for this stuff."

"Ha! He's already paid for it." The saddlemaker went to his cubbyhole desk. "Here. Paid cash." He flipped the bills under Fineens' nose.

A canker formed in Fineen's stomach and he found breathing difficult. He had to get out before Collins saw his expression. Fineen turned to the door and walked rapidly down the street. Collins came out and stared after him, then shook his head and went back inside his shop.

Harness! Saddle! The son of a bitch probably bought horses too; this was Fineen's thought as he walked toward the livery stable. Sonnerman was pitching hay toward the back of the barn as Fineen walked through.

"I want to talk to you," Fineen said.

"Well, I ain't never too busy to do that," the old man said. "What's on your mind?"

"Did Bill Daley tell you to buy him a team?"

"You heard, huh?" Sonnerman chuckled. "I guess he found where she hid the money. He's spendin' it like a drunk Indian."

Fineen's expression was stricken; he knew where Daley got that money and panic crowded him. He forced himself to speak calmly. "Thanks," he said and walked out.

He controlled his urge to kill and compound an already fatal mistake on Daley's part. God, didn't the man understand that this was all it would take to hang them all? Of course he understood that the town would think Daley had found where Ethel had salted the money, and that was all right, because Fineen wasn't worried about the damned town. But Lincoln Mc-

Keever and that insurance detective wouldn't be fooled, not for a minute, and once the house started to collapse, it would be too late to run from under it.

I'll have to get to Daley; this was Fineen's thought as he went back up the street, cutting across to the drugstore. He took the side steps two at a time and pushed open the door without knocking.

Daley and his wife were battling in the parlor; she was shouting and flourishing a vase while Daley cringed away, his arms upraised to ward off the blow about to descend at any time.

Ethel Daley did not hear Fineen approach; he snatched the vase away from her before she knew anyone else was in the room.

"Shut your loud mouth and get out of here," Fineen said fiercely.

She turned shocked, round eyes on him, then backed up a step. "What—what do you mean, breaking into my house?"

"Go on, get out of here! Get out or I'll run you in for disturbing the peace.

"Daley, are you going to let him talk to me like that?"

"I hope he does lock you up," Daley said. "You've gone completely crazy!" He had a cut on his forehead and a smear of blood on his cheek; he dabbled at these with a handkerchief.

Fineen took her by the arm and propelled her toward the door. "I said to go and cool off. Don't come back for an hour, do you hear?"

"The idea, coming in here like this—all right, I'll go." She gave Bill Daley a last look. "But I'm not through with you, you sneak!"

"Yes, you're through," Fineen snapped and slammed the outside door, locking it so she could not come in unexpectedly.

Daley was kicking at some of the mess. "Sure glad you got here, Finley. Jesus, I don't know what got into the woman, I honestly don't. I was sitting here when she came busting in, raving mad."

"We'd better have a talk," Fineen said. "A real honest one, Bill."

"Honest?" Bill Daley stared at Fineen. "Man, we've always been honest with each other." He shook his head.. "I'm going to have that woman put away, damned if I ain't. Crazy, that's what she is. Money crazy."

"What the hell else is there for her, married to a dried-up little prune like you."

"Huh? Finley, you had no call to say that. I thought we were friends." ·

"My friends are on the level with me," Fineen said. "You little runt, did you think you could get away with it? How dumb do you think I am, anyway?"

"Get away with what? Finley, for God's sake won't someone tell me what I done wrong instead of just cussing me out?"

"Don't stand there and play innocent with me," Fineen said. "It's all over town by now, the way you threw money around; clothes, new harness, horses; God, did you try to spend it all in one day?"

"Suits, harness? Finley, you're not making sense!"

"I'm not?" He hit Daley then, smashing him back into a chair. "Getting ready to run out on me, Bill? Leave me all alone to face McKeever, is that it?"

Unmindful of his bleeding nose, Daley said, "I swear to all that's holy, Finley, I don't know what you're talking about!"

"Aw, shut your lying mouth, you worthless little punk! I never wanted you in on this in the first place, you know that. You've got paper guts, that's what you got. McKeever scares you too easy." ·

Bill Daley acted like a man near tears, frustrated tears. "Finley, I'm telling you the truth. I never spent a nickle of that money. Not one nickle."

"You're a liar! You scattered it all over town!"

"Would I be that dumb? Would I? Ah, Finley, listen to me, will you?"

"You're pretty dumb and you're scared," Fineen said. "Sorry, Bill, but I can't afford to listen to you now. McKeever's breathing too close down my neck now. I can't take a chance with you."

"Wha—what're you going to do? Finley, think about this now. Don't do anything hasty now."

"I won't," Fineen said. "You think I'll shoot you here?" He shook his head. "No, I'm too smart for that. It gets dark every night, Bill, and when it gets dark enough, I might take a shot at you. So you watch yourself, huh?

And don't go near McKeever or that San Francisco investigator. One word to him and you're a dead man, because wherever you are, I won't be out of shooting range. Just remember that."

BILL DALEY'S fear was genuine. "Finley, in the name of God, trust me! I'm not a bad man. You've known me for years; I've never done anything wrong."

"I guess you believe that," Fineen said softly. "Maybe we all believe that, you, me, and Wade. You might call that our biggest mistake, trying to go on, respectable, when we killed and stole."

"You're not making sense," Daley said.

"Yes I am. If you're going to be bad, Bill, then be bad all the way. I mean, know you're bad. The trouble with us is that we don't believe we're no good, when really we're as rotten as ever were born."

"I've tried to live right, Finley! You know I have. Hell, before this, I never did anything wrong. Please, Finley, believe me now."

"Too late," Fineen said. "Way too late, Bill."

"All right," Daley said, angry at last. "All right, you loud-mouth, if that's the way you want it. You'd better shoot me now because as soon as you leave I'm going to McKeever and spill my guts. You think I want to worry and watch the rest of my life? By God I'd like one decent night's sleep before I die." He smiled then, his manner cocky. "Go ahead and shoot me, big brains. That shot will bring the town on the run and you'll hang because there isn't a lie in the world big enough to cover for you now." He got up from the floor and brushed his clothes briefly. "I'm going to be generous with you, Finley. Real generous. I'm going to give you some time, say a half hour, to clear out of Two Pines alive."

Finley Fineen pulled his gun and cocked it, then he stood there, thinking this over. He understood the truth of Daley's statement: pull the trigger and he'd be as good as dead. Go, and he had a half hour, which was better than nothing. Still, there was another way, and he tried it.

"I lost my temper, Bill. Hell, if we don't break and run, McKeever can't pin a thing on either of us." He tried a smile, the old friendly smile. "How about it, Bill? Friends?"

"No," Daley said. "Stop fooling yourself. Finley. Mc-Keever will never give up until he's got us. Take the half hour and be thankful for it."

Finley Fineen slowly uncocked his gun and put it away. "Bill, what the hell happened to us? We were going to hold the money for five years. Sit back, safe, while McKeever ground his nose into the ground trying to figure it out." He shook his head. "We did everything right, the shell, the damned gun, everything right."

"No," Daley said. "We did everything wrong, Finley. We robbed a man, and killed him. No matter what else was right, that was wrong enough to wipe out everything else."

"None of us really needed the money," Fineen said, as though he were trying to justify himself. "A man's just got to do something once in a while that ain't been done before. You know that's a fact, Bill. Why can't we face McKeever out? It'll work, I tell you!"

"It won't work," Daley said. "Maybe some other kind of a man could make it work, but not us, Finley." He nodded toward the door. "You'd better get going."

"God, I've got a wife, a business!"

"Finley, you don't have a damn thing except a sackful of money. I hope you enjoy it, wherever you stop long enough to spend it. But you won't stop much. You won't dare. In a half a year's time your neck will have a permanent crink in it from looking over your shoulder." He stood there a moment, then crossed to the door and unlocked it. "I'll start counting when you get to the bottom of the stairs."

"Jesus—" Then Finley Finnen closed his mouth.

"It's a poor way for a man to end, isn't it, Finley?"

Fineen stopped on the stairs and looked briefly. "Yes," he said. "Bill, I've got nothing against you. It was meant to work out this way, I guess."

"It would have worked as you planned," Daley said, "if we'd been more like Wade."

Fineen frowned. "I've thought that, but then, he's dead, isn't he?" He turned then and hurried down to the street. At the bottom of the steps he met Ethel Daley, and he spoke to her briefly. She looked up at her

husband, then came up the stairs, running, crying.
"Come on inside," he said softly. "I've got something
to tell you, Ethel."

18.

LINCOLN McKEEVER was peeling the wrapper from a
cigar when Finley Fineen came down the stair-
way; Boomhauer's nudge raised his attention. They
watched Fineen speak briefly to Ethel Daley, then when
Fineen hurried to his office, Boomhauer said, "What do
you think, Lincoln? Has he nibbled at the bait?"

"A little early to tell," McKeever said. "If we move a
bit too fast now we'll lose it all."

"Yes, and if we poke around, we may still lose."

"That's a chance we have to take," McKeever said.
"Want to finish the game?"

"Not for a while," Boomhauer said. He saw Jim
Singleton come out on the porch across the street and
signaled him. When Jim came across the street, Boom-
hauer said, "Will you sort of keep an eye on Finley
Fineen? Stay out of sight as much as you can though.
I just want to know what he's up to."

"All right," Jim said and walked on down the street.

McKeever's cigar was about done for when Ethel
Daley came slowly down the stairs. She looked up and
down the street before she saw McKeever, and when she
raised her hand, he stepped off the saloon porch and
walked toward her, Charlie Boomhauer tagging along a
pace behind.

There is little attractiveness left in a woman when she
has been crying, but Ethel Daley no longer cared how
she looked. She spoke to Lincoln McKeever. "Bill's upstairs. He killed Doc Harris."

McKeever's glance touched Boomhauer briefly. "I'll
go," Boomhauer said.

Not wanting to draw a crowd, McKeever walked
Ethel Daley to the hotel. He steered her into Nan's
room without a word, then closed the door. Nan came

in from the kitchen and McKeever said, "If you have some coffee on, I think Mrs. Daley would like some."

"Something wrong, Lincoln?"

"Not now," he said. "Just bring some coffee."

"He told me what he did," Ethel said. "I can't believe it. I just can't."

"You'll have to believe it," McKeever said gently. "Bill went off the deep end, that's all. A man sometimes does that."

Nan came back with a tray; there was no more talk until Mrs. Daley had a cup in her hands. "There were three of them, Fineen, Bill, and Wade Stanton. Fineen killed Dalridge. Bill killed poor Doc because he got scared." Her eyes were dull and slow moving. "I just can't believe my Bill would do a thing like that. He's always been such a gentle man, Sheriff."

"I'm not the sheriff," McKeever said.

"It was you he was afraid of," she said. "He told me that."

Nan said, "Lincoln, did Bill Daley confess—"

He waved her silent. "Mrs. Daley, you know what's going to happen don't you?"

"I guess you'll hang him," she said. "He was never a mean man." She looked steadily at McKeever. "I loved him, did you know that? But I never did right by him. I wanted to, but somehow I was always so afraid."

"Of what?"

She shrugged. "Losing him, I guess. I was never a pretty woman, you see. Sweet, everybody said, but awful dowdy. Catching a man can be hard when you're something everybody looks through instead of looking at. Poor Bill, he just couldn't make up his mind, even after we went together for three years. I guess I pushed him into marrying me. A man resents a things like that, you know. A woman's got to give a man freedom if she wants to hold him. I wanted to be that way, but I just couldn't. You fight for something and you want to hold tight to it. Poor Bill, I guess I just choked all the manhood out of him." She paused to drink some of her coffee; McKeever and Nan exchanged glances. "I never should have got on him like I did, after him all the time, taking all his money, but I had to. Some don't know what it is to be afraid, and I was scared I'd lose him to another woman. Mr. McKeever, you've got to understand that to some, hate is as good as love; at least it's something." She shook her head slowly. "I guess I was going to lose him anyway, him spending all that stolen money the way he did. That's what brought it on. He was fixing to leave me and I couldn't help getting mad. You can understand that, can't you, Mr. McKeever?"

"Bill wasn't going to leave you," McKeever said. "You see, I spent that money for him. Me and Mr. Boomhauer."

She stared at him. "You did? Now you've got me all mixed up. You knew my Bill had robbed Mr. Dalridge?"

"I knew it but I couldn't prove it," McKeever said. He did not bother to explain to her; he wasn't sure she was in any condition to understand if he did explain. "Nan, will you take care of her? See if you can get her to lie down and rest."

"All right, Lincoln."

He stepped outside just as Charlie Boomhauer came into the lobby. "I got him in jail," Boomhauer said. "I also notified Kelly and Burgess; they're coming right in." Boomhauer took off his hat and mopped away the sweat trapped there. "He made a full confession. I think we can arrest Fineen now and make it stick."

"Did you recover the money?"

BOOMHAUER took it out of an inner pocket and made a brief fan of it before putting it back. "Eighteen thousand."

McKeever whistled softly. "Didn't Kelly and Burgess claim around forty apiece?"

"They were lying," Boomhauer said, then smiled. "But that's not unusual when trying to collect from an insurance company. "I know where Stanton hid his money too."

"The hell? Did Daley know?"

"Yes," Boomhauer said. "They even worked out the individual hiding places, sort of a test to determine whether it was foolproof or not. Stanton buried his share under the manure pile. I'll have a crew go out there and dig it up as soon as Mrs. Stanton pays off the hands and leaves." He clapped both hands over his breast pockets. "Got a cigar? I'm out."

McKeever offered him one, and a match. "Did Daley say where Fineen was?"

"No," Boomhauser said. "But the man can't be far." He squinted through a haze of smoke. "We've got to get that damned badge off of him. I'll speak to Kelly and Burgess about it as soon as they get to town."

"You want to go over to Fineen's house with me, Charlie?"

"Yes, I think I will." He turned to the street with McKeever. As they walked along, Boomhauer said, "Funny thing about Daley. He talked about Stanton, but not about Fineen."

"Didn't he tell you Finley hid his share of the money?"

"No," Boomhauser said. "And I didn't press him too hard. We'll find that out when we pick up Fineen." He smiled. "I don't think he'll get far with Jim watching him."

Madge Fineen was in the back yard, hanging up the week's washing. When no one answered the front door, Lincoln McKeever let himself in. Then they went to the back porch; Mrs. Fineen seemed surprised to see them coming out the back door.

"Well, do you always walk through a body's house?"

"No," McKeever said. "Where's Finley?"

"How would I know. I hardly seem him anymore, with his sheriff's duties and all."

"Would you come in the house a minute?" McKeever asked.

Madge Fineen frowned. "I've my washing to do."

"You'd better come in," Charlie Boomhauer said, and something in his voice made her put the bag of clothespins down.

She wiped her hands on her apron and went ahead of them into the house. "If you're expecting me to fix coffee, you're mistaken. This is my busiest day."

"No thanks," McKeever said softly. "Will you sit down, please?"

"I like standing," she said. "Get on with it. I said I was busy."

McKeever was suddenly without words to tell this woman what he had to tell her. Charlie Boomhauer said, "Mrs. Fineen, we're going to have to arrest your husband."

She seemed indignant. "For what? You don't have the authority."

"I'm afraid we have," Boomhauer said. "Won't you

please sit down now?" When she settled in a kitchen chair, Boomhauer told her of the charges, mentioning Bill Daley's arrest and confession. Listening to this man talk, Lincoln McKeever learned the power of a persuasive voice, a commanding manner. Boomhauer always spoke softly, yet with finality, with rock-steady assurance; people didn't often argue with him.

MADGE FINEEN listened, her lip caught between her teeth. There were tears to be shed, but she held them back. Finally she said, "I knew he was a bothered man of late. Not able to sleep good, and he didn't eat his meals like he should." She turned her head to stare out the window. "My Finley with blood on his hands?" She pressed her fingers against her mouth. "My Finley. I bore him three children, you know. One died at birth, and two before they could walk. Lung fever. But he never blamed me, not my Finley. I love the man."

"We want you to stay home," McKeever said. "Finley's around town somewhere and we have to go after him. If you want, I'll send someone to stay with you."

She shook her head. "I just want to be alone."

"Are you sure you'll be all right?" Boomhauer asked.

She turned her head slowly and stared at him. "All right? Do you think anything will ever be all right again? God, why did he do it? We were happy, Finley and me. Oh, there were things we both wanted and could never have, but there's always something someone wants that they can never have."

"I guess Finley wanted some things you didn't know about," McKeever said. His nod brought Boomhauer along and they went out the front door.

"That's always a dirty job," Boomhauer said. "Telling some innocent person about a thing like that."

"Don't you get toughened up to it?"

"No," Boomhauer said. "Somehow you never do. At least, I never did."

By the time they reached the main street, the whole town knew about Bill Daley and Finley Fineen. They even understood why Wade Stanton drew against McKeever's drop, and in their way, they forgave McKeever without taking back all the things they had thought about McKeever and Betty Stanton.

Burgess and Kelly stormed into town in their buggy

and stopped by McKeever and Boomhauer. "My God, what a shocking development," Kelly said as he dismounted. Burgess tied the horse, then wiped sweat from his face.

"To think we appointed Fineen sheriff," Burgess said. "Well, that's a mistake that will soon be corrected."

"Yes," Boomhauer said smoothly. "And while you're at it, gentlemen, I would also go over your claims again to make sure the amount filed is absolutely correct." He waited while both men glanced at each other. "A good deal of the money has been recovered and we expect to get the rest of it shortly. I'm sure you understand."

"Ah—yes," Olin Kelly said. "We did check, Mr. Boomhauer, and I'm happy to say that the amount is considerably less."

"Fine," Boomhauer said, smiling. "A little less profit in it for you, perhaps, but it makes for better relations between the home office and the insured."

Jim Singleton came rushing down the street and rudely pushed his way through a thin rank of onlookers. "Lincoln, Fineen's skipped out!"

"What? You're sure?"

"Hell, he saddled a horse and rode out five or ten minutes ago. Heading north."

"Go saddle my bay, and get a horse for Boomhauer."

"My interest is mainly money right now," Boomhauer said, "not that I wouldn't enjoy a manhunt. I'll leave Fineen to you, McKeever. Just make sure you get him."

"I'll damn sure get him," McKeever said. "Go on, Jim. Get that horse saddled."

McKeever excused himself and walked across to the Hanover House. Nan was in the kitchen and she seemed surprised to see him. "Trouble at Fineen's?"

"If I hadn't been so damned busy congratulating myself on how smart I am," McKeever said, "I'd have guessed that Bill Daley bought his life from Fineen for a head start." He took a flour sack and began to fill it with staples.

"You're going after him?"

"What else? He's got eighteen thousand dollars that doesn't belong to him and an appointment with a rope."

"Better take a skillet along." Then she took the sack

away from him. "Here, let me do that. Go have a cigar and calm down. Fineen isn't that much ahead."

"If he gets into those mountains to the north, an hour is all he'll need." He walked up and down the kitchen a few times, then paused to look out the back door. "I should have gone after Fineen as soon as Daley confessed. And I keep asking myself why I didn't. Hell, I'm not afraid of the man!"

"Here's your sack," Nan said.

He took it from her. "Is that all you have to say?"

"Well, what do you want me to say?"

"You're not that dumb," he said and took her into his arms. She raised her lips for his kiss and he held her that way for a long moment. When he released her, he asked, "Satisfied?"

She was on the edge of a smile. "Should I be?"

"You made me come to you," he said. "Isn't that what you wanted?"

"Yes," she said. "Now I'll never pick at you again."

Jim came running through the hotel. He smiled when Nan quickly disengaged herself from McKeever's arms. "The horses are saddled and waiting, Lincoln."

"You can take one back," McKeever said, shouldering the sack. "Boomhauer's not going."

"But I am," Jim said flatly.

"You are not!" Nan said. Then she looked at McKeever, and back to her brother, and a smile raised the ends of her lips. "Pa's .45 is in the drawer behind the counter. But be careful."

With a whoop Jim Singleton ran to get it. McKeever said, "Nan, he'll thank you for that."

"No he won't," she said. "But I guess you were right, Lincoln. The time's come."

19.

THE easy way would have been to telegraph ahead and have the law waiting for Finley Fineen, but Lincoln McKeever wasn't about to take the easy way.

Not this time. He would run Fineen down and bring him back kicking and yelling for the town to look at.

With Jim Singleton at his side, McKeever pushed north, following the game trails and clinging always to the high ground that afforded him the best view. This was a land of lodge pine and underbrush, and rock outcroppings, and his direction often seemed confused, yet McKeever knew where he was going. A few years of working these woods as a logger had sharpened his sense of direction, and at the end of the day, he was miles ahead of where he would have been if he had followed the road.

From the eagle's nest ridge, McKeever stopped to look out across a broad, grassed valley. "He's down there somewhere," McKeever said, pointing. Darkness was not far away, and in the valley a twilight was already falling. The distant gleam of lights marked a solitary place, while a few miles beyond, the road arched upward to cross a timbered ridge.

"If he's down there," Jim Singleton said, "then what're we doing up here?"

McKeever laughed. "Don't you like it up here, Jim?" He nodded toward the lights. "I'll lay you odds that Finley's sitting down to supper there, or at best, he's just finished eating and is getting ready to leave." McKeever's glance went on to the far ridge. "About midnight, Finley'll top that. If he keeps on going, he'll be in the clear."

"It's fifty-five miles to the nearest town," Jim said. "And he wouldn't head there, Lincoln."

"Wouldn't he?" McKeever shook his head. "He has to, Jim. There's a railroad there. Finley's a town man, Jim. He'll stick to the roads and bluff or fight his way through if he has to. And he'll head for a railroad to catch a train East." He jigged his horse into motion. "Come on. I'd like to be waiting in the depot when Finley goes to buy his ticket."

"Hell, we'll have to ride all night to get ahead of him."

"So, we'll ride all night," McKeever said.

During the long hours, the tiring hours, he told himself that he was being a fool about this; how much easier it would have been to wire ahead for a reception committee. But there were certain things that a man had to do alone, and McKeever felt that this was one of them. With a stranger, he might have felt differently, but not Finley Fineen, a man he had known for years. When you've called a man friend, like he had, the personal contact always remained, even up to the scaffold.

Jim Singleton's determination to be a good deputy sheriff overcame his weariness. He offered no complaint at the long hours McKeever put in the saddle, the aching miles traveled, or the briefness of the stops McKeever made.

At a quarter after three, Lincoln McKeever held the face of his watch close to his eyes to read the hands. "We've passed him," he said, the first words he had spoken in hours.

"You sound damn sure," Jim said softly.

"Finley's a buggy man," McKeever said. "Been four or five years since he's ridden astraddle. We've passed him."

"Then we can take it easier, huh?"

McKeever laughed. "When you're chasing a man, Jim, you never take it easy. Especially when you want to come back alive."

He mounted again and Jim Singleton wearily pulled himself into the saddle. They did not stop again until dawn, and only then to watch the sun's first rays make silver cords of a pair of railroad rails trailing off to the faintest horizons.

The town of Buffalo lay ahead and they began to cut off the last of the high ground, angling down to the basin floor. An hour later they met the road and went on into town. Buffalo was larger than Two Pines, a cattle town with a cattleman's indifference to cleanliness and careful planning. McKeever counted eight saloons in three blocks and this alone marked it as cattle bought and paid for.

The depot lay on the south end, but instead of going directly there, McKeever rode down a quiet side street and dismounted to tie his horse.

Jim said, "Wouldn't the stable be better?"

"Finley might go there. I wouldn't want him to recognize our horses."

"If he's so eager to get out of town, he'll go straight to the depot."

"Still I don't want to take the chance," McKeever said. "Feel up to a cup of coffee, Jim?"

"Man, I could do with the pot."

They tried two restaurants and found them closed, but the saloon was open and the bartender was brewing himself some coffee. McKeever placed his hat on the bar and said, "A bottle, one glass, and two cups of that coffee."

While the bartender served up, his glance took in their dusty clothes, and the haggard expression both wore around the eyes. "Been movin' some, ain't you?"

"Considerable," McKeever admitted. He tasted the coffee, then smiled. "Man, you are a genius with the brown bean." He nudged Jim Singleton. "Good, huh?"

"Sure is."

"When do the trains run around here?" McKeever asked.

"Depends on where you're going. There's an eastbound due in around one this afternoon."

McKeever poured a glass of whisky for himself, then shoved the bottle away from him. His glance found the wall clock briefly: twenty minutes after six.

"There's a town ordinance about carrying firearms in the city limits," the bartender said, glancing at their guns. "Just thought I'd tell you that to spare you any trouble."

"I appreciate it," McKeever said.

The bartender waited, then said, "You can check 'em here, if you want."

"Ah—maybe later," McKeever said. He finished his coffee, then nudged Jim again. "Let's walk around."

"Fellas, the marshal's pretty strict about the no gun law."

"Thank you. We'll remember that," McKeever said and pushed aside the swinging doors.

They paused on the boardwalk a moment to scan the street. Jim said, "Where do you plan to take him, Lincoln?"

"Where no one will get hurt in case he starts shooting," McKeever said.

"Catch him on the outskirts of town," Jim suggested. "That way we wouldn't have to worry about that marshal and his no gun law."

"Yeah," McKeever said, brushing his beard stubble. "The trouble with that is that a man is just naturally wide awake when he rides into a strange town. It appears to me that we wouldn't surprise Finley much by jumping him too quick." He shook his head. "No, I'd like to give Finley a chance to get a drink and drop his guard a little. Let's go on down to the depot. We'll wait there."

"How long do you figure?" Jim asked.

"Three hours, maybe four." McKeever looked at him carefully. "Getting jumpy?"

"Some. I never been in this kind of a spot before."

"Well, don't feel bad. A man always gets jumpy at a time like this."

"Yeah? You don't act that way."

"How I act," McKeever said, "and how I feel are two different things." He put his hand briefly on Jim Singleton's shoulder. "I hope you never have to shoot a man, Jim. But if you do, I hope the decision comes quick, in a matter of seconds, when it's draw or die. I don't want you to ever have to know beforehand that killing will be necessary, like I did when I faced Wade Stanton." He let his eyes run up and down the street again. "That way is always bad, Jim. Bad because you have to think about it, before, as well as afterward."

"Stanton was a guilty man," Jim said. "It makes a difference when he's guilty."

"Does it?"

"Sure it does."

"Someday you may find out different," McKeever said. "Come on, let's go down to the depot."

A STATION AGENT was wrestling baggage when McKeever and Singleton walked in and sat down on one of the benches near the front where they could see the street approach. The agent came in, peered at them, then said, "Train ain't due for hours yet."

"We'll wait," McKeever said.

An hour earlier, Jim Singleton had thought of nothing but sleep, now he found it out of the question; he could never remember feeling so alert, so fine-tuned.

"I've been thinking," he said. "You know, about Finley and the others, and what made them rob Dalridge." He shifted, trying to find a nonexistent soft spot on the hard bench. "Lincoln, to tell you the truth, I've felt like doing something crazy. It seems like there's nothing for a fella to do in Two Pines, except hang around and wait to grow up." He grew thoughtful for a moment. "Lincoln, sometimes it's a terrible thing to grow up in a town where everybody knows you. After a time they don't pay any attention to you, or even look at you. Hell, I've had the notion to take a gun and shoot out a half a dozen store windows just so people would look at me."

"But you never did," McKeever said.

"Yeah, I never did. But I thought about it." He looked at McKeever quickly. "Do you suppose that's how it started? I mean, one of them said, 'What this town needs is a damned good holdup'."

"Probably," McKeever said. "That would be Stanton talking, Jim. He was that way, quick to find fault, the first to object; the man liked trouble, deep down inside, only it takes more than a liking for trouble to be a real badman, Jim. Wade Stanton didn't have that."

"You think Fineen has?"

"Yes," McKeever said quickly. "I think he has, but he don't know it yet. And I want to get him before he finds out."

"I don't follow you."

"Well, let's take Wade first. He came after me, face to face, but he didn't want it that way. Pride pushed him, and that liking for trouble. I think Wade expected me to back down. Bill Daley? Yes, he killed Doc Harris, but out of fright and desperation. He fought because he was cornered, nothing else. Whether he actually was or not is not important. What is important is that he *thought* he was cornered."

"And Finley?"

"He killed Dalridge because he enjoyed it. Jim, a man would have to enjoy deliberately clubbing a man to death to do so thorough a job. We all have a sleeping rage in us, Jim. You felt it when you had the urge to shoot out some windows. Finley Fineen had it when he clubbed Dalridge to death with his gun barrel. So when you find a man who lets that rage loose on the world you have a killer, without conscience or hesitation. A man like Finley."

JIM SINGLETON tapped McKeever on the shoulder, drawing his attention to the street fronting the depot. McKeever saw the badge first, the man second. Then the marshal stepped into the depot and took a quick left and right look. He came over and said, "Howdy, gents. Passing through?"

"Yes," McKeever said.

The marshal pursed his full lips and brushed his mustache with his forefinger. "Sorry to trouble you, but we have an ordnance about sidearms. Like to have you check them with the station agent until you leave."

"We won't leave the depot," McKeever said. "Can't you alter the rules a little this time?"

"Afraid not," the marshall said. "Rules aren't meant to be altered in this town." He held out his hand. "I'll check 'em for you and save you the trouble."

Watching this man, Lincoln McKeever saw that he wasn't bucking some soft-headed town loafer wearing a badge. The marshal was a relaxed, easy-mannered man, who always kept his right hand at his side, not too far from a well-worn Smith & Wesson .44.

"My name is Lincoln McKeever, the sheriff from Two Pines. This is my deputy, Jim Singleton."

"Oh? Then I guess you got some kind of identification, a badge maybe?"

"No, I don't," McKeever said. "I expect you'll just have to take my word for it."

"I can't do that," the marshal said. "Let's have the guns or we'll go over to the jail."

Lincoln McKeever cursed this man beneath his breath, yet he held no genuine anger against him; he would have done exactly the same thing in Two Pines. "All right," he said. "Give him your gun, Jim."

Unbuckling his belt, Jim Singleton rolled it around the holster and handed it to the marshal; McKeever was tugging at his own buckle, then it came loose and started to slip to the floor. He made a frantic grab for it, but missed and let it fall. The marshall grunted in surprise as he looked into the bore of McKeever's pistol.

"You learn a new trick every day," the marshal said bitterly.

"Put your gun back on," McKeever said, and when Jim Singleton refastened the belt, he said, "Now take the marshal over to the bench and see that he sets down.

Cover him but don't let your gun show." He picked his own gunbelt up off the floor and put it on, holstering his pistol.

McKeever and Jim Singleton sandwiched the town marshal between them and Jim kept the muzzle of his .45 pressed into the marshal's side.

"Now I'm sure sorry we have to do it this way," Mc-Keever said softly, "but I wasn't lying about being the sheriff. There's a man coming here, or at least I guess he'll head here, and I mean to arrest him. Now you're going to sit right there with Jim's gun on you while I take this guy. Afterward, if you want to ease your mind, you can telegraph Two Pines and confirm my story. But right now you're going to behave yourself, understand?"

"I understand," the marshal said. "But boy, you'd better be telling me this straight. If you ain't, I'll see that you spend a year in jail." He looked at Jim Singleton. "That goes for you too, Billy the Kid."

"That's enough talk," McKeever said softly. "Just be comfortable and act like an old friend, huh?"

20.

AT TEN o'clock Lincoln McKeever's worry began to grow to alarming proportions and he kept his attention on the road leading to the depot. Jim was getting tired of holding the gun and the marshal was getting tired of sitting so long.

He said, "Your bluff won't work, McKeever. If you think you can hold me here until train time, then get away, you're crazy. I'll telegraph ahead and have you taken off and brought back."

"We're not getting on the train," McKeever said.

"Where the hell can he be?" Jim Singleton asked. "Lincoln, you suppose you guessed wrong?"

"No, I don't think so. This is Finley's best chance, if he ever gets here."

When twelve o'clock came, Lincoln McKeever would have given five dollars for a cup of coffee and a plate of

stew. In the back room the station agent cooked his
dinner and the aroma was maddening. The marshal sat
quietly, looking at each of them from time to time.
"What you done?"

"Huh?" McKeever asked, his attention pulled around.

"I said, what was it? Holdup? A shooting?"

"You're out of your mind," McKeever said. "Just shut
up and sit still."

The station clock ticked loudly, monotonously, and a
lazy heat filled the place. Not many people came to the
depot for it was a short distance from the center of
town, and McKeever was thankful for that small favor.

At one o'clock the station agent began to wheel freight
onto the cinder platform, and in the distance, a train
whistle hooted for a crossing. The town marshal said,
"Not much time left, boys."

"I told you to shut up," McKeever said. He pulled
his lips tight and looked out the window. "Where the
hell can he be? Was I wrong?"

"If you were," Jim said, "we'll never catch him with
this much head start."

"I wasn't wrong!" McKeever said tightly. "Damn it,
I can't be! I know Finley too well. He'd think of the
train. He's just not a man who likes to ride, especially
when he has a lot of miles to cover."

"Train'll be here in ten minutes," the marshal said. "If
you want to put that gun away, sonny, I'll see that you
get off light, say only ninety days."

"We'll play this McKeever's way," Jim Singleton said.

They sat there while the train drew nearer, finally
clanking into the station where it sighed to a halt. A few
passengers got down and the baggage car door opened
to take on freight. McKeever watched this activity with
a maddening sense of defeat.

"Lincoln!" Jim's tone was enough; McKeever looked
out the window.

FINLEY FINEEN was cutting across the street, his step
rapid. He had a pair of saddlebags over his left arm and
his pistol was riding on the front of his thigh, where it
would be handy.

With a start, McKeever saw what Fineen's plan was,
and he hurriedly stood up. "Keep the marshal here, Jim,"
he said and ran for the back door of the depot. The

ticket clerk tried to block him and McKeever knocked him asprawl, then charged onto the platform. Fineen intended to board the train without a ticket, buying it from the conductor, then if anyone found out how he had escaped, they would have a tougher time tracing his destination.

Finley Fineen had his foot on the coach step when McKeever ran clear of the building. He said, "That's far enough, Finley!"

For a heartbeat Fineen hesitated, statue-still, his hands raised to the grabrail. Then he whirled, drawing his gun, and McKeever's hand plucked his own pistol free of the holster. He had a slight edge on Fineen, and shot first, but Fineen had the saddlebags before him, chest high, and McKeever saw the bullet bury in the money.

Fineen's bullet snapped at the brim of his hat, then McKeever rolled his thumb across the hammer again, this time shooting a little lower. Fineen grunted as the bullet took him in the stomach and fell back against the coach. He tried to work his gun, but his strength was draining away. Finally he let his gun fall, and followed it ungracefully.

Going forward, McKeever picked up the saddlebags, then rolled Finley Fineen over with his foot. Heads lined the raised coach windows, then the conductor signaled the engineer and the train panted into motion drawing clear of the station.

Jim Singleton came out then, still covering the town marshal. He looked at Fineen, then said, "You're a good guesser, Lincoln."

"Yep," McKeever said. "But he had me damned worried."

The marshal said, "Say, you really were after this fella, weren't you?"

"You're getting the idea," McKeever said. He began to unbuckle the saddlebag. "There's about twelve thousand dollars in stolen money in here." He showed the marshal, who whistled softly. "Have you got a safe where I can put this?"

"Sure."

"My deputy and I are going to get a meal, a bath, and a shave," McKeever said. "Tonight, I'd like to get fresh horses for the trip back to Two Pines." He smiled. "And that'll give you time to check on us by telegraph."

"I don't guess that's necessary now," the marshal said. "But you two ought to carry some kind of identification on you."

"After this," McKeever said, "we will. Come on, Jim. You'll take care of this?"

"Sure," the marshal said. "I'll lock this saddlebag up right away." He looked again at Fineen. "He'll draw a crowd—hey, Fred, loan me one of your freight carts to pack this fella over to the jail."

Five hours' sleep, a bath, a good meal and a shave can change a man's outlook on life; at least it did for Lincoln McKeever. He was not sorry that Fineen chose to shoot it out; in fact he rather expected it. Somehow the thought of taking Finley Fineen back and hanging him in front of all the people who knew him left McKeever with a bad taste.

A bullet was quick, and dying in a strange town with no one to care could be a blessing in disguise.

That evening, with fresh horses and Fineen tied across one, McKeever got his saddlebags full of money from the town marshal, woke Jim Singleton from a sound sleep, and left town twenty minutes later.

They made an all night ride of it; McKeever liked night for traveling, and in the morning they stopped to brew a pot of coffee and cook a meal. When the fire was dirt-covered, McKeever motioned Jim Singleton into the saddle, and drew a mild complaint.

McKeever stayed on the road going back, but he didn't stop often, or for long, and by his manner, Jim Singleton could draw some definite conclusions about this man, the sure way he had of doing everything.

Two Pines welcomed McKeever and Jim Singleton as a couple of heroes, and McKeever was somewhat concerned about how Jim would react to this sudden acclaim. But the young man shrugged it off, put up the horses, then went home. Finley Fineen was taken to his home; McKeever made no statement to Fineen's wife; he left her alone to do her crying.

Charlie Boomhauer was waiting for him at the jail. He took the saddlebag, counted the money briefly, then dumped it into the bottom desk drawer.

"I got the money back from the merchants," he said.

"The company will return it to Kelly and Burglass within a few days; I've wired the home office for instructions." He looked at McKeever. "You look tired."

"Not the kind that sleep will cure," McKeever said. "The town's pretty keyed up, now that it's over. Bill Daley say anything more?"

"Yes, I have his statement, all the details. How Fineen made the gun and Daley the shell." He shook his head. "Lincoln, have you ever sat down and figured out how close these three came to getting away with this? I tell you, it was nearly the perfect crime."

"Except that they got caught."

"If it hadn't been for you, they wouldn't have," Boomhauer said.

"There's always someone like me around," McKeever said. "I hope that didn't sound like a brag."

"It didn't; I know how you meant it." Boomhauer took two cigars from his pocket and offered one to McKeever. "The home office is going to be damned pleased. They might offer you a remuneration."

"I don't want it," McKeever said.

"Don't be a damn fool, Lincoln. Take it." He waved his hands briefly. "I know how you feel. This is your town and you knew these men, but you can't think of that and you know it."

"Yeah," McKeever said. "A lawman is supposed to be hard, isn't he?"

"It sometimes helps," Boomhauer admitted. "I wish I was." He nodded toward the cell blocks. "Daley wanted to see you as soon as you got back."

"All right, but I'm going over to the hotel first."

Boomhauer grinned. "A nice looking girl. I don't understand why you waited so long."

"Because I'm a fool," McKeever said and went out.

H E HAD difficulty getting through the crowd milling up and down the street; they wanted to shake hands and tell him how good he was, and McKeever didn't want to listen to it.

He found Nan in her room; she answered the door quickly. "Jim came home ten minutes ago. I wondered if you'd come here, Lincoln."

"There's no place else I want to go," he said.

She motioned him into a chair, then sat on the arm. "I know you had to kill Finley, and I'm sorry. But it was better than hanging him, Lincoln."

"Yes. I don't want to hang Daley; I wish someone would do it."

"His trial begins Monday," she said. "I suppose it'll be a formality." She fell silent a moment. "I feel sorry for his wife; she'll have to live with this, like dirt that won't wash off."

"I'm going to resign," McKeever said. "All the way back from Buffalo I thought about it. I've got some money saved. Maybe I can find a business that suits me, somewhere away from here."

"Do you really want to leave here?"

He shrugged. "The town's kind of wore out for me, Nan. You know what I mean?"

"Yes. We all feel that way from time to time. You know, there have been times in my life when I've thought of running away with a gambler or a whisky drummer just to be doing it. Twenty years from now people would remember me and shake their heads sadly, yet they'd remember."

He looked at her quickly, his eyes serious. "Why did you tell me that?"

"Because we all see ourselves as being different from what we really are, I guess. I don't think many of us really like what we are, yet we have to go on living with it." She got up from the chair arm and moved around. "Idiots are contented, Lincoln. We're all restless and wandering, even if it's only in thought. After we're married, I'll feel the same way, and I want you to understand it, just as I intend to understand you."

He stood up, hat in hand. "I love you, Nan. It's been a long time since I said that."

"Yes, but it still sounds wonderful." She put her arms around him and kissed him briefly. "Go on now. When this is all over, we'll get married."

"Are we going to fight, Nan?"

"Sure," she said, smiling. "Do you want a wife or a freak?"

He was serious. "Nan, let's not grow tired of each other."

"I don't think we ever could," she said. "Now go on. Come back when you can."

He made his way to the jail; Boomhauer was still there, sitting on the company's money.

"You want the keys?" Boomhauer asked.

"I'm not going in the cell," McKeever said. He took off his gunbelt and laid it on the desk as a precaution against having it grabbed away from him.

BILL DALEY occupied the center cell, away from the windows, in case some citizen decided to hurry justice with a rifle bullet. As McKeever stepped down the short hall, Daley came off the cot and pressed against the bars.

"You got him. I heard the noise in the street. They wouldn't yell and carry on like that if you hadn't got him." He looked around, his eyes wide and wildly rolling. "Well, where is he? Ain't you going to lock him up? He's as guilty as me. More so. He talked me into this. Yes, siree, I didn't want any part of it but Finley made me go along. He's the guilty one. I'm just an innocent man who got caught up in something he couldn't get out of. Come on now. You bring him in here and lock him up!"

"Finley's dead," McKeever said.

"Dead?" Daley stared. "You're lying to me, trying to scare me, that's what you're doing, Lincoln. Hell, I always liked you. We've been friends, haven't we? Good friends. Now you stop this lying to me and bring Fineen in here where he belongs."

"I'm not lying, Bill. Finley went for his gun and I had to kill him."

For a full minute Daley just stared and rubbed his face and shook his head, saying, "No, no, no, no."

"You're all alone, Bill. I'm sorry, but that's the way it turned out."

"Alone?" He grabbed the bars and tried to shake them. "I don't want to be alone!" Tears suddenly began to race down his cheeks and his face twisted like a tormented child's. "Don't hang me alone! God, don't make me hang alone! I don't want to be alone!"

McKeever turned and walked back to the office, shutting the door, yet the sounds of the pleadng, the crying, came through. Charlie Boomhauer raised his head and his eyes were sad.

"I guess he knows now. Really knows and understands."

"Yes. It's too bad a man has to know."

"You going to stay on, as sheriff, I mean?"

McKeever frowned. "What makes you think I want to quit?"

"Because I've had some tough ones too, and I wanted to quit. We all do now and then."

McKeever sat down in one of the chairs. "No, I'll stay, Charlie. This is my town. Besides, I'm going to get married pretty soon." He let his smile start and grow. "A married man has no business being unemployed, has he?"

"Nope," Boomhauer said, rising. "Come on, I'll buy you a drink to that."

THE WIND RIVER KID

1

SHE SAT ERECT on the seat of the buckboard, handling
the reins like a man, with her wrists stiff, her elbows tight
against her sides. She wore a gray linsey dress and a
bonnet tied firmly over copper-hued curls. The backs
of her hands were deeply tanned, as was her oval face;
a sprinkling of freckles peppered the bridge of her nose.
She was young in years, but a lifetime in a rough land
had driven the nonsense out of her until she carried a
perpetually grave expression around her full mouth.

While she drove, she studied the land: sheer mountain rises, thickly furred with tall pine and Douglas fir,
with the winding road the only visible scratch on the
virgin face. The road wound beneath the buckboard's
ironshod wheels, clinging at times to a bare foothold on
the mountain's face.

Finally the road made a sharp turn and dipped quickly
to a valley floor where the town of Rindo's Springs lay,
close-huddled, the hub for a large planing mill, a saw
camp, and the huge lumber company buildings. On the
other side of the town, a slab burner rose to a high
cone, belching an eternal cloud of smoke. Distance did
not muffle completely the rip of power saws, the moan-
ing roar of planers.

She drove patiently, letting the miles fall behind her
as she left the four-mile downgrade and entered the
town. Rindo's Springs was a cross-hatching of narrow
streets flanked by heavy log buildings and uneven board-

145

walks. In the air were the tangy flavors of pitch and coal smoke from the huge steam engines at the company mill.

A recent rain had left the road thick and sticky, and the buckboard's wheels flung mud as she navigated the street. The peeled logs of the buildings were darkly damp, and as she passed the corner saloon, she came under the sharp scrutiny of the porch loungers. She held the team to a slow walk for the length of the street; not that she felt like taking her time, but because she was a woman sharply aware of public opinion and constantly on guard lest unseemly behavior color their judgment of her.

Besides, the streets of Rindo's Springs were too crowded for speed; nearly everyone within a radius of twenty miles was in town. Buggies and saddle horses were packed together, and there was not a single empty place along the main drag's hitching racks.

Aside from the sounds coming from the saw camp, the town was strangely silent; the men who stood along the boardwalk's length did not speak to each other; they presented only a solid-faced patience. She nodded to many, her own men, and ignored the others.

She turned at another side street and pulled up to the hitchrack in front of the jail. Dismounting, she tied her team, then crossed the walk and opened the door without knocking.

The sheriff raised his eyes quickly, then smiled as though relieved. He had a newspaper spread on his desk and his revolver lay disassembled, a scattered pile of oily, metal parts. The girl leaned her back against the heavy plank door. "Ben, with a town full of enemies this is a poor time to take your gun apart."

Ben Colfax leaned back in his chair, his fingers searching his vest pockets for a cigar. He was fifty-some and feeling his age. Tired lines were etched permanently on his face. Even the badge pinned to his shirt front looked tarnished and ready for retirement.

"I have no real enemies," he said mildly. "It's just that a man caught in the middle has no friends." He looked steadily at her, a genuine affection in his eyes. "The voting is over, Bess. Just a matter of waiting now while Judge Richmond and the mayor count the ballots."

"How do you think it's going to go?" she asked.

Ben Colfax sighed and brushed his revolver parts aside to make a place for his elbows. "I went over the voting register pretty close, Bess, and except for the merchants, it's a fifty-fifty chance." He shook his head sadly. "Was your father alive, I'd say we had Rindo licked. He had as much power among his faction as Rindo does in his. But now there's no telling which way the merchants will go. Rindo's direction, probably." He took his cigar from his mouth and brushed his shaggy mustache. "Wish I could help you, Bess. You know I wish that, but I can't."

She pulled a heavy chair close to Colfax' desk and sat down. "Ben, no one on this earth will ever make me believe that Cadmus Rindo didn't kill Pop, or have him killed. And just five days before the election—that's too convenient, Ben. Too close to be coincidence."

He reached across the desk and patted her hand. "Bess, I've been a lawman all my life. I respect the law, and the law heard all the evidence I could gather against Rindo, and the law said he was innocent." He spread his hands. "I've got to respect that judgment, Bess. And you have to respect it."

"I'm going to fight that old man," she said flatly. "Fight him as hard as Pop ever did."

"But keep it legal," Ben Colfax said gently.

She stepped to the door and paused there. "Ben, do you think Cadmus Rindo's keeping this election legal? Who is this man Onart? None of us have even seen him. Have you seen him?"

"No," Ben Colfax admitted. "I haven't. He's just a name on the ballot."

Some of her resentment and hurt vanished as she regarded this kindly man; her voice grew soft. "Ben, you just refuse to see bad in anyone, don't you?"

"Easier to see the good," he said. "I guess I'm weak."

"No," she said. "You're very strong, Ben. And I wish I had some of that strength right now." She stepped outside and closed the door. Turning east, she moved along the warped boardwalk, lifting her skirt and feet carefully so as not to stub a toe on the irregular cracks.

This was a lumber town and the men here were like the timber they hewed, tall and generally big-boned, silent men for the most part, but today the silence was unnatural. She nodded to a few of her friends, but did not stop to speak to anyone. Somehow, all talk seemed used up. The buzz and commotion from Rindo's company lot held the men's attention, for earlier in the day he had closed down for a half-hour so his employees could vote. Now it seemed that they were totally disinterested in the election's outcome, as though they already knew which way it would fall.

The polling place was Murray Burkhauser's log saloon and a group of men stood on the porch. Murray Burkhauser was there, his hands thrust into his pockets, a fine cigar fragrantly ignited between his teeth. He was a tall man, although not overly heavy. Timber had never been his business, and although he had lived in this town four years, he was as out of place as a total stranger, a man in alien surroundings. Kansas City or San Francisco would have been more to Murray Burkhauser's liking, a chandeliered palace with dancing girls and a dozen sweating bartenders, and customers in beavers and ascot ties. Not a log building festooned with elk antlers and smoky ceiling beams, with a banjo and a tinny piano. Yet, for reasons he discussed with no man, Murray Burkhauser had no intention of leaving Rindo's Springs.

When Bess stepped onto the porch, he said, "Too bad women can't vote, although I doubt one more could make a difference now."

She gave him a steady look, holding her temper back. Her glance shifted to the man standing on Burkhauser's left. "You're looking smug, Cal."

"I don't mean to be," he said. He was a young man in his early thirties. His eyes were a deep brown and his skin a tightly stretched covering for good bones. Unlike Murray Burkhauser, Cal Runyon *was* timber, but not the two-dollar-a-day, fall, limb, and buck kind. Timber boss was closer to it, for he wore a pair of cord trousers and engineer's boots, and a manner that automatically told an observant man that he was well paid to exercise authority.

"Where did you find this dark horse Onart?" Bess asked.

"I didn't. Cadmus Rindo picked him." He pulled out a stem winder and glanced at it. "The count should be finished pretty soon." He touched her lightly on the arm. "Will you step inside?"

Her impulse was to refuse, but everyone on the porch looked at her. Bess shrugged and stepped through the door. No liquor was being served, both Rindo and Ben Colfax having agreed beforehand to keep the election a sober one. Along one wall, planed pine booths had been installed, and Cal Runyon led Bess to one. She hesitated, then sat down. Cal Runyon slid in across from her.

"Bess," he said softly, "you're holding a hate as though you liked it."

"Pop's dead," she said dully. "He was all I had left, Cal."

He made a waving motion with his hands, as though searching his mind for a way to get through to her, to crush her prejudice. "You won't listen to me, will you?"

"Why should I?" she asked. "Cal, you work for Rindo, and he was the only man who stood against Pop."

"But not to the extent where he'd kill him," Runyon said. "The old man loves a fight, Bess. But an open fight. Not a shot in the dark."

She placed her hands flat on the table, preparing to rise. "I buried him the day before yesterday, Cal. It's too soon for me to listen to you."

"Would I lie to you?" he asked. "Bess, do I have to tell you how I feel?"

"No, and I don't want to hear it." She stood up and looked at him. "Cal, I'm afraid to trust you now. Almost afraid to trust anyone." Quickly she turned and walked to the door. But there a thought halted her and she came back. "Can I ask you something straight out and get a straight answer?"

"I've always answered you straight," he said.

"Then who is Onart and why hasn't anyone seen him?"

Cal Runyon studied his hands for a minute. "Bess, the old man was mad, at you and at Ben." He looked steadily at her and there was an appeal in his eyes. "I tried to talk him out of this, but he went ahead anyway, putting this man against Ben."

"Ahead with what? Cal, you're not answering me. Where is Onart? No one's seen him."

"He's in jail," he said softly. "Bess, I'm sorry."

Her eyes went wide with disbelief. "Cal, this is a joke!"

He shook his head. "No joke, Bess. I wish it was."

Anger began to fan a warming heat into her face. "Where's Cadmus Rindo now?"

"You'll find him at the hotel," he said. She whirled and hurried out and Runyon got up to go to the door as though he meant to follow her.

Bess turned north along the boardwalk, and at the next corner she crossed over. The two-story hotel sat on the corner, the wide lower gallery fronting the boardwalk. Cadmus Rindo sat in his favorite chair. He was a man nearly eighty, but age had not undermined his spirit nor dulled the razor edge of his mind. His hair was white as was his beard, but he looked at Bess Jamison with the drill-sharp eyes of a much younger man.

"What kind of a man are you?" Bess asked.

"Whatever people make me be," he said flatly. "So you found out about Onart, huh?"

"That was low," she snapped, "running a jailbird against a man like Ben Colfax."

Cadmus Rindo laughed without humor. "Does make Ben look pretty bad, don't it?" Then his laughter vanished. "But keep in mind that Onart ain't a jailbird. Just a common drunk."

She regarded Cadmus Rindo with eyes that mirrored her disbelief. "Why don't I just get a gun and shoot you?"

"Was you a man," Rindo said calmly, "I'd have given you your chance at the inquest the other day." He leaned forward and speared her with his eyes. "A woman ought to stay at home. Get married. Have babies." His eyes pulled into narrow slits. "Stop meddlin' in a man's business." A smile began to lurk behind the snowy thicket of whiskers. "I'll miss your pa. Always gave me a fight for my money."

"You'll find that I can put up a scrap too," she said softly. "And you've given me added reason, old man. What you've done to Ben Colfax will break his heart. What kind of a man are you to do such a thing?"

"Like any other man," he said. "Any damn fool can win a friend, and lose him the same day. But when you break a man's spirit, you achieve something absolute."

"I guess that's your crowning achievement, isn't it? You own the town, the biggest mill, the freight line, and the logging railroad. Now you own the law, all bought and paid for. I suppose you'll make that gunman, Pete Davis, a deputy."

His eyes grew dark and there was an angry set to his cheeks. "Now you understand something. I didn't want to own the sheriff, but you and Ben Colfax made me buy him for my own protection."

"You're completely rotten," Bess said and mounted the porch. She went directly to the clerk's desk, took a key to a room on the second floor, and walked up the steps. Rindo's last remark still stung her and beneath her breath she called the old man many names, and branded him a coward for seeking someone else upon whom he could place the responsibility for his acts.

She could understand why Onart's identity had been kept a closely guarded secret; Rindo's men would vote the way he told them to vote, and Bess's employees would vote for Ben Colfax, regardless of who was running against him. Rindo, she knew, must have guessed that once Ben found out who his opponent was, he would simply have resigned, thereby depriving old man Rindo of his moral victory.

Locking the door, she stripped off her dress and washed her hands and face. Then she sat down on the bed to think, trying to figure out the most gentle way to tell Ben Colfax about Onart. Yet there didn't seem to be a way. She left the bed.

Through the open window she could hear the sounds of laughter along the street; the quit whistle blew at the mill. While she stood there, watching, every man on Cadmus Rindo's payroll drifted into town, clogging the main street, filling the town with swagger and loud talk. She could see her own men down there, easing aside for Rindo's men. Had the election swung toward Colfax, her own men would be kings of the street, filled with victory-built confidence. But defeat robs a man of his strength and makes him unsure of himself; she could not blame her men for drifting to the end of town.

The citizens of Rindo's Springs were staying clear of the traffic. Their vote had been swayed by Cadmus Rindo, and now that the election had teetered his way, they were content to make the best of it. Burkhauser had opened the saloon for business and the bulk of the crowd gathered there.

She saw Cal Runyon leave the saloon porch and walk diagonally across the street toward the hotel. He looked up toward the upper gallery and spoke briefly to Will

Beau-Haven, who owned the place, then passed from Bess Jamison's sight beneath the overhang.

She slipped into her dress quickly as knuckles tapped against her door. She crossed the room, one hand fastening buttons; the other turned the key. Cal Runyon stood there, hat in hand. "You going to let me come in, Bess?"

She nodded and stepped aside. He waited while she closed the door, then tossed his hat on the chest of drawers. He smelled strongly of shaving soap and pipe tobacco and the timber. His face was a canvas on which worry was clearly painted. "Ben knows by now. Some of the boys went to the jail to rub it in." He lifted his hands in a feeble gesture. "I couldn't stop them."

"Did you even try?" She glanced at him briefly, then turned away. "What's the use of even talking about it, Cal?"

"We don't have to be at each other's throats, do we?"

She turned to him suddenly. "What do you want of me, Cal?"

"To marry me," he said simply. "Let Cadmus have the damn place."

"Did he send you here to ask?" Her anger was like an explosion, quick to spring up and quick to die. His expression tightened and she was instantly sorry. "Forgive me, Cal. I didn't mean that."

"It's all right," he said.

Shaking her head, she reached up and brushed the bronze curls away from her forehead. "It's not all right. We're starting to accuse each other. Before we know it, something will be said that we can't forgive. I don't want that to happen." She turned and looked again out the window. "It's not pleasant, knowing that you're beaten. Have you ever known the feeling?"

"No," he admitted. "Things have been easy for me."

She looked around quickly. "Tell me the truth—how can you work for a man like Cadmus Rindo?"

"I've found him honorable," Runyon said.

"Oh, Cal!" Her shock was genuine. "How can you say that?"

"Because I know it to be true," he said. "Bess, don't you see, we're fighting each other. I want to find a way out."

"What way is there?" she asked. "Cal, will you quit Rindo for me?"

"No," he said. "I've worked for the man too long." He

picked up his hat and turned to the door. "What's going to happen to us, Bess? Were all the things we talked about just talk?"

A sudden whoop split the silence and a revolver popped. Bess looked quickly from the window, turning her head both ways. "They've got Ben!"

Whirling, she plunged past Cal Runyon. In the hallway she stopped and gave him a flat, uncompromising stare. "I guess we're already getting a taste of Cadmus Rindo's law."

"I'll go with you," he said quickly.

"I don't need you," she said. "I don't even want you around."

Then she was dashing for the head of the stairs; Runyon followed, then gave up the thought of chasing her.

The crowd on the street had migrated toward the jail. They were howling and discharging firearms into the air. One man was even trying to wedge a span of mules through Burkhauser's front door, while down the street, other mules were being hitched to logging dollies for an impromptu race through town. Bess Jamison hurried across the street, completely ignoring the traffic. One horseman cursed and pulled up short to keep from running her down, only to be plowed under by another who failed to stop in time.

Gaining the opposite boardwalk, Bess walked rapidly, but by the time she reached the corner, the crowd was breaking up and Ben Colfax was not in sight. At the jail door she knocked, for it was locked.

From inside, Ben Colfax said, "Who is it?"

"Bess."

He shot the bolt and let her in, then locked the door again. He had a handkerchief in one hand and was dabbing at a bleeding lip. A swelling over his eye was growing more pronounced by the minute. "I came close to killing men out there a few minutes ago," he said bleakly.

"No one could have blamed you," Bess said.

He shook his head and turned away so she could not see the shame in his expression. "I don't mind a licking, Bess, but the way I was licked hurts. Rindo thought so damned little of me that he ran a tramp against me. He had to rub my face in the dirt."

"It was a cruel thing," Bess said.

"The world's cruel," Ben Colfax said and sought comfort in a cigar. "Did you see how quick the wolves jumped me? A bunch of hired animals." He went around to the drawer side of his desk and lifted a ring of keys. "To think I had him in jail all the time," he said softly. "I'll sure have that rubbed in my face all right." He walked down the short hall to the cell blocks. Bess Jamison followed him.

The young man lay on his back, mouth open, snoring loudly. He needed a bath and shave and a lot more self-respect, Bess decided. Ben Colfax toed him without too much gentleness, nearly booting him off the bunk.

With a startled grunt, the young man opened his eyes and sat up. "Getting kind of heavy with your handling, ain't you?" He looked at Bess. "You the warden's daughter?"

"Keep a civil tongue in your head," Ben Colfax warned, "or I'll bat some sense into you."

Raising a hand, the young man touched a still tender bruise on his cheekbone. "Seems that you already did. You want to try again now that I'm sober?"

"You're free to go," Ben Colfax said. "I'll get your stuff."

He went back to his office. Bess leaned against the bars and studied Onart. Not a bad face, she decided. A little thin, but that was probably from drinking too much and skipping too many meals. Onart's hair was dark brown, straight as a string and badly in need of barbering. He had an oval face, without the heavy-boned ridges so common among thin men. His lips were long and thin, giving his expression a quality of cynicism that seemed somehow out of place.

He returned her stare for a moment, then said, "See anything you like, just ask for it. We carry it in stock."

"Smart, aren't you?" Bess tried to stare him down, but failed. She looked around the cell: a cot, washbasin and a cracked pitcher on the floor.

Ben Colfax tromped down the hall. He had a shell belt draped over his arm and tossed it to Onart. "Now git!"

"You're in a hurry," Onart said easily. "I'm not." He turned the cartridge belt over and opened a small pocket on the back. Thrusting his fingers inside, he sounded it, then looked at Ben Colfax. "I see you found it. There was three hundred dollars in there."

"A likely story," Colfax said. He looked quickly at Bess. "They all try that. Claim you took their money." His attention whipped back to Onart. "Beat it, and if I hear you telling it around that I rolled you, I'll break your skull."

"I'll bet you will," Onart said. He smiled and lifted a booted foot to the bunk rail. Then he split open the sewed cuff of his trouser leg and palmed four twenty-dollar gold pieces. Ben Colfax' face darkened in sudden anger, and Onart's smile turned to a soft laugh. "Here's some you didn't get." Buckling on his gunbelt, Onart settled it on his hip, then expertly palmed the weapon and rotated the cylinder. "At least you didn't steal the shells," he said.

"Ben! Are you going to take that?" Bess Jamison placed her hands on her hips and glared at Onart.

"Call me a liar," Onart suggested. He motioned toward Bess, all the time looking at Ben Colfax. "Go on, tell her I'm making it up, that you don't roll every drunk."

Ben Colfax watched Onart, his expression drawn and hesitant. He looked at the gun Onart wore, and more especially, the way he wore it. Only a select breed of men wore a pistol like that, in a holster trimmed of all surplus leather and cut to ride so that the butt was always cocked away from the hip for easy access. And Ben had looked the gun over carefully while Onart slept in the cell. A gunsmith had plied his trade with cautious skill, hand-honing the lockwork until it was as smooth as butter. The original hammer had been altered and smoothed for slip-hammer shooting. Colfax' summation was that this was a money-making pistol, a for-hire pistol, and the man wearing it was better than most for he was still alive.

Glancing downcast at Bess, Colfax said, "The job never paid much, and a man slips into bad ways after awhile." He shifted his feet and moved his hands aimlessly. "Bess, you wouldn't hold this against old Ben, would you? It ain't like I'd ever been dishonest with anyone here. Just a few bums now and then."

"This isn't the time to discuss it," Bess Jamison said. She looked squarely at Onart. "Things have happened while you've been sleeping in jail."

Her glance toward Ben reminded him of the lost election and with considerable reluctance he unpinned the badge from his own vest and hooked it on the front of Onart's canvas jumper.

"What the hell's this?" Onart asked. "Some kind of joke?"

"We wish it were," Bess said, "but it's no joke. You've been elected sheriff."

The front door shook under a heavy fist and Ben went to open it; then the compounded step of several men came toward the cell block. They were all timber men with their multicolored wool shirts and calked boots that left torn dimples in the plank floor whenever they took a step. They looked at Onart, hard work and trouble blended in their expressions, revealing much of their lives to a single, observing glance.

Bess nodded at the leader. "Has everyone gone home, Jess?"

He pulled his attention away from Onart and looked at her. "Most of them are still hanging around, figuring maybe there was something you wanted to do." He made a curt motion toward Onart. "Is this what Rindo bought?"

"Who's Rindo?" Onart asked.

"The man who bought and paid for you," another man said. He was over six feet tall, shoulders as wide as a singletree, and his arms were sinewed boughs. This man touched Bess lightly. "You say it and I'll put a kink in this fella and take him back to Rindo."

"Let him," Ben Colfax suggested. "I'd like nothing better than to give some of this back to Rindo."

"It wouldn't be any trouble to me," the big man said, speaking softly. "What do you say, Bess?"

She pondered the question, her brow furrowed. To all appearances she was as collected as a housewife selecting the supper vegetables.

Onart said, "What kind of people are you anyway? The law picks a man's pockets and now you stand there talking about wrapping me up in a bundle to send to a man I don't even know."

"You don't mean a thing to us," Bess said flatly. "It's your tough luck this is happening, that's all."

Onart's glance touched each of them, then settled on the husky lumberjack. "You want to fight, is that it?"

"If Miss Jamison says so," the man admitted.

They were all watching Onart, but he had drawn his gun before any of them could move. "Stand still," he said flatly, then edged out of the cell. He nodded his head toward Bess Jamison. "This bulldog of yours got a name?"

"Harry," she said.

"Come out here, Harry."

When the man stepped into the hall, Onart closed the cell door and turned the key. Ben Colfax grabbed the bars and shook them. "You got no call to lock us up!"

Onart laughed. "Fella, everyone in this town is crazy so I don't have to have a call to do anything. No more than you did to lift my money, or you," he looked at Bess, "to egg this ape on to mash in my head." He prodded the lumberjack in the small of the back with his gun. "Let's go to the front office where we'll have swinging room."

"Well now," Harry said, smiling. "I'll go for that."

Bess and Colfax were tugging at the cell door while the other two men stood back in silence. Onart urged the big man ahead of him, and, once in the office, took off his gunbelt and hung it on a handy peg. The rack of rifles on the wall was locked and Onart slipped his own gun into the middle desk drawer and locked it.

"Now we can make this nice and safe," Onart said.

Harry stripped off his shirt and laid it across the back of a chair. His chest was broad and flat, well thicketed with hair. When he stepped toward Onart, his calks left small blond tufts of pine on the floor.

"You mind locking the outer door?" Onart asked. "I wouldn't want you to run out when the going gets tough."

"No chance of that," Harry said. He turned the key and then tossed it into the corner. "You ready?"

"Sure," Onart said. "Let's get it started."

Harry's charge was as furious as a bull's. He plowed around the corner of the desk, all muscle and drive. Onart stepped away, swooped up the lamp and brought it down across the crown of the man's head. Shattered glass and kerosene flew in a wild spray, and Harry went to his knees with enough force to jar the building.

From the cell block, Bess yelled, "Harry! Harry, watch yourself!"

Onart walked around the far side of the desk and

stood slightly behind the lumberjack as he pushed himself erect. There was an oozing split in his scalp. Before Harry could find Onart, the man doubled his fist and planted it in the soft spot behind Harry's ear.

Driven forward, Harry went asprawl across the desk, sliding to the floor on the other side. He landed head and shoulders first, dragged the rest of his long body around where it belonged, then looked at Onart. There was no anger in the lumberjack's eyes, just a new respect and a great deal of caution.

"You want to get up now?" Onart invited.

"I'll get up," the man said. "Just give me a minute."

"Why should I give you anything?" Onart asked, then swept forward, one foot swinging. He caught Harry as the man was trying to rise, and the boot arched him back. He landed flat on the floor, his mouth mashed. "We get rough now," Onart said and swept up a chair.

The down-swung furniture took the lumberjack across the head and shoulders as he was trying to roll. Driven flat, Harry pawed at the floor as though trying to find a purchase somewhere that wouldn't tip and rock.

Onart stepped back and waited, and when the man got enough strength to rise, he said, "One more, Harry," and picked up another chair. He waited until the man was on his feet, then stepped to one side and swung as though trying to cut down a tree. Some kindness prevented Onart from making a complete ruin of Harry's face; he struck him flush in the chest, catapulting him backward across the desk and into the wall.

Bess was shaking the cell door and demanding to know what was going on, so to bring her up to date, Onart half-dragged Harry down the short hall, unlocked the cell door, and pitched him in. Everyone looked at the big lumberjack, then at Onart.

Ben Colfax said it. "Who—are you, mister?"

"Now you ought to know me," Onart said softly. "You had me locked up for a week."

Ben Colfax raised a hand and pawed his mouth out of shape. "Don't get many of the real tough ones in this part of the country." He shook his head. "The name Onart don't mean anything to me, but I guess it should."

"Try the Wind River Kid and see what you get."

For an instant it looked as if Ben Colfax was going to

strangle on his cigar; then he began to chuckle. This soon got out of control and he laughed. Finally he began to cry, all the time laughing in a high, half-hysterical voice. Bess took him by the arm and shook him. "What's so damned funny?"

With a supreme effort, Ben brought his mirth under control. He wiped the back of his hand across his eyes. "By God, that's poetic justice for you, Bess. Rindo elects a jailbird so he can get me out of office, then the man he elects turns out to be the Wind River Kid, as dangerous a man as Doc Holliday or Wes Hardin." He paused to suffer through a dying chuckle. "And I took his money, when all the time I could have got five hundred dollars for turning him over to an Arizona marshal."

"You're too greedy for your own good," the Kid said. He threw the cell door wide. "Go on, get out of here." He pointed to the tarnished sheriff's badge still pinned to his jumper. "Like it or not, this county's got itself a new sheriff."

Colfax left first, then Bess; she edged away from the Kid as though he would suddenly reach out and bite her. The two men who had come in with Harry helped him to his feet and outside. Bess stood by the front door while Colfax leaned against his desk. The Kid unlocked the middle drawer and rebuckled his gun. Colfax was looking around at the scattered destruction. Finally he said, "You could have hit him with the desk too, Kid."

"Didn't need to," the Kid said softly. "Harry wasn't as tough as he thought he was."

"Maybe you're not either," Bess said flatly.

"Lady," the Kid said, "why don't you get married and have kids?" He looked steadily at her, and then she went out, slamming the door. "What eats her?" he asked.

"She has her troubles," Colfax said. "We all do." He looked at the Wind River Kid. "This is logging country, Kid. What brings you here?"

"I need a change," the Kid said.

"Well," Colfax opined, "you got that all right. Never heard of you wearing a badge before." He got off the corner of the desk. "Too bad you had to come here, though. Rindo'll offer you some money and you'll take his orders. I know your kind, Kid. Hired out so long that it comes second nature."

"The same way you've picked so many pockets that you're no longer honest?"

This drove an angry color into Ben Colfax' face, but he kept a tight rein on himself. "You think what you want, Kid. At least the law ain't after me." He stepped to the door, pausing there. "The place is yours and you're welcome to it."

"Where can I find this man Rindo?"

"On the hotel porch if he ain't gone home. You want some advice?"

"From you?" The Wind River Kid shook his head. "You need it worse than I do, mister."

"Suit yourself," Colfax said. "But you'd better get on the right side, Kid. The girl can use you with trouble coming on." He sighed. "She's a good sort, Kid. You got to forget that part in the cell. I don't guess Harry'll hold it against you either."

"I don't have to forget anything," the Kid said. "Go on, tend to your own business."

"All right," Ben Colfax said, "but I'll be around to watch you fall. Don't forget that you don't have a friend in this town. Bess's crowd would just as soon jump you as not, and once Rindo finds out who you are, he'll get rid of you. He's got a man fast enough to shade you too."

After Ben Colfax closed the door, the Wind River Kid sat down behind the desk and tried to adjust his thinking to this new turn of affairs. With eight hundred miles between himself and his stomping ground, any man would consider himself safe, but evidently this was a miscalculation; he certainly had fallen into the exact thing he wished to avoid.

Strange, he thought, that a man of twenty-four could consider his life drawing to a close, or at least the major run of it behind him. That kind of thinking can drive a man across many a weary mile, and in the end desert him, leaving him exactly as he had been, only just a little older and much more tired.

The Kid mentally recounted his two-week spree in Rindo's Springs and was sorry that he'd ever bought that first bottle; whiskey had never liked him and after a good drunk he liked it even less than before.

Leaving the office, he walked slowly along the main street, breathing in the rich odors of pitch and burning slabs from the giant incinerator. A small crowd cluttered the porch of Burkhauser's Saloon and the Kid gave them a careful look before he entered. He wondered if Ben Colfax had spread the word about his identity, then decided that the ex-sheriff would keep still; he wanted others to share his surprise. Probably make him feel less of a damned fool that way.

Ben Colfax was leaning against the bar, and around him were several men, all loggers and none his friends —the Kid could tell by the way they left Colfax standing by himself. The aroma of spilled beer and old cigars whetted a thirst in the Kid and he bellied up to the bar. One of the men turned and gave him a brass-faced stare, his glance lingering on the tarnished badge.

"So you're what Rindo bought?" The man chuckled.

The bartender was waiting, either for the Kid's order or a signal to duck. "Draw a beer," the Kid said; then while the tap sizzled, he glanced at the man. "How much did it cost you, mister?"

"Not a nickle."

"Then keep your mouth shut about how other people spend their money," the Kid said. He had a manner of speaking, in a near whisper, that made men cock their ears and listen. It was almost as though he were determined never to shout or speak up, or repeat what he had said, and because men were afraid they would miss something important, they listened most carefully.

The man next to the Kid stiffened slightly. He was tall and stringy and as tough as the rock hills. No logger, this man. The Kid felt a chord of recognition strike, then he remembered him from Kansas, a gunman, and far from second-rate.

Of course there would be one in Rindo's Springs; there seemed to be one in every town, just waiting for trouble. He tried to recall the man's name, then he had it: Pete Davis. Fragments of the man's achievements came to him, the men he had killed in the course of a brief and frantic career. The Kid knew without thinking that here was a bit of business that would have to be taken care of sooner or later, whether he liked it or not.

Farther down the bar, Cal Runyon shifted his weight and said, "Ease off, Pete. The old man don't pay you to shoot off your mouth."

The Kid looked past Pete Davis and locked eyes with
Cal Runyon. "You somebody important?"

"Not really," Runyon said. He picked up his beer and
came around the cluster of men, edging in between the
Kid and Davis. "I work for Cadmus Rindo, the man
who elected you."

The Kid never took his attention from either man.
Both seemed to be unarmed, but he wasn't sure. Pete
used to carry his gun in a half-breed spring rig under
his coat, and that had never slowed him down. The Kid
lifted his beer, drank, then set the stein aside. He said,
"And where can I find the kind old soul who goes
around making sheriffs out of strangers?"

Cal Runyon nodded toward the street. "At the hotel,
most likely." He pursed his lips and rolled a thought
around in his mind. "You sound sore. Better get over
it. There's nothing to be sore about."

"Sounds reasonable," the Kid said. He took another
swallow of beer, then turned away from the bar. At
the door he said, "That was on you, wasn't it?"

Runyon smiled faintly. "You got any other name besides Onart?"

So Ben Colfax hadn't told. . . . "Ask Pete, he knows
me," the Kid said and stepped outside. Across the street
and a few doors down sat the hotel, and as he walked
along, the Kid studied the building carefully. On the
upper gallery he saw a man sitting in a wheelchair, a
heavy robe over his legs. On the lower gallery he saw
another man and knew without asking that this was
Cadmus Rindo. The old man followed him with his
eyes, and at the barbershop the Kid paused to look back.
He saw Pete Davis leave the saloon and cross over to
where Cadmus Rindo sat. There was a hurried confer-
ence; then the Kid turned his back on it and went into
the barbershop.

Leaning back in the chair, he indicated that he wanted
a shave and a haircut and damn little conversation. The
barbershop was warm and spiced with the fragrance
of shaving lotions, and the barber was a skilled man.

After the shave and haircut I ought to get out, the
Kid thought. After I take care of Pete, he told himself,
then realized that this was the way it had always been:
pushing on, but only after he had taken care of the
business at hand. Although he never thought much about

it, he was always a little amazed at himself for being able to anticipate trouble before it loomed. But he knew that Pete's attitude had warned him. And the way he had eased off at Cal Runyon's order clearly indicated that he was willing to wait. Add it up and it spelled trouble, but that was the Wind River Kid's business, a business in which he handled himself well.

There was not much left of the day when he stepped out on the boardwalk. A gray dusk was settling, building sooty shadows along one side of the street. At the lumber camp, the whistle was shrilling and the ring of gang saws began to tone down in pitch as they were slowed down and shut off.

By some unvoiced call, many people began to form in ranks along the boardwalks, making an unsuccessful attempt to look casually idle.

Pete Davis was standing near the hotel entrance, his hands thrust into his coat pockets. Cal Runyon was on the saloon porch with Ben Colfax, while old man Rindo still sat in his rocking chair, his eyes never leaving the Wind River Kid.

Then Pete decided to cross the street toward the saloon, but he stopped in the middle for another look toward the barbershop. When he saw he was being watched, he bent, picked up a rock, then casually flung it through the butcher's plate glass window. The glass cascaded over the boardwalk, and the butcher ran out, cleaver in hand, shouting dire threats. Then he saw Pete standing there and the anger melted. Mumbling, he backed into his store again and closed the door.

For an instant longer, the Kid just watched; then when Pete looked at him and grinned, the Kid started down the walk toward the saloon. And as he walked he asked himself why he cared. There was more here to aggravate him than Pete's smug smile. He'd run into this before—the feeling a town had when one man had it by the throat and wouldn't let go. Then came the question: Why did he have to do anything about it? Other men saw the same thing and only shrugged and rode on their way, but he couldn't do that. Some basic chemistry in him revolted and he had another fight on his hands.

He stepped onto Burkhauser's porch and went inside. A crowd was waiting. Pete was leaning against the bar, a beer in his hand. His glance was full on the Kid when he stepped up. Pete said, "You gettin' thirsty again, Drunk?"

There was no change at all in the Kid's expression. "I could go for a beer." A waggling finger stirred the bartender to his taps. When the Kid had the beer, he added, "Pretty good throwing arm you got there."

"You saw that, huh? Always wanted to break a window."

"Well you sure did that one," the Kid said. He drank some of his beer. "Now let's go pay the butcher what it'll cost to replace it."

The Kid's voice had been so deceptively soft that Pete couldn't believe he had been serious. He stared for an instant, then tipped his head back to laugh.

His mouth came open, but the sound died in his throat, for the Kid planted a rock-hard fist against the point of his jaw. Pete spun back against the bar, arms outflung, and the Kid caught him as he began to sag.

"Give me a bucket of water," he said to the bartender.

"Nothing here but the slop bucket," the man said.

"Hell, that's good enough for him. Hand it over." The bartender hesitated, then hoisted a wooden bucket. The Kid heaved the suds into Pete's face, bringing him around at least to the point where he could partially support himself. Every man in that saloon held his breath and watched as though he were deathly afraid of missing something. Many of the men were timber workers on Cadmus Rindo's payroll, but the Kid counted on their minding their own business, and he was not mistaken.

Pete was clinging to the bar, nearly unconscious. The Kid said, "Now let's go pay for that window. I asked you nice but you were too thick-headed to hear. I won't tell you again."

He fisted a handful of Pete's collar and flung him toward the swinging doors. Pete banged against them just as another man was coming up on the other side, and the impact sent this man sprawling and cursing across the porch while Pete clung to the louvered panels for support. When the Kid came up behind him, Pete tried to whirl and make a fight of it, but another hard fist in his mouth propelled him backward across the porch, his boots scraping for purchase. His heels caught and he spilled down the short steps to the street below.

The Kid took his time, and when Pete got groggily to his feet, the Kid was behind him, pushing him with stiffened arms.

A throng of interested spectators followed the two men as they headed for the butcher's shop. The butcher came to his doorway, a heavy man with worry in his dark eyes. He wiped his hands nervously on his blood-stained apron. When his glance touched Pete, there was a hint of apology in it, as though he were sorry the man was being put to this trouble simply because he broke a window.

The Kid gave Pete a final push and stopped before the butcher. He asked, "How much is it going to cost to replace the window?"

The butcher looked at Pete, then at Pete's friends, who made up a bulk of the crowd. He grinned but it turned off sickly. "I guess it was all in fun, so I'll replace it myself."

"I asked you how much?" The Kid's voice was soft and easy and even the butcher understood that this man was making a concession—he didn't often repeat himself.

Pete raised his bloody head and looked squarely at the butcher. "Be careful now, Donegan. He caught me off guard. I'll use my gun the next time."

This was hint enough. The butcher spread his hands in an appeal for sympathy, understanding. "I don't want any trouble, fella. Let's just let this go."

"You had trouble when the rock came through the window," the Kid pointed out. "Are you going to make out a complaint?"

"Complaint? Christ no! I've got to do business with these men."

Pete's manner became suddenly assured, even arrogant. He looked around at the crowd and laughed. "Well, Tin-star, you seem to have sunk an ax into more'n you can chop."

"A law's been broken," the Wind River Kid said. "If it ain't on the books, then it ought to be. Now pay for the window."

"He said—"

"I don't give a damn what he said!" the Kid suddenly fisted Pete's shirt front, jerked him off balance, slapped him twice across the face, then gave him a backward shove. He crowded against Pete, his hands slapping pockets until he found the hardness of metal coins. Then the Kid ripped the cloth, scattering money on the floor. "Pick up ten dollars," the Kid said, "and pay the butcher."

There was a hesitation, then Ben Colfax, who stood on the boardwalk, spoke up in a voice that could be heard the length of the street. "That's the new law, boys—the Wind River Kid!"

To many, the name meant nothing, but to a few it spelled trouble. Pete, who had his pride and reputation to think of, looked quickly at the Kid, then bent down and retrieved ten dollars. He thrust the money at the butcher and started to move away.

The Kid took him by the arm and hauled him back. "Get something through your head, Davis. You thought you had a big thing here with the butcher too scared to complain, but the law was still broken, and if I have to, I'll do the complaining for those too timid to do for themselves. I don't give a damn if you break every window in this town, but if you do you'll pay for every one. Not because it's the law, but because it's justice. I know your reputation, but it don't scare me."

Pete waited an additional moment. "You through talking?" He stepped back, out of the Kid's reach. "You can bet I'll see you again soon. With a gun."

"You're smarter than that," the Kid said flatly.

For another moment Pete lingered, at least long enough to convince the onlookers that he wasn't exactly running. Then he wheeled and began to batter his way through the crowd. The Kid stood by the door until the butcher went inside and the crowd began to melt a little around the outer edges. As the boardwalk cleared he noticed a young woman standing there, pencil and notebook in her hand. She looked quite intense, giving him her undivided attention. Ben Colfax was still on the boardwalk and he edged over until he stood close to the young woman. He said, "You axed yourself quite a swath, Kid. He'll get you for that."

Though he had intended to turn away, the Kid pivoted on his heel and came over. He looked more carefully at the girl and she met his eyes frankly. She was younger than he had at first thought, not more than twenty. Her pale hair was wavy and unfettered, falling well past her shoulders.

The Wind River Kid realized that he was staring and pulled his eyes away. To Colfax, he said, "Got any tobacco?" When the sack was passed over, he gave his attention to the manufacture of a cigaret.

"I'd never have tackled Pete Davis," Colfax said gently. "You were lucky he didn't have his gun on. But you can bet he won't go without it from now on."

"Be something to look forward to, huh?"

This made Colfax pause. Then he said, "I learned something about you tonight, Kid. You don't hesitate to jump a man. Most men shy away from Pete's kind. Even when a fight's buildin', they wait 'til the last minute before swinging. But you're different. I'd say you're most eager to meet trouble more'n halfway." He tapped the Kid on the arm, drawing his attention around. "Take a look across the street. There's another man who don't duck trouble."

The Kid turned and, across the brief interval of the street, met the blunt, uncompromising stare of Cadmus Rindo. The man's glance had weight to it, and an open challenge, which was accepted in silence by the Kid.

Finally Rindo heaved himself erect, made a hand motion to a man down the street, then waited there, stony-faced, until his buggy was brought up. He mounted and lifted the reins, wheeling about to stop in front of the new sheriff.

Cadmus Rindo's voice was a soft bass rumble when he spoke. "There was a time when a drunk could be counted on to be nothing more than a drunk."

"Times must have changed," the Kid said easily.

"What are you doing in this part of the country?" Rindo asked. "This is timber. Guns and cattle are a thousand miles south."

"A man gets tired of one thing all the time," the Kid told him.

Rindo grunted and fingered his flowing mustache. "And it was my luck to pick you." He lifted the reins. "But I guess it's a mistake I can correct easy enough. Be gone from this town in the morning."

He drove off down the street and turned out of sight at the next corner.

2

CADMUS RINDO'S ULTIMATUM and departure left a wake of silence, but Ben Colfax broke it when he said, "The old man wasn't fooling."

"I didn't think he was," the Kid said.

"You ought to have let Pete Davis have his fun," Colfax said. "Rindo put him up to that to see what you'd do."

"And he found out," the Kid said. He looked carefully at Ben Colfax. "You don't see what I'm getting at, do you?"

"Can't say as I do," Colfax admitted. He looked at the young woman who stood slightly to the rear of the Kid. "You, Nan?"

"Yes," she said quietly. "I see it."

"Then somebody tell me," Colfax suggested.

"The law was broken," the Kid said. "It wouldn't matter to me whose man broke it, or whether he was fast with a gun."

Ben Colfax cuffed his hat forward over his eyes and scratched his head. "That sounds darn funny coming from you," he said. "There's an Arizona warrant out for you. In any other town you'd be just another Pete Davis."

"That warrant's not for breaking the law," the Kid said.

Shaking his head, Ben Colfax turned and shuffled down the street. The Kid followed him with his eyes for a moment, then turned toward the jail.

"May I walk with you?" the young woman asked.

"Any reason you should?"

"I think so," she said and waited. Finally he shrugged and they turned down the boardwalk together. At the jail he went in ahead of her and put a match to the lamps.

"Close the door," he said, and began building a small fire to ward off the night chill. A few sweeps with his booted foot pushed the shattered chairs into one corner and he drew up the remaining one. "Care to sit down?"

"Thank you," she said. She straightened the folds of her dress and held her pad and pencil in her lap.

He glanced at them, then said, "You a writer?"

She seemed startled. "Oh! I'm Nan Buckley. I run the newspaper."

He went to the stove to shake it down and adjust the damper, for a good blaze was crackling and the cast iron belly was shedding heat into the room. "You think I'm good for a story?"

"Perhaps," she said. "If I can understand why you're so angry."

He raised his eyes and looked quickly at her. The lamplight made her face seem more full, yet the blandness of artificial light could not detract from her radiant complexion. Her eyes were blue; he had been sure they would be. And her lips were full and firm, mirroring her changing moods. They were evenly compressed in this moment of seriousness, and the Kid felt an almost overwhelming desire to see them smile.

"Am I angry?" he asked evenly.

"Very angry," she said. "They could well call you the Angry Man, instead of the Wind River Kid."

"You've got quite an imagination," the Kid said.

Nan Buckley shook her head. "I think not. You were angry when you came to Rindo's Springs. Very angry at yourself, because you tried to drink Burkhauser's place dry the first night. And I understand that you were quarrelsome, and over nothing at all." She paused. "Tell me why you're so angry."

"So you can put it in the paper?" He gathered up the smashed furniture and chucked the pieces into the stove, then closed the door with his foot.

"We don't put everything in the paper," Nan said. "Don't you want help at all, Mr.—ah—"

"Kid," he said. "It's as good a name as any." After digging through the desk drawer, he found a cigar and spent a moment lighting it. Then he planted his elbows solidly on the pine desktop and regarded her through a veil of smoke. His eyes seemed without humor, yet there was a capacity for laughter in them. Finally he said, "You're looking at a man who's worn out. Used up." He smiled and fanned smoke aside. "You ever been tired? Not the kind you can cure with sleep, but bone tired. Tired of living from day to day. Tired of being with the same kind of people all the time." He shook his head. "You wouldn't know the kind I mean. The ones that buy everything, especially unpleasant things."

"There's unpleasantness here in Rindo's Springs," she said. "Are you angry because you ran into the very thing you wished to escape?"

He thought about this, then pursed his lips. "Partly, I suppose." He let the cigar rest idly between his thumb and forefinger. "You know about me? About the Wind River Kid?"

"You're a gunfighter," she said. "Some say you're bad and there's a reward out for you."

He chuckled at her simplified answer. "Do you know what you're talking about?"

"No," she said. "But I want to know. Why did you come here?"

"An accident," he said. "No one sent for me, if that's what you're thinking. I don't hire out anymore like Pete Davis."

"I wasn't thinking that. But this isn't your kind of country, or your kind of men." She raised a hand slightly, half apologetically. "I'm not trying to belittle you, but this is logging country. You won't understand us, and we don't understand you." Her fingers plucked idly at a loose thread on the front of her dress. "You're in a strange position, the victim of an old man's angry prank that somehow backfired in his face."

The Wind River Kid touched the tarnished badge. "Is this genuine?"

"Yes," Nan admitted. "The election was legal. Cadmus Rindo merely put on some additional men at his mill. Enough to sway the election his way."

"You make it sound like I ought to resign," the Kid said.

"I'm sure I didn't mean it that way. But I'd do

anything I could for this town. It's worth saving, even if it meant encouraging you to get Pete Davis into a gunfight and kill him."

"What's in this town that's worth saving?" the Kid asked flatly.

She smiled. "You're a man without a home; you wouldn't have said that otherwise." Then she paused, gaining a slight insight into this man. "Perhaps that's part of your anger. You need a home desperately and can't find one."

His first impulse was to deny this loudly, but he did not. Lifting his cigar, he found that it had gone out, and he rekindled it before speaking. "Being run out of towns gets tiresome. After a man gets a reputation, folks won't take a chance on him." He shrugged. "I had big ideas. Told myself that the only way to get out was to get way out, into a country that hadn't seen my kind and wouldn't recognize it if they did. That was a foolish hope. A man's a damn cow, carrying his brand wherever he goes."

"You're impatient," she said. "If you worked as hard at starting anew as you did to build your reputation—" She stopped speaking and stood up. "Well, it's none of my business what you do."

"It seems that you're making it your business," he said. "What kind of an ax are you grinding on my backside?"

A faint smile lifted her lips and a new sparkle came into her eyes. "I think you might be good for Rindo's Springs. I'd like to suggest something, if I may."

"Go ahead. You will anyway."

"I'd like to write about you in my paper." He frowned, but she ignored it. "Like a word portrait. After all, you're the new sheriff, and people have a right to know what kind of a man they have behind the law." She paused to study him. "There are going to be a lot of lies circulated about you. The best way to stop that is to tell the facts."

"What does this get me?" he asked.

"Nothing," she said, "but it might help Rindo's Springs."

He mulled this over in his mind for a time. "A list of my activities isn't going to read like an alderman's report. Most of it I'd as soon not talk about."

"Then you choose to hide the facts?" Nan asked. "Kid, you want people to accept you, but what do you intend to give them in return? A dubious past? A closed mouth when anyone asks you anything? Anger at them for not understanding something you won't allow them to understand?" She turned to the door. "I was mistaken; I can't help you at all."

"Wait," he said, coming around the desk. "There's an Arizona warrant out for me. If the word got back there—"

"I understand perfectly," she said smoothly. "Kid, one of these days you're going to find out that you can't hide. And once a thing is out in the open, it never is as bad as you imagined it." She picked up his hat and handed it to him. "This is your chance. Are you going to let the people of Rindo's Springs know what kind of a man they have in office or not?"

She waited while he thought about it, and he remembered the other towns he had found that he liked, and left as soon as someone identified him. Moving on could get to be a habit with a man, a bad habit. Then too, this woman had a persuasive manner. He smiled and said, "We'll try it your way, as long as it's painless."

She placed a hand flat against his chest. "Wait. I didn't say it was painless. I just said it wouldn't be as bad as you imagined."

His eyes traveled over her features carefully as though he might find a clue to her thoughts there. "What are you trying to do, reform me?"

"Do you need it?" Her smile lurked in her eyes. She opened the door and waited while he turned down the lamps. He locked the office and pocketed the key; then they turned down the street together. The town was quiet for all the business houses were closed, except for Burkhauser's place, which held a lively crowd. The air was moist and heavy and the acrid smoke from burning wood was almost overpowering. When they drew abreast of the saloon, the Kid became aware of Murray Burkhauser standing in the blackest shadows. The saloon keeper's cigar glowed darkly red, then faded.

"You look like you're in a hurry," Burkhauser said. "Got a minute?"

They stopped. Nan said, "I'll go on ahead and put

on a pot of coffee. You can't miss the place. Second side street."

"All right," the Kid said and watched her move away. When she was out of earshot, he turned to Burkhauser. "Make it fast."

"You've got time for one on the house, haven't you? No?" He shrugged. "Ben Colfax timed that pretty good when he identified you tonight." Burkhauser bent forward as if to make a closer examination. "I expected you to be an older man, if you can judge by the stories." His glance touched the Kid's gun. "Something a little fancier there. Pearl handles, maybe, or a twin on the other hip."

"If you've got something to say," the Kid said, "suppose you get to it."

"All right," Burkhauser said. He cast his cigar into the street where it died in a shower of sparks. "You plan to stay on in Rindo's Springs, or are you going to treat the election as the joke that it is and leave?"

"No joke to me."

Burkhauser frowned. "Kid, this is no place for you. What's in it for you?"

"There doesn't have to be anything in it," the Kid said. "A lot of times there isn't a thing you can put in your pocket."

"You and I differ there," Burkhauser stated. "I like to put things in my pockets. This town has sides, Kid. Better pick one and stick with it."

"Which side are you on?"

"I'm on my own," Burkhauser admitted. "You hate money?"

"No, I get along all right with it. But it's not a disease with me."

Burkhauser chuckled. "You're looking at a man who's afflicted. I'm not alone. The old man, Cadmus Rindo, owns everything around here. It's his town, his bank, and his money in it." He moved his hands in a small circle. "But there's always competition. Bess Jamison's outfit cramps the old man. He'd be happier if she was in some other business besides logging." Burkhauser stepped down and tapped the Wind River Kid on the chest. "This town is made up of the 'haves' and 'have nots'." He paused to smile slyly. "Then there are a few who try to pinch a little from each."

"And that's you," the Kid said.

"I do what I can," he said. "This saloon is mine, and I have a little money spread around where it'll do the most good. But Rindo's the key timber here. Get him and everything will fall down because he holds everything up. You're a smart man, Kid. You rode into this town with a yen to see new places. All right, you've seen them. Now ride on out and let Bess Jamison and Rindo fight. Let everything collapse of its own accord."

"While you pick up the pieces?"

Burkhauser shrugged. "No harm in that." He patted his inner coat pocket. "You could leave about four hundred dollars richer, Kid."

"That's a lot of money," the Kid said. "I'll think about it."

"But not too long," Burkhauser cautioned. "Come and see me in the morning before you leave."

Burkhauser turned then and walked into his saloon. The Kid stood there for a brief interval, then went on down the street. A resentment began to simmer, for few men are flattered when other men offer to buy them; yet this had happened before and he had always managed to pass it off. But somehow this was different, a little more insulting. Perhaps because he had mentally shed his old habits.

He found the newspaper office; gilt letters on the glass paneled door identified *The Rindo County Free Press*. The Kid knocked and almost immediately Nan Buckley came to the door. She did not light a lamp in the front of the shop, but led him through the gloom to the office and living quarters she kept in the back.

"Did Murray try to buy you off?"

"Yes," he said, surprised. "You know him pretty well."

"I know everyone in Rindo's Springs," she said. "All their secrets." She motioned toward a chair. "Want some coffee?"

"Thanks, yes." He sat down and looked around the room. There was a well-worn comfort about everything, the furniture, the flowered rug on the floor, and the curtains over the rear windows. Much of this woman's personality was revealed in the room.

He studied her as she poured the coffee—a graceful woman with a composed face, as though all her troubles were minor ones. After handing him the cup, she took a seat across from him; her hands rested in her lap and she reminded him of a schoolgirl waiting for her first beau.

"You think it's strange, being here in my parlor, don't you?"

"I thought that, yes." He smiled. "I even wonder why I'm here."

"You're a smart man," she said. "Smart enough to realize that this has to be the last town. The Wind River Kid has run himself to the ground."

That she could pin this down so precisely amazed him; then a good reason occurred to him. "You've seen this happen before?"

"Yes," she said. "My father. He ran. He just couldn't stop and admit that he left mistakes behind." She bent forward slightly and her tone became intense. "Please, do this for yourself, no one else. Stay in Rindo's Springs." Then she relaxed, her expression again composed. "This is not like most towns. Here one man owns everything. You saw how it was with Pete Davis and the broken window; all of them were afraid to object. Most people here are like that, afraid. But you're not. The Wind River Kid doesn't owe Cadmus Rindo a cent. The only obligation you have is to yourself. That's why I believe you will be good for this town." She looked squarely at him. "Is this warrant serious?"

"I was in the Chino Valley War," he said. "Is that serious enough?"

"I'm going to print that," Nan Buckley stated. "I'm going through the old files and dig up everything I can that's fact and print it."

"That'll call the dogs quick enough," the Kid said. "For the life of me, I can't decide what you're after." He paused to sip his coffee before it got cold. "A man like me tries to bury everything and you seem determined to dig it out. Besides, I don't know as I like this town. What's to stop me from leaving?"

"Nothing," she said, "unless you want to admit I'm right."

"About there being an end to how far a man can run?" He laughed and set his coffee cup aside. "Paint me any color you want, and I'm still the Wind River Kid. That's something that won't rub off until I'm dead."

He got up, picked his hat off a small table and walked

toward the door. She followed him through the dark shop. "I wanted you to stay so badly," she said. "You are leaving, aren't you?"

"Good night, Miss Buckley," he said and walked back to the jail.

He unlocked the door, then turned the key after he closed it. The lamp still shed a feeble glow into the room and he took it with him into the small ell-shaped sleeping room off the hall. There he settled on the bunk, his hands clasped behind his head.

Most men, he knew, were forty or fifty before they had any genuine regrets, but here he was, twenty-five and wishing he could wipe it all out, forget that anything wrong had ever happened. It's hell, he conceded, to be half an outlaw. He supposed that was what he deserved for tagging along on the fringes of the really tough ones. Still, he could never take a lawless life too seriously; some deep sense of decency had always pulled him clear before the mud got too high on his boots. There had been some shooting from time to time, but a man could hardly be condemned because he was fast with a gun. Besides, the law had called this self-defense, since the others had drawn first.

Still this left an evil tang in the Kid's mind. Every time he rode into a town, the sheriff would advise him to ride on. No one, it seemed, wanted trouble, yet it clung to him like beggar lice.

Joining that Chino Valley bunch had been a fool stunt; he realized it now. Still, the pay had been good, or so it had seemed at the time. A man couldn't look into the future, he decided. How was he to know that warrants would be sworn out against the losing faction? Just another shove to keep him moving, make him like Pete Davis, a real trouble-hunter.

Putting the past aside, he understood that he had no real business in Rindo's Springs. The badge he wore was, as Murray Burkhauser said, an old man's joke, or revenge against Ben Colfax. The Wind River Kid had no right to wear such an emblem of authority.

His talk with Nan Buckley disturbed him more than he cared to admit. She was right; he had gone about as far as a man could go when he had no distinct destination. Yet he could not stay. She was, above all things, an honest woman, and when her paper came out, the Wind

River Kid would be known to all; he believed her when she said she would dig up the facts. He was, he supposed, in the position of the man who had never objected to having his hair ruffled, but was angered when someone disturbed the toupee that concealed his baldness. All men accumulated some bad things during the run of their lives, and even voiced no objection when called bad. But no man liked to have his sins listed in print.

Rising from the bunk, the Kid walked into the main office, set the lamp on the desk, then placed the tarnished badge beside it. Looking at this piece of metal, he felt a genuine regret. Under different circumstances he might have worn it with pride.

The town was asleep when he stepped to the board-walk. Burkhauser's place was still alive, but then most saloons were nocturnal. He walked toward the stable near the end of the street, and in the coal darkness, searched out and saddled his horse. He supposed that Nan Buckley would miss him briefly, but since he really meant nothing to her, she would soon forget that the Wind River Kid had passed through.

He still had a few dollars, his gun, and enough shells. That should get him to San Fransisco. Lively town, or so he had heard. With this thought in mind, he turned out of town and took the west road.

3

BESS JAMISON'S PLACE was in the high timber nearly eight miles northwest of Rindo's Springs, and being a conservative woman who knew the value of a dollar, she chose not to rent a room at the hotel; instead she drove back to her home. The road was little more than a rutted logging trail, and as she wound up the dark slope, thunder rumbled and reverberated through the mountains. Lightning flashed whitely, revealing the timber in brief, ghostly light. When the rain began, she stopped and put up the top to her buggy, then drove on.

Her camp nestled in a short valley, and there were only a few lights glowing in the bunkhouse when she drove across the muddy yard. She was putting up her team in the barn when a man splashed across, stepping high to keep out of the deeper puddles. When he came to the barn door, Bess said, "Go back to bed, Henry. There won't be any work tomorrow."

She went on to the house, half-running in the rain. On the porch she paused to whip the water from her hair and face. Once inside, she stoked the fire in the back room, pulled the shades, then stripped completely and stood before the stove, toasting first on one side, then the other. When the heat had soaked into her, she padded in her bare feet, ladling grounds into the coffee pot. The flickering fire cast glowing lights on her bare flesh, building deep shadows around the smooth curves of her body.

While the coffee boiled she took a towel and dried her hair, then her legs, for the whipping rain had saturated her clothes to the waist. While she dried off, she heard a horseman approach the house. Walking into the other room, she took a robe from a closet and slipped into it as knuckles rattled the door.

"Come in," she called and tied the robe tightly. She held the loose edge to keep it from exposing her legs when she walked.

Ben Colfax stepped quickly inside, beating water from his hat. He took off his poncho and hung it dripping on the hall tree. "Oregon weather," he said sourly, his hands patting his pockets for a cigar. Then he tipped his head back and keened the air. "That coffee I smell?"

"Come into the kitchen," Bess said. She took cups and saucers from the pine cupboard and placed them on the table. "Late for you to be out, Ben. And it's a long ride from town."

"You left too early," he said, then told her about the Kid's run-in with Pete Davis. "Of course Pete'll kill him for it, but not until he's had his fun making him sweat."

Bess listened carefully, pouring the coffee while he talked. Then she sat down across from him, her forearms flat on the table. "It looks like Rindo can't control his own sheriff," she said.

"Well," Ben said, scratching his head, "being the Wind River Kid, he's a little hard to control. The way I hear it, a man could get shot for trying to lean on the Kid when he wasn't in the mood for it."

"Then if he's against Rindo, we need him," Bess said.

Ben Colfax sipped his coffee slowly, pausing now and then to pour some into the saucer to cool it. "Bess, he don't have to be against anything." He reached across the table and patted her hand. "I guess you made a mistake, invitin' Harry to rough him up. This kid can handle himself, fists or guns. Rindo found that out too, and he's ordered the Kid out of town."

"Do you think he'll go?" Bess Jamison asked.

Colfax' shoulders rose and fell. "A man of his reputation hates to be told to do anything. Likely he's made up his mind to stay. He could be a help to you, Bess, was you to play the cards right."

"Tell me how, Ben."

He pursed his lips and fingered his mustache. "Seein' as how I'm no longer the law and don't have to be neutral, I guess I could offer a little advice. No man can work and fight at the same time, Bess. If Rindo and the Kid got to squabblin', the old man might get so busy he'd forget to tend to business." Colfax leaned back in the chair, one arm hooked over the edge behind him. "Your daddy must have been pressin' Rindo pretty hard, to get killed sudden like he did. I still ain't satisfied with Rindo's story. Too pat. Too thin." He got up and went to the stove for a refill on his coffee. " 'Course, Cal Runyon's testimony turned the trick for Rindo. That never satisfied me, either. Cal's a company man, through and through. You know that."

"Yes," she said softly. "And he'll never change, Ben. I've given up hoping."

He came over and stood behind her chair, looking down at her. "Bess, you want to stay small? You want to go on payin' Rindo for the use of his mill? Go on shippin' over his railroad?" He leaned forward and put his hands on her shoulders. "There are merchants in town who want out. You're not alone, Bess. There's all the help you'll ever need, providin' the Kid don't side with the old man. And it looks like he's playing a lone hand, lightin' into Pete the way he did."

"We've got to be sure," she said. "Ben, when we buy chips into this, everything goes on the board, win or lose. I don't want to bet too early. Not until I know who's playing." She fell silent for a time, then when she spoke, her voice was hard. "Pa died because he wouldn't knuckle under to Rindo. I'll never forget that."

"That's the ticket," Colfax said. He came around to his own chair and sat down. "If you need any more money—"

She held up her hand and shook her head. "I'm already deep in your debt, Ben." Her smile was gentle. "I don't know what I'd have done without you. Lost everything, probably. I want to own this land, Ben. I want to own it free and clear, not work it for Cadmus Rindo."

"Well, it ain't as if he's takin' a tithing," Ben said. "He gave your pa permission to log it off."

"It's not the same," she said flatly. "Ben, I'm not the kind who can live by another man's grace. Every time I see Rindo I think that all he'd have to do to get rid of me would be to kick me off with a court order. As long as I'm living like this, I have that threat over me."

"The world's a tough place to live," Ben Colfax said, rising. "Somehow, a man never gets so high he's free of other men. Rindo was here first and put his mark on the country. Ain't hardly a man here that he didn't give something to."

"Give?" She laughed derisively. "Just loaned, Ben. Thats all."

"It gets kind of tiresome arguin'," he said and walked to the door. She followed him. The rain still fell heavily, rippling off the eaves, turning the yard into a bed of mud. Ben wiped his hand over the saddle, planing off most of the water before mounting. "If I see Cal Runyon," he said, "is there anything I should say?"

"Tell him I don't want him hurt," Bess said. "No, don't tell him that. We've said everything that's to be said."

"All right," he said. "Good night, Bess."

He turned his horse and rode back toward town. People, he had to admit, were generally a bunch of fools, not satisfied with what they had. Forty years before, give or take a season, Cadmus Rindo had struck the first ax blow to this country, and within ten years, had carved out a town, and then given it away, building by building. His strength and hard-headedness had built an industry, and a railroad, and incurred more enemies than any man had a right to have.

Of course, Colfax decided, the rest followed as sure as the sun. Men came and looked and wanted, and all the pleasantness vanished while a man's accomplishment became a stone weighing him down, making him struggle to keep what he had built. An old story to Ben Colfax, who had been seeing it or hearing it in one form or another all his life. And a goodly portion of that time had been spent trying to walk the neutral path down the center.

Colfax rode head down, letting the drizzling rain pour off his hat. He was quite surprised when his horse stopped, snorting and quivering. He stood in the stirrups, trying to penetrate the ink shadows. Then suddenly a horseman loomed close, but instead of stopping, spurred past and raced on.

Turning in the road, Colfax yelled and started after the rider, then quickly gave up the idea. He sat in silence, hearing only the prattle of rain which swallowed all other sounds. Finally he rounded his horse and went on toward Rindo's Springs.

The street was dark and empty when he arrived. He rode straight through to the lumber company offices at the far end of town. A guard stepped out of the shadows near the closed gate, his shotgun poised. Then he recognized Colfax and relaxed slightly.

"Cal Runyon around?" Colfax asked.

"There's still a light in his office," the guard said. "Go on in."

The gate was opened and Colfax eased his horse through. He was in Cadmus Rindo's empire now. Around him stood the sheds and machinery which ground out vast quantities of plank and stumping and railroad ties. A huge wagon park sat on the right with several, huge-wheeled logging arches arrayed behind that. Farther off was the mule corral, covering five and a half acres and containing over three hundred animals. The nerve center was the steam power plant, always alive, its fiery maw glowing day and night.

Ben followed the road to the central building, a heavy, log structure, two stories high. He dismounted before a roofed hitching rack and stepped onto the porch. A hallway led him to Cal Runyon's office, identified by gilt lettering on the pine-paneled door:

CALVIN D. RUNYON
GENERAL SUPERINTENDENT
CALIFORNIA-OREGON LUMBER AND MILLING COMPANY

Ben Colfax knocked and heard Runyon's grumbled invitation to enter. Runyon was at his desk, coatless, sleeve-garters holding the cuffs of his silk shirt free of the litter of papers. A fire glowed in the corner stove, crowding a stuffy heat into the room. Runyon looked up when Colfax stepped in, then said, "Surprised to see you, Ben. There's whiskey and cigars on the sideboard."

Colfax flung open a window, admitting a shot of cold air and the pungent flavors of a saturated forest. "What are you trying to do, kiln-dry yourself?" He made an adjustment of the stove, then helped himself to the whiskey and cigars. "Shouldn't do this," he said with a sigh. "Bothers my indigestion so late at night." He eased himself into a chair, shot glass in one hand, cigar between his teeth. "How's Pete's head? The Kid fetched him a couple of good ones."

"I had to cool him down. He wanted to take his gun

and shoot it out with the Kid," Cal Runyon admitted. He pushed his work aside and folded his hands. "Ben, just what did the old man get us into with this Wind River Kid?"

"Trouble more than likely," Colfax said. He puffed on his cigar and tried valiantly to come up with a smoke ring. Finally he gave it up. "What the hell got into the old man, Cal? He spooked?"

"Mad at you and Bess," Runyon said. "Ben, he didn't shoot her father. And when she accused him of it, he swore he'd slap her down hard."

Ben Colfax pawed at his mustache. "Cadmus did some rantin' and ravin', somethin' about kickin' me out of office, this being election time. But I really didn't take him serious, Cal."

"Neither did I," Runyon admitted. "This rocked me, Ben, because I've been relying on you to keep the peace. Cadmus is an old fire-eater, Ben; you know that. Sometimes I think he'll just up and take a rifle and settle his differences. He worries me."

"You ain't the only one," Colfax said. "Couldn't you have stopped him from pulling this fool election stunt?"

"I tried to talk to him, but he wouldn't listen." Runyon chuckled. "He knew I'd be against it, so he kept it from me until it was too late to do anything about it. When he gets his wind up, there's no stopping him." He leaned forward, his manner suddenly serious. "But this Wind River Kid scares me. He doesn't push worth a damn and the old man's liable to get shot for his trouble. We've got to do something about it, Ben."

"Do? Hell, do what?"

"Get the Kid out of town, or get Bess Jamison to cool down for awhile."

"Can't see her doing that," Ben Colfax confessed. "Bess has some real hard feelings toward Cadmus. You blame her?"

"No, no," Cal Runyon said. He got up and closed the window, then stood there watching the rain smear the glass. "Ben, I'm going to be on the square with you. I can do it now because you're on the outside." He turned about to face Ben Colfax. "If anything ever pushed Cadmus Rindo into the fight, he'd fold and this town would fold with him. Rindo gave away a lot, but he took a lot back." Runyon opened a filing cabinet and tossed a thick sheaf of papers on the desk. "These are notes, Ben. All signed by Cadmus Rindo. There aren't a dozen men in this town who don't hold Rindo's note." He waved his hands to include the mill and all the buildings. "Where do you think the money came from to build all this, Ben? Small investors, that's where. Ben, if the old man ever showed the least sign of being shaky, the people who hold his notes would sell out at twenty-five cents on the dollar. If that happened, Rindo's Springs would be dead."

Ben Colfax clung to a thoughtful silence, his eyes veiled and secretive. "Can't he pay 'em off, Cal?"

"In ten years, or five if he was pressed. Ben, the country needs timber. We've grown so fast we haven't caught up yet. Nothing's laid by for that rainy day."

"Rainin' now," Colfax said softly.

Cal Runyon understood what he meant and his face settled into troubled lines. "Ben, I think I know you. You've lived a lifetime being honest and fair to everyone. Will you try and convince Bess that she'll only destroy herself if she tries to stir up trouble now?"

"I'll do what I can," Colfax promised and stood up. Cal Runyon started around his desk but Colfax waved him back. "Know my own way out, Cal. Thanks for the cigar and drink, although I'll likely toss all night."

Walking slowly down the hall, Ben Colfax gnawed the cigar. On the porch he paused to contemplate the rain and the dreary night. His lips drew into a thoughtful pucker; his eyebrows twisted into crooked thickets. "That close, eh?" he said very softly. "Well I'll be doggoned!"

Then he stepped out into the downpour and swung into a soggy saddle.

4

SINCE THAT agony-filled day eight years before when Will Beau-Haven slipped and found his hips hopelessly crushed beneath a logging arch's iron-bound wheel, he had been making it his habit to sit on the upper gallery of his hotel and observe the town of Rindo's Springs. A man with considerable time on his hands soon learns to spend it carefully, and Will Beau-Haven had always considered himself a thrifty man.

Promptly at eight each morning his wife, Grace, pushed him onto the porch in a special, wheeled chair, placed a robe over his withered legs, then left him to watch the town. By his side was a tin pail on which a long cord was attached, and at nine-thirty Will Beau-Haven hailed a ragged-haired boy, lowered the bucket, then watched the lad trot across the street to Burk-hauser's saloon. A moment later the boy returned, the bucket now full of beer. The rope was retied and the bucket hoisted aloft; a coin was dropped to the boy's eager hand.

In this quiet way Will Beau-Haven spent his days, and shortly after one o'clock, when *The Rindo County Free Press* reached the streets, Beau-Haven again lowered his line to receive his paper. Not that it would contain anything he didn't already know, but he was a man who enjoyed having his observations substantiated by the printed word.

Unfolding the paper, Will Beau-Haven read the banner line, then let his eyes jump to the center column that ran the length of the page, printed in type so bold as to prohibit anyone missing it. He read the account twice, then called his wife to the porch. She was a woman in her early thirties, quite pretty in a quiet way. Her dress was brown and severely devoid of trim. She wore her hair simply parted, then coiled into an unimaginative bun on the back of her head. Seemingly she took pains to make herself as unattractive as possible; still, a native beauty refused to be hidden—she could not disguise the appealing bow of her lips, the deep color of her eyes, or the exciting swell of breast and hip.

While she stood there, Will Beau-Haven read aloud the enumerated deeds of the Wind River Kid, and at the completion of this third reading, he still could not decide whether the Kid was saint or sinner. By clinging to the proven record, Nan Buckley had written with startling objectivity, presenting a man no different from most, save that all his dirty linen had been hauled out at one time and aired publicly.

"I think it's a disgrace," Grace Beau-Haven said flatly, "having a man like that in public office. Why, it says right there he's wanted in Arizona."

Then, like most men presented with a flat statement, Will Beau-Haven began to argue with his wife, taking the Kid's side. Standing half-hidden in her own doorway, Nan Buckley observed this, and the duplication of it up and down the main street, wherever men gathered.

Gabe, her typesetter, eased up and said, "Started something, Nan." He waved his hand at the street. "They'll argue this for a month."

"You have to believe in something to argue," she said softly.

The old man looked at her, then his face wrinkled into a grin. "I see it now. Smart. Very smart. The Kid didn't have a friend in town, so you organized them for him."

"Why not?" she asked. "Gabe, I've never seen people agree on everything. But a man has to declare himself before others will take a side, for or against." She reached behind her and picked up a paper. "The Wind River Kid has declared himself. Look at this last paragraph:

'This is the duly elected peace officer of Rindo County, a man no different from other men, no more misunderstood, no more maligned. How are we to judge this man? By the record, or by his conduct in Rindo's Springs? Like all of us, the Wind River Kid must endure the day-by-day judgments of his fellow men. Are you, as a citizen of Rindo's Springs, prepared to judge?'"

"Well," Gabe admitted, "if it was calculated to start argument, you sure done what you set out to do."

"I think I'll take a walk through town," Nan said. A glance at the curdled sky told her that the rain had passed, so she took a shawl instead of a parasol. The street was a mire of mud and a heavy-laden lumber wagon drove through, the wheels gouging deep grooves in the earth. Nan walked slowly along the main street, her ears picking up bits of argument as she passed chattering groups. At a side street she turned, walking along until the street dwindled to a buggy lane, at whose end sat the most imposing home in Rindo's Springs. It had been a year in the building; most of the gable work and gingerbread was hand-carved and shipped overland from San Francisco after a stormy passage through the Roarin' Forties. The house was surrounded by an acre of lawn, and a bronze deer browsed under the stately trees.

Lifting a large metal knocker in the center of the door, Nan rapped a few times and heard the echo boom through the house. A moment later a colored servant came to the door.

"I'd like to speak to Mr. Rindo, please," Nan said.

"He's in the drawin' room, Ma'am."

She knew the way, and when she stepped into the large room, she closed the door. Pale pine panels ran to the ceiling; beneath her feet was a thick, maroon rug. A chandelier, reported to have cost several thousand dollars, hung on a brass chain from the beamed ceiling. The air was saturated with the odor of Rindo's cigars and wood smoke, the residue of a badly drawing fireplace. Cadmus Rindo sat in his deep chair facing a broad window which fronted on the lane leading in. He spoke without turning his head. "Saw you come in." He gestured to the paper flung haphazardly on the floor. "Read that too. What are you trying to start?"

Nan came around and sat down so that she could see his face. "I just wanted the citizens to know what kind of a man you elected."

He looked at her quickly, his eyes tight-pinched and knife-sharp. "So you think he's my man, is that it?"

"You put him in office."

He shook his head, a loose lock of hair bobbing.
His flesh was dark and dryly wrinkled, like old leather,
yet his eyes were as clear as a still pond, and his hands
were without tremor. "I picked a dark horse as a means
of getting to Ben," he said. "But that same horse turned
right around and kicked me when I tried to mount him."

"That was your mistake," Nan said flatly. "Dealing
off the bottom is an expert's business; it's not your
game."

He glared at her. "You going to lecture me?" His anger
was a sham and they both knew it. Suddenly he smiled
and pawed his mouth out of shape. "Nan, you're always
tryin' to beard the lion in his own den."

"I like you," she said simply. "Even when you're as
fretful as a back-sore mule." She fell silent momentarily,
then added, "You've never liked Ben Colfax, have you?"

"No, I haven't," Rindo admitted. "I've always distrusted
a man who was apparently so blamed good all the time."
He moved his hands restlessly. "Damn it, Nan, I only
wanted him out of office, and for no other reason than I
just don't trust him. Didn't give a damn who I elected
in his place either. When I saw the Wind River Kid gettin' drunk in Burkhauser's place, I got the idea of running him against Ben. Be a big insult to Ben." He blew
out a long breath. "Of course the Jamison girl's convinced
that it's all an attempt to buy the law for my side."

"What else could she think?" Nan asked. "Mr. Rindo,
you sicked Pete Davis into breaking that window to
prove you had the law bought and paid for. Only the
Kid fooled you, didn't he?"

"Yeah, he did! I got a right to test a man, haven't
I?" He chuckled. "I sure found out in a hurry too." He
looked steadily at Nan Buckley. "But I did it for my own
pure pleasure." He waved his hands. "The Jamison girl
believes that I want to own the law. Ben Colfax has
always believed that. Consarn it, Nan, it's just that I don't
trust the man!"

Nan Buckley stood up. "I have things to do. Perhaps
I'll stop by later."

"Do that," Cadmus Rindo said. He pulled a bell cord
near his chair and a moment later the servant appeared.
"Show Miss Buckley out, Jules."

Walking slowly down the path, Nan considered Rindo's
conversation. Colfax was not the only man in Rindo's

Springs the old man didn't cotten to; Burkhauser was high on the list. In times past, Cadmus Rindo had never imposed his will on anyone. Nan found it difficult to believe that he had changed his policy. Even George Jamison, Bess's father, had failed to rile the old man past the argument stage.

Nan stopped at the sheriff's office and found it empty. When she saw the badge on the desk, she drew her conclusion and hurried back to the newspaper office. She found a small boy playing on the boardwalk, and after giving him a dime, dispatched him to the stable with orders to have her buggy hitched.

Going to her room, she shut the door and quickly shed dress and petticoats. She slipped into a pair of faded man's jeans and a shirt, then rolled a heavy coat inside her slicker.

From the cupboard she took cold meat, a loaf of bread, and two cans of peaches. Placing these in a flour sack, she added a can opener, knife and spoon. On her way to the stable, she stopped again at the sheriff's office only long enough to pick up the tarnished badge. Her buggy was waiting and as she mounted, the hostler said, "Cloudin' up, Miss Buckley."

"The roof doesn't leak," she said and whipped out of town, taking the west road. A man on the move, she decided, would not retrace his steps, and the Wind River Kid had drifted in from the east. He'd go west, probably to Pendleton, then turn south, toward California.

For better than an hour she drove at a steady pace, and later, when she came to the road leading to Bess Jamison's place, she turned off. The rain was still running off from the highland, and in some places it roared and ripped alongside the road, turning the ditches into unruly torrents.

Rain has always been the nemesis of logging, and Bess' crew was working close to camp, making repairs on wagons and logging arches, getting ready for the drying wind and time when falling would commence.

As Nan wheeled up to the porch and dismounted, Bess came to the doorway, nodded indifferently. No great friendship existed between them, yet there had never been an open animosity either. Bess held the door open so Nan could step into the house. She wiped her feet on some burlap sacks.

"You don't get out this way often," Bess Jamison said. Moving into the drab parlor, she motioned Nan into a hard-backed chair. The room was quite plain; her father had had next to nothing when he first came to this country and time hadn't added substantially to his possessions.

"I was wondering," Nan said, "if you had seen the new sheriff?"

"Only that once in jail," Bess admitted. She bit her lip. "I'm afraid I gave him a rather poor impression. But I was angry. That's why I let Harry try to—well, teach him a thing or two."

"But I understand Harry got the lesson," Nan said. She folded her hands. "That hardly seems important now, Bess. I just talked to Cadmus Rindo and I don't think he tried to buy the law just to get at you."

"He's lying," Bess said flatly. She wiped a hand across her face, then brushed stray strands of hair from her forehead. "I accused him of killing my father, and Cadmus Rindo has never taken a thing like that from anyone. Why does he keep a gunman on the payroll if it isn't to threaten me?"

"Believe me, Bess, he only intended to hurt Ben."

She blew a gusty breath of disbelief through her nose. "Now that's downright ridiculous. Ben's a good man; everyone likes him." She looked steadily at Nan Buckley. "I suppose you talked to Cal Runyon too."

This was supposed to hurt, and it must have found a mark for Nan's chin lifted slightly and her eyes turned brightly brittle. "Cal and I haven't spoken for six months," she said. "I hope you believe that because it's true."

"You're still in love with him," Bess accused.

"Of course," Nan said softly. "But Cal made his choice; I've stepped aside. What are you going to do about him, Bess?"

"That's my business," she said cooly.

"Not exactly. I stepped aside for you, Bess, but I didn't do it so you could throw him over any time you felt like it." She stood up and moved to the door. "Please understand me. You either make up your mind about Cal Runyon, or I'll move in on your territory."

"If he'll take you it'll be second best as far as he's concerned," Bess stated. "He loves me."

"Then you're a bigger fool than I thought," Nan said and went to her buggy. She did not bother with a good-bye. Wheeling out of the yard, she drove the treacherous logging trail to the main road, then turned west again.

The sky was muddy and dreary, and a short time later rain began to fall again. She put her poncho around her legs and listened to the rain rattle on the buggy top. Talking about Cal Runyon had left her with an empty feeling, one she had thought herself rid of months ago.

The road wound through heavily timbered land, and at times clung to the sloped sides of mountains that were veiled at the tops. Once she had to pull to the side of the road to let the Dallas Stage wheel by, high wheels flinging mud, side curtains flapping. The passengers waved and shouted greetings, then passed from her view, leaving her only the drum of the rain for company.

By late afternoon she sighted the half-abandoned town of Sinking Wells. Started ten years before by three Eastern promoters, Sinking Wells was going to be the hub of a vast railroad system linking Oregon with points east, or so the promoters claimed. Within five months, Sinking Wells boasted ten thousand citizens, but the railroad died in the dream stage, and since the citizens had come seeking quick money, they had moved on, leaving four through streets and a score of rotting buildings. Recalling the unsuccessful attempts made to revitalize Sinking Wells, Nan Buckley was convinced that once a town died, it could never be brought back. Her one concern was that Rindo's Springs would suffer a similar fate, and she meant to prevent that if she could.

Driving past the sagging hotel, Nan Buckley pulled in near the one section of hitching rack still standing. The only place of business was the hotel, and this was slowly going to pieces. The porch sagged dangerously and dribbled water through the roof in several spots. Stepping inside, Nan saw that part of the old saloon's bar had been set up in the lobby, and along one wall, bins from the mercantile had been set up to make Sinking Wells a one-man operation.

The owner and sole citizen was an ancient man whose only title to all this was the fact that he had remained behind while the others had left. He looked around when Nan came in, stomping mud from her boots.

"You want a room?" he asked.

She shook her head.

"A drink then?"

Again she shook her head.

The old man mauled his whiskers. "Can't make a nickel that way." He snapped his fingers. "You're looking for somebody? A man, twenty-five or so, brown eyes and hair, and wearin' a canvas brush jacket." His eyes pulled into fleshy slits. "Upstairs. He bought a bottle and that's the last I've seen of him."

"Thanks," Nan said and went up the creaky steps. On the upper landing she paused, looking at the double row of closed doors. Then she walked along, bending down to study each knob. When she found one with disturbed dust, she knocked. For a moment she thought that she had made a poor guess, then the Kid said, "Hell, it's open if you want in."

Taking a deep breath, Nan opened the door and stepped inside. The Kid was stretched out on the rickety bed. Water dribbled down one wall, making a puddle on the floor. Then he swung his feet to the floor and sat up.

"Hello," Nan said.

"What do you want, Miss Buckley?"

"You didn't stay to read my story," she said.

"I already know the story," he said.

Nan walked deeper into the room, picked up the bottle of whiskey she saw sitting on the dilapidated dresser and saw that it had never been uncorked. She put it back.

"Why haven't you opened it?"

"I could have been waiting for company," he said. He sagged back on the bed and placed his hands behind his head. "Why don't you go back to Rindo's Springs where you belong?"

There were no chairs in the room so the Kid moved his feet aside, making a place on the edge of the bed where she could sit. He watched her with unwavering attention, then said, "If people knew you followed me here, they might draw some wrong conclusions."

"That doesn't worry me," Nan said. "Where are you going from here? California?"

"I hear it's nice there. Lots of sunshine."

"Perhaps it's best that you do go," she said softly. "You've gotten into the habit of running and you've tried to drink yourself into forgetfulness. The next thing will be to change your name, won't it?"

This angered him. "Why the hell would I do that?"

"Another form of denial," she said. "If the running can't make you forget who you are, and the whiskey can't, then changing your name might."

"Thanks for the lecture," the Kid said. "If you're through, will you get out so I can enjoy my bottle?"

"Oh, I intend to," Nan said easily. "But I don't think you'll enjoy it any more than you enjoyed it in Rindo's Springs." She clasped her hands together and smiled faintly. "You see, I believe in the Wind River Kid. That may sound strange, having known you for such a short time, but it's still true. Like it or not, you were elected sheriff of Rindo County. Please come back. We need you."

He sat up, facing her. "I can make you leave," he said. "Do you want me to?"

"I'm not leaving yet," she said. "And I think I know—"

He cut her off when he put his arms around her and pressed his lips on hers. There was gentleness in him, but he put it aside for a purposeful roughness, and she submitted to his embrace not stiffly but with a relaxed deadness. Slowly he released her and stood up, his back to her.

"Now I feel ashamed of myself," he said. "You want to hate me, go ahead."

"I can understand you," Nan said. "Much better than you think I do." She stood up and touched him lightly on the arm. "Sooner or later every man on this earth has to declare himself as standing for something. You think that what people think about you can hurt you? No, it really can't. But what you think about yourself can hurt you."

Perhaps because he stood so unmoving she felt that what she said fell on deaf ears; her manner suddenly changed and she became very much in a hurry. Moving to the door, she said, "Well, I've had my say. Goodbye."

He did not move until she started down the hall, then he bolted after her. "Nan!" Slowly she turned around and looked at him. "Nan, I've got a tired horse. Can you give me a lift back?"

Her smile seemed to brighten the drab hall. She came

up to him and took his arm. "Of course. Let's go."

"Wait," he said and went back inside the room. When he came out he was carrying the whiskey bottle. Downstairs he paused long enough to give it back to the old man. "Just hand it to the next dry man who comes through."

"What happens if I get dry myself?" the old man asked.

The Kid grinned. "Don't you know what to do?"

They stepped out into the smothering rain. The Kid got his horse and tied it behind the buggy, then handed Nan up to the seat. He drove into the first gloom of night while Nan tucked the poncho around their legs.

For awhile they rode along without talk, then the Kid said, "You said you understood how it was with me because of your father. You want to tell me?"

"I guess," she said. "He was a newspaper man in San Francisco, but he made a serious mistake: he backed the wrong political candidate. There was an investigation, and a scandal, and when the smoke cleared, Dad was as black as the blackest. So he packed everything that was left and we started moving. Running is the word. As soon as he would be recognized, he'd move again. Until we came to Rindo's Springs. There he stayed and faced the world."

"How was it?" he asked softly.

"Not easy, but he lived like he wanted to live, and he ran an honest newspaper. Last year he died of consumption."

"Too bad," he murmured. "But a lot of him rubbed off on you, Nan."

"I like to think that it did," she said. "Rindo's Springs needed my father, and he needed Rindo's Springs."

"And you think I'm like that?"

She smiled. "I know you are."

A distant streak of lightning cut a ragged path to the earth and thunder boomed. Rain rattled on the tight buggy top and the horses hoofs threw mud against the bangboard. The Kid looked at her a moment, then said, "Nan, I'd like you to know something. I'm not sorry I kissed you."

"I know," she said.

"And you?"

She smiled and shook her head. "Don't pin me down."

He was wise enough to know that he could go no

farther, so he changed the subject. "Nan, do you think I can be a good sheriff?"

"You know the answer to that," she said. "I talked to Cadmus Rindo and he respects you."

This struck him as funny. "He ordered me out of town!"

"That should convince you that I'm right," Nan said. "But knowing Cadmus as I do, I'd say that he'll have Pete try to get rid of you." She took his arm and held it until he looked at her. "I want you to know that I'm for the old man. I believe he has a right to what's his. If anything happened to Cadmus Rindo, the town would die. And dead towns never come back, Kid. Name me one that has."

He paused for a moment, his brows furrowed. "I guess I can't."

"You see? Cadmus Rindo gave nearly everyone there a start, and many of them were men already convinced that they would never get a second chance. In return, they've invested in Rindo's lumber mill. He alone holds everything together. That's why nothing must happen to him, Kid. That's why Rindo's Springs needs you."

"You want a miracle?" he asked.

"If it takes one, yes. Kid, will you talk with the old man?"

"Before or after he runs me out of town?"

This was a question she didn't know how to answer, and he didn't press her for one. They settled back, letting the soggy miles disappear beneath the iron-shod wheels.

5

NAN BUCKLEY stopped at the jail; the Kid had said he preferred the solitary cot to a room at the hotel. Then she drove down the street to the newspaper office while the Kid watched. When he entered the office it was dark and he stumbled about, trying to find the lamp. With it lit, he went into the small room and tugged off his boots. Settling back, he thought about Nan Buckley and that brief interval of time when he had held her in his arms.

The thought contained an element of excitement for him; no other woman had given him that feeling. And he had known a few women, and now that he put his mind to it, could recall several with varying degrees of clarity. There was that Mexican girl in Laredo; he could not remember her name, but he remembered Laredo and Joel McKitrich; the town had been theirs while the job lasted. But a gun job never did last long. In Tucson there had been Helen; he supposed he could have married her if her father hadn't been a judge. What he remembered best about Cheyenne was Jane, but a man can't fight nesters with one hand and marry into them with the other.

A knock at the outer door broke off his reverie and he padded to the front of the building in his stocking feet. He opened the door and was surprised to find Cadmus Rindo standing there, slicker spilling water.

"Kind of late, I know," Rindo said, "but one of my boys saw you come back to town."

"Come on in," the Kid said, closing the door. Rindo shrugged out of his raincoat and took off his hat. He laid these on the desk, then said, "If Nan had minded her own business, you'd be a long way from here by now, and the only one who would have been disappointed is Pete Davis."

"More than likely," the Kid admitted. "That shouldn't make you cry."

"Now, no need to get a chip on your shoulder," Rindo said. "I've been doing some serious thinking since we last met." He glanced briefly at the young man. "Seems that I'll have to get along with you, Kid. At least it'll be better than fighting Ben Colfax."

"Just what's wrong with Ben?" the Kid asked. "Besides sticky fingers when it comes to money."

"Ha!" Rindo shouted, slapping the desk. "So you see it too. Good. Makes things easier for me." He perched on the corner of the desk. "I'll come right to the point. What started out of spite toward Ben Colfax has turned into something else now. I never trusted Ben because he always acted too damn good. No man's really that way. Got to be something wrong or he ain't human." He squinted his eyes. "Expect you're trying to make sense of what I'm saying. Well, it's simple enough. I don't want trouble with you, Kid."

"If you're offering to buy—"

"Oh, for Christ's sake!" Rindo exploded, looking disgusted. "Kid, you think I got horns or something?" He chuckled. "Nan reminded me that I threatened you. Well, I was mad. Any man would be mad when his plans kick back at him." He rubbed his gnarled hands together, groping for words. "I got a sick town here, Kid. Too many people wanting what don't belong to 'em in the first place. I know, I'm an old hog who saw this first and wanted it for himself. That was a young man's natural greed, but I'm not young anymore. Be eighty next month, which is more time than a man's generally allowed on this earth. Gettin' tired too. For some years now I've been wantin' to give away what I worked so hard to get, but it's a hard task to feed a hungry dog when he keeps snappin' at your hand."

"This Jamison woman—you'd give her the land she wants?"

Cadmus Rindo paused with the packing of his pipe and nodded.

The Wind River Kid said, "If you do, she'll take it for

a sign of weakness. That'll spread and every merchant in town will feel shaky because they have their money tied up in your outfit."

Rindo scratched a match across his boot sole. "You see it," he said. "No need to explain it to you. Hell of a mess when a man can't get rid of what he has."

"The Jamison woman thinks you killed her father," the Kid said.

"I didn't shoot him," Rindo said flatly. "Hell, I wanted to bad enough at times, but when I kill a man it's in broad daylight where people can see it." His pipe gurgled when he drew on it and he paused to clean out the stem with a straw he kept pocketed for that purpose. "Takes money to set up a big mill, Kid." He tapped himself on the chest. "I have the mill, so Bess Jamison hauls the logs to me for milling. The trouble comes when the sawed stuff is loaded on her wagons. She scales the logs, and then scales the lumber when it's loaded, then claims that I'm shorting her. Hell, if Pete wasn't around to scare 'em a little I'd have had serious trouble before this."

"Tell her to mill the stuff somewhere else," the Kid suggested.

The old man snorted. "Can't do that, son. Hell, she'd be shooting at me inside of a week. Besides, I'm not after her." He shook his head. "Can't convince her or Ben Colfax of that though. The way they tell it, I just go around crackin' the whip. Anyway, old man Jamison kept accusing me of cheating him by holding back some of his sawed lumber out of every load. I just took it at first, then when he kept it up, I sent Cal Runyon with a message, saying that I wanted to have a talk and settle the squabble. The whole damn town knew there was bad blood between us, so when Jamison got shot on the company steps, I was the prime suspect."

"But you didn't shoot him, you say."

"Hell no, I didn't! Heard the shot, grabbed my own pistol and ran out. A crowd started to gather and then Ben Colfax came up. He grabbed the gun out of my hand and held me for the coroner's inquest. They turned me loose." He studied the grain in his pipe for a moment. "Still, there's a lot of folks who think I did it."

"Ben Colfax one of them?"

"Yep," Rindo said. "That's why I wanted Ben out of

office. He was only interested in gettin' me, not helping the town."

"Well, you sure didn't help it by shoving me down the voters' throats," the Kid said. "Mr. Rindo, you've got to stop doing what's right for people. Let them do for themselves."

"Hell, they'll go under!"

"That's every man's privilege," the Kid said. "You elected me sheriff and I'll keep the peace if I can. But if you pull another stunt like sicking your gunman on me, I'll throw you in jail along with him."

Cadmus Rindo stared at him. "You mean that," he said.

"Try me and see," the Kid invited. "I know Pete feels he's got to even the score, but tell him not to try it with a gun."

Rindo grunted and got up, putting on his slicker and hat. "We'll get along, you and me." He stepped out into the slanting rain and got into his waiting buggy. The Kid stood in the doorway as the old man drove down the dark street. When Rindo turned the far corner, the Kid moved to close the door, then paused when he saw a man leave the shadows across the street. The man hurried across the street and only when he reached the near boardwalk did the Kid recognize Ben Colfax.

"Been makin' a deal?" Colfax asked. Water ran in streaks down his face and his heavy coat was soaked through. He hunched his shoulders, trying to ward off the chill night wind.

"Don't say too much," the Kid suggested. "It's late, Ben."

"Late?" Colfax laughed. "Rindo's bought himself a real tough boy this time, ain't he? Well, I'm pretty good myself; age ain't slowed me down. Just remember that when you get set to crowd me."

"No one's crowding you," the Kid said. He began to close the door, but Ben Colfax flung out his arm.

"Hold on! I'm not through talkin'."

"Tell me about it in the morning," the Kid said and shoved hard on the door. Ben thrust his shoulder forward, again blocking it, only this time, the Kid suddenly released the door, allowing Colfax to plunge into the room.

The ex-sheriff would have sprawled on his face had not

the Kid's fist whistled up and smashed him in the mouth.
Colfax reeled backward, catching his bootheel on the
boardwalk edge. Arms flailing, Ben Colfax landed flat in
the muddy street. The Kid flung the door wide and
looked at the man, waiting patiently while Colfax sat up,
pawing at the mud that clung to him.

"Believe me now?" the Kid asked. He shut the door
then and slid the bolt. An instant later, Ben Colfax ham-
mered on the panel, then gave up and went away. The
Wind River Kid returned to his cot and stretched out
again, this time snuffing out the lamp.

He listened for a time to the rain drumming on the
roof, then sleep tuned the sound out of his consciousness.
How long he slept was a question in his mind when a
heavy pounding on the door brought him bolt upright.
Without lighting the lamps or picking up his gun, he
went to the front office, still half asleep.

When the Kid tried to slide the ash bolt, he found it
jammed and for a moment could not understand this.
Then he realized that someone was putting so much
pressure on the outside that it was wedging the wood
tight. "All right! All right!" he said. "Get your shoulder
off it!"

The weight slacked off and he slid the bar back. Before he could back away, the door crashed in, and the
shadowed jumble of three men tried to crowd through
at the same time. Had they not been in such a hurry,
they would have succeeded in taking him then and there,
but he gained a second's grace, and struck before they
did. His knuckles caught one man on the bridge of the
nose, making him bleat out in pain.

Then all three of the men were in the room; one tried
to tackle the Kid around the waist but before the groping
arms could restrict him completely, he laced his fingers
together and brought both arms down across the back
of the man's neck. With a sigh, the man wilted, but the
Kid got his feet tangled and fell.

The third man jumped him and in the darkness nearly
landed astraddle, but the Kid rolled, taking the man's
knees full on the thigh. He sucked in his breath, fearing
that his leg was broken; at first it went numb, then
started to throb so badly that he was weak with pain.
The man who had taken the punch in the nose was up
again and swinging his boots. One lucky kick caught the

Kid on the shoulder and flung him against the wall. In the darkness identification was impossible; the booted man kicked the wrong man and drew a snarled curse from his partner. They began to grope for the Kid; the downed man stirred and sat up, then got to his feet. He started to say something, then stopped as though he feared the sound of his voice might lead to an identification later.

The Kid held himself absolutely still, blending with the shadows along the base of the wall. His thigh and shoulder sent constant shooting pains through his body, making him strangely light-headed. One of the men stepped close to him and the Kid suddenly reached out and grabbed both ankles, jerking the man backwards, flat on the plank floor. The breath left him in a rush, and the Kid yelled, "I got him!"

Immediately the other two jumped their partner, lacing him with kicks and savage blows. He began to yell and the Kid eased along the wall, moving toward his back room and the .44 hanging there. The man's yelling finally got through to his partners and they stopped pummeling him, realizing that they had the wrong man.

Suddenly, springing to his feet, the Kid made his room in one-legged hops. In a group they started after him, but Pete Davis' voice yelled, "He's after his gun!"

They all made the front door together and fought to get through. The Kid had his .44 now and was swinging around with it. Leveling it, he fanned it empty, realizing as he shot that he was seconds tardy. Several of his bullets brought down glass across the street, and when the booming echoes died, he could hear the fading pound of boots on the boardwalk.

Tossing his gun on the cot, he limped painfully over to the chest of drawers and put a match to the lamp. Then he sat down on his bed and patiently tried to massage life back into his leg. He was sure no bones were broken, but he had suffered a terrible bruise. Only by a distinct effort of will did he bring himself to stand on it. He walked into the outer office and looked around for anything that might have been dropped in the scuffle. Spots of blood dotted the floor, attesting to the effectiveness of the first blow struck; but he found nothing else, not even a torn-off button.

The rapid burst of gunfire had jarred a few citizens

out of a sound sleep; lights were coming on, while across the street, the merchant whose window had been shattered came down in his nightshirt to make a cursing examination. The Kid lit the two lamps in the office, then limped to the door for a look up and down the rain-pestered street. Other than the curious, there was no one resembling Pete and his two tough friends.

He had a choice, he decided. Either Rindo had lied to him and sent Pete around, or this was Davis' own idea, brought about by his impatience to get even. The last possibility seemed a little far-fetched for he was by nature a patient man; his type of retaliation was more apt to be with a gun and in full view of the public. Which left Cadmus Rindo as the main suspect, but the Kid remembered the old man too clearly, the way he looked, and the tone of his voice; it was hard to imagine him lying.

Quite suddenly Ben Colfax came around the far corner, running toward the jail. He hauled up a dozen yards from the door. The Kid said, "You got here mighty quick, Ben. How did you know where to come?"

"I—" Colfax hesitated, then said, "Bein' a peace officer as long as I have sort of gives me a nose for trouble."

"You could get that nose flattened for sticking it in where it doesn't belong," the Kid said. He stood back from the doorway. "Come in."

While Colfax stomped the mud from his boots, the Kid limped into the back room and came back with his gun and holster. Punching out the spent brass, he reloaded the .44, then slipped it into the leather.

Colfax watched the way he favored his leg. "You get hurt a little?"

"Not so bad I couldn't leave a mark or two of my own," he said. His glance touched Colfax' face and the puffed lips. The ex-sheriff was squinting at the Kid, his eyes pinched nearly shut. Softly the Kid asked, "Those your boys, Ben? You teaming up with Pete maybe?"

Colfax was the soul of indignation. "Damn you, Kid—" He puffed out his cheeks and spoke more calmly. "I got nothing against you." He raised his hand to his bloated mouth. "This here I can settle myself."

"Make sure you do it to my face," the Kid warned. He raised his head when quick, light steps sounded on the walk. Then Nan Buckley appeared, a slicker wrapped around her. She was without a hat and the rain made a soggy ruin of her hair.

"What—?"

"Join the party," the Kid invited. His glance touched Colfax briefly. "I don't want to keep you, Ben, so if there's anything on your mind, better say it."

"Came here the first time to offer my help," he said fretfully. "Got a punch in the mouth for my trouble."

"Do I look like I need help?" the Kid asked.

"Every man needs it," Colfax said. "I know this town. I could be a big help to you."

"Would you really, Ben?"

The older man looked squarely at the Kid. "You don't trust me, I can see that. Don't blame you much. Be suspicious myself was I in your place. But it'd be a shame if you let that pious old buzzard talk you into anything. To hear him tell it, he prays every night."

"Could be he does," the Kid said. He glanced at Nan Buckley and found a sparkle of amusement in her eyes. When Ben Colfax looked around at her, she erased it quickly and presented only a bland inscrutable expression.

Ben Colfax was trying another angle. "I'd make you a good deputy, Kid. Been in harness a good many years and I know a few short cuts."

"The next thing you'll be telling me you're honest," the Kid said.

"Ah," Colfax said, "you're still sore about the money that was under your shirt." He pawed at his mouth. "I'll give it back, Kid. Hell, if it makes that much difference, I'll—"

"You keep it," the Kid said. "Consider it a loan, Ben. When I want it back, I'll just up and take it, same as you did."

The soft threat had subtle weight to it and Ben Colfax looked uneasy. "Well," he said, moving toward the door, "I guess I'll say goodnight."

"And better luck next time, Ben," the Kid said.

He was on his way out when he stopped and turned back. "Kid, you don't think I—" Then he saw that talk was useless. "All right, think it then. But proving it is something else, ain't it?"

"If I ever do prove it, Ben, you'll be the first to know."

When Colfax tromped off down the street, the Kid

limped to the door and closed it. Nan Buckley said, "I heard the shooting and I was worried."

"How did you know it was me?"

"I don't think there's anyone besides you in Rindo's Springs who can fan a hammer so the shots just run together, unless it's Pete Davis." Her smile was brief, but tinged with concern. "Those shots had a professional touch behind them."

"Yes," he said, "and the more I think of it, the more I believe that those three toughs had Ben Colfax behind them." He eased himself to the corner of the desk and sat down gingerly, favoring his thigh and shoulder. "I was due for a real stomping, Nan. If it hadn't been so blasted dark, I'd have been on the floor yet."

"Can I print this in the paper?"

He shook his head. "Not just yet. You know the merchant across the street? Good. I'll have to pay for his window and whatever goods was damaged by that hail of lead." He snapped his fingers. "A second sooner and I could have nicked one of 'em. But this leg slowed me up."

"Knowing a little about you," Nan said, "I'd suggest that you keep an eye out for bruises. Likely they'll be wearing a few."

He began to chuckle. "They had one of their own bunch on the floor and were flogging the daylights out of him, thinking it was me."

"It could have been you," she said sternly, "and that's not very funny."

He looked steadily at her. "Nan, we haven't known each other very long, but—"

"No," she said. "Kid, don't say any more now and don't ask me anything." She paused, as though considering something of grave importance. "You'll find out anyway, but I'd rather tell you myself. Until a few months ago I was in love with Cal Runyon, Rindo's head man. But he fell in love with Bess Jamison and I stepped out of the picture. It's still too soon for me to be honest, even with myself. And I don't want to hurt you."

"It's all right," he said. "Are you still in love with Runyon?"

"I don't know," she admitted. "If he came to me tomorrow and asked me to marry him, I don't know what I'd say. The not knowing isn't good. But until I'm sure, it'll have to do." She turned toward the door. "It's late. I'd better get home."

After she left, he slid the ash bolt again, reminding himself not to open it when half-asleep or unarmed. The cot felt lumpy but weariness smoothed it. The pain in his leg and shoulder troubled him and sleep came only in fitful snatches. When he awoke, the gray morning light was streaming through the windows. The rain had stopped and only the drip of the eaves remained.

Getting up, he found his leg so sore that walking was a torture. But he hobbled around, enduring the discomfort, and the enforced use seemed to restore some elasticity. Finally he hobbled out and down the street to the restaurant where he ordered breakfast. Afterward he went to the barber shop for a shave and a bath. When he undressed he saw the huge area of discoloration and sent the barber's boy down the street for some liniment.

The town was coming alive; the mill began its clamor, and along the main street, high-sided lumber wagons hauled toward the railhead five miles west. After his bath and liniment rub, the Kid felt a little better. He paid the barber and had just reached the boardwalk when an excited boy rushed up, panting and trying to talk at the same time.

"Trouble—at the—mill," he said and ran back quickly, as though he were afraid he would miss something.

Speed was out of the question as far as the Kid was concerned, but he headed toward the end of the street at a lope. A crowd began to ease along and he saw Ben Colfax come out of a side street to join this exodus.

At the company gate the guard admitted him, and since Colfax had caught up, let him in also. The gate closed against the curious townspeople, and the Kid cut toward the tie mill. Ben Colfax sided him. "Knew this would happen," he said. "Told you it would."

The Kid spotted the crowd of company men and began to batter his way through. All wagon loading had ceased and men climbed atop the bound lumber for a better view of the trouble.

He could hear the fight long before he could see it. Above the shouted encouragements was the crack of bone against bone. When he reached the core of the gathering he paused; only a fool would rush in without surveying the odds. Automatically he assumed that the trouble had started between a Jamison driver and Pete Davis; he could not help but think how neatly this would disguise any bruises picked up last night. Two men circled each other, both bloody and both eager to draw more blood. One was dragging a whip—that would be the teamster, Bess Jamison's man. Pete Davis was armed with a logging peavey and he had used it, for the sharp metal end was crimson.

From the other side of the circle, Cal Runyon was shouting something about being let-through-here-by-God. At that moment the Kid chose to step in between the two men. He faced Pete Davis, luckily, for the man swung the peavey. The Kid ducked and the pole sent his hat spinning into the crowd. Ordinarily he would have closed with the man, but his injured leg prevented that. When Pete back-handed for another swing, the Kid stepped within reach, drew his gun and chopped the man's forearm with the barrel.

The peavey was dropped immediately and the Kid faced Bess Jamison's teamster. "Do I have to take that whip away from you, mister?" His voice was soft, but no one missed the menace in it. The whip dropped almost silently to the mud.

Cal Runyon burst through then, saw the situation was under control and did not interfere. He waved his hand, bringing two men forward. "Get him to the office, then call the doctor."

But the teamster stood his ground, blood dripping from a cut on his head. The Kid said, "Did you start this?"

"Any reason why I should?"

"Don't get smart with me," the Kid advised. "You can talk here or in jail. Make your choice."

"He shorted me again," the teamster said. "Hell, I can tell a full load when I see one. This is shy a hundred feet or better."

"No one has cheated you," Cal Runyon said flatly. "I can show you the papers—"

With a wave of his hand the teamster cut him off. "To hell with your papers!" He glared at Runyon, and then at the Kid. "Figured you'd side with Rindo. He paid for you."

"Take your load and get out of here," the Kid said. "Go on before there's more trouble."

"Sure, but you won't always be able to do this so easy. One of these days we'll all come in and then we'll get a square deal or there'll be dead men."

He whirled and mounted his wagon. Ben Colfax stepped forward and said, "I know this man well. Maybe if I rode along with him I could talk sense to him."

"Why don't you keep your nose out of it?" the Kid asked.

Colfax smiled. "Why, there ain't nothin' about this that's official, sheriff. You got any objections to lettin' me ride with a friend?" He turned and got into the wagon.

The crowd opened a lane so the wagon could pass. The Kid turned and waited while Cal Runyon dispersed the men back to their jobs. Finally Runyon said, "Damn it, I hate these things."

"Both of you can't be right," the Kid said. "You're sure they're getting—"

"Hell yes, I'm sure," Runyon said. His young face was grave with genuine worry, the face of a man who preferred to live simply and in peace, but whose job was neither peaceful nor simple. "You handled Pete a little rough. Was it necessary?"

"You think I should have let him crown me with that peavey?"

Runyon shook his head. "He's a hothead. I'll try and cool him off enough so he won't take a gun to you. Pete's that way. To really lick him you'd have to kill him."

"I wouldn't want to do that, but his pride may force a showdown between us."

"It's hell," Runyon admitted. "That's the trouble with trying to settle a fight where both men think they're right. The one you lean on always feels that he got the short end." He looked at the Kid. "Can you come to my office?"

"Sure," the Kid said and limped along beside Runyon. After a time, Runyon's curiosity got the best of him. "Did Pete give you that limp?"

"Yeah. Last night around midnight," the Kid said. They entered the main building and Runyon saw that the sheriff had a drink of good whiskey and a fine cigar. Then the young engineer went behind his desk and sat down, cocking his feet up on the edge.

"Ben was trying to help. I suppose you know that," Runyon said.

"No, I didn't know it. He a friend of yours?"

"I like Ben," Runyon admitted. He gnawed on his cigar, his eyes thoughtful. "You know, one of these days Cadmus Rindo's going to get damn tired of this squabble and order a clean-up. Likely I'll be the man appointed for the job."

"Will you do it?"

"Either do it or quit," Runyon said. "But I like my job."

"Even if it included running Bess Jamison off her place?"

Runyon frowned deeply, indicating that he had considered this possibility before. "I suppose you've been told about Bess and me. Fairly common gossip around town." He laughed without humor. "People seem to get a kick out of watching two people tear apart over something they can't help. Like watching a dog fight. I want to marry Bess, but she won't have me unless it's on her terms."

"You mean join her?"

"That's about it," Runyon said.

"What are your terms?"

"The same, only turned around," he admitted. The ease left his expression and a cloud of lines formed on his forehead. "I'll never understand why her father was killed. Before that there was just bad feeling and a lot of talk. Now it's open dislike. Trouble all the time, like today. Every week there's a fight or the threat of one."

"One of these days," the Kid said softly, "a teamster will bring his rifle along. Be sure to call me before Pete Davis makes him use it."

"Have no fear, I will," Runyon said. He paused to study the ash on his cigar a moment. "Did you see what Nan wrote about you in the paper?"

"No," the Kid said.

"Well," Runyon said, unsure of his conversational departure point, "you've been around; let's put it that way." His glance came across the desk very steady. "The fact that you're still here reinforces my first opinion: that you're a man who can draw faster and shoot straighter than most. Of course, there are those who'll treat you like you had the plague. Just something that you'll have to put up with. But while you're letting the cold shoulders bounce off, remember that damn few of us in Rindo's Springs are lily white."

"I've been told that already," the Kid said. "Does that include you?"

"The whole wide world," Runyon said. He walked to the door with the Kid and watched him cross the soggy yard, moving at an easy pace to favor his bruised leg. When the sheriff had passed through the front gate, Runyon locked his office and went to the stable to saddle his horse.

Leaving the grounds by one of the logging roads, he bypassed the town, then met the main road on the other side. He rode at a steady pace and near noon, cut off toward Bess Jamison's. When he rode into the yard, she came to the porch edge, her hands sheltered by an apron.

Runyon dismounted. "There was trouble again, Bess."

"I'm not surprised," she said. "There'll always be trouble as long as your loader cheats us and Pete stands there to make him take it."

He sighed as a man will when he has made up his mind not to lose his temper. "Can I come in?"

Turning, she went into the house and he followed her into the parlor. She sat down but he remained standing, feeling very ill at ease.

"Bess, every time there's trouble, we just drift farther apart. Is that what you want?"

"We can't always have what we want," she said. "I thought we settled that."

"Settled what? That you'd go your way and I'd go mine? Bess, we love each other. Can you just forget that?"

"I can now," she said. "When my father was alive, everything was different. Now this is my fight. Please don't ask me to forget what he stood for."

He shook his head, blocked by this inflexible argument. "I'm not asking you to forget anything. But we have to bury the past, Bess. What is hating Rindo getting you? You've even forgotten how to smile."

"Don't ask me to change what I am, Cal."

He reached down and took her arm, turning her so that she faced him. "Bess, what do you want of me?" He looked confused, bewildered. "Do you want me to quit Rindo? We can get married and move away somewhere. I can get another job."

"Run?" She seemed outraged. "You'd suggest that I run? When I leave here, if I ever leave, Cadmus Rindo will be on his knees."

This was, he already knew, the point where words failed him completely, and no matter how he tried, he could not sway her. So he quickly pulled her to her feet and against him and pressed his mouth on hers. She slapped him once, then began to push at him, but he held her until her arms went around him. She was a woman of flesh and feeling; he needed no further proof than this. His arms hurt her, a welcome hurt for she moaned and clung to him.

But once free of his embrace, the effect of his love was lost to her. The hard inflexibility returned to her expression and she clenched her fists as tears formed in her eyes. "You have no right to try to make me weak, Cal."

"Bess—"

"Get out," she said softly. "Cal, just get out and leave me alone. Don't come back."

"You don't mean that!"

"I do mean it! I have to mean it!"

He stood there for a moment, hoping she would change her mind, but he understood that she could never change; her hate for Rindo had spread through her until it encompassed many things. So he went outside to his horse, mounted, and rode slowly from the yard. He tried to think of additional arguments, but there were none. The pleasantness had vanished from the day, leaving it dull; the enthusiasm he normally felt toward living drifted to nothing.

She was mistaken, and blind to her error. And it seemed to be Cal Runyon's destiny to stand by, a helpless observer, while Bess Jamison skated along the thin edge of self-destruction.

6

WHEN THE WIND RIVER KID returned to his office, he was not at all surprised to find a delegation of townsmen waiting for him. They stood in a close group, severe of expression, very righteous and hard-minded. The Kid had faced other men like these, men who had little tolerance for anyone outside their own restricted sphere.

He closed the door and said, "This looks official as hell."

A short man in his fifties spoke up. "Allow me to introduce myself. I'm Jake Leggett, the mayor of Rindo's Springs." His round stomach jiggled when he talked and he seemed to be eternally out of breath, for he sucked in whistling draughts of air after every sentence. Leggett did not offer to shake hands and the Kid did not seem offended. "These gentlemen are Dr. Carver, Mr. Osgood, who manages the bank, and Judge Richmond."

Of the four, only Dr. Carver thrust out his hand. He smiled and said, "I'm in your debt, young man. You've already sent me some patients." Carver was a dried-out man, wrinkle-faced, and his clothes bore chemical stains, giving him an untidy appearance. He bent forward suddenly and examined the Kid's eyes. "Ever have any trouble with your liver? No? Good. A healthy liver means a healthy mind. New theory of mine. Haven't got it all worked out yet but it's as promising as some of these new ideas."

Jake Leggett cleared his throat, and Dr. Carver glanced at him, then stepped back. "Mr.—ah—Kid, we consider the election most extraordinary, under the circumstances, and we're at a loss as to what to do about it."

211

"You waited too long, didn't you? If you had any objections to Cadmus Rindo's electing his own man, you should have protested before this."

"It's not your place to inform us of our duty," Judge Richmond said stiffly. He was a big, florid-faced man who overindulged himself with food and drink, and he obviously loved the sound of his own voice. "Our purpose, sir, is not to discuss what we should or should not have done about the election, but what disposition should be taken with the officer elected." He cleared his throat to get a deeper, more commanding tone. "I feel that it is quite unfortunate that you are not wanted in this state, sir. If that were the case, a warrant for your arrest would solve our problem of removing you from office."

"So that you could put Ben Colfax back in?" the Kid asked.

"Well," Richmond said, "we know Ben to be an honest man."

"He's a petty thief," the Kid said harshly. "And a man who'll steal a small amount will steal more if he gets the chance."

Richmond momentarily puffed his cheeks and sputtered like a freight train trying to make a long grade. "I consider than an insult, sir!" He looked at Carver, Leggett, and Osgood as though expecting them to share his outrage.

"We're not here to argue the virtues of Ben Colfax," Osgood said softly. He was a very small man, barely five foot three, but he had a commanding face and courageous eyes. "Kid, we can't alter the fact that you have a dubious reputation. Not as an outlaw, you understand, but you have been involved in affairs of a violent nature. Naturally, our primary concern is with Rindo's Springs and that it continue to enjoy a healthy atmosphere. We can't tolerate any threat to that atmosphere."

The front door opened suddenly and Nan Buckley stood there. She glanced at each in turn, then came in and shut the door. Jake Leggett said, "This is a private conversation, Miss Buckley."

"There are few private conversations in Rindo's Springs that I don't eventually hear about," Nan said sweetly. "Besides, when I saw this knot of civic virtue gathering, I just had to join it. What would Rindo's Springs do without the guardians of public honesty and morals?"

Judge Richmond was puffing his cheeks in agitation; his frown was a deep weaving of lines across his forehead. "Kid," he said, "I feel it our duty to get up a petition for your removal. That is the only legal recourse available to us."

This was, the Kid knew, what he had always resented and always tried to escape—the brand of the unwanted, this mass condemnation by his contemporaries. Yet, quite strangely, this time he felt no sense of inferiority; he found that he could face them calmly, without a trace of apology or shame. "Now why don't you do that?" he said. "Give you something to do while the Jamison crowd fights it out with Rindo's bunch. Then when the town falls down around your damned ears, you'll know that at least you did your civic duty."

"I can see," Richmond said, "that you force our hand."

"When you use tactics like that," Nan Buckley said, "you force other people to do the same."

Richmond's face grew stern. "I'll not stand for interference now."

This was clearly a warning that Nan Buckley chose to ignore. "Now, Judge, Rindo's Springs is my town too. Or have you spent so much time in Miles City that you've forgotten? Why, just the other day your wife mentioned how much you go to Miles City. She was wondering what the attraction was. I promised to inquire the next time I went there."

"Ah—yes," Richmond said, his face taking on a deeper hue. His glance touched the others. "Gentlemen, if you'll excuse me, I have important matters to attend to."

"What the devil's more important than this?" Mr. Osgood asked impatiently. "Damn it, Freeman, this was your idea in the first place."

"I'm sure it's being left in able hands," Richmond said hastily and stepped outside.

"Fine howdy-do!" Dr. Carver said. "Well, we three are capable, sensible men. There's no reason we can't get on—"

"Doctor," Nan said innocently, "I was talking to Mrs. Fisher, the schoolteacher, the other day. Do you still

check her physical condition regularly? We wouldn't
want the children of Rindo's Springs to contract a disease, now would we?"

"I'll have you understand—" Carver began, then fell
into a swift silence. Mr. Leggett looked at the doctor,
then at Osgood.

"It seems," he said, "that we are being whittled down,
one by one. Perhaps this is a matter better held pending
until another time."

They all seemed to find this completely agreeable and
after hurried goodbyes left the office. The Wind River
Kid stared at the closed door, then blew out a relieved
breath.

"As a politician," he said, "you don't do bad."

"I told you that I knew this town," Nan said. "That
included the bad as well as the good. Dr. Carver's association with the schoolteacher has been a public joke for
some time. And in Miles City, the judge finds a certain
entertainer at Harrigan's Saloon quite irresistible." She
smiled. "Unfortunately, Mr. Osgood didn't linger or I
would have reminded him that a man of his age shouldn't
chase the female help around the office furniture. And
Mr. Leggett's wife is one of Murray Burkhauser's best
customers—via the back door, that is. Some say that he
has hauled her home in the buggy so often that the horse
knows the way."

"Sounds like a pretty low way to fight," the Kid said.

"It's a dirty way," she admitted, "but it is the way.
Kid, you may not think so, but your way has always been
more honorable. Meeting a man face-to-face with a gun
has a certain dignity to it. You'll find that missing here.
They're all small men, in their souls, and they have to
swing a club or anything they can lay their hands on."

"I suppose," he said and went behind his desk to sit
down. By stretching his sore legs straight out he found
that he could ease the ache.

"Well, I have shopping to do," she said. "And news to
gather, especially about the trouble at the mill." Her
smile began to brighten her eyes. "And what I really
came here for was to invite you to supper. About seven?"

"I'll be there," he said and she went out.

There were no doors in Rindo's Springs that remained
closed to Nan Buckley. She stopped briefly at each business establishment, taking some advertisements, which

were the backbone of her paper, and gathering bits of news to enlighten the social-minded. Beneath the hard crust of Rindo's Springs lay the soundings of social activity. There was to be a box lunch at the church, and the school was putting on a play the next week, and the judge had bought his wife a piano, which meant a recital, probably not much musically but certainly important socially.

By mid-afternoon, Nan had a small notebook darkened with scribbling. She stopped at the general store to place her order for the boy's late afternoon delivery; then she started down the street to the print shop.

As she passed the shoemaker's, Cal Runyon entered the street on his bay. She saw him pass, then quite unaccountably, he wheeled around and came back. Nan stopped and Cal Runyon said, "Is there any reason why we can't speak to each other, Nan?"

"None at all," she said. "You're looking fine, Cal. I haven't seen you for months."

"Because I've deliberately avoided you," he said. "Can we talk someplace, Nan?"

"I was going home," she said. "Perhaps you'd like a cup of coffee."

"Thank you, I would." He dismounted and led his horse down the muddy street. At times, when the hitchracks were bare, he could edge close to the boardwalk and walk beside her, but at other times he was forced to walk in the street.

In front of the newspaper office, he tied his horse and entered with her. The typesetter was taking off his apron. He smiled, said goodbye and left. Nan put her notebook on the scarred desk and led the way into her quarters. Cal Runyon paused in the doorway, somewhat ill at ease.

"You haven't changed anything," he said. "But then, you never were one to change much."

"Steady, Nan," she said lightly and began to stoke the fire.

"I went out to see Bess," he said. "You heard about the trouble?"

"The whole town has by this time," she said. "Bess didn't like it, did she?"

He sighed. "That and a lot of other things. Bess and I have reached the end of something, Nan. There's no use trying to fool myself any longer."

She was ladling coffee grounds into the pot; she stopped and turned to face him. "Are you sure, Cal?"

He did not look at her; instead, he studied the design in the rug. "I should have seen it right after her father's funeral. Bess and I have said goodbye."

Her eyes darkened as she searched his face. "Why are you here, Cal? Oh, I know I invited you, but why are you really here?"

"I made a fool's choice, Nan. I just wanted you to know that." He moved his hands aimlessly. "Too bad a man can't do a few things over."

"Cal, we all wish that. It wasn't easy to take, your telling me that it was Bess Jamison you wanted. I think I was angry enough to have shot you gleefully. The hurt was deep because my feelings were deep."

"You don't know how sorry I am," Cal Runyon said softly. "I've regretted that part of it constantly, Nan, the hurting you."

"I've forgiven you," she said, "if that matters."

"It does matter," he said. He stepped toward her, closing the distance almost timidly. "Nan, you're very beautiful. Do you think that we could ever—I mean, have I placed too big a gulf between us?"

"I really don't know," she said. "We'd have to reach, Cal."

And he did reach, for her. She closed her eyes and stood quietly in his arms while he kissed her face and lips. There were no words now; the conversation was carried on in the language all lovers speak—the faint pressure of the hand, the promise of lips on lips.

The delivery boy came to the back door and knocked, but neither of them spoke. Finally the boy set the box of groceries down and went away. Nan Buckley smiled gently and laid her head against Cal Runyon's chest; his hands stroked her bright hair and they stood that way, completely alone.

Promptly at seven, the Wind River Kid locked the door of the office and walked through the twilight toward the newspaper office. The sky was now clear of clouds and a stiff wind husked down the street, rapidly drying the mud. When he came opposite the hotel, he looked up and saw the darkened shape of Will Beau-Haven, injury-locked to his special chair. Beau-Haven's cigar end made a bright glow as he drew on it and his voice floated down. "Drop up sometime."

"I'll do that," the Kid promised and walked on. He turned the corner and at the dark door of the newspaper office, he stopped. Knocking, he waited a moment and when no one answered the door, knocked again. Behind him, at the hitchrail, a horse stomped impatiently and the Kid looked at him.

A streak of light showed under a far door, and by this he knew that Nan was home. Then the streak of light vanished, as though someone had turned the lamp way down. The door opened, and there was enough light remaining to silhouette Nan Buckley as she came toward the dark front, a robe drawn tightly about her. Pressing her face close to the glass, she said, "I don't feel well. I'm sorry about supper."

"That's all right," the Kid said. "I'll drop by tomorrow."

She turned and went back to her quarters. He waited until the far door closed, then started back up town. Two boys raced around the corner nearly knocking the Kid down. He caught one by the arm and looked into a frightened face. "I'm not going to belt you," the Kid said. Almost without reason, he pointed toward the horse tied in front of the newspaper office. "You know who that belongs to?"

One of the boys made a thorough examination. "Looks like Cal Runyon's bay," he said.

The wind seemed to contain more of a chill than it had a moment before. Slowly the Kid released the boy he held, then gave them each a quarter. Without speaking he walked slowly away. Burkhauser's door was open and very inviting; the Kid stepped onto the porch. From the hotel gallery, Will Beau-Haven called, "Sheriff, you got a minute?"

The Wind River Kid seemed not to hear. The swinging doors gave beneath his hands and he stepped up to the bar. A dozen men sat at tables, drinking and playing cards. A few stood at the bar, but he found a place that looked sufficiently lonesome. The bartender came up, hands busy with his slop rag. The Kid found a dollar and laid it down. "Will that buy pretty good stuff?"

"Damn good," the man said and produced a bottle.

He took it and put it under his coat as though he were half-ashamed to be seen with it in public. At the sheriff's

office, he let himself in and locked the door behind him.
The place was dark and he put a match to the lamp, then
went into his own room and sat down on the bed.

Placing the bottle on the floor between his feet, he
sat hunched over, his face mirroring his gray thoughts.
He was not the sort of man who jumped to a hasty conclusion without looking at all the facts, but this time his
emotions pulled him into a quick judgment. He placed
none of the blame on Nan Buckley; Cal Runyon was the
center of the Kid's bitter thoughts.

A rational portion of his mind told him that it was
none of his business; Nan had already told him about
Runyon and if he had been fool enough to believe all the
fire was out, then he had no one to blame but himself.
Yet too many factors entered into the computation, tilt-
ing it completely off the scale. There were those years
when the wrong business or the wrong friends had
slammed doors in his face, coupled with a certain sensi-
tivity that had always troubled him. These factors added
to the belief that he had at last shed his past served to
drive the bitterness deeper.

Since the Wind River Kid was not much different from
other men who found facing themselves much more
difficult than facing danger, uncorking the bottle of
whiskey was the next logical step. And he took it.

He was not a sociable drinker and he never claimed to
be. Whiskey was akin to a blow on the head; it made him
forget. Yet he could not do that as easily as he thought.
When the bottle was half-gone, all the Kid had gained
was a growing anger and increasing dizziness.

Deserting the bottle, he returned to the street. Burkhauser's place still worked hard to make itself the live-
liest in town, but the Kid had little interest there. His
step was unsteady, partly from his sore leg, partly due
to the whiskey. But his aches seemed to have diminished,
and he persuaded himself that he felt fine.

Turning toward the newspaper office, he saw that Cal
Runyon's bay still stood three-footed at the hitchrack.
His impulse was to bang on the door and demand an
opportunity to avenge a lady's honor, but even drunk he
could see how damned silly that would look.

Waiting seemed to be his best course of action so he
eased into the bakery doorway where the wind did not
bite so much. Time scuffed its feet and he checked his

watch at what seemed to be half-hour intervals but were actually only five-minute breaks. An eternity later, the front door of the newspaper office opened and Cal Runyon stepped out, adjusting his hat to his head.

When Runyon stepped under the hitchrail, the Kid eased out of the doorway. "Hold on there," he said softly.

Runyon turned about. He bent forward to peer through the darkness. "Sheriff? That you? What the devil you doing lurking in doorways?"

"Waiting for you," the Kid said flatly. He stepped toward Runyon and nearly stumbled.

Runyon retied the reins and came to the boardwalk. "You drunk?" He stepped close and then said, "By God, you've been hitting it all right. What's got into you, man?"

"You," the Kid said. He tried to give Runyon a shove backward and only succeeded in pushing himself off balance. "We got something to settle, we have."

"What the devil are you—" Cal Runyon stopped. "Oh, I see." He raised a hand and wiped his mouth. "I don't suppose you'd listen to sense."

"That's right," the Kid said. "She smiled at me, Cal. Treated me like a human being who was as good as the next man." He laughed bitterly. "Then you had to come along and make her as cheap and ugly as all the others I've known."

"Did I do all that?" Runyon asked softly. "Kid, I loved her long before you ever saw her."

"You had a woman," the Kid pointed out. "What do you do, change your mind every week?"

Cal Runyon stepped back under the hitchrack, his fingers untying the reins. "I don't have to listen to that," he said. "Sober up, Kid; then we'll talk."

"Then we'll fight," the Kid said stubbornly. "We're going to fight, Cal."

"I won't pick it," he said. "Come around tomorrow, sober, and then if you still want to fight, I might accommodate you."

"There's no time like now," the Kid said and stepped toward Runyon who waited calmly on the other side of the hitchrack.

When the Kid drew within range, he uncorked a punch meant to be a scorcher, but Runyon ducked it easily. He then hooked the Kid's shirt front with his hands, yanked hard and brought the hitchrail hard against the Kid's stomach. With flailing arms and legs, the Kid went over. He struck the road on all fours as Nan Buckley opened the front door.

"Cal, you forgot to—" She saw the Kid getting up. "What are you doing down there?"

With the solidness of the hitchrack to help him, the Kid got to his feet. Nan stepped toward him, but stopped when Cal Runyon said, "He's got a mad on, Nan. Let him work it off."

"He's been drinking," Nan said, surprised. "Don't hurt him, Cal."

This detached conversation riled the Kid to a fever anger. His charge took Runyon completely by surprise and both men slammed into the horse's hip. Swinging, the horse lashed out with his hind feet and both men escaped by a narrow margin. Downed, Runyon and the Kid rolled beneath the horse, then Runyon came up on the other side, his hands lifting the Kid clear. As the Kid came to his feet he whipped his fist around and hit Cal Runyon flush in the mouth, driving him back.

Even drunk, the Wind River Kid was a better fighter than most men, and Runyon saw this too late. Runyon tried to close, to grab one of the Kid's arms, and took a crack over the eye that split skin, then another that opened his upper lip.

"Cal," Nan shouted, "Cal, can't you grab him?"

"Like a—damned eel," Runyon said, trying to get the Kid's arms pinned down.

There was kindness in Runyon, and this defeated him from the start, for there was nothing but anger in the Kid, anger and a childish desire to even off some of the hurt. Finally Runyon tired of taking this and tried to hit the Kid. He landed a weak blow to the Kid's cheek, but the power was lost when the Kid rolled away.

Runyon took a raking blow across the bridge of his nose and swore. Then, when all else failed, he tried to wrestle his way out of it, hoping that the Kid's intoxication would make him clumsy. But the exercise, the release of anger had sobered the Kid, and he grabbed Runyon around the neck and held him while he flailed him in the face with his fist. This angered Cal Runyon, wiped away his kind intent, but he found a purpose too late, because the Wind River Kid had him on the run, had him on the defensive.

The Kid punched with machine precision, and he hit hard, quickly. Finally Runyon backed away completely and raised a hand to his bloody face. He was nearly out of breath, and quite weary. "Wait," he gasped. "You've licked me—if that's what you—want."

Runyon pawed at the mud clinging to his clothes, mud he had picked up rolling beneath the horse's feet. His glance touched Nan Buckley, a glance filled with apology.

Yet it was the Kid who apologized. "Sorry I butted in," he said and turned away.

"Kid! Wait!"

"Let him go," Runyon said softly. "Talk won't change anything, Nan."

"How did he—?"

"My horse, I guess," Runyon said. "He was waiting for me when I came out.'

Nan pulled her robe tighter about her. "What have we done, Cal? To ourselves and to him?"

"Something we can't undo," he said and mounted. "Get inside before someone sees you."

"Yes," she said, so softly that he could barely hear her. "Before someone sees me. Our kind has to have the darkness, isn't that right, Cal?"

"You'll feel better about it in the morning," he said.

She looked steadily at him for a moment, then went inside, shutting the door. Runyon hesitated a moment, then turned his horse down the street toward the jail. A drunk reeled out of Burkhauser's as he passed, hailing loudly, but Runyon ignored him and went on. Dismounting before the jail, he tied his horse and went inside.

The Wind River Kid was in his small room, stripped to his underwear. He had filled a wooden tub with water and was methodically washing his clothes. When Runyon stopped in the doorway, the Kid glanced at him, then went back to his work.

"I don't like being dirty," he said softly.

"None of us do," Runyon said. "But it isn't long after we're born that we start rolling in it." He took a cigar from his pocket, then offered one to the Kid, who shook his head. "Kid, is this the end of this between us? Or are we going to tangle again?"

"It's the end," the Kid said. The sounds from Burkhauser's drifted fitfully through the walls, and a heavy wagon trundled down the street, building a brief racket. "There's an old pair of jeans and a shirt hanging in the other room," he said. "Mind getting them?"

"Sure," Runyon said. He went out and a moment later came back, laying the clothes on the bed. He sat down and observed the Kid carefully. "You like Nan, huh?"

"She seemed different," the Kid said.

"Different?" Runyon shook his head. "That's the trouble with men, Kid. The one woman for them always seems different from the others. They're not. We're not. All the same, Kid. All born the same way, and most of us die the same, as disappointed as the next man." He paused to examine the cigar ash. "People are always apologizing for what they do," he went on. "What I'm trying to get across to you, Kid, is that neither Nan nor I have to apologize for being human."

"All right!" the Kid shouted. "All right, you made your damn point. Now leave me alone."

Cal Runyon blew out a thin cloud of cigar smoke, then stood up. "You think Nan's sure to end in perdition, don't you?"

"What difference does it make to me? She made her choice."

"Yes," Runyon said, "she did, and I think not too good a one."

He walked out of the small room and into the main office. From down the street came the rattle of a wagon, the snap and jingle of harness. Curious, he stepped to the door for his look.

The darkness kept him from a full recognition until the wagon stopped in front of the jail. From the high seat, Ben Colfax said, "Been out to the mill, Cal. Got some trouble here."

Runyon stepped to the boardwalk, peered up at the canvas-wrapped man atop the load. "He dead?"

"Plumb dead." Ben Colfax took off his hat and ran his fingers through his hair. "This is real trouble. The new sheriff around?"

"Kid!" Runyon turned toward the interior of the office, but the Kid was on his way. He brushed past Runyon, hopped onto the wagon and peeled back an edge of the canvas. The combination of night and a bloody face was not enough to shroud the man's identity; he was the same man who had quarreled at the tie mill.

Runyon too had his look, then spoke briefly to Ben Colfax. "Go get the doctor."

"Hell, he likes his sleep," Colfax said. "In the morning's time enough—"

"Damn it, I said go get him. This is Bess Jamison's man. In the morning we may have a full-scale shooting war on our hands over this."

7

WHILE BEN COLFAX went for a doctor, the Kid returned to his back room, stoked the fire beneath the coffee pot, and when it was hot, drank several cups. Cal Runyon perched on the edge of the cot, gloomily turning the room dense with his cigar. The coffee, he noticed, seemed to improve the Kid's disposition, neutralizing the remaining effects of the alcohol.

Ben Colfax came back and hurried inside. He took a lantern out of the closet and lighted it so that Dr. Carver could make a preliminary examination before the dead man was moved. The Kid and Cal Runyon came to the front door and stood there.

"Exactly what happened?" the Kid asked. Colfax looked around, then climbed down off the load. He cuffed his hat to the back of his head, looked at Cal Runyon, then motioned toward the office with his hand.

They went in and the Kid closed the door. "We got to the railroad siding," Colfax said. "I got down first and went around to the other side of the wagon. There was a shot and he just crumpled over."

"Did you see who it was?" Cal Runyon asked.

Ben Colfax looked at him briefly, then nodded. "Can't be sure, you understand, seein' as how it was dark and all. But he either had on a white shirt, or his arm was bandaged."

"Are you saying it was Pete?" Runyon snapped.

"Said I wasn't sure," Colfax repeated.

Dr. Carver stepped inside. "I'll have him taken to my house if it's all right with you, sheriff."

"Go ahead." After Carver closed the door, the Kid

faced Ben Colfax. "Ben, how sure are you that Pete fired that shot?"

Colfax slapped his hands together. "Thunderation, how can I be sure? I only said it could have been Pete; he had his arm bandaged. And Pete had reason enough; everyone knows how he nurses a grudge. Ask Cal. The fight went sour on him, didn't it?"

"That's all true enough," Runyon admitted. "We'd better talk to Pete."

"You stay here, Ben," the Kid said. He started for the back room to get his gun, then recalled that it had slipped out of his holster and was now lying in the mud in front of Nan's newspaper office. To Ben he said, "Lend me your pistol."

There was a moment's caution in Ben Colfax's eyes, then he unbuckled the gunbelt and handed it over. "You going to arrest Pete?" Colfax asked.

"If there's need for it," the Kid said. He opened the door and then allowed Cal Runyon to step out ahead of him. They walked together toward the company buildings. Finally the Kid said, "What do you think, Cal? Do you believe Pete's the kind of man who'd pot someone off a wagon?"

"No," Runyon said flatly. "I've known him awhile. He takes his fights to a man's face. He's tough and quarrelsome, but he settles things openly."

"If what Ben says is true, then Pete changed his habits."

"I hate to think so, Kid. Too many things are changing around here."

"You're Ben's friend, aren't you? You want me to believe him, don't you?"

"I trust Ben," Runyon said. "You make up your own mind."

"That's my habit."

"I think you look at things too closely," Runyon said. They walked the rest of the way in silence. The main gate guard admitted them and they went to the main bunkhouse. Twenty minutes later, both men were heading back for the sheriff's office, for a few questions revealed that neither Pete nor his horse were where they should be, and the company hostler recalled that Pete had come straight from the doctor, saddled up and ridden out.

When the Kid and Runyon reached the side street on which Judge Richmond lived, the Kid stopped. "I'm going to get a warrant for Pete's arrest."

"My horse is still tied in front of the jail. I'll wait for you there and go with you."

"All right. See that mine is saddled and waiting." He walked away and a moment later turned into the dark path leading toward the judge's house. The place was dark but the Kid pounded on the door until a lamp was lit upstairs and a head showed at a window.

"Who the devil's down there and what do you want at this hour?"

"It's the sheriff," the Kid said. "Open up, judge. There's been an accident."

The window banged shut and a moment later a blob of light descended the stairs and a shadow darkened the other side of the glass-paneled door. Richmond flung it open and the Kid stepped inside. The judge was in his nightshirt, a heavy displeasure mottling his face.

"Couldn't this have waited until morning?" he asked.

"One of Bess Jamison's men has been killed," the Kid said.

"Hell, that can wait until morning."

"Not if you want to prevent a war," the Kid pointed out. "I have enough evidence against a man to go after him. If I can put him in jail before Bess Jamison gets here with her crowd, she'll have to admit that the law isn't all Cadmus Rindo's."

"One of Rindo's men did it?"

"Looks that way," the Kid said. "I want you to issue a warrant for Pete Davis."

"Hmmm," Richmond said, rubbing his face. "We'd best go sure and easy there, sheriff. It won't do to rile Rindo in order to keep from riling Bess Jamison."

"I said I had some evidence," the Kid said. He smiled without humor. "Judge, there's a warrant out for me on even less evidence."

The judge puffed his cheeks and sighed, then went to his desk and filled out the proper papers. He handed them over and said, "This can trigger off a lot of trouble."

"And a lot more if nothing's done about it," the Kid said. He left without further delay and cut toward the jail. Cal Runyon was there, puffing on a fresh cigar, his face pinched with concern. Ben Colfax had his feet elevated to the desk top, a satisfied expression on his face.

When the Kid stepped inside, Colfax said, "Told you that you'd need me, Kid." He chuckled. "I'm an old fire-horse that hears the bell."

"Then enjoy the ringing," the Kid said. He motioned toward the door. "Come on, I want to lock up."

This was as close to being thrown out as a man could get without actually being tossed. Colfax looked angry and offended and full of argument. "This the thanks a man gets?"

"Thanks for what? Come on. We've got to go."

Colfax stood up and moved toward the door. "You taking him, why not take me? Been a lawman all my life and I could give you a lot of points."

"And I've been dodging lawmen," the Kid said. He waited until Runyon stepped out, then locked the door. Ben Colfax stood on the boardwalk, looking for a wedge to open a new argument, but the Kid didn't give him any. Runyon had brought up his horse and he stepped into the saddle. When Runyon swung up, the Kid said, "Go home and go to bed, Ben. I'm not going to make you a deputy."

"You may be sorry for that," Colfax said and shuffled off into the night.

Cal Runyon's frown was deep. "He meant well, Kid. Probably could have been a help."

"I don't want him around," the Kid said and turned his horse out of town.

"You got something against him?"

"I don't trust a thief," the Kid said flatly. "And Ben Colfax is a thief."

For a moment, Runyon clung to silence while he phrased words in his mind. "Kid, I hope you can prove that."

"Do I have to?" He looked squarely at Runyon. "He stole from me and that's all the proof I need."

The flat finality in the Kid's voice froze any further argument Cal Runyon might have had, and they settled down to the ride. The wind snapped along with its chill, but the clear sky held no promise of rain.

There was a lot to learn about the Wind River Kid, Runyon decided, and he discovered a few things during the three-hour ride. The Kid was at home in this element, and he possessed an uncanny sense of direction. In a short

time he gauged the fall and rise of the land, and insisted
upon leaving the road to cut through the timbered sec-
tions. As though guided by an extra perception, he
sought out the small, back trails, the shortcuts, and after
shaving a half-hour off the normal time, stopped on a
high ridge and looked down on the railroad terminus.

Cal Runyon said, "I never knew this way, Kid."

"Pete did," the Kid said. "Any man who's moved
around a lot would have taken the shortcut over the
mountain instead of riding around it." He rapped his
heels against the horse's flanks and started down, wend-
ing his way through the avenues of tall timber. The
ground was wet and soggy and they made no sounds at
all, except for the occasional snapping of a dead branch
or the whisper of pressing through light brush. The
forest was ink-dark, yet the Kid made no mistakes. To
Runyon it seemed that this man had traveled this trail
many times, yet he knew that the Kid was a stranger to
it.

The railroad terminal did business on a twenty-four-
hour basis. The roundhouse was lighted and switchers
puffed back and forth on the siding, shuffling empties
and strings of loaded cars. A railroad-owned town sat
off to the right beneath the crouching brow of a high
bluff. The Kid slanted down off the ridge and once he
hit the flats, ignored the yard section and rode into the
town. Runyon wanted to stop, but the Kid shook his
head and rode the length of the street. The buildings
were all framed with lumber sawed at Rindo's mill,
and all were painted an identical tan. A saloon and
yard foreman's hotel sat on opposite corners, both
brightly lighted. The rest of the town was dark, but
the Kid wasn't interested in the buildings. His attention
was focused on the horses standing nose-in at the hitchracks. He rode slowly down one side of the street, then
turned and came back on the other.

To Runyon, he said, "You would recognize the horse,
wouldn't you?"

"A dun gelding," Runyon said.

"If you see it, you'll be sure to mention it, won't you?"

Runyon gave him an offended stare. "I don't hide my
men, Kid. Get that notion out of your head."

The gelding was found tied in front of the saloon.
The Kid and Runyon tied up alongside and stood for

a moment on the boardwalk. "Are you carrying a gun?" the Kid asked.

"Yes," Runyon admitted.

"Let me have it." He held out his hand and waited.

"Just what is this? Hell, I'm a grown man; I can handle it."

"Come on, Cal. Hand it over."

Reluctantly, Runyon reached beneath his coat and snapped his gun free of a shoulder holster. It was a .38 Smith & Wesson and the Kid broke it open, spilling the cartridges before handing it back. Runyon resettled the pistol beneath his armpit. "What did you think I was going to do, shoot you in the back?"

"I don't want you shooting anyone," the Kid said, starting for the saloon porch. He paused to look over the louvered doors, then went inside. Runyon following a pace behind. A quick survey of the bar told him that Pete Davis was not there; then he saw the man sitting in the far corner, a half-filled beer stein before him.

Moving between the tables, the Kid flanked him, then suddenly scraped a chair aside and sat down across from the man. Pete Davis looked up slowly and said, "Been expecting you." His glance found Cal Runyon. "You believe I did it?"

"I don't know what to believe, Pete." Cal remained standing.

"Well, I didn't do it," Pete said flatly. He locked eyes with the Kid. "You don't believe that, do you?"

"You're here. Your gun's gone. And Ben Colfax said he thought he saw you at the time Bess's man was shot."

"If Colfax says I shot him, then he's a liar." Pete Davis patted his stomach. "And my gun's here, under my coat."

"If you didn't kill him," Runyon asked, "then who did?"

"I don't know," Pete said flatly. "After I left the doc's place, I got to thinking, so I saddled up and came here, meaning to finish what I started without having the law interfere." He looked squarely at the Kid. "I waited around and finally saw the wagon come into the siding. Then there was a shot and Ben Colfax was yelling about someone being killed."

"You saw all this?" Runyon asked.

"Sure, but from a distance." Davis paused to drink some of his beer. "I'm not a fool; I knew this would look bad for me. That's why I waited here instead of lighting out. Besides, Kid, we ain't settled our little difference yet."

"You'll have to come back with me," the Kid said softly.

Davis raised his eyes. "To jail?"

"There'll have to be a trial," the Kid said. "That's the law, Pete."

"They'll hang me." He shook his head. "I can't take the chance."

"You'll have to take it," the Kid said. "Drink the rest of your beer and let's go, Pete. There's no sense trying to draw against me now."

Davis glanced at Runyon. "You going to help him take me back?"

"He's the law," Cal Runyon said. "And his way's best, Pete."

"Not for me it ain't. If a jury don't convict me, Bess's bunch will find some way to get to me." He placed his hands flat on the table. "I've heard plenty about the Wind River Kid, but I'll take a chance."

"You're acting like a fool!" Runyon said.

"Stay out of this, Cal," the Kid said. He stood up slowly. "Let's go, Pete." With great clarity, the Wind River Kid realized that he did not want to kill this man, but if he was forced to shoot, it would have to be clean and for keeps. Watching Pete Davis, the Kid understood that this man was also tired and wanted out, only he couldn't put his pride aside, and because of that there would be no way out.

Yet for a heartbeat it seemed that Pete was going to obey, but then Pete rammed forward with his shoulder, upset the table, and drew his gun. He was a practiced man, skilled, confident that his speed and accuracy were superior to all others.

Cal Runyon jumped back and the Kid grabbed the table as it spun toward him and hoisted it in front of him as Pete Davis let the hammer slide from under his thumb. The bullet puckered the wood, passed through with a rending of slivers, then imbedded in the far wall. Men boiled to their feet, colliding with each other in their haste to get down and out of the line of fire.

Cal Runyon yelled a warning to the Kid, who needed none. Pete was recocking his gun, leveling it, sighting more carefully this time. The Kid knew that there would be no way to take Pete now, and that the table was not stout enough to stop a bullet.

His palm popped against the slick butt as he swept the gun up with tremendous speed, cocking, whipping it waist high, firing in one, smooth, uninterrupted motion. The pistol recoiled in his hand and he held it that way, muzzle up-tilted, powdersmoke a haze about him. Pete whirled half around, the gun falling from his relaxed fingers. Then he settled face down. The saloon was strangely silent and the Kid put his gun away.

"It had to be a killing shot," he said, as if apologizing to the fallen man.

"We know that," Cal Runyon said.

Boots thrashed across the porch, and a big man in a derby hat came in. He was armed with a sawed-off shotgun and a long billy-club. Punching and jabbing his way through the crowd, he had his look at Pete Davis, then turned to the Kid. "I'm Cassidy, the railroad marshal. Who're you?" His glance touched the badge.

"Jim Onart, the sheriff at Rindo's Springs."

"I'll have to make a report," Cassidy said, "since it happened here. You want to come over to the office?"

"Sure."

"I'll stay and put Pete on his horse so we can take him back," Runyon said.

The Kid nodded and followed Cassidy through the crowd. Once on the street, Cassidy said, "I try to keep the desperadoes out of this town. He was a bad one, huh?"

"No, just a man who had to do everything the hard way," the Kid said.

The marshal's office was on the main thoroughfare and they went inside. Another man was there, a tall man in his late thirties. He wore a neat, dark suit and a pearl-handled Colt slung low against his thigh. When Cassidy and the Kid stepped inside, this man stood up. "Marshal?"

"I'm the marshal," Cassidy said. "What can I do for you?"

The man exposed his left cuff, revealing a small, crescent-shaped badge. "I'm Boomhauer, United States marshal."

"Glad to know you," Cassidy said, offering his hand.

"You must have come in on the 11:36 train." He turned to the Kid. "This is the sheriff from Rindo's Springs."

"A pleasure," Boomhauer said, shaking the Kid's hand. Boomhauer had a bland face, the kind usually associated with a careful businessman. His hair was sandy and he had a tawny mustache that drooped past the ends of his lips. "Rindo's Springs, you say? Coincidence, but that's my destination. Perhaps we could ride back together."

"If you don't mind the company of a dead man," the Kid said. He gave Cassidy his attention, yet regarded Boomhauer furtively when the marshal was not looking. Cassidy was at his desk, pen in hand. "What was the dead man's name, sheriff?"

The Kid gave him the facts and Cassidy wrote every bit of it down. Just as he finished, Cal Runyon came in. To the Kid he said, "I got Pete wrapped in a canvas and tied to his horse."

"You want to get some sleep before you start back? Be daylight in another hour."

"I'm in no rush," Runyon said. "If you want me, I'll be bunked down at the stable." He went out and the Kid went to the door, there pausing.

"If that's all, Cassidy, I think I'll find something to eat."

"There's an all-night dining room at the hotel," Cassidy said.

Boomhauer reached down and retrieved a small satchel. "Sheriff," he said, "if you have no objection, I'll join you."

For an instant The Kid surveyed him critically, then shrugged. With Boomhauer walking beside him, the Kid headed back for the saloon. "Trouble is always unpleasant," Boomhauer said, his voice mild and pleasant. "Been with the law long?"

"I've been associated with it for a few years," the Kid admitted. He stepped into the bar and collared the bartender. "Did you pick up that fella's gun?"

"Got it right here," he said and handed it over.

"Evidence," the Kid said and slipped it into his waistband. He turned and went out, Boomhauer at his heels. Across the street, in the hotel dining room, the Kid and Boomhauer ordered a big meal, then settled back to wait for it.

To Boomhauer the Kid said "Rindo's Springs is your destination, you say?"

"Yes." He brought out a yellow telegram and spread it on the table. "Our office in The Dalles received this." The telegram read:

IF YOU ARE STILL LOOKING FOR THE WIND RIVER KID COME TO RINDO'S SPRINGS.

"We checked immediately with the Arizona marshal's office and there is a warrant out for this man. Have you seen him around your town?"

All men find strangeness in discussing themselves as a separate entity, and the Kid had to beat down this uneasiness before he could speak. "You sure this isn't some kind of a joke?"

Boomhauer's shoulders rose and fell. "Sheriff, we never treat a warrant like a joke." He smiled. "You know that we don't try men. We only arrest them."

"What about a description? A picture?"

"No pictures," Boomhauer said. "And the description fits at least ten men I know." The waiter brought their meal and all conversation ground to a halt while appetites were blunted.

"I suppose you'll want to look the town over," the Kid said, forcing an easiness into his voice.

"Routine," Boomhauer said. "Likely you're right; it's a joke." Then his eyelids pulled together slightly. "But again, why would anyone send a telegram? It's never happened before."

"Well, good luck with your manhunt," the Wind River Kid said.

"I've been hoping I won't find him at all," Boomhauer said, quite seriously. "You see, the Wind River Kid isn't exactly what I call a criminal. True, he's fast with a gun and he's left a few stretched out behind him, but those were clearly self-defense, according to reliable witnesses. Unfortunately, the Kid fought on the wrong side of a range war. Now a politically rotten sheriff has a warrant slapped on him." He paused to drink some of his coffee. "Listening to you make that report to Cassidy started me thinking. If I meet the Wind River Kid, I'll have to arrest him, just like you had to arrest this Pete What's-His-Name. The Kid isn't the kind who'll go back to a crooked jury and a paid-off judge." Boomhauer's voice softened. "I'll likely have to draw on him, and then there'll be another dead man."

"Maybe you," the Kid said.

"Maybe, but I've drawn on men before. Good men." He shrugged again, and attacked his apple pie. "But we're talking about the future, and something that might never happen."

"But if it does?"

Boomhauer paused, looking steadily at the Wind River Kid. "Then I'll have to do what you did. That's the regrettable part of our job, isn't it?"

Through the remainder of the meal they talked of other things, and the Kid found much in Wade Boomhauer to admire. The man had been around, and always on the right side of the law. He understood killers and governors with equal clarity, and shading all of his opinions was a fine sense of responsibility and justice.

The Kid paid for the meal and walked to the stable. He talked the hostler out of a horse for Boomhauer, then found Cal Runyon and woke him. Mounted, they left the railroad town and drove for the mountain road that led back to Rindo's Springs.

The day was dull and gray at first, then the sun came out, sucking steam from the earth until it drifted like thick wood smoke. By nine o'clock they shed their coats, and at ten stopped to rest their horses.

Runyon had introduced himself earlier, so he fell into conversation with Wade Boomhauer now. "You after a man?" he asked. He found spare cigars and passed them around.

While taking his light, Boomhauer said. "Got word— the Wind River Kid—was in your town."

Cal Runyon simply stared, then caught himself. He avoided a direct look at the Kid. "Sounds like a crank's work. I know just about everyone in Rindo's Springs."

"Probably so," Boomhauer said, puffing gently on his cigar. "Still, I'll have to check it out."

The Kid indicated that he was ready to mount, but he and Cal Runyon held back, letting Boomhauer go on ahead out of earshot. "Kid, what the hell you going to do? When he starts asking questions, the word will be out."

"There's no hiding it," the Kid admitted.

"There's one way," Runyon said softly. "Rindo still controls the town. If I say so, no one will dare open his mouth."

"That wouldn't shut up all of them." The Kid sighed. "Well, it had to happen and now that it has, I really don't mind it."

"You're a strange one," Runyon said and then pushed forward to side Boomhauer.

8

The Kid took Pete Davis' body to Dr. Carver's house and carried it into his small operating room.

Looking around, Carver said dryly, "My, but business has picked up since you came to town."

The Kid frowned. "That's not funny."

"Well," Carver said, swinging around, "you're in a bad mood!" He opened the canvas covering Pete Davis and examined the bullet hole. "Dead center. This from the hip?" He caught the Kid's scowl and raised his hand. "All right, all right. Just a scientific question."

"Did you take the bullet out of the teamster?" the Kid asked.

"Take all the bullets out," Carver boasted. "Thorough, that's the way I work. You want to see it?" He got a small jar out of a cupboard and opened it. Five bullets lay in his palm, each neatly tagged. "A few of these were before your arrival," he said. "This one came out of Bess Jamison's father." He picked up another. "Here's the one you want."

The Wind River Kid looked at it carefully, then slipped Pete's gun out of his waistband. He read the stamping on the barrel: Colt Single Action Army .45.

"Something wrong?" Carver asked, reading correctly the puzzled expression on the Kid's face.

"Are you sure you took this one out of the teamster?"

"Sure, I'm sure. What's the matter?"

"The slug is from an old .44 American. Notice how light it is? No other .44 is that light. The .44 American is getting pretty rare as a handgun load. Pete's gun is a .45 Colt."

"Then Pete didn't kill—" Carver paused to stroke his

236

chin. "Say, that puts a different head on the beer, don't it?"

"Yes, and you keep it under your hat," the Kid said, turning toward the door.

"You want to see the bullet I'll take out of Pete?"

"No," the Kid said. "I know who put that one there."

He let himself out and walked slowly toward the center of town. Until now there had been no doubt in the Kid's mind that he had shot the guilty man; the way Pete had bolted had convinced him. But now all that vanished like a patch of early morning fog; the physical evidence of the mismated bullets was simple and undeniable. Since bullets were his business, he thought instantly of the possibilities of shooting .44 American loads in a .45. Of course accuracy went to hell, but this had been done before with confusing results. Two things knocked this possibility out as far as the Kid was concerned. First, Pete would have had to do the shooting at over twenty yards and at night; a .44 fired in a .45 was not accurate enough for that. And secondly, the .44 taken from the teamster had well-set rifling marks; that couldn't happen in an oversize barrel.

As the Kid passed the hotel, the clerk saw him and beckoned him in. "Sheriff," he said, "Mr. Beau-Haven told me that if I saw you, to ask you to step up. He wants to see you."

"All right."

"Straight up the stairs and first door to your right."

With a nod, the Kid mounted the steps, listening to them squeak beneath his weight. At the proper door he knocked, then listened to tapping heels approach. When the door opened, Grace Beau-Haven said, "Won't you come in, sheriff? My husband is taking the air on the upper gallery."

She took the Kid's hat and placed it on the sideboard. He followed her through two lavishly decorated rooms. Double doors opened onto the railed gallery overlooking Rindo's Springs. Will Beau-Haven sat in his special-built chair, a robe wrapped about his useless legs.

"This is the sheriff, dear," she said. "My husband, Will."

The Kid shook hands briefly with Will Beau-Haven, then sat down when offered one of the chairs. Grace lingered by her husband, her hands gentle on his shoul-

ders. Her face was composed and her eyes held a
slightly vacant expression, as though her mind were busy
elsewhere. The Kid had noticed instantly her purposeful
drabness. He knew it was not an accident, for she wore
rice powder to disguise the natural radiant color of her
skin. Her dress was a dark gray with only twin ribbons
of black trim bisecting the bodice. And the dress was
loosely fit, almost shapeless. Grace Beau-Haven, he observed, was a neat woman. Her hair, although severely
dressed, was burnished smooth, and she took pride in
her hands. Such a woman, he deduced, would not wear
a misfit dress unless she had a definite reason, and he
could only guess at what it might be.

"Going to rain again," Will Beau-Haven observed.
"You notice how muddy-looking it was at dawn?"

"I'm a poor weather prophet," The Kid said.

"Hard for me to ignore it. Get my shooting pains when
the weather changes." He canted his head to look at
his wife. "How about some fresh coffee, Grace?"

"Tonic for you," she said. "But I'll fix the sheriff some."

When she went inside, Will Beau-Haven glanced at
the Kid. "New man in town. Understand he's the federal
law."

"Boomhauer. Nice fella."

"Not when he finds out who you are," Will Beau-Haven
said. "How long do you think you can keep it from him?"

"I never treated it like it was a contest," the Kid said.

"May be a shooting contest when he finds out." He
looked carefully at the Wind River Kid. "I'll have a good
seat, won't I? The best in town. I sit here, day in, day
out, looking down, seeing everything that's worth seeing.
Don't get a chance to tell what I see, though. People
are too busy to talk to a cripple." He paused and looked
down toward the street, studying Burkhauser's place.
"I see everything that goes on over there. You take that
gap between Burkhauser's and the general store; used to
be a door there, but it's been boarded up for six months
now. Richmond, Colfax and Doc Carver used to use that
door regular, then they suddenly stopped. Been bothering me, not knowing why." He chuckled. "Sheriff, how
much would you charge me to watch all night and see
what goes on in that gap?"

"Something going on?" the Kid asked softly.

"You take a look at all the other gaps between all the

other buildings in town. Filled up with bottles and junk. But look across the street. That gap's kept clean. Make you wonder?"

"Damned if it don't," the Kid said. He turned his head at a slight sound and found Grace Beau-Haven standing there with a tray. Her expression was composed and neutral when she poured the coffee. He added sugar and canned milk, then sat with the cup nestled in his hands.

"Quite a town, Rindo's Springs," Beau-Haven said, as though picking up a conversational thread dropped when his wife came back. "A lot goes on down there. Men pulling against each other, planning to do better—or do worse, which a man can do easy enough all the while he thinks he's doing better." He sighed and drank the tonic she handed him. Then he made a face and set the empty glass aside. "Not many towns like this one, where one man made it and keeps it alive." He waved his hands at the street. "There are men walking around down there just waiting for the old man to die so they can swoop in and gobble up what he's spent a lifetime building. Damn fools! Once they begin fighting over what the other man has, they'll lose everything."

"A man has to stand or fall by himself," the Wind River Kid said. "You can't blame people for wanting that right."

Will Beau-Haven laughed, then leaned forward and tapped the Kid's knee with his finger. "Rindo built all this and picked nearly every man who lives here. That's what I said, picked. Hand-picked." He sagged back. "Maybe it was a kind of cruel joke he played on everyone, or maybe it was because he felt he had to do it."

"You've talked this into quite a thing," the Kid said.

"Talk?" Beau-Haven laughed. "Man, live here. Get to know these people. Look at them. Examine them carefully. They're all imperfect specimens."

"Hell, we all are."

Beau-Haven shook his head vigorously. "Not the way I mean. Nearly every man here is a misfit. Unable to hold himself up, and yet unable to admit it to himself. Rindo looked for that weakness when he allowed them to settle here. Take myself. I was just a muleskinner until I got crippled. Rindo gave me a share in this place because I was useless for anything else."

The Wind River Kid looked at Grace Beau-Haven, opening his mouth to ask her if she approved of this view, but the words failed to come out. She was sitting perfectly straight, her eyes fixed on some inward scene. She appeared to be in a trance.

"She gets like that," Beau-Haven said. "Let her alone and she'll be all right. Lord knows what she dreams about." He took the Kid's sleeve and shook it. "There's something wrong with every man in this town. Nan Buckley's father came here in disgrace. Burkhauser was a gambler whose only talent was dealing off the bottom of the deck. Ben Colfax was nothing, just a man who'd been a deputy and lacked the brains for anything better. I could go on, but it would be the same. That's why we sit around hating Cadmus Rindo, because we know what we are and that we'll never be any better no matter how many chances we have. Kid, you never win a man's heart by sharing your wealth with him. But you show him your weakness and fear and he'll be a friend."

"It seems that I'm well qualified for Rindo's Springs," the Kid said dryly.

"You've already been signed up and initiated," Beau-Haven said.

The Kid finished his coffee in silence while Beau-Haven studied the street. Perhaps, the Kid decided, there was some truth in this bitter judgment, and in the years to come, he might also realize that there would never be anything better. But youth had hope, and he was still young, no matter how worn-out he might feel at times.

When he stood up, Grace Beau-Haven blinked and said, "Leaving? Why, it seems that you only just came."

The Kid said goodbye and Grace Beau-Haven walked with him to the door. "You musn't mind Will," she said. "He's very bitter."

"And you?"

Her eyes became softly warm and dreamy. "We all have our own little worlds, sheriff."

He gave her a brief nod, placed his hat carefully on his head and went down the stairs. As he entered the lobby, the clerk signaled him over. "The marshal who came into town with you," the clerk said, "has number eight. Last room, street side, on this floor."

"Thanks," the Kid said, turning away.

"Oh, sheriff." The Kid turned back. "Miss Buckley's waiting." He nodded toward a sheltered corner and following his eyes, the Kid saw Nan sitting in one of the heavy leather chairs.

Stepping up to her, the Kid said, "I made a big fool of myself last night."

"I didn't come here to point that out," she said. "Kid, what are you going to do about this U. S. marshal?"

He shrugged. "What do you expect me to do?"

"He's catching up on his sleep now," she said, "but then he'll start asking questions. He's bound to find out."

"It's my problem, not yours."

He deliberately closed her out, and her pride made her chin come up. "Of course," she said softly. "I'm sorry I meddled." Quickly, before he could stop her, she got up and walked out.

The Kid silently cursed himself for being a fool, yet his pride gave him little choice. Before, when observing two people in love, he had always considered it amusing when they flung these shaded ultimatums at each other, but now the humor vanished. This thought brought him up short; a man's first realization that he is at last in love is rather shattering.

His anger at her was very understandable now, for it had been a jealous anger. Even the fight with Cal Runyon assumed sensible aspects, and he supposed that everything had been quite clear to Runyon; this would be a source of embarrassment now.

Leaving the hotel, the Kid walked in a roundabout way to Cadmus Rindo's large house and was admitted. Rindo was in his study and he looked around when the servant announced the sheriff.

The old man had his chair drawn up by the window where he could observe a portion of his town. Through the walls filtered the buzz and rip of the planing mill, and even here the pungency of the slab burner perfumed the air. "Sit down," Rindo said. He had been reading and now put his book aside. Very carefully he tamped tobacco into his pipe and lit it. "I've been wondering if you'd come."

"Any reason I shouldn't?" the Kid asked.

"You shot an innocent man," Rindo said. When the Kid opened his mouth to speak, Rindo held up his hand. "I know, you couldn't have done anything else, Pete being what he was. Rather fight than talk. I meant to fire him a dozen times, but never did. Some men just can't take care of themselves, and as long as he worked for me, I figured he wouldn't get into any serious trouble." He brushed his mustache. "Seems I was wrong."

"Another one of your misfits?"

Rindo's head came around quickly; then his expression softened. "You're learning fast, Kid. Yes, Pete was a down-and-outer. In one jail after another. He was pretty good with a gun, though, and took my orders until you came here."

"But you seem sure he didn't shoot Bess Jamison's man."

"Not positive, but I knew that wasn't Pete's way, Kid. He liked to face a man out. He did with you, didn't he? A man he must have known he couldn't beat."

"Yes," the Kid said bleakly. "He made it self-defense for me."

Rindo drew on his gurgling pipe. "Well, you didn't come here to tell me how sorry you feel for yourself. Got a suspect?"

"Any man who hates you," the Kid said.

"Ha!" Rindo slapped the arms of his chair. "Then go take your pick from the voting register."

The Kid considered this for a moment, then asked, "What does Ben Colfax have against you, Mr. Rindo?"

"Nothin' more than anyone else has," Rindo stated. "He's a perennial down-and-outer. Lots of them in this world. I pay no attention to how people feel about me. I understand it and I expect it. You're young, but someday you're going to find out that one good turn don't necessarily deserve another."

Gnawing his lip, the Kid turned several possibilities over in his mind. "Assuming that Pete was telling the truth, that he didn't kill the teamster, then we'll have to assume that Ben is lying. What does Ben stand to gain by telling something that won't hold up? Seems that the risks were pretty great."

"Hold on," Rindo said. "As long as you're figurin' that way, why not go back and figure Pete did do the shooting. He could have changed guns. He could own more than one, you know."

"That's a possibility I hadn't considered," the Kid said. "I'll have to check it." He picked up his hat, thanked

Cadmus Rindo for the visit and started back toward his office.

When he passed the newspaper office, Nan Buckley hailed him and he stopped. She handed him his revolver, holding it by the barrel. "You dropped this last night. I cleaned it good."

He slipped Ben Colfax' gun into his waistband, and his own into the holster. "Thanks," he said and started away, but her voice stopped him.

"Kid, do you hate me?"

"No."

"But you no longer believe in me. Is that it?"

"About it," he said. "Forget it, Nan. You don't owe me a thing."

"I don't believe that," she said. "We all owe something to someone."

He left her and walked slowly along the main street, wishing that he could hate her, for that would simplify everything. As the Kid approached the hotel porch, Wade Boomhauer stepped out. Too late to alter his course, the Wind River Kid stopped.

"Wonderful what a few hours' sleep will do for a man," Boomhauer said. He smiled and looked toward the planing mill as though trying to identify all the blending sounds of saw and planer. "A hell of a racket, ain't it?"

"Pretty noisy, but you get used to it."

"I may not be here that long," Boomhauer said. He patted his pockets a moment. "Sheriff, do you have a cigar you could spare?" The Kid found a Moonshine Crook and offered it. "Thanks. A light? Yes, I can't seem to find matches either." He bent forward, cupping his hand around the flame.

The clatter and rush of horsemen at the head of the street caused both of them to straighten. Bess Jamison was running down in her buggy, while behind her, twenty mounted men made a tight wedge, driving all other traffic to the sides of the street.

She saw the Kid on the hotel porch and pulled up suddenly. The men sawed to a halt behind her and the Kid stepped to the street's edge. Bess Jamison did not bother to dismount. She had a double-barreled shotgun on the seat beside her, and she placed her hand on the stock, near the trigger guard. "We've come for the man who killed Allen. He was my driver."

"You're a little late," the Wind River Kid said evenly.
"The man is dead. Killed resisting arrest."

Bess looked around, at the gathering crowd and at her
own men. Then her attention swung back to the Kid.
"I'm not going to call you a liar, but you're Rindo's law,
and I find it hard to believe."

"I'm afraid you will have to believe it," Wade Boomhauer said evenly. "I happened to be there too."

Bess turned toward him. "And who the devil are you?"

"Boomhauer, United States marshal," he said, making
a slight bow from the hips.

Before Bess could say anything, the Kid slid his easy
voice into the gap of silence. "There'll be an inquest in
the morning. I'd advise you to be here for it." He took
a step closer to the buggy. "And don't bring armed men
into this town again."

"I've got a right to protect myself," Bess Jamison said.

"The law will do that for you," the Kid told her. He
stepped back so she could turn the rig, but instead of
that, she looked at Boomhauer.

"You after somebody?" she asked.

The Wind River Kid tensed, knowing that his moment
had arrived. He tuned so that he faced Boomhauer. The
marshal spoke around his cigar. "We have reason to
believe that the Wind River Kid is in this vicinity."

"Reason?" Bess Jamison laughed. Here was, the Kid
decided, her best opportunity to get rid of him without
raising a hand. In her eyes he was Cadmus Rindo's law,
bought and paid for, and because of that, her enemy.
Few people could resist such an opportunity and the
Kid held out no hope that Bess would pass this up. And
she didn't. She pointed the stock of her buggy whip at
him and said, "There's your Wind River Kid!" Her smile
was triumphant. "Let's see you get out of this one,
sheriff." Lashing her team, she stormed down the street,
her armed retinue following her.

She left a wake of silence. The spectators along the
walk stood absolutely motionless. Wade Boomhauer
took his cigar from his mouth and cast it into the street.
"What about it, sheriff?"

"I'm the Wind River Kid. Can we talk about this,
Wade?"

"Afraid not," Boomhauer said. "You know what I have
to do."

"Just a minute," the Kid said. "Wade, I came into this town as nothing, but now it's changed. I got elected as a bad joke, but it's turned out to be more than that for me. Wade, I need this town and it needs me. You going to take that away from both of us?"

"Can't help it," Wade Boomhauer said. "It's my job, Kid."

"Then I'll have to fight you," the Kid said. "You give me no choice, Wade."

Boomhauer nodded. "Figured it would be that way," he said and drew.

He was good. His draw was clean and fast, the product of long practice, and he was not a fancy gun-handler; he ignored hammer fanning, merely squeezing off when the muzzle flipped level.

But the Wind River Kid was palming up his own gun, the one lavishly tuned by a superior gunsmith. And that gun was in gifted hands. Although he gave Boomhauer the first move, he had him beat by the time the marshal slipped the barrel clear of the holster. No killing shot this time; the Kid put his bullet deliberately in Boomhauer's gun arm, fracturing it.

Boomhauer's bullet went a foot wide, since shock had started to spin him. His gun fell and he staggered back, fingers vising the torn flesh. He would have fallen had not a man stepped down and caught him. The Kid rushed forward, flung an arm around Boomhauer and helped him into the hotel lobby. To one of the bystanders he said, "Get Carver; don't just stand there!"

There was haste in his voice and anxiety, and regret for what he had done. He brushed others aside who tried to help, then tore at Boomhauer's sleeve, exposing the torn flesh and pumping blood. Boomhauer's complexion was chalky and shock made his eyes glisten. He spoke with an effort. "You could have—put that dead center—instead of just in an arm."

"Why did you have to draw on me?" the Kid asked. "Hell, Wade, I didn't want to do this."

"Got a job to do," he said.

From the doorway came the doctor's shrill voice demanding to be let through. He knelt by the Kid and made his examination, then opened his satchel. "If ether makes you people sick, I'd advise you to leave." He handed the bottle and cone to the Kid. "Put that over his nose and add the ether a drop at a time." While the Kid followed directions, Dr. Carver continued his rough-mannered preparations. "Bullet just seems to have nicked the bone. Damned lucky it isn't a compound fracture. Splint? Where the hell did I put splints? You there, run into the kitchen and bring me some kindling." He looked at the Kid. "You do this?"

"Yes," the Kid said. "How much of this stuff do I pour on the cloth?"

Dr. Carver lifted one of Boomhauer's eyelids. "That's enough for awhile." He stood up and began flailing his arms at the crowd. "Get out! What do you think this is, a sideshow?"

They fell back before this shouting attack and when the lobby had been cleared, he came back and set Boomhauer's arm. While he was bandaging it, he said, "If he was after you, I wouldn't worry about it. He'll be a mighty sick man for a few days." He paused to cork the ether bottle. "Be a week before he feels like walking."

"Then I've bought myself a little time," the Kid said and went out.

There was a good-sized crowd still cluttering the boardwalk, but he pressed through and went on to the jail. When he opened the door, he found Ben Colfax sitting at the desk, his feet elevated. He dropped them quickly to the floor and said, "Been looking all over town for you." He got up when the Kid came around the desk.

"Not very damned hard," the Kid said. "What do you want, Ben?"

"If you're through with my gun, I'd like it back," he said.

The Wind River Kid slipped his own gun out of the holster and laid it on the desk. From his waistband he took Ben's gun, crammed it into the leather and handed the whole rig over. Without looking at Ben Colfax he said, "That story of yours about Pete shooting the teamster doesn't hold up. Pete was carrying the wrong caliber gun."

"Maybe he had another," Ben said. He tipped a chair against the wall and sat down. "Bein' a peace officer with years of experience, I'd say that Pete simply switched guns on you. Any good gunman's got a spare."

"You mean he threw the other one away?"

"Ain't likely," Ben said, smiling. "Pete's kind spends

good money on their guns; he wouldn't throw one away.
His horse around?"

"I think someone took it to the livery," the Kid said.

"Suppose we go take a look." He got up. "Don't mean
to tell you your job, but you might as well take advantage of my experience."

The Wind River Kid had a refusal on the tip of his
tongue, but he held it back. "All right," he said, "let's go
take a look."

Darkness was only a matter of minutes away when
they stepped outside, turning toward the stable at the
end of the street. The building was dark except for the
lamp glowing over the arch. They stopped just outside,
both squinting, trying to cut the muddy gloom. Ben said,
"You see if you can find a lantern. I'll try and locate Pete's
horse."

He moved away before the Kid could say anything.
By the time the Kid located and lighted a lantern, Ben
was grumbling and stumbling around one of the rear
stalls.

"Found him!" he called. "Come on back, Kid."

With a glow of light preceding him, the Kid walked
toward the back of the building. Ben was in a box stall,
his fingers fumbling with the lashings of Pete's bedroll
and saddlebags.

"If it's here at all," Ben said, "it'll have to be in his
blankets or bags. Put there before you shot him."

The Kid's glance came around; he was surprised at
Colfax' cleverness, and made a point to remember that
this man was smarter than he looked. "Let me have the
blankets," he said.

But Ben was already spreading them out. "Take the
bags," he said.

Ben was pawing the blankets apart while the Kid
sounded the saddlebags. He found Pete's shaving gear, a
spare pair of socks, then the gun. "Here's something," he
said. "Bring the light around."

With the yellow flow of light over his shoulder, he
read the caliber: .44 S & W American. Finding the gun
made his case as complete as anyone could make it; he
felt a vast relief, for his conscience had been riding him
for having shot an innocent man, even in self-defense.

"He was Rindo's man," Ben Colfax said. "The old man
will have some explaining to do at the inquest."

"I'll need you there for a witness," the Wind River Kid said.

"Be obliged to tell what I know," Colfax said. He kicked Pete's belongings under the feed bin. "People around here know me, Kid. My testimony will give weight to the proceedings." He slapped the Kid on the arm and walked out, his shoulders bent, his head down as though he were studying tracks on the ground ahead of him.

Leaving the livery, the Kid decided to speak to Cadmus Rindo, for in his mind he felt that the old man should be told about Pete's guilt. Facing a coroner's inquest in the morning, Rindo would be at a terrible disadvantage if this proof were thrown unexpectedly in his face. Yet as he walked along the street, the Kid thought of that bullet collection Dr. Carver had. Could any of the other bullets there have been fired from a .44 American?

Dr. Carver was in his library, and he put his book aside when the Kid stepped in. "Sorry to interrupt," the Kid told him, "but I'd like to have another look at those bullets you saved."

"Certainly," Carver said, taking the lamp so he could go ahead to his laboratory. He placed the box of bullets on the table; each tagged and cushioned in cotton. "This one," he said, "was taken from Dale Pritchard, an attorney who was killed here about a year ago."

"How did it happen?" the Kid asked, taking the bullet and swinging around toward the lamp.

"No one knows," Carver admitted. "Knew the man pretty well too. Played cards with him regularly at Burkhauser's." He looked at the Kid and saw his sharpened expression. "Find something?"

"It's a .44 American," the Kid said. He laid the bullet down. "After Pritchard was shot, was that when the card games broke up for good?"

Carver looked a bit uneasy. "You know about that? How the devil——" Then he shrugged. "It's no matter really. Burkhauser, Ben Colfax, the judge, myself and Pritchard had a sort of private club." He paused as a man will when he wants a relatively bad thing to sound relatively good. "We were always hashing over some scheme to take control away from Rindo." He laughed hollowly. "It was really just a way to pass the time."

"Someone didn't think so," the Kid said. "Looks like Pete took his job seriously enough to kill more than one man to keep it. Where was Pritchard shot?"

"Behind Burkhauser's place," Carver said. "The body was found near the gap between the buildings. Someone had been waiting for him."

"I thought that side door was a secret."

"Seems that it isn't, seeing as how you know about it," Carver said. "Ben Colfax investigated for weeks but couldn't turn up a thing." He sighed and wiped his mouth. "Makes me stop and think. Rindo must have known all the time; who else gave Pete his orders?"

"Let's see the bullet that killed Bess Jamison's father," the Kid said.

Carver fished through the tagged lead, then laid another in the sheriff's palm. "A .44 American?"

"Yes," the Kid said. "Can I have these three bullets?"

"That's evidence," Carver said. "Will you sign a paper for them?"

"Certainly," the Kid said and waited while Carver wrote out the description and circumstances pertaining to their removal. The Kid affixed his signature, then put the bullets into a small paper box that the doctor gave him. At the door he asked, "Is Boomhauer still at the hotel?"

"Yes," Carver said. "I intend to check on him later on."

Leaving the doctor's house, the Kid walked slowly toward the center of town. The matching bullets put Cadmus Rindo in a bad light. He knew only the barest rudiments of how business was run, but he was smart enough to know that the moment Rindo was indicted, Rindo's Springs would go to rack and ruin. The notes held by the merchants would be nearly worthless for Rindo could not pay off. The economy of the town would hit the bottom with such a whack that it might never recover.

As he passed the newspaper office, Nan Buckley spoke from the dark doorway. "Lost your last friend, Kid?"

He stopped and turned to her. "Nan," he said softly, "you told me once that you never wanted to see Rindo's Springs die. Well, I have to do what you didn't want done. I can't help myself, Nan."

"What are you talking about?" She stepped up to him and took his arm. "Kid, you've got to tell me."

"Come along," he said.

"All right." She drew a shawl around her shoulders and walked with him to the hotel. They met the clerk coming down the stairs, a tray full of dishes neatly balanced.

In passing, the Kid asked, "The marshal awake?"

"Yes," the clerk said. "Room six. We moved him to the second floor where there's a little more quiet."

The wall lamps puddled a dirty yellow light on the carpet. At the far end of the hall, the Kid opened the door without knocking, then stepped aside so that Nan could enter first. Boomhauer was propped up in bed. His face was gray although a strong dose of laudanum had deadened the major run of his pain. The Kid made a hurried introduction of Nan, then pushed two chairs close to the bed.

"I've got a nerve coming here like this," the Kid said, "but I need help. This job has kept me guessing; I don't know much about the law. All I can go by is what I think is right and wrong." He glanced at Nan, then launched into the history of Rindo's Springs, making clear the town's dependence on Cadmus Rindo. He described in detail the trouble Rindo had with Bess Jamison's father, and with the daughter after the father was shot. Without taking sides, the Kid laid out the rewards and consequences should anyone succeed in dethroning the old man. Then he produced the bullets, filling Boomhauer in on the details, and his suspicions. When he finished, he sat back in his chair, his young face grave.

"I would say," Boomhauer offered, "that you have a poor case against Cadmus Rindo." He put the bullets back in the box. "I have no doubt that a conviction is impossible; you have nothing to link him to the shootings. However, as you say, the town will collapse if you even let out a suspicion that he could have had anything to do with the deaths. Quite a problem. Throws the law books out the window and places everything on a man's conscience, doesn't it?"

"Yes," the Kid said softly. "Wade, some men in this town have been waiting for the day to come when they could make people believe that Rindo was through. Money is waiting to buy up Rindo's notes at ten cents on the dollar, and when that happens there won't be a town. People have to trust each other in order to do business. If I arrest Rindo, the trust will be wiped out. He's an anchor for everyone here. Now, what if I don't choose to sink the town just to get one man?"

Boomhauer's face was thoughtful. "You know the answer," he said. "As soon as I can walk, I'll take over and do the job for you." He let a small gap of silence build. "Kid, I've been in this business for eight years. It's what I wanted to be. You have no right to temper the law with your own feelings; if that happened often, there wouldn't be any law to turn to." He locked eyes with the Wind River Kid. "As soon as I'm able I'm going to arrest you, Kid. I'll come after you again. Maybe it won't be in the arm the next time, but as long as I carry this badge, I've got to try. And if I don't make it, I'll know that somewhere another badge will take up where I left off."

"What kind of man are you?" Nan asked flatly.

"He's a lawman," the Kid said, rising. "And a much better one than me." He opened the door for Nan Buckley and she stepped through. The Kid paused and said, "Wade, I like this town, so I'm going to play this the stupid way."

"I thought you would," Boomhauer said. "Good luck, Kid."

The Kid flashed him a grin and went down the hall with Nan Buckley. When they reached the boardwalk they stopped.

"Thanks for making the decision I wanted you to make," she said. She looked at him steadily, her eyes bright. "And yet in a way I'm sorry because you had to take sides. A compromise has always come hard for you, hasn't it? Perhaps that was what made me like you from the start."

She turned before he could speak and hurried down the street. He waited until she passed from sight around the corner, then stepped off the walk, angling toward Burkhauser's saloon.

HALFWAY ACROSS THE STREET, the Wind River Kid stopped and retraced his steps. Reentering the hotel, he went to Will Beau-Haven's door and knocked, then waited with a growing impatience until Grace opened it. She seemed quite surprised to see him, but stepped aside and ushered him in. She wore an old pair of carpet slippers and they flapped loosely as she led the way to the gallery where Will Beau-Haven was taking his nightly observation of the town.

"The sheriff's here," she said and sat down. Lamplight dribbled through the open door and in this feeble light she resumed her interrupted knitting.

"Thought you'd be back," Beau-Haven said. He waited until the Kid pulled a chair around and sat down. "The town's getting nervous, I can feel it. People here are like a little kid who thinks his father's holding him down. The kid swears he'll up and leave home, but few do because they can't lose pa to lean on. The word's already around that you and Ben found the gun Pete used to kill the Jamison teamster. Pete worked for Rindo and Rindo was quarreling with Bess Jamison. Pretty obvious conclusion there, huh?"

"It's not proof," the Kid said. "No proof at all."

"True," Beau-Haven admitted, "but it's enough to start a run on Rindo's bank. You wait until it opens in the morning and you'll see the line." He turned to his wife. "Hand me that box of cigars there." Then he offered one to the Kid, and a light.

Between puffs, the Kid asked, "Who was Dale Pritchard?"

"So you found out about him?" Beau-Haven shrugged. "A smart lawyer. Too smart maybe."

"Part of the poker club?"

Beau-Haven chuckled. "Doc always did talk too much. Yes, Pritchard was as greedy as the rest. Came here as Rindo's lawyer. Quit him after a year or two and established a private practice. Talk has it that the judge, Ben Colfax and Murray Burkhauser financed him. No proof of it though." He paused to taste the fragrance of his cigar. "Whatever went on at those poker games is all over, sheriff. That door has been boarded up for months now." He turned his head and looked carefully at the young man. "What's so interesting about Pritchard? Most people have forgot about him by now."

"Any man whose death has never been explained is worth asking about," the Kid said. He got up. "Well, thanks for the cigar."

"I'll show you out," Grace Beau-Haven said tonelessly and laid her knitting aside. Her expression was as immobile as cement. The Kid followed her to the hall door.

She said a brief goodnight, then closed the door, listening to his footsteps recede down the hall. When she was positive that he had left the building, she walked back to the gallery.

"Time to come in now, Will."

"Ah, let me finish my cigar," he said.

"Now you can have another cigar tomorrow," she said. He grumbled something and she wheeled his chair toward the double doors. She placed him alongside his bed. With an effort she helped him shift his weight out of the chair. And when she leaned over to undress him, he took her arms and tried to pull her to him.

Her hands set up a gentle but firm resistance. "Please," she said, "you're just getting yourself worked up again."

His expression turned angry and desperate and packed with frustration. "Can I help wanting you with my mind, even though I can't do anything about it?"

She pulled away from him and fussed with his covers. "You have to stop thinking about it," she said. "Will, I've tried not to disturb you."

"Disturb me?" He looked at the ceiling and laughed. "Grace, do you think a sack dress can disguise what I already know?" He clenched his fists and struck his misshapen thighs, his mangled hips.

"I'll get you the tonic so you can sleep," she said and hurried from the room. When she came back, he was staring at the ceiling with dulled eyes. The tonic was downed without protest and he sagged back on his pillow. She turned the lamp down and went to the door. "You'll sleep now, Will. Please try."

"Where will you be?"

"Always near you," she said. "I bought a new book called *Ben Hur*. Perhaps you'd like to read—"

"No, no," he said, waving his hand. "God knows you have so little pleasure, Grace; I'd not deny you that."

"Goodnight, Will."

He did not answer her; he rarely did. She closed the door softly and went into the parlor. The hanging wall clock ticked steadily on and she glanced at it: a quarter to nine. Early, she thought, and settled down with her book.

When the Kid stepped into Murray Burkhauser's saloon, heads turned, gave him a brief glance, then swung back to their own interests. He sagged against the bar, signaled for service, and the bartender edged up. "A tall beer," the Kid said. "Murray in the back?"

"No, he's playing cards over to Judge Richmond's house."

The Kid successfully masked his interest. "Oh, with Doc and Ben Colfax?"

"You got it right," the bartender said, moving away.

Toying with his beer, the Kid considered this for what it was worth. The door Beau-Haven said was no longer in use did not mean the end of the poker games, or the talk that must pass back and forth. The game went on and the Kid was certain that the stakes were not always on the table. But four-handed poker was a poor game; a fifth member made it more interesting. Dale Pritchard had been the fifth. Now the Kid wondered who had taken his place.

Finishing his beer, he went out and down the street. Traffic was light, a few horsemen and fewer pedestrians. At a quiet corner, the Kid ducked down a dark side street, walking slowly until he came to the alley behind the saloon. Dodging litter, he made careful progress until he came to the gap between the saloon and the store. To make sure he had the right place, he took a quick sight through and saw the upper gallery of the hotel. With half a mind he noticed that Will Beau-Haven was no longer at his post. Easing into the slot, the Kid found it free of debris. Normally such an opening would be a catch-all for stray whiskey bottles, but here everything had been carefully picked up. The night was ink here and he gently felt along the wall of the saloon until he found the boarded-up section. All along the Kid had felt that he was onto something important here, but now he felt a keen disappointment.

Still, he made a careful examination with his hands, and oddly enough, found that all the boards were cut to exactly the same length. This struck an off-key chord in his mind, for he knew how haphazardly a place was usually closed up—a carpenter did not bother with exact measurements and cuts.

Yet this was a good job, tight-fitting and perfectly laid out. Returning to the alley, the Kid found a tin-can lid, then returned to the section of the wall and carefully tested the ends of the sawed boards. The lid went in deep, clearly outlining a doorway.

Satisfied now, the Kid found a piece of paper and wedged it carefully into the crack. Tomorrow he would come back and look for it. If it was still there, he would know that the door had remained closed. If it had fallen, then he'd have to lay plans to find out who used the door.

Leaving the alley, he walked down the quiet street toward Cadmus Rindo's house. There was a light on in the old man's study and the Kid knocked. A moment later the servant admitted him. Rindo was sitting by a small table, reading. He put the book down and waved the Kid into a chair. "Sort of been expecting you," he said. "I hear tell you found Pete's other gun."

"Yes," the Kid said flatly. He took a chance and added, "That same gun killed Bess Jamison's father and Dale Pritchard. Do you know what that adds up to?"

"That I ordered it done," Rindo said. He waved his hand. "Don't matter. I'd be accused of it anyway."

"Some people will say that it's proof enough."

The old man's eyes squinted. "What do you say?"

"It doesn't make much sense," the Kid said. "Hell, of all people you know best what'll happen here if there's open trouble. Shooting Bess's old man was a sure way to start it. So was killing the teamster. Unless you're trying to put yourself under, you'd have no reason to have 'em killed."

"That's my whole point," Rindo said. "No matter how Ben or any of the others twist it, I'd gain the least by starting trouble." He smiled. "Being as you're a man who's seen his share of trouble, I was counting on you to see it." His humor vanished. "How does it look' up town, Kid?"

"Not good," the Kid admitted. "Beau-Haven thinks there'll be a run on the bank in the morning."

"I'd better call Cal Runyon," Rindo said and rang a small bell to summon his servant. When the man appeared, Rindo said, "Go to the company office and fetch Cal Runyon here."

The servant turned to go, then faced around again. "Beggin' pahdon, suh, but Mistah Runyon's ovah to the judge's house playin' pokah. This is Thursday, suh."

"Go get him anyway," Rindo said, sagging back as the servant went out.

The Kid was relieved when Rindo clung to a brief silence, for he was trying to fit Runyon into the poker club, to attach some meaning for this small but very select group. Somehow, in his mind, this group had become synonymous with Cadmus Rindo's troubles.

He looked up suddenly and found the old man's sharp eyes reading him. Rindo said, "You play poker, Kid?"

"Probably not the way Runyon plays," the Kid said. He leaned forward, his curiosity out of control. "Old man, don't you care?"

Rindo started to chuckle. "Kid, if I jumped every time a rabbit rustled in the brush, I'd be jumpin' all the time. Cal Runyon's a human being. And don't you forget it." He leaned back in his chair and folded his gnarled hands in his lap. "For nigh onto forty years now, I've put up with this sort of thing. Sure, I could ride herd on these folks, but there's no need to. Give 'em their chance to talk and plan and scheme and get frustrated. As long as I'm alive, there's nothing they can really do."

"They can kill you," the Kid said.

"That's likely," Rindo said. "But who's goin' to do it? Ben Colfax? Naw! Ben don't want to get hung while everyone licks up the gravy. Oh, Ben'd like to see me dead, but he wouldn't do it."

"What about Burkhauser and the judge and Doc Carver?"

"Same thing," Rindo said. "They've been talkin' about

it for a long time, but they still haven't settled that one important detail: who's going to pull the trigger." He sighed and packed his pipe. "Son, you're settin' there, mind a-churnin' away, trying to figure out who killed who. It does bother me, the way you always keep lookin' for a man's dark side. Why should you look for something we all know is there? Look toward his good, son. Life's a lot more pleasant that way."

"I can't make up my mind," the Kid said, "whether you're a great man or a damn fool."

"A blend," Rindo said. "Just like all other men." He turned his head when steps crossed the porch. "That'll be Cal." He got up and poured a drink and had it waiting when the young general superintendent came in. Runyon nodded to the Kid and picked up the glass. Rindo asked, "How was the game?"

"Dull," Runyon admitted. He checked his watch. "I hope this won't take too long. I'm thirty-seven dollars in the hole, and I'd like to make it back before midnight."

"Maybe I can add a little fresh blood," the Kid suggested gently.

"I'd like that," Runyon said. He drank his whiskey and looked at Cadmus Rindo.

The old man said, "Before the bank opens in the morning, take that eighteen thousand that's in the company safe and transfer it to the bank's vault. The Kid here heard a rumor of a run."

The Wind River Kid stared, for this was not what he had expected. When he opened his mouth to protest, Rindo smiled and shushed him with a wave of his hand. "Son, when there's going to be a run on a bank, there's nothing like money to stop it. If a depositor's scared, his philosophy is: if you have it, I don't want it, and if you haven't got it, I want it now." His glance touched Runyon. "See that the money gets there." He pushed himself erect. "Bedtime, gents. And, both of you, stop stewin' and get a decent night's sleep."

Cal Runyon and the Kid left the house together, taking another back street toward the judge's place. Runyon walked in silence for a time, then said, "He's a great old man, Kid. I'd like to see him outlive all of us."

"He may at that," the Kid said.

The shades were pulled in the judge's parlor, but fragments of light squeezed through at the bottom. Runyon went in without knocking and they looked around, surprised to see the Kid with him. Burkhauser pulled up a chair and said, "I hope you've got cash. My luck's terrible and some new money will look good."

Judge Richmond nodded and Carver peered over his glasses. Ben Colfax mumbled a greeting, then put his attention on the shuffle. "Stud," he said. "A dollar ante."

He flipped the cards with a certain clumsiness, one to each man, all face up except his own. The Kid had a queen showing so he bet another dollar. "That-a-boy!" Burkhauser said. "Go slow here. Remember the poor working man."

Again Ben Colfax put out a round of cards, face up. Runyon drew a ten to match the one he got on the first round. Ben Colfax peeked at his hole card, then said, "Make up your mind, Cal."

"I'll go two," he said and slid his money onto the table. Richmond licked his lips and looked at the five and six he had; he seemed to have difficulty deciding whether to stay in or drop out. But he was a long-shot player at heart and put in his money.

Again the cards went around. "There's whiskey if you want it," Burkhauser said. No one seemed to care for a drink. Burkhauser was moodily studying his cards while Ben Colfax contemplated two jacks. The Kid had a queen and a pair of nines.

"Jacks bet," Colfax said, "ten dollars."

Richmond threw in his hand and the Kid could not help thinking how right Rindo was: the judge for one did not have the courage to kill a man. Murray Burkhauser made a great fuss over his cards, but he was too conservative to take chances; his went into the discards. Runyon played it out, as did Carver and the Kid, only Carver was lost before he started. He was a man who tried to reduce the game to scientific principles, ignoring the strong character of the players.

When all cards were out, Runyon and Carver gave up, after contributing thirty-five dollars apiece to the pot. The Kid looked at Ben Colfax crouching over his cards. Colfax had his pair of jacks and an ace showing, against the Kid's pair of nines and the solitary queen. "Jacks, ace bet," the Kid said.

Ben took his time, making the wait tedious even for those already dropped out. He did not look more than once at his hole card, implying that it was so good as to become unforgettable. His flat glance touched the Kid, then he said, "How much you got there?" indicating the coins by the Kid's elbow.

"About a hundred dollars."

"That's my bet," Colfax said, thrusting that amount to the center of the table.

The Wind River Kid began to dig into his pockets and came up with some bills. He added this to the gold, then said, "Raise you seventy-five."

A muscle twitched in Ben Colfax' cheek and his eyes pulled together slightly. Murray Burkhauser said, "Put up or shut up, Ben. You've been tapping us all night."

The Kid waited; then with a growl of disgust Ben threw in his hand. His hole card was a deuce of spades. Scooping the money toward him, the Kid counted it, put most of it away, then took the deal. "Five-card draw," he said, "since it's dealer's choice."

He played for an hour and a half, winning some, losing some, but generally winning from the judge and Cal Runyon. Carver's mathematics were confounding, for the man played a straight game, so straight that it was confusing. Carver was a sure-thing player and the moment he suspected that the cards were falling wrong, he dropped out.

Burkhauser had been a professional too long to play for anyone but the house. He possessed no individual daring, especially when betting his own money.

The real study was Ben Colfax, and the Kid bent all his mental faculties trying to keep abreast of the man. Twice Colfax drew to an inside straight and made it. Given the slightest chance, Ben Colfax would either make his cards or bluff the others into submission.

At a quarter to twelve, Murray Burkhauser yawned and slid back his chair. "Closing time," he said. "I've got to see if the bartender made back what I've lost."

He got into his coat and said goodnight. The Kid glanced at his watch while Cal Runyon said, "Hey now, big winners don't walk out so easy."

"I can spare an hour or two," the Kid admitted.

"An hour for me," Colfax said. "Way past my roosting time." He looked around the table. "Who's got the deal? Doc? Let's get 'em out then." He spun a dollar onto the table and leaned back, smiling at the Wind River Kid.

When the wall clock struck eleven, Grace Beau-Haven put down *Ben Hur* and went into her bedroom. There she kindled a small fire and heated water for her bath. She undressed and stood before a full length mirror, studying herself. Shed of the drab and shapeless dress, she was a woman alive and beautiful, with a body delightfully turned in flawless curves. Her breasts were high and firm, her hips boyishly trim and her muscles as smooth as a runner's.

Impatient with the heating water she dumped it luke-warm into a large pewter tub then lowered herself into it. Her bath was leisurely and after blotting herself dry, she sprayed her neck and shoulders with cologne. Afterward she re-hid the bottle on the top closet shelf.

From a hidden alcove she took out a dress that was pale blue and as light as a cloud. She shook it just to hear the silk rustle, then giggled, so profound was her pleasure.

Donning fragile silk - underclothes and lace-trimmed petticoats, she moved gracefully about, humming in an almost breathless way. Finally she slipped into the dress, fought the row of tiny buttons up the back, then put on a pair of light shoes.

The clock had struck the half-hour some time before and she turned the lamps down before opening the hall door. No one was in sight and she moved toward the back entrance, which was always kept locked at night. Inserting a key, she let herself out, then relocked the door. A flight of steps let her down to the mud-black alley. She took the stairs carefully, yet rapidly, for she had a long-standing familiarity with them. Moving swiftly down the alley, she avoided noisy traps of litter, then stopped at the first cross street. All the business houses were closed and no one occupied the boardwalks. Quickly and unseen, she crossed to the other side, and halfway down, entered the alley.

Only by conscious effort did she keep herself from running, and with each step her impatience increased until it became almost unbearable. At a gap between the buildings she paused, but only for a second. Then she turned sideways and began to edge through. At the boarded door in Burkhauser's wall she scraped twice with her fingernails, then listened to his approaching step on the other side.

10

As WAS HIS long-established habit, Murray Burkhauser closed his saloon at eight minutes to twelve on Thursday nights. He took the cash from the bartender's box and carried it to his office. A turned key closed him off from the rest of Rindo's Springs and after putting the cash away, he ignited a cigar and waited.

Frequent glances at his watch kept him informed of the exact time, and when he heard two faint scratches on the wall, he lifted a metal wastebasket and placed it over the desk lamp. With the room smothered in darkness, Burkhauser stepped to the bookcase, pulled it from the wall so that Grace Beau-Haven could enter, then closed it quickly.

He then removed the metal basket from the lamp before the odor of heated metal grew thick in the room. With only the single light pushing at the darkness, they put their arms around each other and stood that way for many minutes, their lips locked, all else forgotten save their own driving passion. There was a touch of obscenity in the way Murray Burkhauser loved this woman: his hands pulled at the rounded flesh as though trying to devour it. His kiss indicated a passion starved beyond control, and he breathed heavily through his nose like a wrestler struggling to free himself from an inescapable grip. His animal hungers overwhelmed her until she merely submitted to his anxious hands, probing, caressing, fondling. There was no balance to his ardor, no scheme or semblance of order to his passion-mad thoughts. He would break off from a kiss to bite her on the neck, then abandon that to grind her body against his; he was a demented bee running amok in a flower

garden, overwhelmed, unable to steady himself for a
moment to drink from a single blossom. There was little
satisfaction to this love; perhaps that drove him so
furiously. His mind was riveted to only one thought
finally and he pressed her back until she rested on his
leather couch.

Grace Beau-Haven's hands pushed at him, trying to
check his headlong rush, but he was beyond restraint.
As before, she gave up and tried instead to match his
insanity. The wall clock ticked loudly and Burkhauser's
breathing was a deep whistling as his lips sought the
hollow of her throat. She knew this man and what he
expected, so she moaned a little and bit him on the ear.

This seemed to be a sort of signal for he got up
hurriedly and turned down the lamp until the room was
thick with shadows. Her dress rustled as she stood up
and Murray Burkhauser tore impatiently at the buttons
on his vest and shirt.

"Hurry," she said softly, and this drove him to a frenzy
of haste.

At four o'clock Murray Burkhauser got up and searched
out a cigar. He padded about, naked and bare foot, the
strong odor of sour sweat heavy in his nostrils. Fumbling
about on his desk, his fingers contacted a cigar and he
hastily put a match to it. In the glare he looked down
at his body and felt a strong revulsion. Whipping out the
match, he slipped quickly into pants and shirt.

This too seemed to be a signal, for near the shadows
by the bed, Grace sat up, then began to shrug into her
petticoats. Murray Burkhauser turned up the lamp and
let the new light fling harsh shadows across his face.

"What time is it?" she asked.

He walked over to the wall clock and peered at it.
"Quarter past four." He stood there puffing on his cigar.
His upper body was thick and roped with muscle and
dark tufts of hair peeked through the open front of his
shirt. "Are you all right?" he asked.

"Yes, I'm fine." He helped her fasten the back of her
dress, then stood there watching her as she put on
her shoes. He wondered if he had hurt her; sometimes
he did, forgetting his strength, bruising her; once his
fingernails had drawn blood.

"Do you want me to go with you?" he asked softly.

"No. Someone might see you."

Suddenly she put her elbows on her knees and looked at him. "Do you know how deep hell is, Murray?"

"What kind of crazy talk is that?" he asked. "Grace, you're not going to have one of your spells, are you?"

"No," she said. "I won't embarrass you, Murray. I know what appearances mean to you."

"Grace—"

"Don't start lying to me," she said quickly. "Don't start telling me that you want to marry me, because I know you don't. I merely serve a purpose in your life, Murray, and if I didn't, some other woman would."

"That's not true!"

"It's true," she said. "Murray, we just don't care about anyone but ourselves. We'll never do the right thing, because the right thing just isn't in us. Down to hell, that's where we're going." She giggled and this frightened him slightly, for her balance was precarious at best. "I don't know why I keep coming here, but I suppose it's because I need you. I don't love you when I leave. Just hate you because you always prove to me what I really am." She gathered the remainder of her things and went to the bookcase. He didn't want to argue with her; his only emotion now was one of impatience; he wanted to be left alone. She stepped down to ground level. They did not speak; goodbye was a needless word. Swiftly and silently she moved down the narrow gap.

Rindo's Springs was asleep; still she used caution navigating her way back to the rear entrance of the hotel. She was an expert at stealth, having practiced it for so long. Unlocking the door, she glanced down the hall, saw no one, then went quickly into her own rooms. The lamp still burned and she began to put her clothes away carefully.

Then she opened the connecting door that led into Will Beau-Haven's room. The side lamp by his bed was flickering, nearly out of kerosene, so she refilled it from a two-gallon can kept in the closet.

Will Beau-Haven lay on his back, his features immobile. For several minutes Grace stood there, looking at this man she had married. Then she reached out and touched his cheek and felt the waxy coldness there. Her eyes regarded him quite calmly, then she said, "I'll get you another blanket, dear."

When she tried to tuck the quilt about him, he felt

strangely unyielding. A trembling started in her legs and worked through her until she shivered uncontrollably. She lay down beside him, her hand stroking his cold, bloodless cheek.

The sun woke her and she stared at the reflection cast on the ceiling by water in the washbasin. She felt very cold and when she got up her body ached and each movement was painful. Then she staggered into the other room, her eyes immobile in a stiff-set face. Carefully she dressed in the drab, ill-fitting dress, fixed her hair in its severe fashion, then powdered her face until her complexion was chalky. "I'm very modest," she said aloud. "A woman has to watch her appearance, men being what they are. But I really prefer gray; it's my best color."

Suddenly she went to the closet and took out the lovely, hidden dresses. Carrying them to the heating stove, she stuffed them inside. A rolled paper and a match sent them roaring up in smoke while she stood there with a rapt expression, smiling and watching the hungry, bright flames.

When the fire died to a gray ash, she walked to the hall door and stood there, a drab, pathetic figure. The clerk was bustling about his duties in the lobby and he looked up, smiling when he saw her. "Good morning, Mrs. Beau-Haven."

Her expression was curiously wooden but her voice was quite deep. "Please send up breakfast for two."

The clerk nodded and she went back into her room. Standing by Will Beau-Haven's bed, she idly brushed his hair. "The sun's out this morning; you'll feel better when you get warm."

Finally the clerk came in with the tray. "Just set it there on the table," she said. "Will you help me get him into his chair, Joe?"

"Sure," the clerk said and followed her to Beau-Haven's bed. He looked at Beau-Haven, his eyes growing larger and rounder. Then he gave Grace a startled glance. "Mrs. Beau-Haven, he's—dead!"

"No, he's just chilled," she said softly. "He'll feel better when he gets in the sun, Joe."

Like all sane people confronted with madness, the clerk regarded her with a tinge of fear. Slowly he backed toward the hall door, then made a dash for the stairs, yelling in a quavering voice.

11

SHORTLY AFTER DAYBREAK, the Kid left his lumpy cot in the sheriff's office and took a walk around town. A swamper was plying his broom on Burkhauser's porch, and down the street the butcher was opening his shop. After cruising both sides, the Kid eased into the alley behind the saloon, then into the gap between Burkhauser's and the store. He found his piece of paper on the ground and picked it up, a thin smile on his face. Quite understandable now was Burkhauser's pointed departure from the poker game.

Leaving the alley, the Kid walked to the restaurant and there had a heavy breakfast. By seven o'clock, a good crowd was developing on both sides of the street. Waiting for the bank to open, he decided, and ordered another cup of coffee.

Nan Buckley came down the street, looked in the window, then came in when she saw him at the counter. "I stopped at your office and you weren't there," she said. The waiter looked at her and she added, "A cup for me, Wong." Her fingers fastened in the Kid's sleeve. "What can we do about this?"

He shrugged. "Nothing. Did Bess Jamison come into town yet?"

"I haven't seen her. Besides, I don't give a damn about her. But there can't be enough money in the bank to pay off the depositors."

"Keep your voice down," he said, and finished his coffee. He swung around so that he faced her. "Why don't you just sit still and see what happens." A quick consultation with his watch told him that time was advancing. "I have an inquest to attend."

"You're awfully calm," she said half-accusingly, as though she envied him this display of unconcern.

The Kid left the restaurant. Pausing on the boardwalk, he looked at the crowd growing near the bank. Mostly small depositors, he judged; very few businessmen were there. This gave him some heart, for if Rindo could stand the strain of paying off for two hours, the word would get around that he had the money. And as he had said, if he had it, they soon wouldn't want it.

Returning to his office, he found Dr. Carver there. The little man's usually grave expression was even more cloudy and he kept drumming his fingers against the edge of the desk.

"Too much poker?" the Kid asked.

"Agh," Carver said. "I've been waiting for you." He took a sheaf of papers from an inner coat pocket. "Here's the report on Pete. You'll need it for the inquest."

"Thanks," the Kid said. He nodded toward the crowd around the bank. "If you have anything in there, you'd better get it out."

"There are other things to worry about," Carver said. He started toward the door, then stopped. "I don't suppose you heard, but Will Beau-Haven took too much medicine last night. On purpose. I found the empty bottle by his bed this morning."

"Dead?"

"Very. Happened around midnight, I'd say." He shrugged his thin shoulders. "He was a sick man anyway. It's his wife I feel sorry for. She found him and it must have snapped her reason. Hopelessly insane, I'm afraid."

He went out in the bustling way he had, as though there were a thousand things he had to do immediately. The Kid sat down on the corner of his desk, his eyes thoughtful.

Then on impulse he picked up his hat, left the office and walked along the main street until he came to Burkhauser's saloon. As he drew near, he became aware of hammering somewhere in back and a strange excitement charged through him. He felt as though he were nearing the end of something important.

The bartender was alone, bent below the counter rearranging his beer kegs. The Kid hurried through and went into the back where Murray kept his rooms. Burkhauser's door was open and the Kid stepped inside. The hammering was coming from the other side of the bookcase. He looked around, seeing the fine furniture, the ornate drapes and desk. Then he walked over to the bookcase and by feeling the vibration, located the door. A tug opened it and he smiled into Burkhauser's startled face.

"Doing a little carpenter work, Murray?"

A moment passed before Burkhauser spoke. "Wait there," he said. "I'm coming in."

"Good," the Kid said and shoved the bookcase closed again. He heard the rear door slam, then Burkhauser's step in the hall. When he came in, he slammed the door and threw the hammer in the corner.

Murray's expression said that he wanted to know how the Kid had caught on. The young man smiled and said, "Will Beau-Haven told me about it."

"That snoop!"

"Dead snoop," the Kid corrected. "It's peculiar how a man reaches conclusions. It all started with the poker club, before Dale Pritchard was killed. Beau-Haven said the door hadn't been used, yet the gap was kept clean. That struck me as odd, Murray. In my work the odd things can save your life." He patted his pockets for a cigar and when he failed to find one, took one of Burkhauser's. "Last night I stuck a piece of paper in the crack of that door and this morning found it on the ground. It fell there when the door was opened."

"Damned smart," Murray Burkhauser rumbled.

"You haven't heard the real smart part yet," the Kid said. "I kept asking myself why a man would leave an old group like your poker party to keep a midnight appointment. The answer was obvious." He smiled. "A woman, Murray. The answer had to be a woman." He shrugged and slapped his thighs. "You know, that discouraged me. It really did. All the time I hoped I was uncovering the group of men who were plotting to take Rindo's hair, and then it turned out that the door was for a woman. Real discouraging."

Murray Burkhauser stared, his mouth a fleshy O. "Plotting against—Jesus, we want to save this town!"

"Now that sounds pretty thin, Murray. But no mind now. When doc told me that Beau-Haven committed suicide in the night, and that his wife was out of her mind, I got a hunch. Ever have a hunch? No, I can see that you're a percentage player. So I came here, and sure enough, you were boarding the door up, which meant that it wouldn't be used again. Why? Because Grace Beau-Haven could never use it again."

The Kid had laid enough ammunition into the black to recognize a score when he made it; Burkhauser's bluff ran out, leaving him full of trouble. "You got a few things twisted," Murray said, pouring himself a glass of whiskey. He drank, then stood deep in thought for a moment. "I guess I know which side you're on, Kid. The town's side. And believe me, that's the only one that matters a damn to me." He looked suspiciously at the Kid. "Must sound bad, coming from me. I've lied and cheated all my life, and told myself that I wasn't really that way at all. But that was a lie too. Funny thing about a weak man. He can't stand without help. That's why Pritchard, Carver, Richmond, Colfax and me formed a little club. Bess Jamison's old man was raising hell; we could see a split-down-the-middle fight coming, and had an idea what it would do to the town. So we got set up for it, pooling money, intending to buy up enough to save Cadmus Rindo when he got forced to the wall."

"But Pritchard got killed," the Kid reminded him. "You waited a long time before taking in another man."

"We had to be sure! Hell, it couldn't be just anybody!" He wiped a hand across his mouth. "That run on the bank won't work, Kid. It won't work because a bunch of us deposited another thirteen thousand dollars this morning before it opened." He laughed with pride and he stood a little straighter. "Rindo can keep paying all day and never run dry. When people see that, they'll stop asking for their money."

This was a possibility that the Kid had completely ignored, that men could be trying to save the town as well as grab what they could for themselves. "Is this straight, Murray?"

"It's straight," he said. "But you can't say anything about it."

"No, I can see that." He looked squarely at Burkhauser. "Now we come to the door."

"I made it," he said. "We had to have a place to meet that wasn't public. After Pritchard got shot, we figured that someone was on to us, so we never used it again." His glance was guilt-filled. "Then I got better acquainted with Grace. It was a rotten thing from the beginning, but I couldn't stop it. I don't think I wanted to stop it."

"Well, it's been stopped now," the Kid said. "Murray, do you think one of Rindo's men killed Pritchard?"

"Hell no! I heard about you matching bullets, but there's something wrong there, Kid. Pete wasn't a back-shooter for anyone, certainly not Cadmus Rindo. A gun-man yes, but not an alley artist. He was proud of the fact that he faced his men."

The Kid glanced at his watch. "The inquest is going to begin in a few minutes." He got up and stepped to the door. "Thanks, Murray. Now I don't feel so alone."

"Wait! Kid, you don't owe this town anything. Why are you fighting for it?"

"Maybe for the same reason you are," he said. "I get a feeling here that I'm really better than I think I am. A good feeling, Murray. Hate to lose it."

He grinned. "People ain't so bad, Kid. Even when they're sonsabitches."

"You're right," the Kid said and left.

The crowd at the bank was a noisy one, now that the doors were open and the cashiers were paying out as fast as they could count it. The sight of people emerging, counting their money, had a healthy effect on those trying to get in. Snatches of talk reached the Kid; one man standing near the crowd proclaimed in a loud voice, "Hell, they got it stacked up a foot high in there! More gold and paper than you ever seen before!"

Using these signs as a basis for judgment, the Kid suspected that the run was due for a short life. With this thought he turned and walked toward Judge Richmond's house.

A block away he could see that the clans had gathered; Cadmus Rindo's expensive buggy was parked by the white picket fence, as was Bess Jamison's mud-spattered rig. Surrounding these were the saddle horses belonging to Bess' men. They were standing in a tight group, stern-faced and silent. As the Kid walked by, they gave him blunt stares, but he could see that they had taken his earlier warning to heart; their weapons were in saddle scabbards.

Ben Colfax and Cal Runyon were standing on the judge's porch, talking, and when the Kid walked up the path, they broke this conversation off.

"Damned sad about Beau-Haven," Runyon said. "He worked for Rindo before I came here."

"Tough on his missus," Colfax murmured. "Doin's about ready to start, Kid."

They went into the judge's parlor and found the warring factions seated on opposite sides of the room. Bess Jamison stared at the Kid, her expression hostile. She and Cadmus Rindo, he decided, did not actually hate each other, but they had passed so many acid remarks back and forth that neither was willing to take anything back for fear of appearing weak. The Kid took a chair near Dr. Carver, and Judge Richmond rapped for order.

The proceedings went along smoothly, if not a bit dryly. Ben Colfax gave his testimony, and the Kid had to back him up with the physical evidence: the bullet taken from the teamster's body, and the matching gun that had been found in Pete's saddlebag.

Twice Bess Jamison got to her feet and started to protest, but Judge Richmond tolerated no nonsense, and she lapsed into an angry silence. There was only one verdict possible under the circumstances: the teamster had been shot and killed by Pete Davis as a result of a quarrel that had taken place earlier. This seemed to outrage Bess, but Richmond moved on to the next business at hand, the shooting of Pete while resisting arrest.

This was a simple matter and was dispensed with in short order. Dr. Carver spoke up. "I have the extracted bullet, judge. Do you want to enter it as evidence?"

"I think not," Richmond said. "Mr. Runyon was a witness to the affair." He rapped with his gavel and brought the inquest to a close.

Doc Carver nudged the Kid and dropped the bullet into his hand. "Keep it as a souvenir."

"I don't want the damn thing," the Kid said, but Carver was already moving away to talk to someone else.

Bess Jamison was one of the first to stalk out, followed by Ben Colfax. While Runyon edged over to speak to the Kid, Colfax took Bess by the arm and steered her to the edge of the porch. They talked for a moment, then walked down the path together, stopping near her buggy.

She gave Colfax a weary smile and said, "Damn little satisfaction I got out of that, Ben. A man killed on each side."

"I know, I know," he said. "The sheriff is quite a fella. Gets his teeth right into a thing." He took off his hat and glanced at the sky. "Cloudin' up. Rain before night-fall." He replaced his hat and looked toward the porch. "Notice how close the Kid stays to Cal Runyon and Cadmus Rindo? Guess I don't have to tell you where the gods are sleepin'."

"Figured it would be that way when Rindo bought the election." She glanced at her men still standing idly by. "Don't run off, Charlie, Hank. The old boar's got to come out of his nest sometime."

"Wait now," Colfax said. "This ain't the place to start trouble. The Kid will stop it."

"Just let him try," Bess said. "We'll walk all over him."

Cadmus Rindo chose that time to come out of the house. He saw Bess and her men gathered by the gate, but came down the path as though he had it all to himself. His steps were slow and measured, the only concession he had made to his advanced years. At the gate he glanced her way, then turned his back on her and walked to his buggy.

This manner of aloofness offended Bess Jamison. "Old man!" she said sharply.

He pivoted slowly and gave her a calm stare. "Were you speaking to me?"

"You know damn well who I'm speaking to," she said. Detaching herself from her friends, she came over Rindo. "I guess you could afford to lose Pete Davis, but I couldn't spare my man. So I hardly call it a fair trade."

His voice held a hint of anger. "You speak of dead men as though they were dollars and cents passed back and forth." In disgust he turned from her, but she took his shoulder and spun him around again.

The Kid raised his head in time to see this storm brewing; he started down the path with rapid strides. Cadmus Rindo was saying, "Don't ever put hands on me again, woman!"

"This is what I think of your threats!" Bess whipped her hand across the old man's face, driving him back against the front wheel. The Kid had the gate open and was passing through when one of Bess's men, thinking to do her a favor, tried to stop him. The Kid sledged the man along the shelf of the jaw, spinning him into his stunned friends. Before anyone could stop him, he yanked Bess by the hair, then stood between her and Cadmus Rindo.

When she made the mistake of trying to strike the Kid, he shoved her with the flat of his hand so hard that she nearly fell. "Get out of town and cool off," he said.

"You're not running me out! Rindo's paid flunky, that's all you are!"

"I told you to get!"

Cadmus Rindo's anger was in full bloom now and there was this insult to balance before Bess Jamison left town. He tried to push the Kid aside, and when he couldn't, walked around him, shaking his fist at Bess. "By thunder, you got me riled now! I put up with your pa and I've put up with you, but danged if I will any longer! You git, and don't come back! If you ain't off that property in twenty-four hours, I'll drive you off!"

"You just come ahead!" she yelled. "You'll get more'n you can handle!"

"Shut up, both of you!" the Kid snapped.

"Huh?" The idea alone was a shock to Cadmus Rindo. For a moment he thought he had heard incorrectly, but he hadn't; the Kid had told him to shut his mouth. And he had the nerve to repeat it.

"I said shut your fool mouth." He ignored the old man, facing Bess Jamison. "Now get out of town before you raise a fuss you can't get out of. Take your friends too."

"I'll go when I get danged good and ready! You want to try to throw me out?"

"You'll cool off better in jail," he said and grabbed her arm before she could break away. Her men made a start for their horses and weapons, but Cal Runyon drew his .38 and said, "I wouldn't interfere with the law if I were you fellas." His voice was soft but the warning was sincere. They remained rooted.

Cadmus Rindo began to cackle and dance a jig; his patent leather shoes raised a tawny cloud of dust. "That's the kind of law I like," he yelled. "No fuss or feathers to it." He shook his fist at Bess Jamison. "Got your comeuppance, didn't you? Remember what I said, twenty-four hours!"

"Another word out of you," the Kid said, "and you can share the cell block with her."

"Huh?" Rindo said, his offense renewed. "You go plumb to hell! I do as I please."

The Kid hooked his fingers in the old man's coat and pulled him against Bess Jamison. Then he shoved both of them ahead of him, his arms stiffened. Cal Runyon brought up the rear, a heavy frown on his face, while Bess' entourage tagged along with Ben Colfax.

Had the Kid stopped shoving for an instant, he would have found his prisoners uncontrollable, but he kept them off balance and fighting each other more than they fought him. A spectacle like this drew a crowd; this was more exciting than a run on a bank. The danger there had dwindled to nothing, but the Kid wondered if he hadn't created a new and more deadly crisis.

Cadmus Rindo was being led to jail like a miscreant drunk and the Kid pondered the effect it would have on the citizens of the town. Most of them were laughing and cat-calling; there is nothing more comical to peasants than when their king loses his seat and falls from his great white horse.

At the jail a thoughtful citizen threw the door open and the Kid's shove propelled them both into the center of the room. The Kid whirled and locked the door while Ben Colfax began to pound on it.

"Let me in, Kid! Damn it, open up in there!"

Ignoring him, the Kid motioned toward the cell blocks down the hall. "All right, let's not waste any time about it now."

"Think you're smart, don't you?" Bess turned to Cadmus Rindo and glared for a moment, then her anger vanished, leaving her face strangely pleasant, just a pretty girl who found continuous anger a trial. "Well, as long as we're in the same boat, I can't say that there was favoritism, can I?"

She entered the cell meekly enough and allowed the Kid to lock the door. But when he tried to lock the door on Rindo, the old man became slightly panic-stricken. "Say now, this has gone far enough! By God, this is my town! My jail!"

"Then you hadn't ought to mind spending a little time in it," the Kid said, turning the key in the door. He went back to his office and let Ben Colfax in. Colfax looked grave around the mouth and kept stroking his mustache with his forefinger.

"Damn," he said, "but I never thought you'd lock up the old man."

"Don't we have a law here about disturbing the peace?"

"Yeah, but who pays any attention to it?" He took off his hat and scratched his head. "Jesus, as if there wasn't enough excitement for one day with the run on the bank and all."

"How did that turn out?" the Kid asked, then was interrupted by a knock on the door. "Go see who that is."

When Colfax unlocked the door, Nan Buckley stepped inside. "Is it true? Do you really have Rindo in jail?" She appeared to be on the verge of tears. "Oh, how humiliating! Are you trying to break his heart?"

"It'll heal quicker than his head," the Kid said. "The crowd gone from the bank yet?"

"Yes," she said. Someone else knocked on the door and at the Kid's nod, she opened it.

A very agitated judge stepped quickly inside. Colfax turned the key again. Richmond puffed his cheeks and patted his chest gently. "Kid, this is highly irregular. I believe both parties can be released on their own recognizance."

"Maybe in the morning," the Kid said easily. "That way I'm sure of having one peaceful day."

"You mean you intend to keep them together in jail overnight?"

"Why not?" the Kid wanted to know. "Judge, here are two hellions who say they hate each other. Can't stand the sight of each other, to hear them tell it." He spread his hands innocently. "But due to an unfortunate disagreement with the law, they're forced to endure each other for twenty-some hours. Now it seems to me the main trouble is that they've never had a chance to sit down and either settle their differences or work up a genuine hate for each other. Well, I'm giving them that chance now."

"Most irregular," Richmond repeated.

"But a sound idea," the Kid insisted. "Judge, could you get them together for a talk?"

"I doubt it," Richmond admitted. "You saw them a-while ago, dog-eyeing each other."

"That was in public," the Kid said. "A jail cell can be a mighty lonesome place at two in the morning when you can't sleep. You may hate the man in the cell next to you, but he's still someone to talk to."

"This from experience, Kid?" Colfax asked sarcastically.

The Kid looked quickly at him. "That election is still sticking in your craw, ain't it?"

The native resentments Ben Colfax held so close were evident in his eyes for a moment, then he drew his lids together, shutting them off from everyone. "I didn't like it," he said. "What the hell you expect?"

Judge Richmond shook his head and turned toward the door. "You have strange ways, sheriff. I haven't quite made up my mind what kind of man you are."

"You mean because I haven't taken sides?" He folded his arms across his chest. "Which side are you on, judge? Rindo's? Or the girl's? Or maybe you believe as I do, that neither of them matter; it's the town that's important."

Judge Richmond studied the Kid. Finally he said, "We all have sides, young man. A good side, and a bad one; we're an infernal blend. Occasionally it's difficult to say which side is predominant."

He went out quickly and Ben Colfax searched for an excuse to linger. "If you need me for anything—"

"I don't want a deputy," the Kid said. "How many times does a man have to tell you a thing before you understand it?"

This was calculated to sting, and it did, for angry color came into Colfax' face. He whirled to the door and slammed it after him. Nan Buckley said, "That was deliberate, Kid. You still don't like Ben, do you?"

"Less every day," the Kid said. He picked up the keys to the cell block and dropped them into his coat pocket. "Can I buy you a cup of coffee?"

"I'll make a better offer," she said. "Come home with me and I'll fix you something to eat."

He laughed and opened the door. "You'll never have to ask me twice," he said.

Traffic on the street appeared normal, and the groups gathered on the boardwalks were still laughing and discussing Rindo's arrest, giving the town a solid ballast; the earlier top-heavy condition seemed to have vanished.

At the *Rindo County Free Press* office, the printer and his devil were working on the paper, patiently setting the type in long sticks. Nan and the Kid passed into the rear; he took a place at the table while she stoked the fire. A gentle thought came to her and her lips pulled into a smile. "The town's come alive since you came here."

"Most of it unpleasant," he said, thinking of Pete and the desperation with which he had gone for his gun. "Do you believe all stories have happy endings, Nan?"

"Yes," she said. "Even the ones that seem sad to us. Happiness is relative. We usually gauge it from our own point of view, though." She placed a frying pan on the stove, added a dab of bacon grease, then cracked four eggs. "What are you thinking about, Kid?"

"The old man," he said. "He told me he wanted to give away what he owned before he died. I believe him."

"That sounds like something he'd do," Nan said.

"I've been doing a lot of figuring," the Kid admitted. "And I get some damned odd answers." He enumerated them on his fingers. "Now you take the original trouble between Bess's old man and Rindo. That was just talk until he was shot. But we know that Rindo didn't do it; I believe him when he claims he hired Pete as a threat, not to shoot anyone. Then the shooting of the teamster, that wasn't his doing either. Nan, I think both of them are victims of someone else who's got a lot to gain by seeing them get into a shooting fight."

She slid his eggs onto a plate, then sat down across from him. "But who'd do that?"

He shrugged and began to eat. "Did you ever think about money? I mean, what is money?" He fumbled through his pocket and brought out a paper bill. "Look at it. Just a piece of paper with ink on it. What makes it valuable?"

"It's backed by gold," she said.

"Oh, sure. If you take it to a bank, they'll give you gold for it. But suppose you're out on the desert and pay a man with this. The only reason he'll take it is because he has faith in what's behind it. At one time we all agreed to accept this as a thing of value. Hell, it could have been pieces of cut rock or beads, like the Indians used. The way I see it, Cadmus Rindo is that silent guarantee behind everything here. As long as he remains as is, Rindo's Springs will survive."

"But he's so old, Kid. He's bound to die before very long."

"Dying won't matter. That won't destroy what he was." He shook his head. "The danger is in his being undermined, making people doubt his backing. There's a difference between dying and being destroyed, Nan. And someone is out to do just that to the old man."

She remained silent while he ate the remainder of his eggs. Then she got up and poured him a cup of coffee. While he added sugar and milk, she observed him carefully. Finally she asked, "What happened to the Wind River Kid?" His eyes came up, surprised and a little puzzled. "You're not the same man, you know. The Wind River Kid was wise and tough and looking for trouble. The sheriff is quiet and thoughtful and never hunts trouble." She clasped her hands together and smiled. "You like Rindo's Springs, and I think the town likes you."

He liked the way this sounded, especially because she had said it, but then he remembered Cal Runyon and his pleasure vanished. She was quick to catch his changing moods and noticed this, but she failed to understand it. The Kid finished his coffee and got up. His manner was somewhat hurried as he gathered his hat and coat and turned toward the front of the building. She walked with him and at the door said, "I wish you liked me."

"Like you?" He ignored the printer and the scurrying devil. "Nan, it would be better if I could hate you." She stood near him, too near to ignore. Quickly he pulled her the rest of the way and folded his arms around her. She offered no resistance and didn't try to turn her face away from his kiss. The warmth and desirability of this woman ate at him, breaking down the walls of his resolve until he believed that her lips contained a promise for him alone.

When he released her, she looked steadily at him. The Kid said, "I don't think I ought to come here again." Before she could answer, he turned and started down the street. She came to the boardwalk's edge, her hand lifted as if to call him back, but then she thought better of it and went back inside.

Walking toward the restaurant, the Kid cursed himself for a fool. Any man was when he made love to a woman who belonged to another man. At the restaurant he ordered two meals and took them to the jail. Unlocking the barred doors, he placed a tray in each cell.

Bess Jamison said, "I suppose I should thank you for this."

"Is there anyone you aren't sore at?" the Kid asked.

"Just what did I ever do to you to deserve your smart talk? Tell me that."

"I don't have to like you," Bess said.

"And I don't have to take your smart mouth," the Kid told her. "Is it because I took the election away from Ben that you're peeved?"

"That's part of it," she admitted.

"Then why blame me? Did I have anything to do with it?"

"I guess you didn't," she said, after a pause.

"Then keep your tongue off me," he said, making his voice as tough as he could. That tone commanded respect from her and she kept watching him closely. "Get something straight: you don't have a solitary kick coming. When your teamster was killed, I caught the man who did it. You got justice all down the line, so stop your belly-achin'." He turned then and looked into the adjoining cell at Cadmus Rindo. "I suppose I've got to listen to you complain."

"The meal's good," Rindo said mildly. "No complaint."

"When are we going to get out of here?" Bess asked, her tone meek so he wouldn't misunderstand.

"You don't get out until the judge says so."

"When will that be?" Rindo asked.

"I'll try to find out sometime today," the Kid said, locking the doors again.

"When I get out, I'm going to take that badge away from you," Rindo promised. "You were just a drunk in jail when I pinned it on you. Just a gunfighter looking for a place to roost."

The Wind River Kid chuckled and went out, closing the separating door. After his step receded, Rindo said, "Damned smart guy."

"You elected him," Bess said dryly. "Stew in your own juice."

"Well, he's better'n Ben Colfax," Rindo snapped. "A dog's better'n him."

"How would you know? Any man that'd kill another—"

The old man flogged his thighs with his palms. "Jesus, are you still harpin' on that?" He made a disgusted noise with his lips. "The Kid didn't teach you a damned thing, did he? You still blame anyone in sight. Damned hollow-headed female, you can't recognize the truth when it's told to you!"

His voice had a genuine ring of truth which she could not completely ignore, and because the Kid had only a moment before shattered her anger, she had little left to color her thinking. "Who else had a reason to kill Pa?" she asked.

Rindo flung his hands in an aimless circle. "Damned if I know. I ain't even goin' to argue about it. Think what you please. Can't waste time tryin' to talk sense to someone who ain't got any."

Without realizing it, he was using a most successful attack, for Bess was not the kind of a woman who liked to be ignored or brushed aside. Her determination to talk now became almost an obsession. "Mr. Rindo, if I promise not to get angry, will you talk to me about—that night?"

For a moment it looked like he was going to refuse; then he blew out his breath and nodded. "No harm in it," he said. "But what's there to talk about?"

"About Pa," she said. "I don't think you understood him at all."

He stared at her, then laughed. "Didn't I? Hell, I had his number when I saw him come down the road in that old wagon. Everything he owned was patched, even the dress you had on, some hand-me-down you hoped no one would notice. Know him?" Rindo shook his head, amazed at her lack of perception. "Girl, there's a mark a man wears when he's a failure and too proud to admit it. I knew your father. Understood him, that's why I gave him timber of his own to cut; his kind never could work for anyone else, and didn't have the sand to stand up for himself."

He looked at her, challenging her to dispute this harsh judgment. "Girl, I didn't have to kill your father. If I'd wanted to get rid of him, all I would have had to do would be to blow hard and he'd have fallen down." He put his hands on his knees and bent forward, his voice softly spelling this out for her. "The thing that always bothered your pa was that he figured I'd not given him enough. It wasn't enough to work land and share the profit. He had to own it outright. That's been your belly-ache all along. Callin' me an old hog, a tightwad." He laughed. "Think, girl. Be honest for once in your life. You knew your pa. Had he owned the land, he wouldn't have lasted a year. He'd have gotten the itch to move, to look at greener grass, and you'd have lost everything again."

She studied him with tear-bright eyes, for this was not a nice picture of any man. "How you must have loathed him!" she said.

"Still can't see your own nose, can you? No, I understood the man. And I had enough understanding to take his mouth and all the bricks he flung at me. Didn't feel sorry for him; he did that, enough for everyone. Girl, I was the only real friend your father had."

"Ben's been a friend," she said. "A real friend. I think that's why you dislike him so."

"Like tryin' to punch through a stone wall, talkin' to you," he said. "I know Ben's talk. He's convinced you that I'm afraid you'll get too big, take me over. Do you believe that?"

"What can I believe?" Bess asked. "Who can I believe?"

He stared at her, then got up and rattled the cell door until the Wind River Kid came back. "Got pen and paper?" Rindo asked.

"There's some in the desk," the Kid answered. "Going to make out your will?"

"Already done that," Rindo said. "Fetch me the writin' stuff."

The Kid returned to his office. A moment later he passed pen, ink, and paper into the cell. Cadmus Rindo carefully composed a neat page, then passed it back through the bars. "Read it," he said, "then sign it as a witness and give it to her."

As the Kid looked over the document, his interest sharpened. "This is a clear title to the property Bess is working. You sure you want me to sign it?"

"Sign it and give it to her," Rindo said.

After affixing his signature, the Kid passed it through the bars to Bess Jamison. She seemed stunned. "Why?" she asked softly. "After all this trouble, why?"

Rindo turned and looked at her. "Can't talk to you, so I'm teaching you the hard way. You've got what you said you wanted, but you won't hang onto it. There's too much of your father in you. I gave it to you so you could lose it, as he would have lost it. And when it's gone, pack your wagon and clear out of the country. I've done my last favor for the Jamisons."

Bess sat down and stared at the deed. She looked at

the Kid, but he only said, "You're on your own now." Then he turned and went back to his office.

Seated behind his desk, he pondered Rindo's sudden and daring decision. The old man was no fool; there was grim purpose behind this move, and the Kid tried to fathom it. Of all those Rindo had helped, the Jamisons had come closer to building a power than anyone else. They cut a lot of timber in the Jamison camp, and there was another twenty years of logging in that section. Properly handled, that camp could take over in the event Rindo went under, and this thought touched off a new train in his mind.

Rindo knew that there was a quiet middle man working to ruin him through Bess Jamison, and the Kid had the notion that the free gift of the deed was a move to smoke that man into the open where he could be seen. A dangerous chance to take, the Kid decided. Too much of a chance for him to ever take, but then, there was the primary difference; Rindo being the kind of a man he was had carved an empire for himself while lesser men struggled just to live.

On impulse, the Kid left the office and went to the hotel. He found Wade Boomhauer reading. The young marshal put his magazine down and motioned toward a chair.

"How's your arm?" the Kid asked.

"Hurts like blue blazes," Boomhauer admitted. "Kid, I think you're sorry you shot me."

"Yes, I am." His fingers plucked at the brim of his hat. "You hear about me putting the old man in jail?"

Boomhauer chuckled. "The clerk wears out the steps bringing me the news." His laughter faded. "Think that was smart?"

"Yes," the Kid said. "I thought it was the right thing to do."

"As long as you believe that, you can't be far wrong." He paused to listen to the customary sounds drifting in the partially opened window. "The town's got a nice sound to it," he said. "Are you going to be able to hold it together?"

"Maybe."

"Kind of a new twist for you, isn't it? As I hear it, you've wrecked a few towns."

"This beats wrecking," the Kid said. He got up restlessly and put on his hat. "I may drop in and see you later."

"Then I'll look forward to it," Boomhauer said. When the Kid was half through the door, he added, "Taking you back is going to be one of the worst jobs I ever had."

The Kid's eyes were serious. "I'm not going to give you any more trouble, Wade."

"I figured that, which is what makes the job so bad."

The Kid closed the door and went down the stairs and through the lobby.

From his position on the boardwalk, he saw Cal Runyon leave the company yard, ride partway down the street, then turn onto the side street where Nan Buckley's newspaper office was. This brought back an old bitterness and he scuffed across the street toward the jail.

Faced with an extremely empty afternoon, the Kid lay down on his cot and tried to sleep, but found it difficult. His mind kept swinging around to Nan Buckley, and visions of her in Cal Runyon's arms kept pushing to the fore, tormenting him almost beyond endurance. He was a fool, he told himself, to even consider for a moment that any woman could love a wanted man. Back in Arizona that crooked sheriff would have a judge waiting to give him four years. When he had served his time, he could drift again, without roots, without direction.

Sleep came unexpectedly and when he awoke he found the room growing dark. As he lighted the lamps, the door rattled beneath a man's heavy hammering and he opened it.

Five of Bess Jamison's men stood there, rifles and shotguns tucked in the crooks of their elbows. "She's been in long enough," one of the men said. "Let her out!"

"Come back in the morning," the Kid suggested. "I'll let her out then."

"We figure a few hours won't make a big difference," the leader said. He was a burly man, heavy in the face, with arms and shoulders thickened by a lifetime of felling timber.

"You fellas figure on breaking her out?" the Kid asked mildly.

"If you make us."

"Well," the Kid said, in a resigned voice, "I'm not going to buck armed men." He turned casually toward the door and the men began to surge forward, confident that this was going to be easy. Only the Kid turned the last step into a plunging leap that carried him inside. He slapped the oak door and slid the bar before they could react. Instantly they set up a clamor and he went to the gun rack, broke open a double-barrel shotgun and fed two brass, double-O buckshot loads into the chambers.

Then he went back to the door and suddenly flung it open.

The first man crowded forward, but stopped when the twin bores pressed hard against his chest. "Makes a big hole," the Kid said. "Want to see?"

"Ease back there," the man said to his friends. "Hal, will you stop that goddam shoving?" He looked apprehensively at the Kid.

A pushy man in back said, "Hell, Otis, break into him!"

"That's easy for you to say, but I got the barrels against my chest." This man remained motionless for a heartbeat longer, then edged back. At the boardwalk's edge, they lingered to save face, then shuffled off down the street.

Finally the Kid closed the door and put the shotgun away. Sitting down, he pillowed his forehead against his palms and let out a long, relieved breath. From the cell block, Bess Jamison called to him and he got up to see what she wanted.

"I thought I heard Otis' voice out there," she said.

"He wanted to break you out," the Kid said.

"Oh dear, now you don't think I put him up to that, do you?"

"No, but someone has done a lot of convincing somewhere along the line."

"I know that now," she said. Her look was contrite. "I've caused you a lot of trouble, haven't I?"

"Goes with the job," he said.

"Can I—do you suppose I could talk to Ben Colfax?"

"I haven't seen Ben all afternoon," the Kid admitted. "But if I find him, I'll say that you want to talk to him."

12

SEATED AGAIN at his desk, the Kid turned his thoughts to Ben Colfax, the longtime friend and advisor to Bess Jamison and to her father before his death. Ben had a winning manner all right, but you couldn't condemn a man because he talked well. Then there was the matter of the poker games; Ben must have put in his share to stop the run on the bank.

The Kid rubbed the back of his neck, uncertain about his own speculations. While he thought about it, a bell began to toll insistently down the street, and he went to the front door to look out. Even as he stared down the street he heard Rindo's shout. But he had no time for Rindo now.

At the far end of town, the company buildings were making a high glow against the night sky, and a crowd began to race along the street at the firebell's call. The Kid broke into a run, pushing people aside who got in his way. Panting up to the main gate, he found it open and the guard absent. The main building was a sheet of flame and crumbling timbers, and company men were dashing about, trying to discover some avenue of attack. Sparks flew as the rising heat caused a wind, and other buildings caught. The crew at the stable drove the mules out of the compound as the haystack suddenly flared up.

The Kid searched for Cal Runyon and found him with Ben Colfax. Both men were studying the destruction as the Kid joined them. "What started this?" he asked.

"Wish I knew," Runyon said. "Ben was waiting for me in my office and I had scarcely closed the door when the bell rang." He turned to a man racing past. "You there! Get the men out of the yard! She's a goner!"

Talking was nearly impossible with the sound of the flames mounting to a roar. Runyon edged away, moving toward the main gate. The Kid and Colfax followed and when they could talk again, Runyon said, "I've got to see Cadmus Rindo!"

"All right," the Kid said and headed for the jail, "Will it be a total loss, Cal?"

"We may save something. All the livestock got clear. The buildings are gone, though."

"Going to be hard on Rindo's pocketbook," Ben Colfax opined.

"We'll make out," Runyon said, clearly indicating by his tone that he didn't want to talk about it.

"Sure knocks the props out from under the town," Colfax said. "The old man won't have anything to pay all the money the people have invested in him."

"I'll bet that makes you cry," the Kid snapped. "Why don't you go home, Ben? We don't want you around."

They were at the jail and went inside. Before the Kid could close the door, Colfax eased in. He had half a notion to throw him out, but he lacked the time. The Kid handed Runyon the keys to the cell block and the young superintendent went on ahead. The Kid could hear him talking.

"The buildings are all gone, Mr. Rindo."

"That bad, huh?" Springs squeaked as the old man eased off the cot. Then the cell door opened and Rindo came into the outer office.

Ben Colfax shifted his feet and said, "Mind if I talk to Bess?"

"No," the Kid said, then remembered. "She wanted to see you."

Colfax shuffled into the back and Cadmus Rindo sat down on the corner of the desk. "How did it get started?" Rindo asked.

"No one seems to know," Runyon admitted. "But of course there hasn't been time to talk to anyone and get a straight answer. Mr. Rindo, does this close us down? I mean, can we stand it, financially?"

"All empires are built on a shoestring," Rindo said flatly. "No, we can't float through this, not without the people's help. And they'll look after themselves first. Can't blame 'em. They're human."

From the rear came Bess' clear voice. "—but I tell you he gave it to me. No strings attached, Ben."

Then Ben Colfax came out of the cell block section and leaned against the wall. His eyes were tight-pinched and he looked carefully at Cadmus Rindo. "Nice thing you done, givin' Bess a clear title."

Rindo looked at him briefly, intolerantly. "What the hell is it to you anyway?"

"Considerable," Ben Colfax admitted. "You see, I got an investment there. Matter of fact, it's more'n an investment. You could say that I practically own it now, with this legal paper in my hand."

"What the hell's he saying?" Cal Runyon asked. He looked from the Kid to Rindo and then back to the Kid.

"Ben's been lending money," the Kid said.

"Just my generous nature," Ben said. "People like Bess and her pa have no business sense. Since I'm their friend, I handled it for 'em." He eased away from the wall. "Anyway, I'm still in business, and you're fresh out, Rindo." He smiled. "You shouldn't have run the Kid against me. I didn't like that. But then it gives me more pleasure to knock you down, old man."

"Get out of here," Rindo said. "I hate a sly man, and you've always been a sneak."

"Ah, that's hard talk," Colfax said. "But I'll go because I'm a man who don't want trouble." He stepped to the door and opened it. "Still, if you need money, come and see me. I'll buy up some of that paper these good folks are holding and when I get enough of it, I'll take over what's left of your mill."

"Where the hell did you ever get any money?" Runyon asked.

"Well," Colfax said, "I've been a peace officer a long time now. Must have arrested six or eight thousand drunks in my day. Always did like to pinch a drunk. Rarely ever give me any trouble, and most of 'em still have a little salted away on 'em someplace. Now and then I'd be disappointed and find only a quarter or a dollar. But over the years, even that counts up."

Cal Runyon was near enough to spit, and he did. Colfax' face turned concrete hard and he slowly raised his hand to wipe his cheek. "Shouldn't have done that," he said. "A bad thing to do to a man."

"Get out of here," the Kid said tightly.

"I'll see you too," Colfax promised and closed the door.

A deep silence filled the office for a time, then Cadmus Rindo smiled and said, "Look bright, boys. We rode high as hell while we stayed on her. We got no kick 'cause we got pitched off." He stood erect and stretched. "That cot's damned uncomfortable, Kid. Am I free to go or do I get locked up again?"

"You can go," the Kid said gently. The old man's courage in the face of disaster was a warming thing to see. Runyon still had the cell keys so the Kid said, "Go get Bess. Tell her she can go too."

When Runyon went down the hall, Rindo said, "Too bad you don't have some laid by. I'd like to see you buy up some of that stuff under Ben's nose."

"I wouldn't buy it," the Kid said. "Not because I don't think it would be a good investment, but because I still think I can save the town for you."

Rindo snorted. "Miracle worker, eh?" He turned as Bess came into the office. "You want to cheer, you go right ahead. Your friend's done a good job."

"I'm not cheering," she said softly. "I'm just ashamed for being so blind."

"A human failing," Rindo said and left.

Runyon said, "My place is with him, Kid." He glanced at Bess. "Are you staying in town?"

"If you want," she said.

"We have a lot to talk about," he said. "All right?"

"All right, Cal."

Bess dropped wearily into a chair, her expression troubled. "A lot of terrible possibilities are occurring to me," she said. "Are you wondering if Ben paid Pete to kill my father?"

He was surprised for it was almost as though she had read his thoughts. Going behind his desk, he opened the middle drawer and brought out the box of tagged bullets and spread them on the desk. Two he could ignore for they merely marked the fatality of itinerants. The other three merited his concern. He spaced them out in their correct order: Pritchard's first, then Jamison's, and finally the teamster's; he felt a pang of shame because he didn't even know the man's name.

Then he recalled the bullet Doc Garver had given him at the inquest and sounded his pockets until he came up with it. He laid this too on the desk, with no

more than half a glance, but that was enough for a man
who had made guns and bullets his business.

For a full minute he stared at the bullet. Bess Jamison asked, "What's wrong? You look odd."

"This *is* odd," he said. "If Doc hasn't made a mistake
with his tag, I shot Pete with his own gun. And that's
impossible because I didn't find it until I came back to
Rindo's Springs."

He pawed his mouth out of shape, flogging his mind to
recall—then recollection came full bloom and he slapped
the desk with the flat of his hand. "How damned stupid
can a man get!" He turned and looked at Bess's ex-
pectant expression. "I didn't shoot Pete with his own gun.
I shot him with the one Ben Colfax loaned me after I
dropped mine in the mud in front of the newspaper
office."

"I—I don't understand."

"And I'm just beginning to," the Kid said. "Bess, I'll
try and put this together for you. First, Ben shot your
father. Yes, he did, and I can prove it. And he shot the
teamster, then swore it was Pete who did it. When he
brought the body back to town, he loaned me his gun
so I could go after Pete. Then when he heard I was
comparing bullets, he had to do something to make the
case complete against Pete. He must have gone to the
stable, put his own odd-caliber Colt in Pete's saddlebag,
the one chambered for .44 American, then led me by the
nose so I'd find it." He shook his head. "Guns are my
business, and I guess there isn't a caliber in the handguns
that I haven't shot at one time or another, but I'll be
switched if I noticed any difference in weight or recoil
when I shot Pete. Ben probably weighed the butt just
right to make it balance." He wiped his hand across his
mouth. "Then too, the gun being a Colt threw me off;
it felt right and natural to my hand. And when a man
gets mixed up in a shooting scrape, he's too keyed up to
notice a little thing like recoil. You know, it all fits in
because Ben's got the nerve to take a long chance like
that, slipping in the murder weapon right under my
nose. I played poker with him once and I watched him
fill inside straights. The man's cool and he won't break
under fire." The Kid smiled. "When I started to compare
bullets, Ben must have had a bad moment, for I was
walking around with the murder gun on my hip. But he

never lost his head." He stood up slowly. "Better get on over to the hotel, Bess. I've got a man to arrest."

"Do you think he'll—fight?"

"Yes," the Kid said. "Ben'll fight. He played a quiet game for mighty big stakes, and he still has a chance to win. That's the bad part of it."

"I—I don't know what to say. He seems like a stranger now, as though I never really knew him at all."

"Perhaps you didn't," he said. "Bess, how much do we really know of anyone? We think we do, putting all kinds of interpretations on what they say and do, but do we really know them?"

"I suppose not," she said and went to the door. "Should I tell anyone what I know about Ben?"

He considered this briefly. "Yes, spread it around. Let's see if we can make Ben run."

After she left he took his revolver and checked it thoroughly, for in a short time now, he would need it. He felt a desire to go outside and feel the pulse of the town, but he was afraid to. The fire at the mill would shatter the strength of these people and he found little pleasure in the prospect of seeing them go down.

This would be more than the end of a town. This was the end of Jim Onart, a man with self-respect; after tonight, if he didn't make a fatal mistake with Ben, he would be the Wind River Kid, riding back to Arizona with a pair of handcuffs on his wrists and a most undecided future.

While he sat there with his dismal thoughts, the first rumble of thunder sounded in the northeast and a moment later a few raindrops splattered on the roof. Soon it set up a dull roar and made sagging patterns on the front windows.

A miserable night, he decided, then put on his hat and coat and went outside. He wondered if Ben Colfax was moving around, trying to make his quick deals, buying up Cadmus Rindo's notes. Very likely. The man wouldn't waste any time; he'd glean his reward here as avariciously as he swept poker winnings into his corner.

The street was empty, as far as traffic went, but most of the stores were still open and the Kid started his rounds, hunting. He chose the dry goods store first because it was the closest. The proprietor was a prune-dry man and about as angry as one man could be. He puffed and glared at the sheriff and snapped, "If you're after the old man's notes too, they ain't for sale!"

This attack, out of nowhere, rocked the Kid. "What's the matter? Ben's money no good?"

"Damned right it's no good! Worthless! I spit on it!"

"Ben's been here then?"

"Twenty minutes ago. Was I a bigger man I'd have flung him into the street."

Bewildered, the Kid left the store and started up the street. He stopped at three places and was surprised at their vehemence. In the butcher shop, the rotund butcher said, "You think I'd kick a man who's down? That ain't a very good opinion of me, sheriff. Hell, I've been down too. You think I'd ever forget what Rindo done for me?"

A glimmer of hope began to warm the Kid. By the time he covered the other side of the street, he began to understand these people and their mass, concentrated outrage. How many plots had been hatched here to wrest control from Rindo he could only guess. How much time had they wasted, complaining, threatening; this was a mystery to him. And he had blamed them, thought them evil, when all the time they had been merely human. It had never occurred to him that these people would unite, but they had, arming themselves against this intruder, Ben Colfax.

And Cadmus Rindo was right after all. He had given his best to all men and because of this, they offered him the best in return. People, the Wind River Kid decided, were magnificent if only a man stopped long enough to notice instead of digging at the dirt that was under every man's fingernails.

He wondered if Rindo knew how these people felt. The man must know or else he would never have been able to live out his advanced years under so mellow a philosophy.

But this was no time to wax sentimental; the Kid pulled his mind back to Ben Colfax, for the news was out now and circulating like wildfire. From down the street, the Kid saw Judge Richmond and Dr. Garver moving head-down against the rain. They saw him at the last minute and veered toward the shelter of the overhang.

"You're the man we want to see," Richmond said. He pulled a folded paper from his inner pocket. "Here is a warrant for Ben Colfax' arrest. Do you need any help?"

"I can handle it," the Kid said. "That's what the county pays me for."

"We can get a citizen's committee," Doc Carver said. "God, I never saw them so riled before!"

"Their security has been threatened," Richmond said. "For twenty years I've been a public servant and never an election has passed but what I wasn't cussed and booed. But that's our privilege, sheriff."

"Getting Ben is my job," the Kid said.

"And it won't be easy," Garver said. "What can we do to help?"

"I've been thinking about it," the Kid admitted, "and I've come to the conclusion that there's too many people on the streets. If you gents could move around and ask the merchants to close and lock their doors, but leave the lights on, I could have this town to myself. Simply by keeping everyone indoors, I can catch Ben a lot easier."

"And if there's any shooting, no one will get hurt," Richmond said. He was a practical man who considered the chances carefuly. "Ben's pretty good. He doesn't make much of a point of it, but he is."

The Kid moved his hand impatiently. "See how quick you can clear the street."

They hurried on and the Kid turned toward the hotel. Without understanding why, he felt the need to talk to Boomhauer. He knocked and went in. The clerk was there with the supper tray and the latest news. At the marshal's nod, the clerk left, then Boomhauer said, "A good job, sheriff. You ought to be proud of it."

"Not finished yet," the Kid said. "I got the merchandise laid out but there's still the wrapping."

"Ummm," Boomhauer said, smiling. I've been tangled in those strings myself. Made any plans?"

"I've got the judge and the doctor clearing the street. That way, with just Ben and me moving about, I'll know who to shoot at."

"A sensible move," Boomhauer said. "Can I offer a little advice, Kid?"

"That's what I came here for."

Boomhauer propped himself up on his elbow, then pushed until he sat up. Then he opened the front of his long underwear and exposed an old bullet wound on his chest. "Thought I'd show you this first to make an impression," he said. "Kid, this is going to be different. No walk-up here, and it's the first man that sees the other, not who is fastest."

"Figured that," the Kid said. "But I shoot straight enough."

"And if you're thinking that the other man might not, then you're not as smart as I thought you were. Kid, you're a lawman tonight, not a gunfighter defending his reputation. Forget the damned code or whatever you go by and think. You got a rifle?"

"No," the Kid said.

"Mine's in the closet. There's a box of shells in the canvas satchel. That rifle's a .50-110 Winchester Express and she'll shoot through six inches of oak. Eight rounds, instead of five, and you don't have to get into pistol range." He reached out and took the Kid by the sleeve. "If he gets behind a door, your sixgun is worthless. Go get the rifle."

The Kid obeyed and was impressed by the gun's murderously efficient lines. He checked the magazine and found it to be full. He put the box of shells in his coat pocket, but Wade Boomhauer had a criticism. "Take the shells out of the box and carry them loose. If you need 'em, you won't have time to fool with the box."

After doing this, the Kid said, "This doesn't give Ben much of a chance, does it?"

"This evens your chances," Boomhauer said flatly. "Kid, you've got to tree this lion on the ground of his choosing. Looking for him gives him a tremendous advantage." When the Kid tucked the Winchester under his arm, Boomhauer asked. "Can you shoot that?"

"Pretty good," the Kid said and moved to the door. "Thanks. You knew what I needed."

"Be careful and think," Boomhauer said sternly. "It cost me this dimple on the chest to find out what I just told you."

A smile was the Kid's answer and he tromped down the stairs. The clerk had locked the front door and he let the sheriff out, then turned the key behind him. A glance at the street was sufficient to show that Richmond and Carver had done a complete job; the Wind River Kid was alone with his adopted town.

What was the best way, he wondered. Taking each side in turn, or the alley first? The alleys, he decided, for he had no way of knowing where Ben was hiding. And he was fairly certain he would be hiding now. Or perhaps not; the Kid was recalling the poker game— much of the man had been revealed in those few hours.

Ben, he felt sure, would not run; he was not the kind who backed down. No, he'd want to square this, just as surely as he tried to win back a lost hand at cards.

But where would a man in his position wait? Not the stable; too crowded. The street too was unlikely. Then the Kid hit on it and started for the burned-out company yard. The rain had done more in fifteen minutes toward putting out the fire than all of the company buckets put together. As the Kid approached the still open main gate, he observed the clouds of steam rising from the black rubble. There was an almost constant hissing as the rain sought out still-live embers.

The night was ink dark here, and he moved into the main yard, angling toward the spot where the main company building had once stood. Farther out, the barracks remained intact; bright squares of light indicated that they were occupied. For over a half-hour he moved around carefully but saw no one. The stable area was devastated, and he searched there thinking that perhaps Ben would take one of the horses. Leaving the stable, he cruised about what was left of the saw and planing mill. The fire had destroyed everything but the heat-bent machinery; this loomed black and useless now.

The Kid put the barracks out of his mind; Ben Colfax would want a dark spot. In an hour, he had covered the whole grounds and found nothing, which puzzled him to the point of disappointment for he had been sure that Colfax would take refuge—

He stopped and stood absolutely motionless. In the rush of hunting his man he had failed to take into consideration the things he had learned about Ben Colfax: the man's cold nerve, his desperate courage. And on the heels of this came the jarring thought that Ben would never run and hide. He would play with a man, double back on him, turn the hunter into the hunted.

The Kid stood in the muddy yard, looking about, trying to determine a logical place to make his stand; he was determined not to let Ben Colfax pick it, yet the man would if he could. Doubling back, the Kid ran past the ruined slab furnace and on to the fire-damaged machinery, there stopping. He paused to still his breathing and wipe a hand over his face. The night was thick with black shadows, and the Kid felt like a country yokel trying to pick the shell that hid the all-important pea. Colfax was in possibly a dozen spots; the Kid could only move about and take a chance on Ben missing his first shot.

As he approached the burned-out harness shop, the Kid stopped, for he saw an odd-shaped shadow. He had the rifle in his right hand and started to lift it, then stopped when Ben Colfax said, "Nope, nope! Wouldn't do that if I was you."

He eased into the clear then and the Kid saw that Ben Colfax did not have a gun in his hand. "This going to be even, Ben?"

"Well now, no draw is ever really even," Ben said. "The trouble with you young fellas is that you don't take an older man's advice. I told you a couple of times that I was pretty good, but since I didn't pull on everyone, you thought I was lyin'."

"You're a pretty good liar, Ben."

"In some things I be," Colfax admitted, "but in others I ain't." He chuckled. "You want to look at yourself, you'll see that I've got you on the hip for sure. A rifle ain't your weapon, son, yet you're standing there holding it in your sixgun hand. Now you ain't free to draw your sixgun, and you're going to be clumsy with that rifle, so I'll let you just go ahead and make up your mind which one you're going to use. When you go for either, I'll get you." He lifted his right hand a little. "You go ahead any time you're ready, Kid."

Some decisions, the Kid decided, were already made for you, and he did not hesitate. Flipping the rifle from his right hand to the left, he drew and knew that he was beat before the pistol started to slip from the leather. Ben Colfax hadn't been lying about his speed and the Wind River Kid launched himself into the mud as Ben shot. The bullet struck either his gun or his hand; with the sudden numbness he could not be sure which had been hit.

He was in the mud and rolling and Ben shot twice more before the Kid could heft his rifle into play. Then he was too late—Colfax was running, dodging amid the wreckage, and then he was gone.

Sitting up, the Kid looked at his right hand and saw

that he was not bleeding. He found his sixgun but it was hopelessly jammed. Thrusting it back into the holster, he stood there and wondered where a man went from here. Was he going to do this all over again, smoke Ben out again, or let the man go, giving it up for a bad deal. The answer was simple; he'd hunt Ben until he found him.

Hunt where? Where, he asked himself, would a man go and be sure he was safe? The answer was so clear that it became a little frightening. Breaking into a trot, he slogged across the muddy yard and headed for Cadmus Rindo's house. The rain had soaked completely through his clothes now but he was hardly aware of the discomfort.

Out of deference, the citizens of Rindo's Springs would leave the old man alone in this hour of tragedy, and a safer place couldn't be found if Ben wanted to hole up. And Ben was smart enough to figure this out.

Approaching Rindo's house, the Kid circled once and saw that it was brightly lighted, which in itself was unusual. There was no way, the Kid decided, in which to sneak into the house; the windows shed light on the grounds all around the house.

So he used the bold approach, knocking on the front door. A moment later he heard Rindo's shuffling step, then the door opened. The old man said, "I'm tired, Kid. Come back tomorrow."

The absence of the servant warned the Kid that he had pulled in a good hand. Now all he had to do was play it into a winner. Rudely he brushed past the old man and stepped into the hall. Common sense told him that Ben was close at hand; he'd never let the old man out of his sight. Rindo licked his lips nervously and because he offered no nod, the Kid was positive that his guess had been a good one.

The library was out; an arch opened up there. On the other side was a heavy oak door that led to another part of the house. At the end of the hall another heavy door was slightly ajar; the Kid needed no other clue.

Suddenly flailing out with his arm, he caught Cadmus Rindo in the chest, flinging him against the wall. Instantly the snout of a pistol came out of the door crack and the Kid worked the lever of the Winchester.

Ben Colfax got off the first shot, a good one that snapped past the Kid's cheek and buried in the woodwork. Then the Kid touched off the .50-110 Winchester Express and the room bulged with the concussion. He didn't stop to see how good his shot was, just worked the lever hurriedly and puckered the door five times, showering that end of the hall with splinters.

There was another shot fired, when Colfax caved at the knees and triggered one off into the rug. The door flew wide and Colfax sprawled, bleeding from four ragged holes.

Slowly, Cadmus Rindo picked himself up from the floor and rubbed the spot where the Kid had hit him. Then he slapped his ears to still the ringing. "Damn," he said, "when you come in I liked to had a stroke! You'd have never shot through that door with a six pistol."

The Kid walked over and looked down at Ben Colfax, shot through and through. Then he turned to the old man. "He couldn't buy one dollar's worth of paper," he said. "The town turned on him like a pack of wolves."

The old man tipped his head forward slowly and stood that way, his chin nearly touching his chest. In a moment he hauled a huge blue handkerchief from his hip pocket and blew noisily. "Damned wet weather," he said. "Can't take it like I used to."

"I'll send someone over to get Ben out of here," the Kid said. Rindo nodded once and the Kid let himself out. With the cold rain against his face, he realized that he was sweating. He cradled the weighty Winchester in his arms and then walked back to the hotel.

A great sadness pressed on him, and yet a new sense of peace helped lift him. This was the end of the road. As far as a man could go, and it really didn't matter now what that Arizona judge handed him, for he had taken his place among men, and proved to himself that he wasn't as bad as some people thought.

He found Richmond and Carver in the hotel lobby. In a quiet voice, he said, "Send a couple of the boys to Rindo's house to pick up Ben."

"He was there?" Carver blurted out.

The Kid nodded. "Probably figured to shoot the old man after he got me."

"We owe you—" Richmond began, but the Kid was moving away toward the stairs. At the judge's nod, Carver went out.

Not bothering to knock, the Kid let himself into Boomhauer's room. He found the marshal sitting up by the window, pants and boots on.

"That's a good rifle," the Kid said. He set it carefully in the closet, then took the shells from his pocket and replaced them in the box. "In a couple of days you'll feel good enough to travel, huh?"

"Maybe," Boomhauer said. "How do you feel, Kid?"

"Feel?" the Kid shrugged. "Better. Better than when I came here."

"Well, you gave these people a little of yourself," Boomhauer said. "Not many men can do that." He turned around and looked at the badly tarnished badge sagging from the Kid's coat. "Why the hell don't you polish that thing? Where's your pride?"

"Just a temporary job," the Kid said. "Besides, it'll tarnish again."

This seemed to make Wade Boomhauer a little angry; he gave the Kid a blunt stare. "Don't you learn anything? Jesus, man, we all tarnish. One of the biggest jobs in life is to keep polishing." He closed his mouth when a knock shook the door. "It's open."

Nan Buckley stepped inside, her face grave. "They told me I'd find you here, Kid." Her glance touched Boomhauer, wished him long gone, then swung back to the Kid. "Were you going to leave without saying anything?"

"I saw Cal Runyon heading toward your place today," he said. He shook his head. "We'd better not say anything more about it, Nan."

"Don't you want to hear what I have to say?"

Now she was testing his fairness. He said, "Sure, Nan."

"I told him that we'd made a mistake," Nan said. "I told him that I loved you, Kid. I said that when you went to Arizona that I was going too, and when you got out of prison, I'd be there waiting to marry you."

The Kid looked at her with the expression of a man who had been stoned between the eyes. Wade Boomhauer cleared his throat and they both looked at him as though they just recalled that he was there.

"He accepts," Boomhauer said, smiling faintly. "Miss, whenever a man looks that stupid, he's accepted." He made a motion toward the night stand. "I had the clerk bring me a telegraph blank. Would you hand it to me, please? And the pencil there too."

With an effort the Wind River Kid performed this

simple service, then watched as Boomhauer wrote his message. He handed it to Nan Buckley and said. "You run a newspaper. Are there any misspelled words there? Got to keep official correspondence neat."

She read it, a tense expression on her face. When she finished she said, "Can he read it too?"

"Sure," Boomhauer said, patting his pockets for a cigar. The message read:

> United States Marshal
> Tucson, Arizona Territory
> Unable to locate Wind River Kid these parts.
> Believe original information to be false.
>   (signed) Boomhauer, U.S. marshal

The Kid handed the message back. "Why, Wade? What about all that stuff, being a lawman and doing your duty?"

"You damn fool," Boomhauer said without anger. "I just did it. Now get the devil out of here and let me enjoy my cigar and my view of the town."

"We'll have a quiet funeral for the Wind River Kid," Nan said softly.

"Make it real quiet," Boomhauer said. "I want to sleep late in the morning."

He laughed when they went out, closing the door.

Will Cook is the author of numerous outstanding Western novels as well as historical frontier fiction. He was born in Richmond, Indiana, but was raised by an aunt and uncle in Cambridge, Illinois. He joined the U.S. Cavalry at the age of sixteen but was disillusioned because horses were being eliminated through mechanization. He transferred to the U.S. Army Air Force in which he served in the South Pacific during the Second World War. Cook turned to writing in 1951 and contributed a number of outstanding short stories to *Dime Western* and other pulp magazines as well as fiction for major smooth-paper magazines such as *The Saturday Evening Post*. It was in the *Post* that his best-known novel, *Comanche Captives*, was serialized. It was later filmed as *Two Rode Together* (Columbia, 1961), directed by John Ford and starring James Stewart and Richard Widmark. Sometimes in his short stories Cook would introduce characters who would later be featured in novels, such as Charlie Boomhauer who first appeared in ''Lawmen Die Sudden'' in *Big-Book Western* in 1953 and is later to be found in *Badman's Holiday* (1958) and *The Wind River Kid* (1958). Along with his steady productivity, Cook maintained an enviable quality. His novels range widely in time and place, from the Illinois frontier of 1811 to southwest Texas in 1905, but each is peopled with credible and interesting characters whose interactions form the backbone of the narrative. Most of his novels deal with more or less traditional Western themes—range wars, reformed outlaws, cattle rustling, Indian fighting—but there are also romantic novels such as *Sabrina Kane* (1956) and exercises in historical realism such as *Elizabeth, By Name* (1958). Indeed, his fiction is known for its strong heroines. Another common feature is Cook's compassion for his characters, who must be able to survive in a wild and violent land. His protagonists make mistakes, hurt people they care for, and sometimes succumb to ignoble impulses, but this all provides an added dimension to the artistry of his work.